Sherryl Caulfield was born in south-east Queensland, Australia, where she currently resides with her partner. She has also spent several years living in New Zealand and Hong Kong and was inspired to write The Iceberg Trilogy following a holiday to Canada.

Come Full Circle is her third novel.

Also by Sherryl Caulfield

The Iceberg Trilogy:
– Seldom Come By
– Come What May

Praise for The Iceberg Trilogy

Seldom Come By is a haunting love story set against the windswept coast of Newfoundland. The story draws you in from the opening lines and takes you on a compelling journey across time and continents, through love, loss, heartache and healing. It is a beautiful and memorable story – a great accomplishment and a wonderful read.
Julie Fison, Author

Descriptive, detailed and quite the page-turner, Seldom Come By focuses on the lives of Samuel and Rebecca (and their families), the beginnings of their romance, their separations, their ups and downs. A very good debut and one well worth reading for lovers of historical fiction and romantic historical fiction alike.
Romantic Historical Reviews

Seldom Come By is an exquisite tale of love and loss, forgiveness and healing..
The Eclectic Reader

I adore historical novels and this is one of the most well written ones that I have read in a very long time. This book was just like the icebergs that the author described: beautiful, breathtaking and the story just flowed much like I imagine the icebergs do through the water.
Goodreads Librarian

I was transported to another life, another time. I laughed, I cried, I held my breath in anticipation, I sighed with delight and ultimately felt extremely fulfilled at the close of the novel. I liken Sherryl's first novel to Paullina Simons' The Bronze Horseman in its claim over my life and heart; its beautiful and gripping story; and its wonderful writing.
Beautiful Bizarre Magazine

The author did it again, I love this book. I read Seldom Come By and was excited to see Come What May available. This book is every bit as good as the first of the trilogy. It held my interest the entire way through and left me wanting more. The characters were so real. Read this series and you will not be sorry. Sherryl Caulfield has become my new favorite author.
Amazon Reviewer

I loved the first book, something so different from what's often offered in the romance genre. Seldom Come By was a deep, epic family story spanning generations. Come What May is another very emotive book, full of wonderful descriptions of places, people and events. I was so saddened sometimes – but I love that in a book, one that makes events and people seem so real that I'm upset for them. Another cracking read, to savour and cherish.
Jeannie Zelos's Reviews

Come What May, the second book in the Iceberg Trilogy, is simply a masterpiece. Sherryl Caulfield will blow you away with her depiction of the vastness of the Canadian landscape and the depth of human emotion her characters grapple with. It's a humbling read as you are drawn into the literal and figurative wilderness. Sherryl's ability to depict great loss and great anguish had me dumbfounded and utterly captivated. While I enjoyed the first book of the trilogy, Seldom Come By, Come What May moved me more – it's continued to haunt me long after I finished it. If you enjoy epic novels spanning generations, if you like being transported to another time and place, this is the book for you.
Jennifer Collin, Author

Come Full Circle

SHERRYL CAULFIELD

First published in Australia in 2015 by Cedar Pocket Publishing
This edition published in 2015 by Cedar Pocket Publishing
PO Box 654 Coorparoo 4151 Australia
www.cedarpocketpublishing.com

ISBN 978-0-9923759-7-3
Cover design by Sherryl Caulfield and Mark Squires.
Cover image purchased through DepositPhotos.
Photograph of Sherryl Caulfield by Lucid Photography.

Discover other titles by Sherryl Caulfield at: www.sherrylcaulfield.com

For brothers everywhere, especially my own,

Greg and Jesse

Overtures

Canada, February 1995

1   Touching the void

In one short page she tries to bridge the silence of twenty-five years:

Dear Jonathan

I trust this note finds you in good health. I am well. British Columbia is now my home, education, ironically, my profession.

A gifted young lad I know shows great interest in ornithology. He is considering: Zoology at the University of British Columbia; Biology at the University of Western Ontario; and – surprise, surprise – The Avian Science and Conservation Centre at McGill.

I was wondering if you or your contacts have any advice or opinions one way or the other as to scholarships, reputation of various faculties, their facilities, and employment prospects post study.

He comes from a small coastal community. Any of these options will be of significant change.

I hope everyone is well.

She asks after no one. After all this time, after everything, she's lost that right. Her closing salutation:

You know what you mean to me.

And then her full name in an illegible scrawl:

Evangeline

It seems obscure, impersonal this note of hers. Something that has taken her five days to write that should have taken only five minutes. It would have been far easier to have called, for she had located the number through Information as a means of finding Jonathan's current address. Which was just as well. He had moved. But she never had any intention of calling. Initially she had tried Victoria Hospital, hoping to send the letter there. But as she had suspected, her seventy-seven year-old brother had long retired. It was 1995 after all.

She doesn't call because...she who rejected them, now fears being rejected in return? She doesn't call because...she will be impelled to ask after people she most likely can't cope hearing about...or doesn't care? She would rather remember them the way she remembers them.

But why does she make contact in the first place? Sitting in front of her dressing table mirror she asks herself this question. Her searching eyes, green-blue pools of intensity; her face, not pale like many women her age, but seasoned, wind-worn; her head, clad in a faded white wimple and veil, an aging bride of Christ. Other women who wear such coverings shy away from mirrors. But not Eva. In her mirror she can have a conversation. With herself. Just herself. But never aloud. God forbid that someone might hear and think her mad. No, there is not a person on earth privy to her inner thoughts.

It's true what they say about mirrors. If you stare long enough and hard enough, they become unflinching. You find the truth you seek. She is reaching out because she is letting go. Once, she was all alone in the world, but that was of her choosing. This time, it is of another. She craves her solitude, yet she yearns to hold the hand of another who has also let go. Or is there something else? That this young man should know he is not alone in the world. That she should know the same. Eva exhales then shudders.

She wanted to drive two hours north and post the letter at Prince Rupert and mark her return address care of Poste Restante. But she knows she can never do that. She is asking something of her brother, and in return she must offer something of herself. A word. The name of a town.

That is all she will provide. And a post office box number.

On the main road, at the start of their drive, there is no letterbox signifying a dwelling. Yet the house is there all right, at the end of a pot-holed, two-kilometre gravel road. It is submerged in a never-ending forest of yellow and red cedar, western hemlock, and Sitka spruce. Two yellow-leaved, now bare-leaved, silver birches in the front of the house, planted years ago as a nod to her childhood, the only exceptions.

Her room is on the second floor of the unpainted A-frame wooden house. She overlooks the driveway so she can see the seldom comings and goings, but, in any event, their dog, Axel, warns of any intruder well before any uncertain knock.

Behind the house is a narrow trail that leads to a rocky outcrop overlooking the Pacific. Nearly another kilometre north is a beach of fine pale sand, strewn with tired driftwood, beyond that, tidal pools and more headlands, the meandering path eventually winding up in Kitisak. If ever she has reason to go to town, she rarely drives, preferring to stride down the road and the eight kilometres of highway into town, then return via the coastal path. The fewer people seeing her walk out their gravel road the better.

For some inexplicable reason, Eva always senses she is being followed. It haunts and infuriates her. She is forever glancing over her shoulder yet sights no one. Still, she never stops walking. It is one of her few necessities in life. As is her wimple.

She never leaves her bedroom without it. Never. A pair of jeans is her other de rigueur. Today, she pulls a fleece vest on over her long-sleeved shirt and zips it up. Downstairs, she will add her down jacket, gloves and her sorrels.

It is late February, the days are lengthening and the temperatures just above freezing. Still, snow is everywhere. The sky is grey, the sun feeble as it tries to poke through. It is a normal west coast winter's day in every respect, except for the letter she carries with her.

3

2   *Abiding memories*

Rebecca awakes and opens her eyes. What she sees in the early grey light of morn is less clear than what she has seen in her sleep.

She could not pinpoint exactly when her vision started to change but in the last few months her world had become so clouded she felt every day was spring in Newfoundland, where if you left the door open the fog would crawl into your house like a left-over ghost from Christmas and stay for an hour till it suddenly vanished.

Today, all that would change. The cataracts were coming out and new artificial lenses were going in. They would be made of plastic and it was that fact that had long deterred her. In his most placating voice, Jonathan had said, 'Mother you have fillings, metal in your body, what's a little bit of plastic?' So today was the day. No doubt tomorrow she would belong to the throng of post-operative patients who claimed, 'I should have had it done years ago.'

Once recovered, she would be quick to pick up a paintbrush and maybe go back to reading books. Lately she'd listened to audio books. For Christmas Morton had sent her *A River Runs Through It* and recordings of some of Gary Paulsen's stories: *Hatchet*, *Dogsong*, and *Dogteam*. How she had enjoyed those. Meant for children and young adults, but really anyone who was a canine lover would be enthralled.   Did-you-did-you-did-you-did-you-did-you-did-you want it to go on forever? Yes, she howled like a husky. I did. I do. She smiled. That book was her son's life.

Soon she would once more clearly see their street of maples verdant in their new season growth and hear the return of the warbling vireo, but while spring brought many birthings to the world – from the delicate bud of the first larch leaf to the wobbly life of baby foals and the pure innocence of new-born seals – it was those illustrious icebergs conceived in the arctic north that delighted Rebecca the most. They were the ultimate outpouring of nature's strength and might as it brought new life into the world.

She was unlikely to be seeing any of them in Montreal when they removed her eye patches, but, God-willing, this summer she'd go back to Newfoundland and once again see sparkling majestic shapes that painted the seascape with their truly unique form. For now, she would have to settle for the excitement of being able to watch vivid images on the Discovery channel, being able to see the face of her eldest son, not just touch it, and being able to read the newspaper, and any letters that wound their way to her. Yesterday, Jonathan had to read to her Gene's letter, such as it was.

She wondered what he made of matters. They hadn't spoken of Gene in years. They never wondered any more. She was certain Jonathan had given her up for dead. But Rebecca had long felt in one small ventricle of her weary heart that her daughter was still alive.

There was a part of her that wished they had never received Gene's letter. To receive such an impersonal note after all these years was more galling than silence. Rebecca always hoped she would see her daughter again under happy circumstances. She always hoped that as the years progressed her daughter would have cut her aging mother some slack. That Gene would have remembered she had lost enough children along the way and that it was hurtful for her to add to the tally with her prolonged absence. That Gene did not, only seemed to confirm what Rebecca had long feared – her daughter's mental health was and would always be variable. How she managed to hold down a teaching job confounded her. Once Rebecca got to that unavoidable conclusion she could set aside her hurt and feel pity for her daughter's untameable demons and her unhinged life. She could say: it was of comfort to hear from her.

And now they had an address. She wondered if she should send on to her the small stash of letters she had of hers, boxed away in her bottom drawer. Ones written between Gene and Sonny back in the early fifties and again in the sixties. She had her own box of letters written during the Great War. Odd the way she had ended up minding Gene's, the way her mother had minded her letters from Samuel.

When they packed up that house in Winnipeg, Gene and Sonny's letters were the only items she said she would take. Did she sense then that she would be a caretaker? She read some of them once. After three years. Like hers, there was nothing remarkable about them unless falling in love was remarkable these days. Most outpourings of love only fluttered the hearts of those directly involved. Hers had certainly fluttered. More than fluttered. And so it should have. Falling in love was the privilege of youth like innocence was the privilege of childhood. Though these days when she looked at the young it seemed sex came easier than love. In her day it was the opposite.

Last night, in her dreams Samuel and Sonny visited. Their presence mingled with recessed thoughts stirred by that letter they had just received. She dreamed of the first time they had gone to Lake Temagami, Samuel and her, their daughter Abigail, then an excited three-year old, and Jonathan, twelve. On the first night after the children had gone to bed she and Samuel had stripped off, wrapped themselves in towels and run down to the lake for a moonlight swim, dodging the little black flies and insects that buzzed around them. Every so often they had to dunk their heads under the water to lose them.

'What did I tell you all those years ago?' Samuel had said. 'And this is not as bad as it gets. In spring they are like a black mist.'

'I can put up with a few black flies for this,' she had said, wrapping her wet naked body around Samuel's.

'Me too. But we are going to have to keep that screen door closed and we are going to have to cover ourselves all over with insect repellant during the day.'

'All over?' she said with a laugh.

'You'll have insect bites on your private bits before this holiday is over. Mark my words. They are incessant. They are ceaseless. They are insidious.'

'Like you used to be,' she murmured.

'Yes,' he drawled. He waited, his mood somber. 'The love making has continued.'

'But not how it was before. Or how it was after Abby was born.'

'I know.' His voice sad. 'I'm sorry. I can be that way again. It can be that way again. I want to. I just thought you needed some time before you could move on. Every time I made love to you, you would end up crying. I didn't think it was helping.' It has been seven months since their beautiful son Henry had been born, lived for one day and then died.

She kissed Samuel's neck then rested her head on his shoulder. 'I know. I'm sorry. But I'm hoping here I won't cry and here it can be like it used to be. Remember Boston when we got so caught up in each other we forgot that we were trying to make a baby.'

'I remember.'

'I want it be like that again. Can we try on this holiday to get back to those two people we were in Boston?'

'Yes,' said Samuel, thickly, 'God, yes. Starting right now.'

They made love in the lake then he danced with Rebecca on the small jetty while he sang Cole Porter's *You do something to me*' and they draped towels around each other like Algonquin shawls. After, he carried her into the house where they made robust love in a solid bed hewn from native timbers and the only cries from Rebecca were breathless ones to the night sky meant for his ears only.

These were the random memories that sometimes came to a nonagenarian lying in the folds of sleep. Thank God she still had her memory. Memories, memories – secrets that no one could touch.

Thinking of Lake Temagami reminded her of a conversation she'd once had with her son-in-law. Sonny had rung a few months before he disappeared asking after the place they had once vacationed at when her kids were young. He'd said Gene had mentioned it to him way back in 1950 when they first met, but she had not remembered the name, a cabin on a lake in the middle of Ontario somewhere. Did she recall the place? She did. Sonny had said, one day if ever he was over that way he might check it out. She wrote providing him with the details but told him she didn't know if it was still there, still available for holiday rentals, let alone how to book it. The last time she had been there was in 1938. So much could have changed. So much did.

When she and Wyatt had gone through all of Sonny's paperwork, they had never found that letter. It wasn't something that had clicked at the time. Only now.

3   *How like her brother*

Her brother did reply. Two months later. Just when Eva had decided nothing was to come of her letter. It was pages long, almost a university paper in content and execution. A well-researched report based on consultation with distinguished colleagues from his McGill days, academics who gave their own unbiased views. It included a summary of likely in-province and out-of-province student fees at the various institutions, known scholarships, from whom and where to apply, an overview of each university community and the attraction of the surrounds. Plus, there was his own personal recommendation that perhaps the young lad in question would have a stronger desire to study the birds he was most familiar with – from his home province – given that was likely what piqued his interest in the first place.

And then, strangely, an offer to accommodate the young man in his own home at no cost, should he be accepted at McGill, until he could find more suitable accommodation. Her heart warmed when she read that. But then it froze.

At the end, was a postscript:

P.S. We are alive and kicking – even Mom.

Even Mom! That shocks her. She thought for sure she would have passed away.

The words lay heavy on her like the pressure on a floodgate. But she is not about to release any valve. She waits and hopes the knowledge will dissipate, that that childish pressure of conscience, of mistaken familial duty will evaporate like water in the height of summer, every day the volume a little less. It's as if her mother is taunting her:

"While you live, Evangeline, I'm not going anywhere."

She has Jonathan to thank for some of her brightest days and her mother for her darkest. How paradoxical that she still can't have one without the other.

Before she read the postscript she was preparing a response, a thank you for your efforts. But those few words thwart any impulse. Finally, a few months later, when school results are in and university applications accepted she sends a postcard.

Thanks for everything. UBC it is.

There was never any question.

Australia, November 1995

4   Storms in Sydney

When it rains she will cry. Her own emotional weather vane tells her so. When the rumbling, tumbling deluge comes pummelling down she will stare out at the heavy drops splattering on King Street and realise it has come to this.

Right now Lindsay's inability to cry is adding to her anguish. That she, two years ago, could be so blissfully engaged and now so blithely un-engaged of her own making and not bitterly upset makes her primary emotion one of anger – at herself – that she could have let a dead-end situation continue for so long – as if all along she knew the outcome.

It is five o'clock in the afternoon, the height of a Sydney summer. Yet today no daylight has been saved. She is sitting on a bar stool in the Forum Hotel, her back to patrons, idly staring at the road. The concertina windows are wide open. The wind is bringing the storm with it on its wings. An empty chip packet skitters along the footpath, dry leaves twirl in tiny whirlwinds, her cosmopolitan sweats in the warm breeze. The sweltering summer day is refusing to tolerate any more. Just like her. She knows when the rain hits the road it will rise in steamy vapours. It's that very change she's looking for, wanting for herself. To have the crying, the grieving over with. To move on to another state.

Her thoughts are being punctuated by the tragic and the euphoric; the great pendulum swings of her life. The 16th August 1976, the day they officially gave her father up for dead after weeks of searching. One year to the day that Elvis Presley died. There was bitter sweetness in that. Her father being such an Elvis fan.

The 26th September 1983, actually the 27th September on this side of the world. She'd only been in Australia a few days after finishing university and backpacking through South East Asia, landing in Sydney just as Alan Bond's syndicate wrested the famed America's Cup away from the USA for the first time in 132 years.

How could any Canadian not be overjoyed at that? What a victory! She became an Australian the day Bob Hawke announced, "Any employer who sacks a worker for not coming in today is a bum." Did she go to work that day? Nope, she didn't have to, but even so, she went to the pub and fortune smiled on the brave. There she struck up a friendship with Kristen, K, who became her first real friend from down-under, her dearest friend whom any minute would be arriving to help strike the death knell.

Next was Australia's Bicentenary, when her sister Shane on her first Australian visit, on the night of 26th January, 1988, announced she too wanted to move to Australia. This country that made them both feel they could start their lives anew. And then that ominous date, which dear friends we will all soon gather to mourn the passing, the 23rd September 1993. The night Sydney won the 2000 Olympic Games bid, triumphing over Beijing. The champagne flowed, Darling Harbour went off, the Greenwood pumped, and the breakfast queues at Maisy's were outside and around the corner. There was singing. There was dancing in the street. There was dancing on tables. And in the tipsy teetering, while they were giddily swaying to '*Throw your arms around me*', he said, 'Marry me. Marry me, Lindsay. We'll never forget this night."

Nope, even now we will never forget it. Today, there's no shouting. And blue has a different meaning. What a way to mark the eve of her thirty-third birthday.

As a teenager, Lindsay always thought she would be a mother by the time she was thirty. That day had long sailed past. But two years ago she did have high hopes that by this birthday she would at least be on her way. How bizarre that she had been.

A year after his inspired proposal Lindsay started trying to get Martin to commit to a wedding date. But the words "wedding", "babies" and "a suitable home" became increasingly taboo. Invariably they would end up fighting. You would have thought she was the one who had first suggested getting married – not the other way around.

Three months ago they had gone up the coast to Port Stephens for a long weekend determined to have a happy time like they'd had in their earlier days. And what had happened? She had left her pill packet behind. A fact she didn't discover till the morning after. What was she going to do, buy condoms for the rest of the weekend? Wouldn't that go down well! So to avoid a scene she said nothing and did nothing. She came home and took the pill every 12 hours to catch up, ignoring the instructions in sixteen different languages.

But then when she was meant to bleed she barely bled, only the faintest watered-down smear. For three weeks she tried to ignore the fact, to not think or feel anything. To have wanted to be a mum for so long, yet to not be living her image of domestic bliss was something she could not face. Eventually she bought a pregnancy kit and left it in her drawer for a week. She always thought the day she peed on that stick would be one of awed delight and thrilling anticipation. Reality couldn't be further from the dream. She couldn't bring herself to tell him.

Two weeks later she woke in the middle of the night with a pain so intense Martin had to rush her to the Royal North Shore hospital. He assumed it was her appendix. She wasn't about to correct him. After all, it could very well have been.

In Emergency the young doctor asked her was it possible she could be pregnant. 'Yes,' she gasped between stabbing pains. 'I'm in a relationship. I have sex. Anything is possible.'

'Lindsay's on the pill,' Martin explained for the doctor's benefit.

The doctor's buzzer went off. He glanced at Martin

before walking out of their curtained cubicle. 'Oral contraceptive is not 100% reliable,' he said over his shoulder.

Martin had thrown Lindsay a grave look, which the attending nurse didn't miss. 'You know,' said Nurse Searle, checking Lindsay's vitals, 'pregnancy often happen for a good reason.'

Lindsay looked at the nurse who no doubt had seen it all. Vaguely she was aware of her squeezing her wrist. They took blood tests, protein samples, urine tests; administered morphine. Martin had gone home and gone to work by the time the results came back. She was pregnant all right. 'I had my suspicions,' Lindsay admitted.

'Well, you wouldn't have suspected this,' said a new doctor. 'It's an ectopic pregnancy.'

That would be right, thought Lindsay, as if that was her punishment for her small act of deception. Coming out of herself she asked, 'What do we do about that?'

'I'm afraid we have to remove the fetus. The longer it stays the more you risk losing the whole fallopian tube. In extreme cases you could lose your life.'

This doctor was full of good news today. Lindsay swallowed. 'So when do you operate?'

'Soon. I want to monitor you for another six hours – your pain suggests your body is already taking matters into in own hands.'

In mild protest Lindsay said, 'but there's no sign of bleeding.'

Five hours later she was cramping and bleeding like she never had before. Her sister Shane was with her by this stage, wiping her brow.

Martin turned up with a dozen yellow roses. Shane updated him. Lindsay was focusing inwards yet she still managed a glimpse of his initial expression before he managed to hide it. 'You look relieved,' she mumbled.

'I am relieved,' he said smiling for her benefit. 'That you are okay, will be okay. That we caught this in time.' It sounded like she had had a malignant lump removed.

Yep, she had gotten pregnant for a reason all right. As it transpired, it was one of the best decisions she had ever made. How long would her untenable life have dragged on otherwise?

5 A drinking and pinking session with the girls

Fee arrived first, followed by Kristen, then Ange who kissed her on both cheeks.

'I tried to call you,' muttered Lindsay.

'I believe you. Shane tracked me down. My mobile's got liquid ingress.'

'It's got what?' asked Kristen.

'Liquid ingress.'

'From the rain?' Fee queried.

'No! At least not yet.' Ange rolled her eyes.

Lindsay couldn't help herself. 'What did you spill on it this time?' she asked.

'Nothing.' Ange eyed the disbelieving faces. 'Honest.'

'Well, who told you it had liquid ingress?' asked Kristen.

'This Indian guy at the Optus shop in North Sydney. I've only had this phone for two weeks and the sodding thing kept cutting out, so I took it into him and demanded to know what was wrong with it.'

Kristen narrowed her gaze at Ange. 'I bet you terrified him.' Ange was 1.55 metres at best. She wore her short, ever-changing hair gelled and spiked to give her more height. Kristen on the other hand was 1.77 metres tall with long black glossy hair that she wore any which way on a whim.

'Ha. Ha,' Ange replied, the limit of her biting. 'So today he calls me and in his heavily accented voice says, "Madam, I'm terribly sorry to inform you that your phone has liquid ingress." She pauses for effect, her eyes wide. "Moisture!" he declares.

'And I go, "How could that be? I haven't spilt anything on it. Scouts honour."

'"It's a mystery then, but lucky for you it is covered by warranty and we can replace it." He says, "Madam, have you been to the tropics on holiday? I've heard sometimes humidity can do things to phones."

'And I go, "that's very interesting. But no I haven't been to the tropics." But what I don't tell him is I've been taking the phone into the bathroom every morning and leaving it on the vanity while I shower in case Alex calls.'

'Is he still away?' asked Fee.

'Yes!' She sighed. 'This project in Auckland is dragging on and on and on. And so there you have it, the tropics have come to Lane Cove. What do you know? Steam and phones don't mix.'

'Great, I'll stop ironing,' mumbled Kristen.

'Anyway, enough of me. How are you?' Ange smiled at Lindsay. Her eyes flashed compassion like a lighthouse.

Lindsay knew she wasn't asking after her physical health. She raised her eyebrows. 'I've felt better. I've felt worse.'

'On a scale of one to ten how unhappy are you?'

'Not as unhappy as I should be. At least not over him.'

'Good, that means we don't have to be that unhappy either.'

'You sound decidedly cheery,' said a decidedly uncheery Lindsay.

'You're off the hook. And I don't have to pretend to like him any more.'

'You never liked him?'

'Not really.' But before Lindsay could ask why, Ange said, 'Look, here's Shane.'

Her sister hugged her; their heads pressed together, Lindsay's ash brown and layered, Shane's sandy, fringed and pony tailed. 'I'm sorry.' She whispered. She didn't need to say another word. More than anyone Shane knew how her heart was held together. 'Did I miss much?'

'Ange was doing her usual to turn this wake around,' volunteered Kristen.

'Now, come on! Lindsay deserves better, that's all. Don't you agree?'

'Abso-bloody-lutely,' said Kristen.

'Too right,' said Fee.

In her sister's defence, Shane said, 'He was better than the last two.'

'He didn't count where it counted though,' Lindsay replied. The unpalatable truth had become painfully clear over the past fortnight.

'When did you ask him to leave?' asked Ange.

Lindsay looked into her near empty glass. 'Last night.' She raised her vivid blue green eyes to look at her friend. 'He didn't love me. He only loved the idea of me. He never wanted to be the father of my children.'

They all nodded their heads in slow, silent agreement.

'Next time,' said Kristen, 'don't get engaged. Just get married for Christ's sake.'

'Oh you're a fine one to talk,' admonished Fee. Despite her husband doing the dirty on her, Fee was still their blue-eyed, beach-blonde, wholesome girl next door. Kristen on the other hand was one of those enigmatic women who didn't particularly care about boyfriends, only lovers. The eldest of seven children, she didn't particularly care about children either.

'I am. You want to know why?' she asked, brushing strands of hair away from her face with red lacquered nails. 'Because I,' she paused, 'can distance myself. You know what men do with engagement rings? They use them like a lay-by sticker in some fancy store. They say: I reserve you, but I'm not going to marry you just yet, because someone better might come along. And you're not going anywhere now because – look – I've just signed you up.'

'She's right,' said Ange. 'You've seen the light and extracted yourself in time. That on-hold card was destined to become sepia over time. But make sure you keep the rock, Lins.'

'I just don't understand what I did so wrong? Did I crowd his space too much? Or do you think he was waiting to see what sort of woman I would turn into?'

While they tried to apply themselves seriously to Lindsay's question, Fee said she wasn't one for handing out advice, however, in the next breath she added, 'I'd say if anything you gave him too much free rein. Would he ever give up a Friday night with the boys? Remember when you were given that week-end away at the Anchorage in Port Stephens as a bonus and he insisted on making it a Saturday and Sunday night affair rather than a Friday and Saturday escape.'

How could she ever forget **that** weekend? It was the beginning of the end. The whole idea was almost laughable. For the benefit of her friends she said, 'I know he enjoyed time out with his friends, but then I like my girl time too.'

'The problem Lins is I'm not sure his time out was as monogamous as yours.'

Everyone gaped at Kristen. 'You know that for a fact?' ventured Shane.

'I don't want to hear,' said Lindsay holding her hand up in a stop signal before Kristen could reply. 'I just want to know what sort of world we are going to end up with if men don't want to give up their bachelorhood, if men don't want to father children?'

'You've got the term wrong, I'm afraid,' said Kristen, 'You mean raise.'

You're right,' she mumbled dryly. Taking a sip of her drink, she looked at Ange. 'You shouldn't delay. Lex could always change his mind you know.'

'Nup. No chance.'

'Aren't you smug?'

'I am, but you're right. Jason who I work with is the epitome of the man you are talking about and get this, six years ago he discovered he had an eighteen year old son.'

'How did that come about?' asked Shane.

'Apparently, on his eighteenth birthday the lad in question's mother told him who his dad was and where to go looking for him. Turns out Jason knew all about Rhonda and her baby but said at the time their relationship had been very casual and not exclusive and so "seventies man" and didn't believe the child was his and wanted nothing to do with either of them. But now twenty-five years later he has this fabulous relationship with his long lost son. They go sailing and drinking together, rugby matches at the Stadium and he's about to become a grandfather and couldn't be more overjoyed at the prospect. And it's just been handed to him on a plate.'

'See!' Lindsay felt validated. 'That's exactly what I mean. The injustice of it all. They don't want to raise them but enjoy them, yes, when it suits them.' She took another sip of her drink. 'So, what's the subtext?' asked Lindsay, 'that I should be looking for a man in his forties? That by then they might be ready for fatherhood.'

'Gotta love that spirit, she's out of the corner already.' Kristen was grinning like the proverbial feline.

'Maybe you should be looking for someone in their early twenties,' suggested Ange.

'You think so?'

'Yes. Maybe if you get them young enough they have more romantic notions, there's been less time for their independence and selfishness to take hold.'

'Huh!' said Fee. 'That wasn't the case with Brad. He decided after the fact that he hadn't sown enough wild seeds when he was young.'

'Maybe Ange's got a point,' said Kristen suddenly capricious. 'When you think of Ross…'

'Who's Ross?' Ange sounded crushed, as if she were the last to find out.

'Aha, got you there.' Kristen threw back her hair and gave Ange a teasing wide-eyed stare.

'Ross was a guy I hooked up with not long after I moved to Australia,' explained Lindsay.

'And?'

'He was gorgeous. Like Jerry from Skippy the Bush Kangaroo.'

'Tony Bonner! I used to drool over him,' said Fee. 'Did you have that show in Canada?'

'Every afternoon.' Shane clicked her tongue twice.

'Yes,' drawled Lindsay. 'He was so Jerry, so respectful, so wholesome, so serious.'

'How serious?' asked Fee.

'Oh he wanted to marry me alright.'

'Did you love him?' Fee drew the word 'love' out. She was always gunning for love.

'She loved him,' said Kristen.

'Well, what stopped you from you marrying him?' Ange stared pointedly at Kristen.

''No, I did not.' Kristen was indignant. But then she conceded. 'I will admit, however, to divided loyalties.'

'Problem was,' explained Lindsay, 'he was Canadian and wanted to move back. But after two winters here I decided I never wanted to spend another winter in Canada again.'

'Canada's a big place,' said Ange, her voice laced with its usual optimism.

'Yes,' agreed Shane, 'and winters last for six months.'

'Even in Vancouver?' asked Ange.

'I could live in Vancouver,' said Kristen dream bound.

'It was beautiful when we visited, K,' said Lindsay, 'But in winter it's grey and wet for four to six months of the year. It's like Ireland. There's a reason the country's so green.'

'Back to the topic of suitable men, please,' said Fee. 'Out of all the men you've ever dated, which one have you loved the most?'

Lindsay stabbed her lime with the straw. The truth was so galling: that the best parts of her life were so far back in her past. After nearly a minute she said, 'I'd say him.'

'Canadian Ross! Why?' Fee was full of questions today.

'Because he had the makings of a good man and he reminded me of our father. But at twenty-four years of age I wasn't going to be marrying my father.'

'But there you have it,' said Ange, bubbling over in excitement at the ingenuity of her own answer. 'You're looking for someone just like Mr. Marlow and no one has ever measured up.'

'Is my bar too high do you think?'

'No, not at all, but are you sure you're not searching for your father? Maybe you've got unresolved father issues.'

'I don't go out with men twenty, thirty years my senior!'

'That's not what I mean.'

'Well does Shane have the same issues?' quipped Lindsay.

'Clearly not! She's happy with Mr Sumi Aida, her holistic healer,' said Ange.

'I would be over the moon if Lins were to marry a man like our father,' said Shane.

'Let's raise a toast to Sonny Marlow,' said Fee. 'Clearly the man was a giant among men. Maybe you have to go back to Canada to find the man meant for you.'

'What if,' said Ange, her eyes animated, her hands animated, 'Ross were to walk through the door right now and say, "I still love you, I've loved you all these years, will you marry me?" Would you move to Canada now to marry him and have his babies?'

'Do you want me to move back to Canada?'

'Abso-bloody-lutely not,' declared Kristen.

'Don't be ridiculous,' said Fee.

'I was merely trying to divine what is most important?' whined Ange.

'How about you divine us some more vodka, Angeski?'

6 How to skip a birthday

Lindsay cancelled her birthday. On Saturday 18th November 1995 she drove to Brooklyn and went sea kayaking by herself on the Hawkesbury river, between banks barnacled with eucalyptus, around Dangar Island, underneath Mooney Mooney bridge on the look out for the white breasted sea eagles she so adored, looking for her very own Cuillen. Years ago, *The Stonor Eagles* had been a farewell gift from her Uncle Morton when she first left Canada to travel overseas, a subtle reminder perhaps not to forget her homeland. It was still one of those books she would take with her to the desert island. She always told herself, if Cuillen could survive, so could I.

Saturday night she caught a movie by herself at Mosman, *A Walk in the Clouds*. Not the world's greatest movie, but oh to be Victoria Aragorn, oh to have chivalrous Paul Sutton, Keanu Reeves, as one's beau. But she was more like Susannah Fincannon losing her heart to unattainable Tristran Ludlow, Brad Pitt, in *Legends of the Fall*. Screw them. Screw them all.

On Sunday Lindsay rose early and went to Balmoral to go running twice around the circuit, swim between the headlands and have coffee and bircher muesli at one of her favourite cafes before the crowds arrived. To get a carpark close to the beach at Balmoral you had to go early. Balmoral was one of Sydney's most popular harbourside beaches and boasted two of Sydney's most exquisite restaurants, Bathers and Watermark, crowd pleasers anytime of the day. You had to book weeks in advance to get a table by the window at either establishment. Lindsay only dined there on very special occasions, like last year when Martin had taken her to one for her birthday. Certainly, not today. Lindsay liked to arrive before the crowds. Early didn't phase her; she liked to witness the day breaking and although she relished the climate in Sydney, particularly after years of long Canadian winters, she still preferred to exercise in the cool hours of morning.

It often surprised Lindsay just how busy the place could be at 6.30 am on a Sunday morning: Hung-over, bleary-eyed parents with their hyperactive toddlers would already be at the park shadowing their kids as they climbed in the giant fig trees at the water's edge, one hand above their head to push a wayward bottom back up towards a sturdy branch, another, gripping their long black life-line in their takeaway cups. Joggers would be running with their Labradors and German Shepherds, while the elderly would be walking their Jack Russells and Shitzus, along the boardwalk, oblivious to the toned, bronzed, women in black tights power weaving with their girlfriends, oblivious to the parents double-parked on the road dropping off their kids at the sailing school whilst racing into a cafe for their caffeine fix, freshly baked croissants and a copy of the Sun-Herald. Balmoral was Sydney in a vibrant microcosm – admittedly not as vibrant as Toronto – mostly a waspish suburb without the beer, urine stains and waves found at Sydney's more famous beaches. It was for these reasons Lindsay was pleased it was her local – though she would have welcomed a little more ethnicity in the mix.

On her way to Wollstonecraft to Shane and Sumi's she stopped in at Neutral Bay to go to the bottle shop and the seven-day-a-week florist. They had just received a delivery of white butterfly ginger flowers on long stalks all the way from Cairns. Sumi would love those. She bought a dozen.

Sunday lunch at Shane and Sumi's was an institution with friends boasting his Japanese teppanyaki rivalled anything from Suntory. Today, at Lindsay's request, they had decided on a very private family affair – just the three of them. When he opened the door Sumi bowed in greeting, his ritualistic endearment. As always he leant forward, kissed her on the cheek and hugged her but this day he didn't release his hug straight away. His sympathy flowed through his Tai Chi arms as they folded her in his brotherly embrace. As was custom, Lindsay left her shoes at the front door and followed Sumi through to the sanctuary of their outside courtyard, a beautiful bamboo haven with a shallow water feature around four sides and a small wooden walkway that you walked over to their outside living room.

Shane gave her a kiss and a passing hug. 'How are you, today?'

'I'm okay.' She pulled an ice-cold New Zealand sauvignon blanc from her bag.

Her sister glanced at it. 'Feel like an alcohol free strawberry daiquiri for starters?'

'Perfect.' Lindsay smiled.

'How's Martin? What's he up to?'

'Martin is mute and hopefully by tonight he will be mute and gone.'

'Where's he moved to?'

'He's put all his stuff in Tom's garage and plans to bunk down there for a few weeks till he finds something or decides to give his tenants their notice.' Lindsay caught Shane's eye. 'No major dramas really.'

'I suppose you're glad you never ended up buying a property together?'

She nodded slowly. 'His resistance has I guess been a blessing and my apartment is all mine.'

'Have you paid your mortgage off already?' Shane asked, surprise in her voice.

'No, but in three years time I plan to. Every bonus I get I throw at it.' Lindsay was a channel sales manager with Cisco, a global IT company. Thirty-year old Shane was an osteopath with a Holistic Health Clinic that had locations in Newtown and Bondi Junction. Four years earlier she'd gone to San Francisco for six months to study Cranial Osteopathy from an octogenarian expert with The Cranial Academy. That's where she met Sumi, second generation American born Japanese, a younger, better looking, equally as green version of David Suzuki. Midway through lunch, Lindsay said to him, 'Tell me, Sumi, master sensei, what do you think I should do at this juncture?'

Wiping his face with his serviette Sumi took his time before he spoke. 'I think you should give your body and your spirit time to recover. Be relationship free for a while. When was the last time you were relationship free for twelve months?'

'Twelve months,' she gulped. 'Ah, when I was seventeen. I didn't let myself look at any boys until after I finished school. I thought Dad would be sorely disappointed with me if I bummed in my studies.'

'And since then there's been a steady stream,' surmised Sumi.

'Yes.' Shane answered for her sister.

'See Lindsay, you are a like a field that a farmer is trying to farm. It takes time to find the right crop and even with that, you have to rest the field every few years, plough the crops back in, let them decompose so the soil can maintain its fertility and nutrients. Rest your soil. Give yourself a breather. You don't need to worry about being alone forever, that won't happen to you.' He smiled encouragingly.

'I don't enter relationships because I'm afraid of being alone.'

'I'm not saying you do. But I imagine relationships come easy to you. I can't imagine the average Australian male not finding you attractive. But your physicality is a double-edged sword. Once you may have had a laissez-faire attitude about relationships, easy come, easy go, but since you've wanted a serious relationship, have you been as discerning as you needed to be?'

'I'm inferring the answer is: "Clearly not".'

Sumi shrugged. 'Do you know why you have chosen the men you have in your life?'

Sumi's questions could be so pointed at times. But they were good for her. Lindsay exhaled while she ruminated over her answer. After a while she said, 'I'm not saying this

28

is the case, but Fiona wonders if I have been searching for someone like our father and that I have unresolved father issues.'

'The two might be correct and they might also be completely unrelated.'

'I'm with you on the latter. We totally adored our father. The only thing unresolved about our father is he's no longer with us. When he died, the bottom fell out of our world. Unfathomable issues around our father – yes – but not unresolved.'

Sumi leant back in his chair and stroked Shane's back. 'So, what are those unfathomable issues?'

'What's unfathomable?' In weary exasperation Lindsay said, 'our father died, as you well know. Mysteriously. His plane crashed or was sucked up by aliens. One minute he was in our lives, the next he was gone, after a private charter from which he never returned. No sign of his plane or his body ever again.'

'We heard from him though,' said Shane. 'Lindsay heard.'

'When?'

'On his way back home. He stopped to refuel and called us from an airport.'

'What did he say?'

'Not much.' Lindsay paused. 'Everything.' The word loaded with emotion. Lindsay was surprised the emotions were still so close to the surface, twenty years after the fact.

'Cryptic?'

'Yes.'

'Did he sound normal?'

'Yes and no. Sumi, our father was an excitable man. He was never normal to other people. We had a banner in our house that said, "Opportunities do not wait for slow thinkers." He'd walk in the door and yell, "Where are my favourite two girls in the world?" He'd say, "What did you do today, you big winner?" He'd ask, "What do you want to do this week-end? The sky's wide open!"'

Shane chuckled at that. 'Or,' she said, 'He'd go, "Girls,

have I got a surprise for you this weekend."'

Lindsay laughed sadly at the memory.

'And did he keep his word? Were they good surprises?'

'Almost without exception.'

'And how does this relate to his last phone call.'

'He called and said, "I have the most amazing news. The best news in the known universe."

'"What?" I asked him.'

'"I can't tell you," he said. "I have to show you." And then he told us he would be home the next afternoon and we would leave the morning after that. And to let Nana know we would be away for a few weeks.'

'We were staying with our grandparents. It was during school holidays,' Shane said for Sumi's benefit.

'He never showed,' said Lindsay, her voice trailing off.

'Tell me again how old he was?'

'Forty-eight,' said Shane.

'And you were... ten?' said Sumi, running his hand down Shane's straight hair. 'Making you, fourteen,' he said looking at Lindsay.

'Not quite,' said Lindsay.

'And there's nothing that's ever been reported or come to light since?' Both girls shook their head. 'Where was he when he phoned you?'

'Sault Sainte Marie. They suspect his plane crashed into Lake Superior.'

'Hence, no sign,' Sumi surmised. After a pause he asked, 'What did you think the adventure was going to entail?'

Shane sighed as her eyes caught Lindsay's. 'The things we came up with for that. A new floatplane. A paddling trip in the scenic wilds of the Yukon.'

'Kayaking with the Beluga whales in Hudson Bay,' said Lindsay. 'A trip to Canada's Arctic to see the polar bears.' She shrugged as she plucked a lone piece of avocado out of the bottom of the near empty salad bowl.

'Do you want to hear my theory?' asked Shane.

'You have a new theory about Dad?'

'No, moreso about you.'

30

Lindsay shrugged. 'Why not? It's the week for theories.'

'When you think of our experiences with men who do you think of most?'

'Our father, of course.'

'Yes and what do we think of him?'

'He was a wonderful father. He was the light of our life. He was busy, ran his own company but he always made time for us. We never went without anything. We had better holidays than all of our friends, and,' she paused, 'we loved him fiercely.'

'Yes! We embraced his enthusiasm and made it our own. As a family we were so conscious of what we had because we were so conscious of what we didn't have. We knew the sacrifices he made, the balls he juggled to be there for us. We weren't like other children. We were aware, not ignorant and we did what we could to ease his workload, relieve his stress – you much more than me. You had too much responsibility thrust onto you at too early an age. You became my mother. You became Dad's right hand girl. Your parenting instincts were prematurely developed. And that's probably how you still are today. Maybe around you men don't feel needed because you're so competent.'

Lindsay reflected on Shane's theory. 'It's possible,' she said at last. 'So do you think I look for men who need mothering?'

'No, I wouldn't necessarily say that. But I think most of the men you've been with have had a very complacent outlook and maybe have even taken advantage of you. They've looked at you and thought, "Lins will be right. She's a trooper." Because you're such a coper. You're not needy.'

'You're right. I'm not. I'm a survivor.'

'Exactly. And they all know it.'

'They don't see your vulnerability,' said Sumi.

'Who does?' Her voice bitter. They looked at each other, their eyes astute. Then tears sprung to Lindsay's. The storm broke at last. Two days after the fact.

Choices

December 1995

7   Such a pity about work

Eva would rather not work. But she knows she'd rather not stay home and become what she once was: uninspired, idle, dying a slow death

In her youth Eva was largely an outsider. She didn't mind being a loner as long as she had her brothers to count on and she could live an industrious life. After secondary school she had seriously considered being a nun. It wasn't until twenty years later that she pursued that path. Instead, she studied history and geography and ended up with a government office job.

Then in her thirties, in another life, she trained to become a secondary school teacher.

In this, in what she regards as her third life, teaching is on the periphery, a routine chore she has to do each week to get through life, like doing the dishes.

When she relief teaches she makes one concession towards the profession that pays her, replacing her favoured denims with long, non-descript skirts. At school, they call her Sister Eva. It satisfies. A few years back when she had the phone connected her radius of available schools increased. She now drives to Salvern if required, occasionally Terrace. Much to her disquiet there are a lot of unhealthy teachers, or teachers with sick children, training commitments, union meetings, stress leave, or sports carnivals, for she has averaged two days a week for the past twenty years.

She has regularly been offered full time and permanent part-time positions and she has regularly turned them down. Of course she could do with the money, but she can't do with all those people day in and day out, the faces becoming familiar. The children who mistakenly think you are someone you're not. The ones who creep up on you, get inside you when you least expect it. And you are left with emotions and complications you don't want. Relief teaching has distance and variety, no lessons to plan, no assignments to mark, no feedback and disappointments to give. And the marking work she does do suits her entirely.

As a former subject master she has secured herself contract work with the BC Examinations Review Board. She reassesses hundreds of exam papers by final year secondary students, ensuring the marks from Port Hardy to Prince George, from Kelowna to Victoria are consistent, that no teacher has been more lenient on their students than others, that standards are upheld. Massive mailbags arrive at the local post office for her and are returned by her as she works round the clock for a five-week period in December-January and May-June each year. She gets paid for each paper she reassesses – the quicker she can turn them around, the more they send her. It is an intense period, the adrenalin surges. No relief teaching during these blocks. Other teachers ask how she manages.

'I manage,' she replies. She regularly has nights where she doesn't sleep. Where she's awake, roaming the rooms of her house.

But something about those long feverish days and nights remind her of her youth, of those youth studying and sitting for their exams, of him now sitting university exams. In those times she re-lives the sense of exhilaration and escape that comes once the mountain of exams has been climbed. There is something about her ability to slog through such a slush of paperwork that proves to her that she's still got it. Whatever 'it' is: her energy, her mind, her agility, her relevance perhaps.

After each period there is a burnout, a crashing, a crevasse that opens up, which she falls into. Usually by then it is holidays and to her relief the lad is off with friends or relatives, or as is the case now, staying on in Vancouver – their first Christmas apart. When she is exhausted she doesn't have the energy to keep her mind at bay, her defences are down; she is watchful and fearful and sleeps fitfully while her frantic energy burns out. It can take days for her life to unfurl from such eddies and return to the calm currents of normality.

This year when she resurfaces Ken invites her over for Christmas and, like every year, won't take no for an answer. She is family, he insists. And truth be told, she more or less is. She forces herself to go. Tells herself things will be all right once she gets there and why shouldn't they be. They have spent years with the Robinsons and their extended Haisla family. Except this year she is alone and he is spending a week at Squamish with the family of a friend he has made from university. Orphans the two of them. Joni Mitchell's *River* is stuck on replay in her head. She wishes she had a river she could skate away on.

8   *That which is freely chosen*

Lindsay decided to take Sumi's advice. She decided to abstain from any romantic entanglement for at least nine months, as long as a baby gestates, to see if she could regenerate herself. The energy she would normally expend on dating, she would expend on herself – trying to work out the unfathomable workings of her life.

She signed up for The Landmark Forum. She sat through: "When was the last time you told your parents you loved them? You need to stop blaming them for your life." Moving right along. "What does it mean to be a human being? The insignificance of life. Humans as ants. Life is nothing. Life is everything." It wasn't the uplifting experience others had talked up. It was just a spiral of questions – lunch with Sumi paled in comparison – with the supercilious facilitator perched on his high stool at the front answering every good question from the floor with an infuriating and more ambiguous question in return. In the end it felt like something she had to endure. The fact that other people had depressing lives and damn bad luck and fractured relationships and convoluted problems that they often contributed to, was of no comfort to Lindsay whatsoever. She had no interest in vicariously knowing their details. She had built her bridge a long time ago.

She read *'You can heal your life'*, *'Men are from Mars, Women are from Venus.'* She read *'The Rules'*, all thirty-five of them. She read Deepak Chopra and Khalil Gibran. And then she said to herself, *'Just give me some Pat Conroy, some Michael Ondaatje, some Cormac McCarthy, anything that she'd read in her Reading Through The Wines book club. Give me real life, raw and gritty. Give me fiction full of bleeding hearts more real than any therapy, factual or theoretical.'

Shane suggested she try a new practitioner at their clinic.

'What does this guy do specifically?' Lindsay asked.

Shane handed her his card. 'He's a psychologist and a counsellor.'

Dr Marcus Brookes. Choiceworks. *Making your choices work for you.* What the hell! What did she have to lose?

She booked herself in for a six o'clock session on Wednesday evening. On arrival he offered her rice and sesame infused green tea and a small plate of cut fruit – Sumi's influence on the clinic knew no bounds. That night, and over successive weeks, their sessions became a retrospective of all the major male relationships in her life. But rather than groan at the thought, there was something about this older, mild-mannered man, his large sailor hands, his athletic build, his earrings, his flower power youth that made the peeling back of the layers not too unbearable. His questions were searching and searing at times, but never judgmental.

They started first with Canadian Ross then moved on to Charlie. Charlie was Mr Easy-going. Whenever she asked him what he wanted to do, his reply was, 'up to you.' He was a coaster, a cruiser, his dope-addled mind masking the fact that he couldn't make a decision to save himself. It took him six months of Saturdays to decide what car to buy. He was the ultimate procrastinator. Their relationship was fuelled by frustration, laughter and the odd joint.

Next, Michael, father of two, reeling from his wife's confession that she was in love with another man, struggling to piece his life back together, afford two three-bedroom homes and schedule time for Lindsay in his busy planner that could change at the drop of a hat if one child was sick and he needed to cover. He was a broken man. At times the revenge sex was good but at times it was unfeeling and empty, as if she were a vessel being used. And then there were times when he looked at her with eyes that said, 'you women are all the same, aren't you? You can't be trusted. The only ones I can trust are my children.' Too misogynistic for her.

Michael was followed by Steve from Perth, a long distance affair, the GI – geographically isolated – relationship, or as her friends liked to call it, the geographically impossible, nothing military about it. Long distance relationships were fraught with challenges, agreed Marcus. 'You don't get to see what your partner is really like. You avoid dealing with problem areas.'

Lindsay countered him. 'We didn't really have any problems, except we weren't living in the same place.'

Marcus countered Lindsay. 'So you never had a moment where you disagreed strongly with what he was saying and decided to shut up because you thought, why spoil our forty-eight hours together?' There was no hiding from Marcus. 'See in those types of relationships you never learn to problem-solve as a couple. You have an unrealistic view of your compatibility because when you're together your life's a twenty-four hour a day party. When did you two first get together?'

'About six months before the America's Cup was raced in Freemantle.'

'Coincidence or convenience?' He didn't wait for an answer. 'Party on top of party. Party twenty-four seven. When did the relationship end?'

Sheepishly she said, 'Not long after the competition ended. It was like Australia's loss took the wind out of our sails.'

Then came Anton the pleasure seeking, serial sex addict. She had no problems identifying him. He'd told her, he and his partner Sonia believed affairs were healthy. That it was unrealistic to expect one person to fulfill all your sexual needs. They upheld only one rule: no falling in love. She glanced across the crowded bar and saw his Sonia head to head and foot to leg with another man, exchanging whispers and thought, why not. She knew from day one, the relationship had no future but the sex was so good, so throat-parchingly, nerve-endingly, crampingly good. Why would any sane woman retreat? But then after he asked Kristen if she wanted to be involved in a threesome she realised the guy was completely and utterly insatiable. Ben was almost as bad, almost as good, oh hammer and tongs, on the hunt for pure gratification. When she discovered he had cheated on her with not one, not two, but three other women he announced he had never promised her exclusivity. That was a lesson in taking something for granted.

After Ben, Lindsay went through a dry patch of detox and purification whilst she became seriously attached to Damian, who was seriously attached, as in married, to Trudi who didn't want to have children, but he did. She became his best friend, his shoulder to cry on, secretly hoping he would stop trying to accept the bed he had made and instead pack up and lie with her. He did leave his wife eventually, but by then she was three men down the line starting with Glenn, the commitment phobe, the product of an inimical divorce, the son of a volatile father who treated him and his siblings and his mother abominably. He never wanted to turn into his father and inflict on any woman or child what had been inflicted on him. He lived his life in fear of imminent failure. A man in emotional lockdown. Her heart ached for tortured Glenn.

Ubaldo was the Italian playboy, from Leichardt, the home angel street devil. His meals, his clothes, his room were all immaculately and unquestionably taken care of by his mother Rosalba. Why would any hot-blooded Latin male ever leave that mother ship?

Then came Adam, on secondment for twelve months from the United States, the GI relationship in reverse. Lindsay was the stopgap until he returned to his real relationship. Then came David whom if she stayed with would have turned her into an adventurer widow. He loved life and exploration more than he could ever love her. His weekends were non-negotiable, climbing and abseiling, camping and bush walking (which she all quite enjoyed), in training for his next Himalayan expedition which every year would drain his entire annual savings. David had a beautiful heart.

Unlike Victor. His was made of Australian iron ore and hit her like a wrecking ball. Part of her felt she was still recovering from Victor. She told Marcus she got swept up in his grandiose sense of self-importance. It wasn't until months into the relationship did she discover all the bald-faced lies. He made national rugby selection, told her he captained the Australian under 21 rugby team and spent two seasons playing in Europe, till he damaged a disc in his back. She finally got to meet one of his Rugby buddies who set her straight. Victor told her he'd turned down a Rhodes scholarship to take up a two-year assignment working for Richard Branson in the Middle East. The people he knew, the things he'd done, the aura he carried with him into a restaurant. 'But, in the end,' explained Lindsay, 'I came to see he used anyone and everyone, even his own family.'

'Your classic narcissistic personality disorder,' said Marcus, nodding sagely.

Stunned, Lindsay asked, 'There's a term for that?'

'Yes. Steer clear of those types at all cost. They suck the very soul right out of you, a Faustian trap to be avoided.'

Lastly Martin. Martin ended up being a male version of Kristen. How did she not see that before now? Because Martin was the youngest, where Kristen was the eldest? The product of a big family he felt so claustrophobic with so many people around him, he would always be a perpetual chain dragger when it came to adding any more family of his own. It took her three sessions to get through all the men who had had any bearing on her life. When she finished she asked, 'Are any normal men left? Any straight men?'

Marcus laughed but he didn't answer. Instead he asked, 'Do you have the occasional one night stand?'

'No,' she said, maintaining eye contact. 'I don't go there. I only have a relationship with a man who I want to have a meaningful, potentially lasting, relationship.'

'But do you see that with all of the relationships you've had, there's been very little potential there at all. Whilst each of the men you've dated can be typecast differently, the pattern is the same. You fall in love with men who will not or cannot make a commitment to you. They are either involved with someone else, still recovering from a bad relationship, afraid of commitment, or don't love you enough to want to offer you something serious and lasting. They are all unavailable.'

Willing participants? Yes! Undeniably bonkable? Yes! Available? No? I'm a walking magnet for unavailable men thought Lindsay. Doomed from the outset. There had been times in the past when she had cried with Kristen and Fee and Ange, cried that she was such a pathetic failure with a capital F.

You're not a failure they had told her.

'Then why do all my relationships fail?' she had asked.

'You're looking at it all wrong,' Ange declared. 'None of them was right for you.'

But now in the soft shadows of Dr Brooke's Bali-styled consulting room, with the lemongrass scent burning there was no evading the luminescent light.

'What's wrong with me?' she cried. 'Why do I keep choosing people who can't love me?'

'Bravo, Lindsay,' said Marcus, overjoyed in the face of her pained despondency. He reached for the box of Kleenex. 'We have made real progress today.'

'We have?' she sniffed. 'How's that?'

'You said choose. You didn't say, Why does this always happen to me? You're not a victim here. You're an active participant. And now that you see all this, we can start on the real work: Why do you keep choosing people who can't love you? Why do you sabotage your prospects like that? How can you change so you can make choices that work better for you?'

'Why?' She sighed, her hands pressed against her eyes.

9 *Leave it to the birds*

Eva has few passions. Beachcombing is one, the other, taxidermy of the feathered variety. Strangely the two often collide.

But before taxidermy came rescuing injured birds. When the boy was six they spent a morning together walking along the beach and searching in the speckled rock pools at low tide. They found a young osprey, its feet trapped in fishing line. They managed to hold the frightened creature while they untangled and cut away the constricting knots with an oyster shell. The bird squawked incessantly until they realised its wing was broken and they inadvertently had been inflicting more pain while holding it so firmly. It hopped gingerly away. She and the boy continued beachcombing, but when they returned they found it being attacked by egrets and terns.

'Eva, what are we going to do? It can't save itself, it can't fly away.'

'It's called survival of the species. Darwin's theory. The strongest in nature survive by killing off the weakest.'

But before the egrets and terns could decide who was the victor a bald eagle came swooping towards them. Had she been by herself she would have stepped back and watched the spectacle with interest but with the boy's eyes already pleading at her, she only had one choice. He had seen the eagle too and he'd already seen too much death in his short life. Snatching the osprey up she yelled, 'run' as they raced in the direction of the woods.

He wanted to put it in the henhouse.

'We won't have any fowl left,' she said. 'Goodbye eggs. No more toast soldiers.'

'What are we going to do about its wing?'

'Nothing.' She paused. 'I have no idea how to set a bird's wing.'

'Can we take it to the vet?'

'I'm stretched for doctor bills as it is. Vet bills you can forget.'

'Can't you fix it?'

'What am I? Archangel St Raphael, the patron saint of healing?'

He looked at her blankly.

'Can you ask your God to fix it?' He was getting more and more upset by the minute.

'We'll pray,' she said, squeezing his shoulder.

They went round and picked up Ken, the boy's adopted Grandfather, and then they drove to the refuse tip, scrounged up some chicken wire and some stakes and built a pen for the pitiful flightless creature and wouldn't you know, it survived. Its left wing was forever crippled. They'd watch it take off and it would beat its right wing twice as much as a way of maintaining its course, counteracting its skewed balance.

In those watchful, hopeful days, Eva knew the bird's recovery and hesitant departure was not the end but the beginning. The boy had discovered birdlife and at the age of six, his calling in life. It was a marvel that one so young could have such trenchant clarity, such intense passion.

His quest for knowledge was boundless. She borrowed books from the Prince Rupert library on ornithology, the anatomy of birds, the identification of birds, birds throughout history. Together they pored over the feathered markings; the migration patterns; the nesting habits; their wingspans; their life spans. Every year for his birthday she would buy him a new book, *A Bird-Finding Guide to Canada. The Birders Guide to British Columbia. Stokes Field Guide to Bird Songs*, a tape compilation.

Then he decided he wanted to keep his own birds. 'No,' she said, fending off a shiver. 'Birds are meant to be free, not kept as caged creatures.' She knew he would agree.

'Injured birds then?' he asked.

There was no local wildlife rehabilitation centre, no raptor rehab place but Ken had been a bird lover all his life and once had kept his own raptors. Ken was happy to share with him all he knew about bird lore, about beating brush and flushing quarry. At eleven years of age, the lad cut down fir saplings, scrounged more chicken wire and somehow sweet-talked Ken and two other men into helping him construct two large pens in a clearing off the trail between their house and the coast.

'I don't own that land,' she warned them.

'I won't tell anyone,' said Ken. 'If we have to pull it down one day, so be it.'

And so while the boy tagged along on hunt and training sessions with red-tail hawks and kestrels, peregrines and Harris hawks, Eva applied herself to the art of taxidermy.

After all, not all injured birds of prey recovered. And she was just as much in awe of their feathered friends as he.

She needed some help to begin with. She'd read enough books but some of the mechanics she just couldn't visualise. She wanted instruction from a professional. She found a weeklong summer course in Longview Alberta run by a Reginald Palmer, a seasoned taxidermist, to be held in the science lab of the local high school. All up she and the lad were away for four weeks. They packed the stationwagon and drove to Prince George, then through Quesnell, Williams Lakes, Kamloops, through Banff National Park, Canmore, almost all the way to Calgary before heading south to Longview. On the return trip they went up the Icefields Parkway through Jasper. She liked Jasper. She liked the feel of it on her tongue.

They camped at national park campgrounds, where eager, well-fed squirrels abounded and timid wapiti occasionally visited. They cooled down in mountain streams.

'Who taught you all about camping, Eva?'

What was she going to say? My father? My brother? My husband?

'People who are no longer of this world.' She paused. 'I learnt a bit here, a bit there, but I've forgotten plenty.'

There wasn't much for the lad to do in Longview. For five days he had to either join her in the class, read, or walk around the school grounds. Dead birds didn't interest him as much as live ones.

But after that week, Eva knew about skinning and fleshing, about anatomy and engineering. She knew how to handle washing and tumbling and drying of bird skins, how to position mounts with proper attitude, shape and design. She learned how to prepare manikins with either hand-made excelsior bodies or cast urethane bodies, how to construct necks, and how to rebuild muscle and skull structure using either original skulls or cast headwork. She sewed and wired and then when all was ready, learnt how to position and secure a completed bird in its own habitat.

Over the years she became quite a master at taxidermy. Part of the back porch was added to and closed in to accommodate a workshop for her creations. Ken and his pals came back to help with that. 'Are you sure you own this land now Eva?' he jibed.

She has a reputation, but not by name. Her birds are on display at the local heritage centre and surplus mounts are for sale in the gift shop. Surprisingly they sell. In the past she would occasionally accept private commissions, often against her better judgment for it would become something more than just the bird, there was another human involved. But the lad used to encourage her and become excited about her accomplishments. Now she's somewhat ambivalent about it all.

The birds she can't part with loom large in her lounge room. A great grey owl on a branch. It glares at the unsuspecting when they enter the front door. A golden eagle, perched on a rock, and her first ever attempt, a Steller jay.

Now the cages are all empty, the birds free. They have grown up, grown stronger, taken flight – just like him.

10 A door she doesn't want to open

The most exhilarating hour in Lindsay's week was the hour she spent with Dr Brookes, studying her own Pandora's box. Who knew one's own life could hold such thrall? Something from the Forum bubbled up. The Johari Window. You don't know what you don't know. Now it had relevance.

Lindsay had two of the three classic symptoms that made her prone to choosing unavailable partners.

1. As a child she felt abandoned by a parent. Therefore she was predisposed to repeating this pattern as an adult by finding partners who also couldn't be there for her.

'How did Shane escape that?' she asked.

'Because,' said Dr Brookes, 'you never abandoned her as a child. You were her de facto parent. The person who was her rock.'

'Our father never abandoned us. Abandon implies free will. He had no free choice in the matter.'

'That I don't dispute, but did you miss your father when he was gone?'

'Of course!'

'Did you feel this overwhelming sense of loss, of grief, of wondering why me? Why us?'

'Yes, yes, yes!'

'Did you want him to come back?'

'I'm not even going to answer that,' she said.

He said, 'the word is not important. What's important is the feeling and what you suffered. That was undeniable. That was crippling.'

2. She was afraid of intimacy. She wasn't sexually or physically abused as a child. She didn't have her boundaries

violated, but sometime after her father died, somewhere in the dark black abyss of her pain, somewhere in the midst of resigning herself to the loss of the man she loved so unconditionally, she decided never to let anyone get that close to her ever again. In the days and weeks following her father's death there came a moment when her old life ended and a new one began. As an unconscious method of protecting herself from pain, Lindsay would choose male partners with whom she could never have a truly committed and intimate relationship. Yet, conversely, she was too trusting in relationships. 'You're prone to measure all men by your father,' said Dr Brookes. 'But not all men have your father's integrity. Not all men come to you with their arms wide open, their palms upturned offering their unguarded heart and their unconditional love.'

Lindsay brought up Shane's theory.

He rose and grabbed a book by Barbara De Angelis and laid it on the table. 'Read it. Shane's right. You'll soon see that your understanding and memories of happiness and contentment and love equal your home life with your father and Shane. And furthermore, that your home life equalled you taking care of everything. Ergo love for you equals taking care of everything. When you are taking care of everything you think that is how and when you will find the happiness and contentment and love your heart most desires.'

In dawning realisation, Lindsay whispered, 'When I'm taking care of everything, what's left for the people around me to do but take what I'm offering. And take and take.'

'Exactly. And if they are not the kind that give in return like your father, you will continue to give more and more hoping eventually they will reciprocate in kind.'

That had a name too. The "Going Home Syndrome."

At the end of one long session Lindsay said, 'I understand everything we've been talking about. I see it all clearly now. But what I don't see is how do I change my future choices. Is it just a matter of me being conscious, of thinking with my head and not my heart?'

'No, it's not, I'm afraid. If you went out in the world now armed with the knowledge you have you would still likely commit the same mistakes. For change to be effective it needs to not just be intellectually driven but also experientially driven, be that a process of driving away from something or driving towards something. You may have understood it all, but have you dealt with it all? Do you understand your pain? Because until you understand your pain, until you feel it and give voice to it, you can't move on because you don't know what you're moving on from.'

He waited. 'Have you processed those two reasons?'

'I think so.' Though moments later Lindsay glanced his way and asked, 'What do you mean exactly?'

'Tell me how these two symptoms have impacted you?'

Lindsay exhaled. 'The way I reacted to my father's death was to make certain decisions deep in my psyche about the way I live my life in order to protect myself from future pain.'

'A good textbook definition, Lindsay. But I need more. How old were you at the time?'

'Thirteen and a half.'

'And where were you when your father died?'

'I was with my Dad's parents. They lived not far from us on the outskirts of Winnipeg.'

'And did you ever go back to your family home?'

'Yes.' She swallowed. 'Once.'

'Okay, take me back to the house in Winnipeg. Take me back to the time you walked through the front door knowing your father would not be following you, knowing your father would not be inside.'

Lindsay looked at him. After several moments, Marcus said, 'When did you go back there?'

'Two days before my father's funeral.' She paused. 'Everyone thought that would be best.'

'Did you want to go?'

'Yes,' her eyes met his, 'mostly, because that place was Dad.' Lindsay did not continue.

Marcus waited. 'Talk me through it,' he said.

Lindsay could only stare at Marcus feeling like she couldn't breathe, let alone speak. Finally, she surrendered an 'I can't,' and started to cry.

In a gentle voice, Marcus said, 'You don't want to, that's different.'

'I don't want to.'

'I know, but do it anyway. Take me back to that house.'

'Please don't make me do this.'

'I'm not going to make you do this. I'm going to sit here and wait patiently until you decide you are ready to do this.'

Lindsay sat and cried in silence for ten, fifteen, twenty minutes. She had no idea how long she wrestled with her mind full of the image of their wooden front door, of the narrow rippled glass panel down the side, her Uncle Jonathan – always Uncle Jay to her, her Aunty Belle, and Aunty Abby, her Nana and Poppa Marlow, Shane, all in formation behind her. Eventually Lindsay whispered, 'It was horrible. It wasn't our home anymore. It was so quiet.' She gasped for a breath. 'It was so empty, but I could still smell him. I could smell his aftershave. I could smell the sweat on his unwashed clothes in the laundry. I could see the unopened mail addressed to him.' She lowered her head as heavy tears fell on her lap.

'Keep walking through the house, Lindsay, I'm holding your hand.' And he was, without her knowing it; Dr Brookes had come to sit next to her on the couch.

'His pajamas were still under his pillow. Around the collar I could still smell the soap he used. The bed was made from weeks earlier. It wasn't warm anymore. I wanted to see his indentation there. I wanted to see it tossed and rumpled like he'd just got up. And vaguely in the background I heard Shane calling out Dad, Dad, as if she hoped he was hiding in some cupboard about to jump out and surprise us.'

'And how did you feel, Lindsay? What was the thing you felt the most?'

Lindsay closed her eyes. The twenty-year caulk on her emotions was being stretched to breaking point, the pain surging, her voice rasping. 'That my heart had burst into flames. Such fire, such agony. I couldn't breathe and I thought that's okay. I will die and when I die I will be with Dad. But I didn't die and I think that was the most unbearable part.'

'That you had to go on living without him.'

'Yes,' cried Lindsay, releasing Dr Brookes' hand to press her own hands to her face, holding inside the memories. She and Shane had cried themselves to sleep that night on their father's double bed.

Dr Brookes let her cry. He let her re-live and re-vent her emotions. Later, much later, he asked, 'and what happened after that?'

'We moved in with my father's parents.'

'Did you want to live with your grandparents?'

'We didn't mind. They had lost their son. They didn't want to lose us as well. Aunts and uncles on my mother's side offered to take us, but in the end they acceded to my grandparents' wishes.'

'What about afterwards, months afterwards? Aside from the heartache, did you feel any anger that your father was gone and you were left behind?'

'Months and months of sadness,' she whispered, 'we just continued to miss him. It was like the sun was permanently eclipsed. Our days were never as bright or as colourful or as happy again.'

'Even to this day?'

'Even to this day.'

11   *I am the plane circling the sky*

Not long after that painful night, Lindsay spent another tearful one with her sister. They had moved into their grandparents by this stage. The room they used to sleep in, on average one night a fortnight, was now their permanent room. Their Nana said she would turn over her sewing room so the girls could have a room each but Lindsay and Shane had both looked at each other and said they wanted to share. No one argued with them.

One night sometime after they had gone to sleep, Shane crawled into Lindsay's bed and asked, 'Can you still see Dad's face?'

'Yes,' whispered Lindsay.

'There is a little movie in my head of the morning he left,' said Shane. 'He was happy wasn't he?'

'Yes,' whispered Lindsay.

'Remember he was singing.'

'*Let Your Love Flow* by the Bellamy Brothers.'

'No he wasn't, he was singing Neil Diamond, *What A Beautiful Noise.*'

'Are you sure?' asked Lindsay.

'Yes, because after he sung clickety-clack he started singing something else, clipperty clop, which isn't in that song normally.'

'When did he sing that?'

'As he was getting into his truck.'

Lindsay could have sworn he was singing something else. And that upset her doubly, that she could lose those last memories of her father by not having been present to their last minute together. She felt like her heart was being squeezed every minute of every day. Reeling had become her way of life. How do you go on living after your father, your only parent has died?

Lindsay was just a few months shy of fourteen and till then she had never given her future much thought. From time to time she would think about the future with respect to holidays. When the next one was coming up – were they staying put, would their Dad have some time off or would they be going to stay with one of their relatives. Nothing about that life fazed or disappointed her. She felt that whatever they did, they would end up having a good time. But now Lindsay felt she was staring down a long endless road with no destination in sight and, distressingly, she had very little motivation to walk it. She plodded through her days. She couldn't imagine much of her old life in her new life up ahead.

The morning they had stood and watched her father leave they were at their grandparent's place and even their Poppa and Nana were outside waving him off. It was school holidays and their father had told them months before he couldn't take as much time off this summer as he'd been the one to have a long holiday the summer before when they went to British Columbia. All he could manage would be a couple of weeks together away somewhere. They were happy with that.

Lindsay wished she could find that feeling again, of not being disappointed, of being accepting and assured that come what may, she would enjoy the company of family and the experiences they shared. She wished she could ask her father for advice on how to keep on living. She felt out of everyone her father would know. She tried to find something to hold on to. It was his smile and his wave as he drove off that day.

'You know what I've decided,' whispered Shane sometime later.

'What?' she whispered back.

'He's still up in the sky.'

Lindsay smiled in the dark, thinking, if only.

'Whenever I see a small plane I tell myself it's Dad. He

can't come down but he's still with us from time to time, flying over to check on us.'

'That's lovely,' said Lindsay, tears trailing out the sides of her eyes, marveling at how her young sister had been able to work out something she had not, something her father would have told them.

That October their Uncle Jay and Aunty Belle flew in for Thanksgiving. Together with their grandparents, they drove to Riding Mountain National Park and rented out a log cabin on the shores of Lake Audy. After a clear, windless day they had an early dinner on a jetty jutting out in the lake as the sun set over the water, painting the sky in a rich palette of blues and oranges. The surface of the lake at sundown was so still it seemed the wharf was stretching into the sky. And then as if orchestrated a small light aircraft flew overhead. Shane had looked at Lindsay then come over and hugged her, the two of them crying but laughing a little as well.

That weekend had been a turning point where Lindsay realised that the life she had with their father wasn't completely over. Her Uncle Jay was determined that some of their treasured childhood experiences would continue. His and Aunty Belle's youngest child, Andrew, was now twenty. For all intents and purposes they were childfree again, yet they saw Lindsay and Shane as more than just their nieces. That they had surprised them by flying in and taking them away for Thanksgiving meant everything. It was what their father would do – turn up and surprise them with something he had planned but never hinted at.

One morning she and Shane were sitting with their Uncle at the end of the jetty, their feet dangling over the edge, when Lindsay said, 'Tell us about our father, Uncle Jay. When did you meet him?'

He told them then about his first medical expedition to the West of Hudson Bay to Churchill, Maguse River, Alder Lake and Rankin Inlet. How their father was only twenty-years old but had flown Jonathan and his Grandfather there so they could administer to the local Inuit population.

'I remember your father saying to me: "I never really feel I know a country or its people until I can get up into the skies in a small aircraft and witness the lay of the land." That's what we did that summer.'

'Your father died before his father too, didn't he?' asked Lindsay, recalling a detail from her distant past.

'Yes. He died when I was twenty-one.'

'At least you had twenty-one years with him,' mumbled Shane.

'That, I did,' said Uncle Jay, 'and like you, they were all good years. I was luckier than my brother and sisters.'

'How old was he when he died?' Lindsay asked.

'Forty-four.'

She inhaled softly. 'He was younger than Dad.'

'Yes,' he drawled. 'He was.'

'Do you remember him?'

'Of course.'

'What do you remember about him?'

'Lots of things.'

'Tell us a memory,' begged Shane.

'Well, I remember when I was Lindsay's age we lived in Toronto and Dad I used to go skate sailing on the frozen lakes in winter. We each had our own sail. They were about seven feet high and about six feet across – a bit like the shape of a giant cicada wing with a bar across the middle and another one at one end that you'd use to hold the sail and move against the wind to adjust your course. We'd hold onto that bar and let the wind blow us across the lake. See who could go the fastest. It was exhilarating. You would go much faster than you would skating normally. It was the one thing that made me enjoy windy winter days.'

'Was it scary?' asked Shane.

'In the beginning, but it was more thrilling than scary and it was something Dad and I did together. Abigail, Morton and Gene were too young to join us – they'd stay home with Mum. It was our special thing.'

'Do you miss your father?' asked Lindsay.

'Some days. But there's many a day I feel he's with me.

Whenever I step outside on a bright blustery winter's day I feel him saying to me. "Good day for a skate today, Jonathan".'

Some weeks later their Uncle sent them a poem. *Do not stand at my grave and weep.* Lindsay and Shane read it over and over till they knew it by heart. Shane even added her own stanza:

I am the plane circling in the sky,
a reflected wing catching your eye.

12   The elephant in the room

Another week, another session. 'Last week was a big week,' said Lindsay by way of opening.

'Yes we started to deal with your pain.'

'Started?' queried Lindsay.

'Started. And let me tell you we have to spend a lot of time back there before we can move forward to the pain of now.'

'The pain of now?'

'Yes. How your current choices are hurting you, costing you big time, stopping you from attaining your heart's most fervent desires. How you are letting the injured and well-intentioned but misguided motives of a fourteen year old determine your happiness as a thirty-three year old woman. I'm not going to begin to tell you of the pain and hurt and anger and forgiveness we still have to work through with the present day you.'

Lindsay swallowed the lump back down. 'I'm not going to begin to tell you that I don't want to know.' But secretly she was intrigued. 'Do I have multiple personalities?'

'No. You are just as mentally stable as the next person, albeit possibly slightly more damaged.'

'What was that you said about forgiveness?' she asked.

'To start with, you need to recognise that by your father's ill-timed death, he completely and utterly destroyed your home life.'

'I don't blame him for that.'

'On a conscious level you don't. But let me assure you, you wouldn't be human if on a subconscious level you didn't scream against the injustice of what happened to you, if you didn't blame him for irrevocably destroying your

58

precious family and the only home you ever knew.'

Lindsay stared at him. 'One day, not today, not tomorrow, we need to face that unflinchingly and look at how you can forgive your father for dying.'

'O merciful Jesus,' Lindsay whispered under her breath.

At times, when she and Shane went to Montreal to stay with their mother's mother, Granny Becca, she would take them to Catholic Mass in the Notre Dame Cathedral. It was Canada's largest cathedral and could accommodate up to 7000 worshippers. Its west tower, The Perseverance, housed Le Gros Bourdon, a huge bronze bell – the largest in the world. It weighed 85 tonnes and was only rung on important occasions. Her grandmother had told them she could remember it ringing to mark the end of World War II in 1945.

Lindsay never heard it ring but she always wanted to. One year, Shane and Lindsay had spent Christmas in Montreal with their father, Granny Becca, Wyatt, Uncle Jay and his family, Aunty Abby and all their Toronto relatives. They had gone to midnight mass. It was a magical evening.

The sisters learnt about prayer from both their grandmothers, their paternal grandmother being perhaps even more devout than their Granny. On another visit, Lindsay had drilled her Granny Becca on God. Do you have to believe in God? Why did she believe in God? How can you prove there's a God? And, did God take her father away from them?

It has been a long conversation that carried on for several days. What Lindsay appreciated about the conversation was her grandmother's honesty – she had struggled with her beliefs – and her willingness to say: "I don't know" or "You can't" to some of Lindsay's questions. At the end of the week Lindsay had decided that God wasn't a father she could relate to, besides she had a father she adored – but Jesus she could admire. He didn't judge people, he got on with everyone, he associated with people others wouldn't, he suffered, he forgave, he died and lived once more. He was a role model and a symbol of hope.

Marcus was looking at his notes, absently tapping his pen. 'Today I want to go back to what we addressed a few weeks ago, one of the reasons for your ill-considered choices when it comes to suitable male partners being, as a child or in your case, adolescent, you were, quote unquote, abandoned by a parent – your father.'

'Yes,' said Lindsay.

'What's the story with your mother?'

'My mother?' Lindsay was surprised. She never spoke of her mother to anyone. 'My mother is dead.'

'You know that for a fact?'

'Well, no.'

'When was the last time you saw her?'

'When I was three years old.'

'What do you know of this woman, your mother?'

'The barest details.' Lindsay sighed. 'What can I tell you? Really I only have one image of my mother, sitting trancelike staring out the window. She was like a statue. Like Salem's wife. When Dad walked in the door at the end of the day he would put her in bed and take care of us. That's what I remember. I actually have stronger recollections of my Granny Becca than I have of my mother from that period in my life.'

'Granny Becca being...?'

'My mother's mother.'

'What do you remember of her?'

'She lived in Montreal but she and Wyatt, her husband, our grandfather, would come and stay with us sometimes while Dad was away working and they'd take us out on picnics in the park and we would ride swings or Wyatt would take Mum somewhere, like to a movie, while we would stay home with Granny and play.

'I remember her standing at the bottom of the ramp outside the back of our house, in the middle of summer, her skirts hitched up into her underpants, laughing and clapping at Shane and I as we slid down this khaki-coloured tarpaulin that she had the hose running on, adding dishwashing liquid so we would slide down even faster and in the end she joined us going down headfirst in all those suds. She must have been well in her sixties at the time but it didn't stop her. She was the one who played with us. Mom never did.'

'What happened to your mother?'

'She was sent away to hospital. Committed.' Lindsay shrugged, raised her eyebrows.' You know, fruit loop.'

'What was her condition?'

'I don't know exactly. Some kind of depression, I think.'

'So your mother abandoned you too?'

'No! She wasn't there to begin with. She wasn't well. She was a sick woman.'

'Lindsay, you're so stoic. You're so understanding. So forgiving on so many levels, always the adult. But have you ever considered in all your rationalising, in all the coddled whispers you overheard when you were a child that you may have disassociated yourself from yourself. I doubt you've ever given voice to the anger and hurt and confusion and the insensibility of your three-year old self.'

Another thirty-minute discussion ensued. Eventually, they moved on. 'So you haven't seen your mother for over thirty years. Do you ever wonder what became of your mother?'

Lindsay grimaced. 'Rarely. I mean when people mention Mother's Day I think mother, what's that?'

'But do you ever wonder if she's still in an institution or if she's somehow managed to rejoin society and live a semblance of a normal life.'

Lindsay exhaled. 'For years I thought she was hospitalised... in a wasted state. But when I was eight, I discovered she had been out for over a year.'

'She was well and chose not to be a part of your life?'

'I never said she was well. She disappeared. We never heard from her. She may have committed suicide, who knows? But clearly she chose not to be a part of our life.'

'How do you feel about your mother choosing to not be part of your life?"

'I don't feel about it.'

'If it were possible, would you welcome her into your life now?'

'That's a big unknown.'

Doctor Brookes eyed her. She eyed him back. 'I would welcome my father back tomorrow unquestioningly. My mother doesn't stir any emotion in me.'

'None, whatsoever? I find that hard to believe.'

Minutes later, Lindsay said, 'Maybe incomprehension. I never knew her. I never understood her motives.'

'Granted.' He paused. 'This week I'd like you to spend some time thinking about your mother. Thinking about what happened to her, what she did and how that made you feel. Write down everything that comes to you. For now, tell me, who were the people who loved your mother?'

'I don't know, her family, I guess.'

'You guess?'

'I was four or five, come on I don't know.'

'Let me ask you a different question. After your mother disappeared from your life, who from her life was in your life?'

'Our granny. Wyatt. Uncle Jay. Aunty Abby. Aunty Belle. Occasionally Uncle Morton.'

'Were there any of your mother's friends?'

Lindsay shook her head, all of a sudden wondering, how come her mother had no close friends.

'And did you have good relationships with your mother's relatives?'

'Yes, of course. They loved us. They showed their love for us. They spoke of their love for us.'

'And do you think these people loved your mother in the same way? I mean, it doesn't seem likely that they would not love their daughter or sister but love her offspring.'

'No,' Lindsay drawled, 'it doesn't.'

'And why do you think they loved her?'

'Because she was family.'

'You think that's a universal law? You think people don't have a choice in whether they love their family members or not? You're a classic case in point as right now

I doubt you love your mother.'

'She doesn't feel like family.'

'It would seem your mother still felt like family to her family. It would seem that her family loved her. And they chose to continue loving her despite her neglecting her children.'

'Yes, I can see that. They never said a bad word about her.'

'What about your father? Did he say a bad word about her?'

'No,' said Lindsay groaning. She covered her face trying to stop the images pressing up against her eyes. 'He made us write letters to her that we would never send. He'd just put them in a box along with our drawings and photos he'd keep for her. He tried to keep her alive for us as if he hoped one day she would come back.'

'And she never did.'

'No,' she whispered.

'Did he talk about her often?'

'Once a month at first, then not much, maybe a bit more in the latter years. I think it was the rose-tinted glasses effect.'

'Did your father ever meet anyone else?'

'Not that we were aware of.'

'Does that not strike you as odd? He was a handsome man by all reports. Energetic, a go-getter. Sounds like lots of women would have found him attractive. It's interesting that he didn't form an attachment to someone, don't you think?'

'Maybe he was like me. Unlucky in love.' Dr Brookes gave her a look. 'Alright!' She put her hand up to stop him. 'I haven't been unlucky. I've been ignorant and uninformed.'

'Good.' He smiled encouragingly. 'For now I want to stay with your mother. It seems to me and I could well be wrong, that your mother was well loved by her family and husband. Does that seem the case with you?'

Once upon a time Lindsay would have said, 'So?' as in

big deal, big difference. But now she wasn't as ambivalent as she once was. Softly she said, 'Yes.'

'Why did they love her so? Why did they show her so much compassion? Why did they cut her such slack?'

'I don't know.'

'Does that not awaken some sense, that all is not what it seems. That there's something you're missing. Something that you weren't told, or didn't know. Maybe something the people who loved you were protecting you from because of your age?'

'Yes,' she whispered.

'When was the last time you talked about your mother to the people who knew her best?'

'So long ago, I can't remember. Never?' She filed that in the talk to Shane on the weekend file.

'What was your mother's name?'

'Gene.'

'Gene,' he repeated. 'Back to my earlier question, if Gene were alive and you had the opportunity to meet her now, would you be interested?'

'She'd be a complete stranger to me.'

'A complete stranger who, if she were sane, might be able to unlock some of the enigma of your childhood. A complete stranger who could enhance the life of your father, who could enhance your life maybe in a myriad of unseen ways.'

'But what would happen if her re-entry into my life had the complete opposite effect. I mean I wouldn't want to meet this woman for her to tell me my father was a notorious womanizer and that caused her irreversible depression. My father was a saint and my memories of him are sacred. I never want them desecrated in any shape or form.'

'That's highly unlikely, but even so you could set boundaries.'

'I don't think so.' Lindsay wasn't at all interested.

'Does her health not stir some degree of curiosity? The possibility that she could have some medical condition, depression and the like, that might be hereditary?'

'I don't need her for that. I could find that out from Uncle Jay.'

'When did he last see her?'

'I don't know. Sometime in 1969.'

'Well what does he know of the last thirty years?'

The answer hung unspoken between them.

'When was the last time you saw your Uncle?'

She wiped her brow. 'Four, five years ago.'

They paused while Dr Brookes made fresh tea. As he poured, he asked, ' Have you ever wondered why it is you are wanting a partner to have children with? Yet your father did such a superb job of being a single parent. Why is the image of the husband and wife so important to you? Is there some pull there towards your mother or is it because you want what you didn't have yourself?'

Lindsay twirled the warm teacup in her hand, blowing to cool its straw-coloured contents. After some minutes she said, 'I think it's because I worry about what will happen to my children if something were to happen to me.'

Dr Brookes sipped his tea. 'I think you're right. But you're forgetting, Shane. She's no longer your baby sister.'

13   Titania, Queen of the fairies

Her mother was not a topic Lindsay and Shane had spoken about with much interest or regularity as children or teenagers with their father or any relatives for that matter. Maybe they had a handful of conversations. A year or so after their father had disappeared she remembered asking her Uncle Jay to tell her something about their mother.

The first thing he told her was that she had lived in Geneva and worked for the United Nations. The fact seemed to verge on the outlandish – hard to imagine her incapable mother had once held such a capable position. The idea seemed so preposterous until he said in the next breath, 'Yes she was a member of the United Nations Commission on Human Rights that drafted the Declaration of the Rights of the Child that was adopted by the General Assembly in 1959.' Now that thought seemed utterly ridiculous – her mother a luminary on the rights of the child!

Lindsay needed something more conventional and believable. 'What else can you tell me?'

'Gene was a very good singer. She could have trained to be a mezzo-soprano except she wasn't happy in the limelight. She liked being part of the choir. She would sing solo under sufferance as long as she stood within the choir not separate to it – that way she felt less conspicuous.

'I remember once when she was sixteen, she and Mum joined Belle and me for a week's holiday on Mazinaw Lake. We were out canoeing and picnicking one day when we beached our canoes and walked up this gorge. I started yelling in the chasm and it echoed and ricocheted off the limestone cliffs. When I stopped, Gene started singing

Amazing Grace and the three of us were dazzled by the effect of her voice in that chamber. I wish there was a way I could have recorded it. She had a beautiful voice your mother, the timbre so rich yet surprisingly powerful.'

'Did she sing with our father?' Lindsay asked.

'Sometimes,' Uncle Jay said. 'They had lovely voices the two of them.'

Lindsay had forgotten all about that conversation until a decade later, in her early years in Sydney she had a meeting with a client in a building on Martin Place. Partway though the meeting she heard the most unusual sound as if someone had just turned on at full volume a CD of a classical diva singing Puccini. 'Sounds like an opera singer,' Lindsay commented.

'It is,' said one of the guys in the meeting.

'Are they practicing for a performance?' she asked. There was a small stage in the Martin Place mall reserved for regular lunchtime concerts. But here it was four p.m. in the day.

'No,' said one of his colleagues. 'It's a deranged opera singer. She walks through Martin Place singing out her lungs, using the acoustics of the buildings as a massive chamber to amplify and reverberate her singing. Always late in the afternoon, as if she wakes up from the turps and goes on her jaunt.'

Lindsay's initial reaction was how quaint, how novel, till something about the story seemed hauntingly familiar. Suddenly she felt light-headed. She took a sip of water. 'What does she look like?'

'An old, skinny version of Stevie Nicks, wearing green elfin-like outfits and tawdry make-up. She rarely wears shoes – even in winter.'

'Does she come through every afternoon at four o'clock?'

'No,' said another guy. 'Only about once a month, but always around this time.'

Lindsay wanted to postpone the meeting immediately to run down stairs. But she couldn't. Afterwards she went down to Martin Place and bought a coffee waiting for the mysterious mad woman to return. She never did. But from that day on, Lindsay always made her appointments in Martin Place for around 2.30 in the afternoon and one day, months down the track, after one of her meetings she heard then spotted the mysterious waif of a woman, skipping and dancing through Martin Place like she was walking through *A Midsummer Night's Dream*.

Boldly Lindsay walked out into the main thoroughfare and stared at the crazed and hagged fairy queen as she frolicked towards her with a vacant look on her face that failed to spark a flicker of recognition. It wasn't her mother. At least not the mother she could remember. But later Lindsay wondered, had she wanted her to be?

14   Her spells

Menopause was hell. How could any sane women go through menopause and not come out agitated and moody. Eva found the smallest thing could upset her and exhaust her patience with herself and everyone, everyone being the lad. It had a lot to do with putting an object down and not being able to find it again. She used to think the boy had moved things on her. Not intentionally or maliciously, but borrowed something, like a pair of scissors and not put them back where they belonged, or where she'd last left them. She'd ask him and he wouldn't have a clue. He'd get up and go looking for the said item...usually to find it in some place she couldn't ever remember leaving it.

And that started to unravel her...as if there were someone else or something else in her house stirring up trouble. She'd twirl around trying to catch them. It.

Occasionally, she would yell, 'Leave me alone! Get out of this house!'

Occasionally the lad would be around and ask, 'Are you talking to me?'

'No!' she would say, as if that was a ridiculous idea.

'Who then?'

'Never mind,' she'd reply. 'I thought I saw a giant mouse. A rat most likely.' She'd shudder in pretense.

But she knew. When she started talking out loud it was a sure warning sign of what was to come. She would ring up Beth or Sarah or the mother of one of his friends and tell them she had a migraine coming on and ask if they would mind him coming to stay for a few days. Huh! That phone that she didn't want, that he did.

As soon as he was gone, she would walk into every

room of the house, casting her eyes back and forth, saying, 'Come on, show yourself.' She would go into each room, ten, twenty, thirty times. She never counted the entries and exits but it became an uncontrollable compulsion. 'I know you're here!' she'd yell at empty rooms, at silent walls.

But while she was searching, they were still, and when she was still, they weren't. So she'd have to sit quietly on the stairs or on the lounge or on the stool at the kitchen bench.

In quiet, biding moments, she'd see black figures blurring past her, swooping at angles. Out of the corner of her eye, she'd catch their dark shape, almost after they had whisked by. She never actually saw them coming, or saw them being, she just saw them going.

She wondered if they – it? - was the angel of death, waiting, swirling, trying to intimidate her so she would do what she had never quite managed to do before – so he could claim her. Or was it the evil force that she could never seem to outrun, snickering, 'I've got my eye on you, on him.'

She never knew how they got in, for she never heard them. And it annoyed her that the dog wasn't alert to them either. Some watchdog he was. There would be days when she would be so berserk that she'd just get up and leave, telling them they could have the house. Just don't burn it down, she'd warn. At the back entrance, she would pause for the final part of her concession and say, "I'll be back later and when I am, I want my house back without any unwanted and unwelcome guests thank you very much.'

Often the fresh air, the frantic walking, the need for oxygen, would start to sooth her: the Pacific silver firs with their large cones like stout altar candles upright and at the ready; the white spruce trees, seldom found in the northwest but two in the forest near her home, their crushed needles in her palm, a calming disinfecting balm. When she'd return, she'd close all the curtains to keep the dark out, and the light in, flicking on every switch on her way past.

After a few days the lad would return. He'd never call.

He'd just turn up. It was as if he were waiting outside and knew when it was fine to join her again.

'You okay?' He'd ask.

'Yes. Thank you,' she'd reply. 'It has passed for now.'

She'd try and repay the families that helped them by reciprocating in her good spells, letting him have friends over for sleepovers, bird training, the usual stuff teenagers got up to in British Columbia, but as much as she tried she could never relax with other people in her home. The best she could do would be to retreat to her room, or the workshop, hand over the house to him as if it were his house and she a guest and the one practically overstaying her welcome.

15 An unexamined life

The questions Dr Brookes raised were questions Lindsay had held at bay for decades. But now they swarmed around her like a disturbed hive of wasps that kept on growing and growing and growing. And it wasn't just the questions about her mother. It was the whole process. Almost as if she'd gone to Fred Hollows for surgery so the cataracts were removed from her eyes and she saw questions within questions within questions, culminating in how well did she know Lindsay Marlow? Who were the people, what were the places and events that had made her who she was today?

It wasn't as if Lindsay had lived a shallow life. She had lived a very full and active life: an MBA from the University of Sydney, a graduate of Sail Australia, a multi-year entrant in the 111 kilometre overnight Hawkesbury canoe classic, her open dive master ticket. It just wasn't a life of deep introspection. But now Socrates had come knocking at her quiescent door. What she didn't know about herself was monumental. What she didn't know about her family was astronomical.

After her father vanished she and Shane lived with their grandparents in Winnipeg while Lindsay finished school. Then she stayed on in Winnipeg while Shane finished school, studying business at the University of Manitoba, even though she would much rather have studied in Toronto or Montreal there was no likelihood of her abandoning Shane at fourteen years of age. But as soon as Shane graduated and Lindsay returned from her down under adventure they headed east where she secured an internship with IBM in Toronto and Shane enrolled in osteopathy. Two years later, she set off on her grand world tour, starting with California, then Mexico and Hawaii where she nabbed a position crewing on a boat that sailed across the Pacific to Rarotonga, Fiji, New Zealand and then Sydney, and there she had stayed. She'd only been to Canada three times since she left; two of those trips to see her Dad's ailing parents before each of them had passed away. Most of her history, most – in fact all – of the people who knew about her, who could help her understand the labyrinth of her life, were half a world a way, living lives that were diminishing by the day.

Lindsay talked about this at length with her sister. Sumi was also privy to their conversations. In the prime of their life, from distant Sydney, Australia, they inspected their childhood and came to one undeniable conclusion: even though they never really had a mother and even though they lost their father way too early, they never felt like orphans. They were always with family who loved them. Looking at their life through the mature eyes of normal functioning adults they came to understand one thing clearly: they were fortunate indeed to have family there for them when they needed them. As teenagers in turmoil they had not been aware. Now, as adults, they had been awakened. That July the sisters took a three-week vacation to Canada before it was too late

Discoveries

July 1996

16   Granny Becca

There was a family tradition that they had growing up with their Granny Becca that went as far back as Shane and Lindsay could remember. As part of their birthday present each year, they would get to sleep one night with their grandmother – when she came to visit or when they visited her. They would lie in bed together and tell each other countless stories only stopping when their yawns got the better of them. Even if they happened to be visiting Granny Becca at Wyatt's place, he would have to vacate the bed to let them take up this night of privilege with their Granny.

It was from their Granny they learnt all about Newfoundland years before they ever visited the place. She told them how folk at a place called Bird Island had once heard a loud thunderous growl, in a deep sepulchral tone, an out-of this world noise that had rumbled around and alongside and practically inside everyone, striking all who heard it with fear and foreboding. The people had sought immediate refuge in God, praying for deliverance from the heavens above, fearing that their world was about to split open and cave in. When all it was, was the sound of an iceberg colliding into a sea cliff and crashing into the cold Atlantic.

How Granny Becca had chuckled telling that tale. She was an expert on icebergs. One look at her paintings was testament to the fact. 'You don't always see them first,' she warned them. 'Some days you hear them first like the people on Bird Island – other days you feel them first.'

As a little girl, Lindsay couldn't understand how that could be – she had images of walking right bang smack into an iceberg. 'Well, yes, that could happen,' said her Granny, 'but unlikely. No you feel them first because they drag with them a mass of chilled air – it's like when you open the door to the freezer you get a blast of cold air – an iceberg is the same thing. But some days,' she told them, 'you can't see them because the fog's that thick. It's then that you feel their presence if they are close enough.'

Because of her stories Lindsay was always intrigued by icebergs and that island called Newfoundland though she did wonder if her Granny was prone to exaggeration when she talked about the fog being like pale fairy-floss that you almost separated with your hands as you walked through it. Lindsay used to wonder if it tasted a little bit like fairy floss too.

However on her second visit to Newfoundland when they flew into St John's to visit Granny's eighty-one year old sister, Rachel, in the summer of 1977, one year after their Dad had gone, there was a day when Lindsay had to get out of their hire car and walk up to a street name and come back and tell Granny Becca what the street was as they couldn't read the sign through the fog.

Despite their misgivings she and Shane had enjoyed themselves that holiday. It was reassuring for them to see two sisters in their eighties still taking walks with each other – albeit their Great Aunt Rachel with a walking stick – but their own grandmother still had a vitality about her that they admired and a way of always including her granddaughters in whatever she was doing.

After seeing their Granny with her sister, Lindsay asked, 'Did our mother get on with Aunty Abigail?' The question took her grandmother by surprise.

'You know, I think after Gene left school they got on very well. They were better friends as adults.'

'Do you think Aunty Abby misses her?' Shane had asked.

'We all miss her,' their Granny had said.

'Do you think our father's with her now?' Lindsay had asked.

From the back seat of the car Lindsay had seen her

Granny and Wyatt exchange glances. Eventually her Granny said, 'I don't know what to hope for that in regard, Lindsay.'

'Why did our father fall in love with her?' Shane had asked.

'I don't know his exact reasons,' their grandmother had said, pausing for a few moments, 'but I think there was a strength and an independence to Gene that we all admired, coupled with a rawness and a certain vulnerability that made you warm towards her. Your mother was a woman that rarely complained or gossiped. She kept her own counsel on most matters – at times much to our annoyance – sometimes we would have liked her to have divulged more.'

Lindsay wanted to know when her parents first met.

'In 1951.'

'Why did they take ten years to marry then?' asked Shane.

'That is one of the great mysteries of Gene's life. We never knew.'

'I think it was to prolong our entertainment and frustration,' mused Wyatt. 'Let me tell you something about your mother and father girls,' he continued. 'It was like watching theatre sports except your Granny had to throw back a few glasses of brandy before she could see the humour in it.'

That afternoon their Granny saw the humour in Wyatt's comment.

Shane wanted to know what was so funny about it.

'We were all on holiday in Parry Sound and your father arrived with a beautiful Cree woman called Kristina whom Morton took an instant likening to. I think she was the first woman he'd taken any interest in since he'd had polio five years earlier. To make himself seem more enigmatic he spent half the holiday talking in sign language to your mother, Gene, because that is what they used to do as kids. Now Kristina was a woman who had been used to other white woman looking down their noses at her and when she met Gene she was completely unprepared for Gene's reaction – your mother liked her and it appeared she was genuinely happy for Sonny to be dating her. You see after Jonathan took Gene on a trip north when she was seventeen she became very enamoured with first nation people. In many respects she liked them more than white people. Anyway, while Kristina liked your father and he liked this Kristina woman very much we all felt he liked Gene more and perhaps the reason he had brought Kristina with him on holiday was to make Gene jealous but that plan soon backfired. Kristina was quick to understand what was going on so she played along with your Uncle Morton's advances in the hopes that she would make your father jealous. At the end of that holiday no one ended up with anyone even though deep down your mother liked Sonny very much and he her.'

'So how come they didn't get together then?' Shane wanted to know.

'Because your mother at that time had an offering to go to Geneva and she chose to do that instead,' said their grandmother.

'She chose a job over our father?' asked Shane in disbelief.

'The job was actually a great honour – she was the first Canadian woman ever to be offered that position. I think your father understood that your mother needed to do this first and then she would be happy to return to Canada and marry him. And he was right. Your father understood your mother very well – better than any of us.'

But he never understood why she left Lindsay wanted to say. She remembered one winter's night when she was ten and it was just her, Shane and her Dad at home watching Elvis Presley's Aloha from Hawaii Concert and part way through *Unchained Melody* her father had got up and walked into the kitchen. He was gone for quite a while, so long that Lindsay couldn't understand what he was doing – he loved Elvis. She had pushed the rug off her lap and gone to the kitchen doorway and there was her Dad in front of the sink, staring out the black kitchen window. She could tell he had been crying. She didn't know what to do. 'Dad,' she said, 'are you coming back in soon?'

He sniffed and said, 'In a minute,' as he turned on the tap and washed his face. And though they didn't say anything to each other, Lindsay knew something about that song was painful to her father and she felt it had something to do with her absent mother.

17   The secret life of Rebecca Olsen Dalton

In July 1996 Lindsay and Shane flew to Toronto and stayed three nights with their glamorous sixty-nine year old Aunt, Abby, and Uncle Will. On Sunday they had a large family lunch – like Thanksgiving in July – with all their cousins who were much older than they and had children in their twenties. They spent two late nights catching up with university friends and Toronto friends from more than a decade ago and then one morning over coffee with their aunt they started to talk about the day their father went missing and their life afterwards: all of the vacations Abby had included them in as teenagers – to Prince Edward Island, to Quebec, to New York even. For the way the girls lived their lives after their father's disappearance was to spend their school terms in Winnipeg with their father's parents – he had no siblings – only cousins who would involve them in various week-end outings – and they would spend their holidays with the extended family of their non-existent mother: their Aunt Abby in Toronto, their Uncle Morton in Saskatchewan, and in Montreal their Uncle Jonathan, always and only called Uncle Jay by them, and their Granny Becca and Wyatt, when he was still alive.

They got out photos of all their holidays. They laughed, at times through tears, and, in a quiet moment and absolute solemnness, Lindsay and Shane thanked their aunt for all she had ever done for them, for being there for them when it counted, for making them never forget they were family. And then they broached a topic that they hadn't broached ever with their aunt – not because it was taboo but because for years it had seemed moot – that of their mother. Had she ever seen or heard from her?

'No,' she said. 'I wish I could tell you "Yes". For you and for me. I've missed her these last thirty years. We weren't close growing up. That was more a reflection on me. I was six years older than her and in my youth more interested in my own life. We didn't become close till she was in her twenties. And then as you know the illness took over and she left us, and then she truly left us.'

Their aunt hunted round for some earlier photos: one of her with their mother, taken one summer in what they were told was their great Grandpa Dalton's garden in Toronto a year before Gene went to Europe – Lindsay and Shane had never seen it before; another one of Gene on skates with two little boys – a six-year old Anthony and a four-year old Stephen.

'She taught my boys to ice skate,' said Abby. 'She had so much more energy than I ever had. Once a month she would come and visit. They adored her. They missed her when she went abroad. I missed her. She used to look after the children on a Saturday evening so Will and I could go out for dinner together. She was a very thoughtful sister in those days and on the ice she was an expert. She could speed skate, skate backwards, twirl, skate with one foot up in the air behind her like a ballerina. In winter she skated every week-end along the Rideau Canal when she lived in Ottawa.'

They spent most of the remainder of their time talking and asking questions about their mother and poring over letters that were thirty and forty years old. Letters Gene had sent Abby in earlier years. Letters Granny Becca had sent Abby in earlier years. Lindsay discovered that Doctor Brookes was right. Her mother was well loved and well missed by her family and she had never done anything to incite their criticism or incur their disrespect.

They caught Via Rail to Montreal where Uncle Jay met them at the station. Standing in front of him they were acutely aware of how much they missed him even though they exchanged letters three or four times a year. He was like their second father, at seventy-eight, their second grandfather. They couldn't believe they had let five years go by without seeing him.

He looked well. He stood tall. While his thick straight hair was silver, his brown eyes were warm and bright and his face clean-shaven – he certainly didn't look anywhere near eighty, nor sound anywhere near eighty. Lindsay decided if she ended up with a man who looked that good at his age she'd be a very happy woman indeed. He was the epitome of your old-fashioned, dashing gentleman, a little bit of Cary Grant in Montreal.

Her uncle's home, like most in his street, was a large two-storey affair made from stones and mortar with an impressive fireplace at one end, and solid dark wooden doors at the front entrance and the garage. In the height of summer however it was largely hidden by two tall sugar maples, part of a dazzling green vertical verge that made Mont Royal one of Montreal's leafiest suburbs.

Aunty Belle, eight years younger than their uncle, stood in a short-sleeved multi-coloured dress at the top of the internal garage stairs, her eyes and teeth flashing. She had the table already set with tuna and salad sandwiches for lunch. Outside the dining room window the garden was a rich tableau, the flowering clematis either side of the arbor created a waterfall of purple, the fuchsias and cardamines in full bloom. It felt so good to be there, so comforting. The place really did feel like their second home, except there was no Granny Becca. Where is she, they asked?

'Would you believe, in Newfoundland?'

'No way!' said Shane.

'Does she still go back there every summer?'

'We've been trying to convince her to cut it back to every second summer,' said Aunty Belle. 'Some years we're successful, but she insists it's the summers in Newfoundland that help her survive the winters in Montreal.'

'Who's with her?'

'Two women from Deception take it in turns to stay four days on and four days off with her. In June we take her out there and spend the first week with her, help her get settled and we go out and bring her back in August. Our St John's cousins visit her as well and family from Salvage. She's never really alone.'

'Amazing,' said Lindsay.

'Does she still paint?' asked Shane.

'Yes. Slowly. Though she's got twenty-twenty vision now days, new ocular lenses don't you know.'

'That's right, I remember you writing about that. The better to spot those icebergs with!'

'Exactly. Do you know one of her paintings sold for $250,000 at auction last month?'

Shane gasped. 'That's the cost of a two-bedroom unit in Sydney.'

'And here.'

Lindsay laughed. 'We need to up our insurances on her pictures.' They both had two of her iceberg paintings. 'How quickly can she churn them out these days?'

'She only manages about six a year. She sleeps a lot during the day and lies awake a lot during the night,' noted Belle. 'She's getting old.'

'At ninety-six I'm not surprised,' said Lindsay.

'Ninety-seven on Sunday.'

'That's right! We were hoping to celebrate with her,' said Lindsay, her voice trailing off.

'You will. We're flying out there on Saturday. We're going to surprise her.'

Tears came to Lindsay's eyes. And her sister's. She looked at her uncle and whispered. 'Thank you.'

That afternoon after they had unpacked and had a second cup of tea, Lindsay made their announcement: After all these years, she and Shane wanted to talk about their mother.

Uncle Jay exchanged looks with his wife. 'What about your mother?'

'We want to get to know her. I only have the vaguest recollections of her. Shane has none. We want to know the woman you knew for the first thirty-six years of her life.'

'And you too, Aunty Belle,' piped up Shane. Turning to her uncle she asked, 'When was the last time you saw her?'

He held his breath for a few moments before exhaling. 'In 1969 at the sanatorium on the lake. Just before she left.'

'Will you take us there?'

'You want to go there?' He paused. 'What for?'

'To see the places she's been. To try and understand what she's been through. It's time,' said Lindsay.

'Okay.' He nodded. 'I will tell you everything I know of the first thirty-six years of your mother's life.'

'Will it be ugly?' asked Shane.

Her uncle shook his head. 'That depends on your definition of ugly. Sad at times.'

He dug out old black and white photos, some dating back to the 1930s and used them as markers to jog his memory, to paint a picture for them as vividly as his mother's famous iceberg creations. He led them upstairs to the attic, to old shoe-boxes full of family letters, their mother's school reports, her university papers, knick-knacks she had collected over the years. They pored over her handwriting as if they could glean something about this stranger from the form and curve of her letters, wishing that the lettering were as familiar to them as Uncle Jay's.

They discovered their uncle was not only the custodian of anything of any value that ever belonged to their mother; he was also the custodian of anything of any value that ever belonged to his mother. The attic was chock full. Alone and upstairs, in the cramped airless room draped under two faded sheets, they made the most amazing discovery of all: two beautiful life-size busts of a male and female nude – from their hips to their throats, a male and female in their absolute prime. Lindsay pulled the curtain back from the window while her sister pulled the sheets back from the statues.

'Incredible,' she whispered. 'Who do they belong to?'

'And how much must they be worth? Two burnished black models like something out of The Tate in London.' Shane ran her eyes over them, Lindsay her fingers.

'Did you ever see a more beautiful male and female specimen?'

'Never,' whispered Shane.

On the woman's behind, Lindsay discovered three scratched letters: ROD and the year 1925.

'That can't be!' exclaimed Shane.

'It must be!' exclaimed Lindsay. 'Rebecca Olsen Dalton.'

'Well I'll be. Granny Becca, you racy lady.'

Lindsay was spellbound. 'Have you ever seen anything more sensual in your entire life?'

'No,' whispered Shane in awe. After some moments she said, 'who's the man? 1925. It can't be Wyatt.'

'Her husband?' And sure enough they found the initials SRD.

'Wow.'

And although Lindsay knew absolutely nothing about those busts she knew absolutely everything. In the inescapable beauty of those silent forms she came undone.

That afternoon they heard the story of Samuel Rousseau Dalton, Uncle Jay's father, their mother's father, Granny Becca's first husband. And in the hearing of Samuel and Rebecca and Jonathan's story, they heard their mother's and learnt the significance of the years 1941, 1950, 1967, and 1969.

18 A little something on the side

When he was fourteen and more than capable of taking care of himself Eva used to give the lad a free rein on the summer holidays. He would do odd jobs around the place and then be off: kayaking trips with his buddies, hiking in the mountains, bird watching, camping, fishing, having a boy's own adventure.

While she would be having her own.

One day on restless impulse, she threw an overnight bag together, got in the wagon and drove. And from there it started. And it isn't so much the travelling or the things she sees, but the people she meets, or, in her case, doesn't meet, that spurs her on. She stays at backpackers, or hostels, not ones that have a bar with music blaring all night, but ones that cater for a more diverse clientele. Ones whose guests aren't interested in ticking off the attractions they've seen or the things they've done. Rather, ones who like to linger and savour a place. Travellers, not tourists.

Now that she lives alone again, she can indulge this whimsy whenever she feels like it. Discovering her country through the eyes of strangers. She likes to listen to their voices, to their accents, to their stories, but she has no desire to engage in a single conversation. She likes to imagine their occupations. With the ones that are alone, she wonders what sent them out in the world by themselves. What compulsion, what restlessness, what desire?

She wards off people well. How many Sisters of Christ do you encounter in a hostel? Like a Salvation Army officer, most people think a nun is there to help, they're approachable, a kind ear in need, with no strings or obligations. But it is interesting what she learns. People shy away from her like they shy away from the police. It's as if they walk into a glass wall and rebound, 'My God, is that who I think it is? What is she doing here?' they wonder. And to shock them further, she lights up a cigarette – a habit she loosely dabbled with in her twenties and dabbles with again in her sixties.

Sometimes she reads a book. At other times she positions herself adjacent to the main doorway so she can eyeball the unsuspecting who walk through. She has no problem making eye contact. At times her eye contact can be excruciating. Penetrable. And unsettling. In this she derives a quiet satisfaction: that her stares and silences have such power. She smiles inwardly but never outwardly. A smile is an invitation to a stranger and Eva never extends invitations.

She has always enjoyed being by the water even though she has an aversion to boats. Almost as much as she has an aversion to planes…so eavesdropping on backpackers who are half her age, sometimes, young enough to be her grandchildren, is pure voyeurism.

She recognises that in a sense it represents a need for some social interaction, but she doesn't dwell on it beyond that. If she were of a different generation, a different temperament, she could be like Aritha van Herk's Arachne and have indiscriminate and forgetful sex with strangers, then move on to another town. But that is not her. She is a sinner but not in that way.

So like a judge, she has her circuits that she goes round, a night in one town this week, a few weeks later, a night in another town, exploring the streets by foot during the day, her wimple and veil flapping in the breeze. It's a senseless waste of time, of money, of gas. She doesn't know why she does it, what she is hoping for or when it will stop. She only knows she must derive some form of pleasure from it else why does she do it. Perhaps she derives pleasure from being away from her home, from being brave enough to venture out, by herself, after all these years.

19 Phone calls in the dark

Midday Saturday they picked up a minivan at Gander airport and headed north on Route 330 to Gander Bay following the signs to the Fogo Island Ferry, onto Route 331 then 335. Uncle Jay drove. Lindsay and Shane had only ever been to Newfoundland twice before: their first trip when they were ten and seven respectively; the second, that lost summer, the year after their father was lost to them. Then and now the landscape was unlike any they had ever encountered: a distinct lack of trees, not completely devoid, but noticeably absent; hills and hills of pale yellow summer grass waving between grey and glinting rocky bluffs; wooden houses in clusters close to the coast; and, if they were lucky, if the distant impenetrable fog rolled away, maybe an iceberg or two on the indifferent sea. The sighting of an iceberg could change the mood of the place entirely.

It was a forty-five minute ferry ride to Seldom Come By and from there another thirty minutes to Second Chance Island bypassing the main village of Deception, further round to the northeast cove and the sparsely vegetated cliffs that belonged to the Crowe family for over one hundred years. The perfect spot to view the late spring and summer icebergs that came drifting along Iceberg Alley.

In the fifties when the former Rebecca Crowe, started coming back to the island the stage was dilapidated and the house in much needed repair. Over the years she and Wyatt and local workmen had upgraded the facilities, adding a tank for running water, a septic toilet and internal bathrooms, a gas stove in the kitchen, and a generator. In the 1980s the electricity was finally connected. At the head of the cove there was already a small runabout tied to the stage. They disembarked and as Lindsay eyed the stone and cement stairwell she thought, good job we left the wheelie suitcases back in Montreal.

'You two, go on ahead and surprise her,' urged their Uncle.

'Not before we take most of these bags up the hill,' said Lindsay.

Outside the painted wooden house Shane decided on a whim to knock on the step-less front door – even though their Granny had long added a verandah to the side, in a nod to tradition, the front door remained as it was, serving little function. After a few moments Shane knocked more loudly.

'Louder,' said Lindsay. 'She's old, remember.' Shane thumped the door.

Finally a white head appeared through the kitchen window, above the planter box full of summer herbs. They looked at her as she squinted at them. A crackly voice said, 'It's obvious you two are not from around here. Where are you from?'

'Sydney, Australia, Granny Becca.'

She gasped. 'Is that you, Lindsay and Shane?'

'It sure is. I thought Uncle Jay said you had your eyes done.'

'I did, I'm just not believing them.'

'Well believe them. We've come back to visit you at long last.'

'Hallelujah,' she said.

They ran inside and hugged her as tightly as they dared, her frame frail. She was shorter than Shane now but still taller than Lindsay's 1.65 metres, her shocking white hair as they remembered it, in a stylish bob, the tips just brushing her jawbone. Her hands were more bony and distended, but her eyes were still their beautiful turquoise colour, though as they would discover, the new lenses eerie at night refracting the light at a certain angle. She would often be quiet for long spells, her eyes a long way away, or a long way back in her past. But she was still their granny, her carriage so noble, yet so endearing, and being there with her, clutching her hands and smiling into her damp eyes, they were overcome with wondrous pride and heartfelt memories, with unspeakable joy and undiminished love.

Over dinner, Granny Becca asked, 'who's going to help me make pancakes for breakfast? Don't all volunteer at once.'

'It's your birthday, Granny. You rest up. We'll cook you a feast,' said Shane.

'Good' she nodded. 'Don't forget the bacon and the berries and the maple syrup. And some cream. Do we have any cream?'

'I've got everything we need,' said Belle, tapping Granny Becca on the hand.

'Thank you, dear. It wouldn't be my birthday without it.'

'I never knew pancakes were a birthday ritual for you, Granny,' said Shane.

'There's a lot about me you don't know.'

Everyone broke into laughter. 'Is there?' said Shane, in gossipy overtones. 'Do tell. For starters we want to hear all about your trip to Paris in 1925.'

Lindsay, who was sitting next to her, leant across and kissed her on the cheek and softly said, 'we want to hear all about your first kiss. Do you still remember that, Granny?'

Rebecca chuckled. 'Like it was yesterday. That's the beauty of old age. You can't remember what you had for dinner the night before, but you remember the halcyon days of your youth.'

Shane, half in jest, said, 'What if I didn't have many halcyon days?'

'I'm sure you had some.' Rebecca glanced at Lindsay and Shane, all of a sudden her expression pained. 'Pray tell me you had some. At least with your father. At least with some lovely young man who swept you off your feet.' Their Granny had suddenly become very anxious.

Lindsay reached out to comfort her. 'We have lived and we have loved. Shane better than me.'

'Good. I'd hate to think everything was ruined for you.'

'No, we have much to be grateful for,' added Shane. 'Look how we have turned out. Look who we are with tonight.' She gave everyone her best smile.

'I hope so,' Rebecca sighed. 'I wish I could have done more for you kids. I wish I could have done more for your mother even.'

'I'm sure you did what you could, Granny.'

'I could never seem to make her see things differently, no matter how hard I tried or what words I used.'

'That wasn't up to you, Mom,' said Jonathan. 'You tried. She was the one who had to choose to see things differently.'

Their granny went quiet as if she were resigning herself to the fact all over again. Then to their surprise she murmured, 'I don't know. Maybe it would have been better if I'd never said anything.'

'What did you say?' asked Shane.

'I don't know now and I don't even know if I knew then. It's just this feeling of helplessness that comes over me at times, a sense that what I said or did, didn't actually help. Maybe it drove her away even.'

'Mom, stop doing this to yourself. This is a pointless exercise. You remember what Gene was like. Even from a young age, she kept things to herself as if she was shielding everyone around her.'

'I remember all right, and what would end up happening? She'd just end up hurting herself the most. But the question I have is: what was she protecting us from in the end? When she was young we found out. But as she grew older we never did. How could we help her make it better when she never told us what to fix?'

That was the perennial question. Even as a child Lindsay felt that. It was good to be finally talking about the elephant in the room. But what could they hope to uncover now. 'When was the last time you talked to her?' asked Lindsay.

'It must have been at the sanatorium when I visited her with Wyatt. Let me think about that.'

The conversation moved on. They cleared the table, did the dishes, made tea and sat back down to enjoy a cuppa with a biscuit slice Aunty Belle had brought with her. Shane was talking to Belle about Sumi, Lindsay to her uncle about the chances of catching some fresh cod when Rebecca started tapping her teacup with a teaspoon, wanting their attention. Clearing her croaky voice she said, 'I remember. I remember the last time I talked to your mother.'

They all smiled in encouragement.

'It was a few days after your father went missing. She rang me.'

Lindsay's eyes leapt from her granny to a perplexed Uncle Jay. 'Are you sure, Mom? This is the first we're hearing about it.'

'Of course I'm sure. She rang in the middle of the night, the long distant pips echoing down the line.'

'Then why didn't you tell us back then?'

'Because there was no point. It was the briefest conversation. It wasn't going to bring Sonny back and I doubted it was going to bring Gene back. And I was right. I never heard from her again. So why bring it up? Why plonk that in the midst of what we were trying to cope with at the time?'

'Well, what did she say?' he asked.

Lindsay studied her Granny closely. Her eyes were piercing, almost as if she were a sorcerer able to call forth spirits or force someone to do something against their will by the sheer intensity of her gaze.

'She said, "Mom, Sonny died?"'

'I said, "Yes dear, it appears so."'

'She said, "I don't want to believe it."'

'And I said, "None of us do." And then after a few moments she hung up.'

'That was it?' asked Lindsay. 'No hellos? No goodbyes? No other questions?'

'No, that was it.'

'Unbelievable.' Lindsay exchanged a frustrated glance with her sister and Uncle Jay.

That night, those few lines replayed incessantly inside her head. After the shock of her granny's disclosure came the anger. Lindsay didn't want to understand her mother's pain and what she'd been through. Hell no. Who was she kidding? She wanted answers and, damn it, after everything she and Shane had been through, didn't they deserve them?

Back in Montreal the sisters spent one whole day at the central post office looking through every telephone directory in Canada for an E or G or an S Dalton or Marlow. They went through nearly two hundred phone directories and ended up with forty-eight possible names. They went back to Uncle Jay's and started calling. With those they got through to they got nowhere. They tried again and again, but being the height of summer, many families were away. Before they returned to Australia they wrote letters to the ones with no answers or the ones who had an answering machine, all the while a part of Lindsay was thinking, I could have spoken to her and she could have lied to me, denied me even – I wouldn't know. I don't even remember what her voice sounds like.

Whilst they were at the central post office they took down the contact information for the Registrars of Vital Statistics in each of the provinces and territories. They wrote requesting any information on the divorce, marriage or death of an Evangeline or Gene Marlow or Dalton. They put the return address care of their uncle in Montreal. They wrote thirteen letters in total.

Over breakfast one morning they discussed with their uncle, as a last resort, the possibility of locating a directory of all the mental institutions throughout Canada. He told them he could get a listing through McGill University's Medical School but he was discouraging. 'At her age, if she's in an institution I'd say she would have deteriorated quite badly and I'm not sure there would be much joy for you in going down such a path.'

They agreed, but nonetheless were not deterred, saying if she was in an institution at least they knew then where she was. And with that they said it was time they went to

Freshwater, the Asylum at Saint-Placide on the northwestern shores of Lac des Deux-Montagnes, run by the Sisters of Providence. Lindsay didn't know anything about asylums. The word was synonymous with lunatic. Which made her think of Pink Floyd and *Dark Side of the Moon* and that was apt she thought: a dark alien place. Forbidding. What she pictured was an imposing red brick boxed building, a cross between a prison and a school, with small windows, something sterile and soulless.

What she found was far from that. It was almost a small village, the main building like the Trapp family home in *The Sound of Music*, washed in a soft yellow, then lots of little two-storey cottages fanning around it – azaleas and lavenders and other shrubs dotted here and there, a wide empty field in front with trees along the lakeshore. Contrary to what she was anticipating, she didn't feel disheartened being there. She gave Uncle Jay a hopeful smile. 'This is better than I was expecting,' she murmured.

'We wanted your mother to get well,' he said. 'We wanted the best for her.'

The warmth of the surrounds unfortunately did not transcend to the on-duty supervising registrar, Sister Dominique, who was decidedly officious, refusing at first to give them any access to their mother's records.

'They're private and confidential. I'm afraid the only people entitled to see them are her doctor and the patient herself.'

'Didn't you admit her?' Shane asked her uncle.

'Yes, but I wasn't her doctor while she was here.'

Lindsay arched one eyebrow.

'We felt it would not be in Gene's best interests for either Wyatt or I to have access to her medical records. We wanted her to feel safe here so she could confidentially work through want she needed to work through and not fear any repercussions or reprisals from her family.'

'A wise decision,' noted Sister Dominique.

'Yes, but it's long past.' Uncle Jay looked at her directly. 'Can you please help my nieces with information on their mother? They have a right to know. It could have some bearing on their life.'

'I'm sorry, but our rules are there to respect the rights and confidentiality of our clients.'

'Come now. They haven't seen their mother since 1969; in fact they never saw her whilst she was interned. After twenty-five years of no contact there is a case for declaring the patient dead, is there not?' Lindsay noted her uncle did not mention the 1976 phone call.

'Do you have a death certificate?' She waited momentarily. 'No. Well I'm sure you understand why you can't access her records?'

'Do you have the official 1969 discharge record for my mother?' asked Lindsay. She knew that they didn't. Her Uncle had told her that just the other week. 'Would that be "No"? Would we be right in assuming you still have her in your care and can take us to her as I'm sure you understand we'd very much like to visit her.'

The sister was clearly galled at her impertinence. Unfazed, Lindsay continued. 'My family entrusted her to this institution and you can't account for her? How do you make amends for that?'

Jonathan interrupted, 'Excuse me sister, if I may?' He placed an envelope on the table. 'Inside, you'll discover I am my sister's power of attorney and as far as I know, it has never been rescinded. You can check your records for that and if that is the case, I would like to see my sister's records and you have my word I will exercise my discretion as to who else I share that information with.'

Sister Dominique picked up the envelope. 'I suggest you take a walk around the grounds and come back and see me in half an hour.'

They went down to the waterfront and strolled along a wide path set amongst the poplar trees, birches and black cottonwoods. Occasionally Shane would bend down and pick up a pebble and skim it across the lake. They saw a pair of loons madly paddling towards their not so secret nest. They asked their uncle for some of his memories of the place from over twenty-five years ago and how they may have treated their mother. He said he didn't know a lot of the details. Anti-depressants. Psychotherapy. After she came through that first time, we trusted them to provide the treatment she needed to get well again. During her first hospitalisation, she was still a minor, that's why we were more aware of her treatment. The second time we were made aware on an as needed to know basis.'

'And?'

He stopped walking and looked at the two of them.

'ECT.'

Lindsay stared at her uncle unflinching, then her sister. She inhaled and turned towards the lake. None of them spoke.

They got limited access to Gene's records: her discharge notices – those they had – and her admissions for 1950, 1967 and 1976.

'1976,' they all echoed.

They looked at the date. Not long after their father's disappearance. Voluntary re-admission. Voluntary discharge. The short admission form noted, "Fearing a relapse of serious depression, the forty-three year old patient, Gene Marlow, readmitted herself for counselling and observation." Her treatment: mild sedatives. Under Observation they found one sentence: "Patient spends a great deal of time outside, lying on the grass, staring up at the sky." She discharged herself four months later.

'That's interesting, isn't it?' asked Shane, 'in light of her phone call to Granny.'

'I'd say it had some bearing,' said Jonathan. He picked up the paperwork and perused the information again. Lindsay studied his profile. After some moments he breathed out one word. 'Morton.'

'What about Morton?' she asked.

'He helped admit her in 1976.'

Now **that** was interesting.

That night they rang Morton but got no answer, perhaps he was in the barn with his dogs, so they rang his next-door neighbour, Paul Ainsley, and asked him to pass on a message. Paul was the nephew of Wyatt Kingston, Granny Becca's second husband who had passed away in 1980 at the age of eighty-nine. Since 1950, Morton had lived near Lumsden, Saskatchewan in Wyatt's small modest home, which he inherited upon Wyatt's death, along with a small acreage. Their Uncle Morton lived quite a reclusive life. Lindsay could clearly remember a holiday she and Shane and her Uncle Jay had had with Uncle Morton back in June 1979, when the four of them paddled around the Bowron Lakes Canoe Circuit. He didn't say much that trip, he rarely did. But he was a loveable uncle all the same – he spoke with his eyes and his smile and his hands. He spoke to them through animals.

He phoned the following evening and spoke first to Belle, then briefly to Lindsay and Shane, and finally Jonathan. They'd agreed earlier that Uncle Jay would be the one to ask him about the admission. Lindsay and Shane tried to hover patiently in the background waiting for the short conversation to be over.

'It would appear your mother was a silent witness at the service we held for your father,' their uncle told them as soon as he hung up.

'And no one saw her?'

'She didn't want to be seen. By Morton's account she was up in the gallery with the organist and the choir.'

'So how did she and Morton meet?'

'She slipped a note under his windscreen and asked him to meet her outside at a cafe. When they met she asked him to drive her to Freshwater. Said she needed to go back and couldn't drive herself.'

'Oh, to be in that car,' exhaled Lindsay in exasperation. 'What did they talk about?'

'That, I can tell you,' said Jonathan. 'It was about as long as the conversation she had with Mom. She said, "Please don't ask me any questions Morton. I can't talk. You know what that's like. Please just drive. You can tell me about your life if you like." '

'That's it?'' Lindsay covered her face with her hands. After a while, she slowly dragged them away. 'Is she her brother's sister or what?'

After some moments Shane asked, 'What happened when they got to Freshwater?'

'When they arrived he asked her if he could get her anything. She said, "No." He asked her did she want him to write to her. She said "No." He asked her if he wanted to let anyone know. "She said, if you love me, please don't."

'Then he asked her did she want him to come back and collect her sometime and she said, "Thanks, but I can manage the leaving." And so they said their goodbyes. He told her he loved her. And she said. "I know. Love you too." And that was all.'

'And has he heard or seen from her since?' Lindsay asked.

Uncle Jay held her gaze. The answer she wanted to hear silently swinging between them. 'No,' he said at last, his voice ragged. Then he dropped his head. His sigh said it all.

Stirrings

September 1996

20   *A different tune*

Eva never wanted a phone.

'What kind of backward people are we?' he had asked her.

'I don't want people ringing me, disturbing my peace.'

'Who's going to ring you?' he had asked and stared at her, his eyes speaking the truth. She had no friends, acquaintances perhaps, whereas he did have friends, and relations. Hence, why he wanted a phone.

'I tell you who,' he continued, 'the school could ring you to check if you are available for relief teaching, instead of making me your go-between, passing notes back and forth.'

'Interesting you should mention the school,' she countered. 'Last time I was there having lunch with Mary Hampton, she was telling me about all these telemarketers who were ringing her at home night and day trying to sell her things, time shares in Miami, computers for dummies and other such nonsense – see, my point exactly.'

She told him they couldn't afford it. That was partly true.

'I'll earn the money for it.'

And he had, working Saturdays in the salmon hatchery. She relented and in relenting she let him put the phone in his name. It was her backhanded gift to him. Her way of saying, this is for you, not me.

But now she silently thanks him for the phone so they can talk twice a week. She rings him on a Wednesday night. He calls one day on the weekend.

Now she asks him, what he's listening to. Previously whenever he put on a CD she would march out the house, walk in any direction, away from the head hammering intrusion of his music in her home. As he'd gotten older, he'd gotten bolder.

'Oasis,' he says. 'Jeff Buckley, Hallelujah.' He pauses. 'You still listening to Leonard Cohen, Joni Mitchell?'

'Yes. And yes.' She smiles down the line. 'K. D. Lang too.'

'Can you even tell them apart?'

'Enough!" she threatens. 'You still listening to Alanis Morissette?'

'You oughta know!' he belts out. 'Hey!' he says, his voice full of excitement, 'here's one for you Eva. You're going to love this.'

'Wait, I don't have a pen.'

'You don't need one. Her name is Eva.'

'Eva, you don't say. Just Eva. Like Madonna?'

'No. Eva Cassidy. Live at Blues Alley. It's jazz.'

'Jazz? How did you come to hear jazz?'

'From one of my lecturers. He's a cool dude. Said it was his best find this summer.'

Stormy Monday becomes her theme song. Written for her, for him.

21 She can still feel anger

Eva had played Jonathan once and she had played him again. For the first, she was deeply ashamed. It was back in 1969 when she was in the sanatorium run by the Sisters of Providence. She was well, ready to leave and re-enter the world. A week before her scheduled release she had asked Jonathan for some money, maybe one hundred dollars, so she could go with one of the nuns to the local town and buy small gifts for the women who had become her friends. It was an innocent, innocuous request. Who wouldn't buy it?

But she took the money, disguised herself in a nun's habit, a scapula, a wimple and veil – a canoness on the run – and vanished. No discharge, no signature, no trace.

That first time was an act of desperation. The second time was an act of weakness and callousness. Sheer folly. For that, she was annoyed at herself. Deeply angry. And now she had been served her just desserts.

Eighteen months ago she had sent him that bizarre letter out of the blue about a young boy she supposedly taught. The communication had nothing to do with the content. It was a purely selfish missive on her part. She didn't care about making overtures of reconciliation, of getting his hopes up suddenly, to dash them just as suddenly. All she wanted was a response from her brother, an embrace of sorts, an assurance.

But by making contact she had extended an invitation into her graces and acceptance had come that day in the form of a letter she had just collected. She carried the letter with her as she walked home. She felt sure it would contain a death notice. But no sooner had she read it was she out the door again, walking towards the beach away from the letter and all it contained.

Dear Gene

We had a visit this summer from your daughters, Lindsay and Shane. A visit from them in itself does not warrant a letter to you. We have certainly had plenty of visits from them over the years, shared holidays and the like.

However this visit was different for a number of aspects:

This was their first visit in more than five years. I'm presuming you do not know that they both now live in Sydney, Australia, and have done so for the past decade. They certainly don't know anything of your existence in British Columbia.

Their main reason for visiting, it would appear, was to locate you or at least find out what happened to you. They asked when was the last time I saw you and I truthfully told them in June 1969.

Naturally I felt desperate about not telling them that a little over a year ago I discovered you were living in a remote part of British Columbia. I badly wanted to pass on your particulars for them to get in touch. But as you had walked away from them once, I realise this decision and choice is yours and yours alone to make. I don't want you to feel threatened as if your privacy is about to be violated and invaded.

It can be a difficult journey to walk towards someone again but the knowledge that the other party is walking towards you hopefully makes the journey shorter, more bearable and perhaps even exciting in its anticipation. From the little I could glean from your first letter, you sounded well but your lack of correspondence afterwards suggests you have no desire to re-establish connections with your family. That saddens us immensely, but we respect that is your decision and want you to know that despite everything we would welcome you back anytime with loving arms. Maybe a day goes by, but certainly not a week, without me thinking of you.

In the letter I wrote I said we are alive and kicking – even Mom. Still today she continues to amaze; her body perhaps even more capable than her mind.

I did not say: "we all are alive" for we did lose one we loved like a brother – Sonny – back in 1976. I'm not sure if I wanted to spare you that news or if I had decided you were beyond caring. However, I now realise that the latter was not the case and that you had indeed called Mom in shock and clearly upset after you heard the news – something she had omitted to tell us till this summer.

So with all this out in the open I would like to make a plea on behalf of those who cannot make a plea themselves. Your daughters have been without a mother for thirty-odd years, without a father for more than twenty. They are not needy, overwhelming young children any more, they are not teenagers who know everything, or self-centred young adults in their twenties. They are well-grounded, compassionate women in their thirties. Women whom you would be proud to call your daughters, and would enjoy getting to know. Give up the memories you have of them and make new ones. Give them a chance. If not for them, then for me.

With all my love
Jonathan.

Eva paces to out blitz her thoughts, to stop herself from screaming, from breaking the cap on the genie bottle and releasing all the fear and injustice, the anger and the madness. She has spent most of her life making an art form of forgetting but even so her memories haunt her, wake her at night, stealing a ride on an unrelenting wind.

Still, she can't remember ever calling her mother after what had happened. Yet intuitively she knows it is the truth.

Why did she call her mother?

Because her mother also lost her husband, unexpectedly, tragically.

What solace had she found in that short conversation? It was as fleeting as her letter to Jonathan, a quick grasping of hands.

Inside Eva there is an icecap where things are frozen over. Whole lives in fact. But all of a sudden Eva feels a crack in one part, where her mother is trapped. This person whom for a large part of her life Eva has held responsible for her own unhappiness, her undoing, her undeniable destiny, this woman had kept her phone call a secret. Had respected it for the painful, private moment that it was. Her mother had honoured her. An act of mercy rather than manipulation. What was she to do with that?

And what of the girls? Of the girls she has little memories. She was a zombie when she should have been making memories. Most of the memories she does have are second hand. But unlike what Jonathan thinks, her thoughts of the girls are not unpleasant or distasteful. They are something entirely different.

22 Let me tell you about anger

Back in Australia, as she drives to work listening to her latest CD haul from Canada – Sarah McLachlan, The Juno Award winners, Cowboy Junkies and Robbie Robertson – Lindsay can't seem to switch off the recording of her mother's phone call to Granny Becca:

"Mom, Sonny died?"

"Yes dear, it appears so."

"I don't want to believe it."

"None of us do."

Click.

Her mother's statement was infuriatingly puzzling. As was her behaviour. Lindsay longed to have been the one who took that call because she wanted to hear the intonation. In the obscure clarity of her grandma's raspy retelling she heard her mother's refusal to believe it, her incredulity. As if she didn't want to admit the veracity of it. But now Lindsay was hearing the emphasis on the 'don't want'. As if she didn't want to let that news in, for if she did, something else would surely follow.

It was as if her estranged mother saw her father very differently to how they expected her to see him. As if, she, Gene, experienced the same sense of anguish they all had: the injustice that his life was over, the inability to accept that. If she accepted it, might she then feel compelled to accept some responsibility for her daughters? By refusing to accept it, was she refusing to accept any responsibility. These questions remained unanswered. As did the question of how did Gene happen to find out about their father's death? From where did she place the call? Why did she call? And this: why did she only contact them the once?

And that was the thing that upset Lindsay the most, the thing that prevented her from getting closer to any truth: if their mother, Gene, was sane enough to call her mother, Rebecca, about her former husband, Sonny, sane enough to care about that fact, how could she not be sane enough to ask about Lindsay and Shane? Did the suffering of her thirteen and eleven-year old daughters not enter her head? Not register.

For the first time in her life, Lindsay felt unspeakable anger towards this heartless woman. An urge to reach out and grab this crazy, uncaring stranger by the throat and yell: What is your story? What the hell were you thinking!

It was all she could talk about with Dr Brookes. The incomprehensibility of her mother's actions. The indefensibility of those actions. Her own impassioned conviction of how differently she would have acted under the same circumstances.

A few months before she had gone to Canada Lindsay had stopped talking to Kristen, Fee and Ange about her sessions with Dr Brookes. She was beginning to sound self-obsessed even to herself and they were beginning to reply to each of her self-revelations with platitudes which, although weren't intentionally insincere, didn't add anything to her personal discovery. It was selfish of her to spend what time they had together naval-gazing about her problems. Besides the focus had shifted. Ange was pregnant. No wonder she had been so smug last November, the cagey little monkey.

But now that Lindsay had returned and Ange had delivered a little boy they called Harry Zappa – 'Zappa? Zappa? Where did that come from?' Lindsay asked. 'Alex liked the sound of Harry Zappa King…what can I say?' Ange replied – and Lindsay had told them of her latest scoop, they were equally gob-smacked.

'She didn't!' said Ange.

'She did,' said Shane who had joined them.

'Far out, how does that make you feel?' asked Fee.

'As you can imagine, completely and utterly invisible.'

'Completely and utterly unloved,' said Kristen 'And unwanted.' She reached across and squeezed both her friend's hands in her own. 'But we love you girlfriend. You too, Shane. We love you so much. You are so meant to be here.'

The girls were once more on board and boy did Lindsay feel justified.

'Am I over reacting?' she asked Dr Brookes. 'Am I being unfair, judging too harshly?'

'One might argue a case for that if everything was known and out in the open. But at the moment you are being very real and anger is a natural response.'

'Healthy?' she queried.

'Yes, healthy. At this stage, I'd go as far as to say necessary.'

'Necessary for what?' She knew enough by now to know there was always a next stage.

23 The rational and the irrational

Growing up with a brother as a doctor Eva had a peripheral appreciation for the sciences. Certainly through personal experiences she had an appreciation of biology in the form of vaccinations and how life-saving those discoveries could be. Anatomy interested her as well.

Chemistry on one hand was mostly a mystery to her. There were topics she understood on a macro level through discussions with other teachers around the staff room over lunch, poring over textbooks. She understood that in chemistry the composition, behavior, structure, and properties of matter were ordered and could be defined, as too could the chemical changes. You could write a formula on a piece of paper, test it and know that it was absolute. When it was explained to her that chemistry was like a cryptic crossword: there could be only one answer, she understood the concept completely.

Biology on the other hand was a little less black and white. Organisms, cells, molecules did evolve, did mutate. They followed certain laws of nature and then at times went inexplicably haywire. But she found the plant and animal kingdoms fascinating and forgave its irregularities.

Human nature however was something radically different. And it was not something that could be isolated and studied under a microscope. For Eva, it was something that was blurred and twisted with unseen forces – some other nature, some other entity – that shamelessly targeted people and families, repeatedly, while others were immune, passed-over.

Eva was thirty-three before she learned the whole truth about her family and saw the truth for what it really was.

Not that there were skeletons in the closets, but that there were skeletons in unmarked graves.

How was it that her Grandma Crowe, should lose all her four sons in childhood, yet her three daughters survive? How was it that her Mother should lose three sons, yet her sister, Aunty Rachel, lose none?

How was it that she, Eva, should suffer like she did? But her sister, Abigail, go unscathed? Why did her life have to descend into darkness from which she barely escaped, from which, some days, she barely managed to keep from her doors and windows?

Why did these things happen and why did they set in motion patterns and reasoning and self-fulfilling prophecies and write their own laws for the way things are and the way things will be?

Eva understood natural disasters like earthquakes and hurricanes; normally there was a logical, scientific explanation. But she didn't understand one off freakish accidents; not why some people drown, while others survive; not why some babies live and some die; not why some planes fall out of the sky for no apparent reason while others don't.

On the surface she didn't understand that at all. She never would. But even still, she understood what it meant for the future.

How was it that none but her could see that there was a bad seed somewhere in the line of women descended from the Olsen's, her mother's mother's family. That one woman in every generation would be cursed and carry the cross for the family's sins? In her generation she was that woman, which meant that one of her own daughters – Lindsay or Shane – would also fall victim to unforeseen tragedies because of this unknown plague hurled at their house from some mysterious sorcerer.

How did one stop this chain of ill-fated command? That was what she tried to do by severing ties with her daughters. By removing herself from their lives when they were young, before they could be tarnished by her black curse. The curse of the Olsen's. This was not about her; it was never about her. The only way it was about her was her wanting it to end with her.

Once, she erred from her path and set off to find her husband and girls again, but that ended in catastrophe. Before she knew it, their father had fallen from the sky. If that was not a warning, what on God's earth was?

In all that she held holy, why would she re-establish the link, especially now when her daughters were entering that stage in their lives when they were more susceptible to malign forces outside of their control.

She knew. She saw it. How could they not see it?

She steeled herself never to think of her daughters, her fear that just a mere random thought from her could spark with an evil spirit loitering nearby to close the connection. That the mere act of her thinking of her children in one part of Canada could have devastating effects to those children in another part, or, as she'd just discovered, in another part of the world. The Angel of Death was no discriminator of geography. This was the power of the curse and she knew in her lucid moments, it was this she was constantly wary of – the reason she continually glanced over her shoulder, trying to catch the slinking specter, trying to forewarn herself, so she could protect her offspring – not that she would run away, rather, that she would face it with all her fury, gladly offering herself up and paying the price in exchange for her progeny living whole lives rather than broken ones.

She knew she has been a wanderer in the wilderness. She was like the prodigal daughter who they wanted to welcome back home, when really they should lapidate her. They couldn't see that by allowing her in, they would cause their own destruction. She was more deadly than the Trojan horse.

How could she ever possibly explain all this to any of them and have them understand? Have them not commit her, again.

She writes to Jonathan and tries.

24 Just impossible

Doctor Brookes sets new homework for Lindsay. Movies. How satisfying it was to watch a movie because it was therapy. She would watch them with Shane, every week a different movie. After a while she discovered they were all wrapped around a central theme – impossible choices. That Doctor Brookes was cagey at times too.

An Affair to Remember. She chose his life over her desire.

Tess of the D'Urbervilles. She chose disclosure and fairness over silence. She chose a moment of love and death over a life of servitude.

Anna Karenina. She chose her lover over her son and husband. She chose a life authentic rather than one untrue. They had to follow that with *Doctor Zhivago.* How could they not? 'Excellent,' said Dr Brookes. 'Make sure you see *Titanic* while it's still showing.'

Yuri chose his destiny. He chose beauty and life over abhorrence and death. Rose chose love over life. They had to move their movie night to Saturday. It took more than a day for her to get over each one.

'What are you doing to me Doc? I spend my whole week-ends crying.'

'Good,' he said, 'keep watching. Keep crying.' But his voice was earnest. No perverse pleasure there.

Sunshine. Kate chose to leave her daughter with the only things she could. 'So unlike my own mother,' Lindsay declared the next week.

'Granted, but Kate was "aware".'

After *Sunshine,* Sumi wanted them to watch *Ikiru.*

Born Free. Joy chose to give up Elsa. Lindsay wasn't convinced she would have been that strong. They weren't ready to leave Africa. They watched *Hatari!* Baby elephant walk. It wasn't on the required viewing list, but what the heck.

Then *The Nun's Story*. After that they had to watch *Change of Habit* – Elvis's comeback movie, for themselves and for their father.

Then, the most harrowing of all: *Sophie's Choice*.

'Can we stop now Doc? I can't take any more.'

'We can stop for a while.'

'I think I need to go on anti depressants. I feel like I'm Holly Hunter in *Broadcast News* – I know that wasn't on the list either – but I have times each day where I just burst into tears in sadness and I don't know what – grief, maybe. All this pain in the world that people don't know about, people don't see, or don't care. What's that all about?'

'Catharsis.'

He was a pillar of peace, she, a blithering wreck.

'We are making progress Lindsay.'

And they were. They were. Somewhere in those dampened weeks her inflamed sense of righteousness died down, her burning anvil of blame cooled. As her dormant empathy became no longer dormant her compassionate conscience came to the fore. Lindsay cried for other people's impossible choices, for their pain. She cried for her own, for her bruised soul, for her unknown mother and her unknown choices and her unknown pain.

25   The sins of the father

It appeared her daughter had reverted to using her full name. Laying on her bed with countless pillows propping her up, a crocheted rug over her lap, Rebecca read and re-read Evangeline's latest letter. It was a marvel to hold onto paper that had so recently come from her hands after nearly twenty-five years of resounding silence.

There was a part of Rebecca that would like to have put pen to paper herself, to also wave the olive branch that Jonathan and Shane and Lindsay were so eagerly trying to extend. But Rebecca no longer trusted herself to say and do the right thing. And the last thing she wanted to do was to sabotage any progress that they might be making.

Once, she had tried to console Gene on not having given birth to a baby boy. It was not a conversation she initiated, rather, one she found herself embroiled in, and unbeknownst to her, her consolation became an ill-timed, ill-formed explanation that had unleashed untold and irreversible damage. At the time Rebecca had no understanding of her daughter's state of mind, no understanding of how her daughter could take lemons and sugar and water and rather than end up with delicious lemonade end up with something akin to arsenic.

It wasn't until a conversation they later had in early 1969 at Freshwater did Rebecca come to realise that Gene saw herself as cursed. Rebecca had reflected wryly on that at the time. A mother's natural instinct was to deny such a statement, to reassure one's child, irrespective of how old they were, though part of Rebecca did think, "*You* see yourself as cursed. I could give you cursed.' But she hadn't because her daughter was clearly fragile and there was no denying that Gene had painful secrets and hidden sorrows, which Rebecca and Jonathan and doctors could only partially unveil, but notwithstanding that, she did. Tragically their well-meant words only seemed to add fuel to an invisible fire.

Timing was everything. Knowing when to speak and knowing when to be silent. Rebecca's mother, Morna, strangely had a gift for it. Though Rebecca almost wished that what her mother had told her on her deathbed at ninety-nine years of age, she had told her many years earlier. Then, Rebecca may have formulated a different view of the world, one that her daughter couldn't morph to the degree that she had. For Rebecca did think that for some inexplicable reason, she and her mother had been dogged by insidious bad luck. Her mother and her did share a bond of sorrow. The sorrow that only a mother could know. And although Rebecca didn't like to admit it, there was no way to hide it, she thought it was because God was a jealous God – he didn't like the fact that she, Rebecca, had loved her human family more than her spiritual family. And that riled Rebecca, for she vehemently believed that she was not alone in that regard, yet how she had been punished, how she had suffered.

It wasn't until 1969, until the man walked on the moon, did her mother shed new light on matters. Her mother too had spent years contemplating the question why.

When she first started telling the story, Rebecca thought it was about another woman, a relative of sorts, who also seemed incapable of escaping mulish misfortune. But afterwards, when she talked with her ailing mother, they decided it was something altogether different.

Morna told her a story that Rebecca's father, Silas, had shared with her after he and she had lost two young boys, Paul and Isaac, through a drowning in the mid 1890s, before Rebecca was born. It was something shared in a rare moment of intimacy, in the depths of their heartbreak. Without preamble her father had come out and said, 'The sins of the fathers are visited on the sons.'

'What sins?' Morna had asked.

Without flinching he had said, 'I killed my brother.'

Morna had tilted her head and looked at him questioningly, but not completely with surprise. And Rebecca had to admit, had he told her, she would have done the same. Her father had come from Labrador and in all her life she never met a single one of his relatives.

'By accident?' Morna had queried.

'No,' had been his reply. 'I had four brothers,' Silas had explained. 'The eldest was Jeremiah. He was a law unto himself. I don't know how he could have been my brother even. We never got on,' he told her. 'But to my parents he was their worshipped first born.' Silas had one sister, Dorcas. She had a good friend called Tamar who Silas also happened to be friendly with. One day he had hoped to marry her.

But when Silas was nineteen and Tamar was seventeen, Jeremiah came upon her when she was alone and raped her. Silas maintained it was a malicious act wielded for the sole purpose of provoking him. And it had. In fury and rage Silas had killed his brother. He then ran away with Tamar. Rebecca heard how her father's sister, Dorcas, was the only one who ever understood and forgiven him.

Just over nine months later Tamar died in childbirth. Silas told Morna he never knew if the child she carried was his or his brother's, but he'd felt his brother's hand in her death all the same. Over time he said he tried to think of it as God's will that she and her baby were taken from him, in order for him to leave all that behind and start life anew somewhere else – with Morna on Second Chance as it so transpired.

When Morna first shared this story with her, Rebecca had sat there amazed but not judging, sensing her father's burden but not being burdened by it, until something overwhelming and unavoidable crashed through her being.

'Oh my God. He's cursed us all,' she had cried out.

'Yes,' Morna had said. 'Our sons pay the price of his sin.'

In her mother's room, in her sister Esther's home, as she held her pale hand, Rebecca and her mother talked at length about that shocking revelation and they decided that that was indeed the case. The sins of the father were being visited on the sons. It was only the males whose lives happened to be cut short. And it wasn't to do with bad luck. It wasn't to do with the choices Morna and Rebecca had made, the actions they had taken: that was completely immaterial. It had everything to do with a vengeful and prophetic God and the one – okay maybe two – mistakes of Silas Crowe. Where was forgiveness and clemency in that?

And later, after her mother had peacefully passed away, weeks and months later in fact, did Rebecca wake up and think: where is the justice in that? He commits the sin, which generations and generations suffer for, whilst he is no longer around, no longer living to witness all the suffering down through the ages. Meanwhile, we, his descendants, are punished for something we didn't do. How does that work? Now at the age of ninety-seven, with her daughter Abby's boys approaching forty-eight and forty-six, Rebecca felt that perhaps her family had at last repaid Silas' debt. She sent up a silent plea, please, please.

In the early days of a Montreal winter, Rebecca vowed once more that if she ever made it to Heaven she was going to have a serious talk about punishment.

All her life Rebecca had railed against accepting her fate. There had been many times when she questioned her faith; she wasn't certain how welcoming the Almighty was going to be. In her dreams and her prayers she mostly remembered her loved ones and prayed she would be reunited with them. In her senectitude Rebecca didn't fear death. When people you loved dearly had gone ahead of you, you didn't fear death like you once had. She only feared missing the welcoming party, of not being able to find the ones she so desperately missed on earth.

26   Predictable and Unwelcome

Dearest Gene

Thank you for your sincere and considered reply. I'm sorry that is your decision for now. I know at heart you are a deeply caring person. That was borne out in your letter. And despite all that I know, and all that I don't, that has always been true, Morton being a classic case in point.

You think the situation is best left as it is, that your daughters and everyone are better off without you. But that is not how we see things. Your presence adds to our life Gene. It is your absence that subtracts from it.

I know you believe you can't give Lindsay and Shane what they want. You may well be right. But can there not be a middle ground where you can give something of yourself and they will accept your offering and be happy with that?

May I suggest you consider starting a purely letter-based relationship with your daughters and see how things transpire from there. You don't have to justify your actions, your past or your current position. Just write to them like they are pen pals you are corresponding with for the first time and tell them a little bit about yourself and your life. I am happy to be an intermediary if you wish to protect your privacy.

Please be open to this possibility.

With love and hope

Jonathan

27 What can she say?

The guilt of knowing she raised the boy when he was an orphan yet turned a blind eye to her daughters when they were orphans, had plagued her for years.

In the beginning she justified it with: "I'm not fit to be anyone's mother."

Then: "I could get depressed again. I could turn into my mother – how she was after Dad disappeared – why inflict that on anyone?"

And there was no evading this dread: "Every day with them would be a horrific reminder of what I did to their father. It would all be too much for me."

The prospect of being a single parent with depression dying to infiltrate, menopause looming, she didn't want to take the chance. Lindsay and Shane were with family and friends, she told herself, with people they knew and loved and trusted. I don't mean anything to them. And what I have to offer will be substandard to what others can give them. They have their lives all ahead of them, full of opportunity. They are better off without me. And on many levels she was right.

When she wrote in the letter to Jonathan, "my life is complicated," the boy was a large part of that complication. Showing her up for the absolute hypocrite that she was. Not wanting to have anything to do with her old family but wanting everything to do with her new one: him. But in her mind with good reason, all part of a well calculated stratagem to keep them safe.

Still, there is no peace for her. Here is Eva's conundrum. If, and it's a big if, if she could write to her brother and convince him (and let him convince all the others) of the machinations of not just the world she lives in, but the world all her family lives in and are bound by, then Jonathan, having that knowledge, doesn't change squat. It doesn't give him the power to fix things, to stop anything tragic from happening. For she knows that she is a tragedy magnet. So it is a pointless exercise in futility. See. Too big an if.

She can barely entertain the idea of the arguments she knows they would hurl back in her face if only they knew the truth and if only they had the chance.

"You have this boy who is alive and well and untouched. Nothing has happened to him!"

And she would reply, "YET! TILL NOW! I hope and pray he'll be like Jonathan, he'll be immune."

In those drifting moments before sleep, when some people lie there and think of what they achieved that day, Eva would lie there and think: I survived. We survived, as if she were living in Treblinka.

They will not see her view. They cannot see her view. All they can do is see the world from their own prism.

She can hear their cries, "You're mad. You're selfish. What did we ever do to you?"

She can see. She knows. In their eyes, her position is unarguable.

How can she believe one thing, while everyone else believes another? That thought just does her head in even more, sucking her into a vortex that at times she can barely make sense of or take any responsibility for.

She doesn't reply.

28　She's alive

When Lindsay and Shane returned to Australia after their trip to Canada in July 1996, this they knew for certain: their mother was alive on the sixteenth of December 1976 – the day she discharged herself from Freshwater nearly twenty years earlier.

That Christmas Lindsay received in the mail a card and letter addressed to her and Shane from Uncle Jay and Aunty Belle. Inside, amongst tidbits of news and updates he had written: 'I can confirm your mother is still alive. I'm sorry I can't confirm anything else.'

Lindsay set a driving record from Contra to Wollstonecraft. Thank God the Spit Bridge was not up. It was news too big to share on the phone. But that night at 11.30 Sydney time, 7.30 am Montreal time, they did pick up the phone, their excitement overflowing.

'Has that made your Christmas?' asked their uncle.

'Yes, it has,' said Lindsay. 'Which one of the letters yielded the reply?

'Strangely the information came to me in a rather surprising and unconventional way.'

'Which was?'

'At this point in time I can't say.'

'Oh Uncle Jay, come on,' urged Lindsay.

'I'm sorry. I would if I could.'

'Do you have an address?' asked Shane.

'I have a means of contacting her. She is being very cautious and I'm not sure what will come of our overtures to re-establish any connection.'

'Why do you say that?' asked Lindsay.

'She wasn't very forthcoming in her reply to my letter.'

'What did she say?' asked Shane.

'Well, she thanked me for letting her know that her daughters were safe and well and leading successful lives in Australia, but beyond that she said she thought it best that the status quo remain as it were, for everyone's sake.'

All parties on the line were silent until Shane asked, 'How did she sound in the letter?'

He laughed dryly. 'I'm not even going to attempt to determine that.'

Lindsay wanted to know why he thought she was taking such a stance.

'I'm sure there are many reasons which I doubt you and I will ever have the privilege of knowing. I'd hazard a guess that one of them might well be the thought of facing her long-neglected daughters is terrifying, too much for her to bear, and, as you know, mental fortitude was never one of her strengths.'

'Strangely forbearance is,' said Lindsay.

'So do we need to take the fear away for her?' asked Shane.

'That's easier said than done.'

'What if we were to write to her and tell her we don't blame her or hold her responsible for anything. That we just want to be friends,' said Shane. 'I mean that's the truth. I don't.'

'I know you don't Shane but I wouldn't mention the word blame. It's just as likely to set her off. Perhaps what I would do is just write to her and tell her about your lives. Start with a clean slate and write a letter to a stranger whom you want to become your friend. Maybe that's too much to hope for at this stage, perhaps more like someone you would like to have a dialogue with.'

'Good advice, Uncle Jay. Any more tips?'

'Yes, she's not unintelligent your mother. Just furtive and unpredictable. But don't let that deter you. Send me your letters and I'll send them on.'

29 Why won't they take no?

It had been two years and two letters since Eva first made contact with her eldest – certainly not long-lost – brother. And now he had made contact with her a fourth time, quite a short letter in fact, enclosing another letter that contained some photographs of her daughters. She read the letter but it took her over a week to look at those photographs.

In his covering note, her brother had penned:

You wrote to me in February 1995 about a young man, a virtual stranger, whom you would like to help on his way. Can you not do the same and more for your daughters?

30   Her all in one word

His name is Ryan. He is not a stranger. He is family to me. And has been for twenty years.

... If only she dared.

He was her best friend, Mary's, adopted son, born in Vancouver at a time when she had not been in a fit state to travel south. Mary was physically and emotionally bereft having just delivered, co-incidentally, a stillborn child she had carried almost to full term. Her husband Billy did not want to leave her side. They had phoned Gene asking if she would mind bringing the baby to them. She had been planning to head north anyway and start a new life in Kitisak close to her best friend. Of course she would do what she could to help her godforsaken friend.

Three years later Mary's gynaecological problems magnified. The effects of more than a decade of pregnancy strains on her body yielded to the invisible cancer gene that had been passed down from her mother. Ovarian cancer, that most silent of killers, became a parasite in her body. A shortness of breath was the first sign something was amiss. Within days they discovered her non-smoker's lung cancer was not the primary.

Mary fought the disease in the way only a valiant mother can. She had a radical hysterectomy, radiation therapy on her lungs, chemo in her veins. Gene would take it in turns with Mary's sisters, Beth and Sarah, to drive her to Prince Rupert for her weekly appointments. Billy buried his heartache and helplessness in booze. After Mary died they had to take him to an alcoholic clinic in Prince George to dry out.

On her death bed Mary told her five-year old son he was

adopted. Her telling was beautiful and unexpected. She asked Ryan did he think anyone else could love him as much as she did.

He had said no.

She said: 'Well trust me, one day a young woman will move you in places you didn't know could be moved, but before that, trust me, other women will love you like I have loved you.' She paused and wet her lips. 'Do you know how I know this?'

'No.'

'Because you are so loveable and from the moment I laid eyes on you, you took up the biggest place in my heart. I know your father and grandfather had the same reaction. I'm sure Eva and my sisters did too.'

'Now I want you to know how you came to me. I couldn't give birth to a baby myself for I could never make a healthy one. I had to rely on the kindness and generosity of another woman to give me her baby. I understood she was a teenage girl. I never got to thank her. I only got to thank Eva who brought you to me with such care and devotion. It doesn't matter how we get our children. It only matters that we love them. And look how much I have loved you.'

Ryan had sat there, holding Mary's hand nodding in solemn agreement.

'So now at this point I have to hand you back to Eva for her to look after you because you still need a mommy. When you're older you might want to live with your father – that's up to everyone to decide. But I want you to know that I know Eva will love you well and for you to trust her in that love.'

It shocked Gene that Mary had never asked her before she broke this news to Ryan. Later she said to her, 'Did you not want one of your sisters to raise him as their own?'

'Eva,' she said, 'There's no guarantee that they won't get what I've got. I don't want him shunted around. And you can't tell me you don't love him.'

Eva had stared at her unable to deny her.

'This is my dying wish and my whole family supports me in this. They will help you.'

She looked up and saw Mary's father, Ken, staring at her. He nodded his head and blinked slowly, decreeing that this was to be. He never said a word but she knew what he'd say if he did.

31 Forgiveness in sight

Lindsay's sessions with Dr Brookes continued week in and week out. She could not imagine her life without them. They were clarifying. They were affirming.

They worked through all her latent anger issues with her mother. Incredible to think that a year ago she wasn't aware she had any, but once tapped it was amazing what flowed to the surface of that well. Lindsay never knew the source of her mother's pain. But she came to appreciate it was real and that she, Lindsay, hadn't caused it. She wasn't responsible. She wasn't to blame herself. For her entire life, Lindsay had carried around the belief that she had been a burden to her mother. How damaging that mindset had been to her self-worth. And deep down inside Lindsay had blamed her mother for lumping that burden on her but Lindsay came to see she had lumped that burden on herself. Such a relief the day she offloaded it.

Who would have predicted the places he would take her to? To the conflict inside her she felt over trying to reconcile her love for her dad with his no longer being there – such an innocent unavoidable severing of trust. She was haunted by images of her father being trapped in a plane, not being able to open any of the doors, his parachute not working, his anger, his heartbreak. She didn't think fear would have played a part in his end. Only fear for them. How could her feelings rate compared to the poignancy of his realisation?

But at last she gave words to it: "Dad I'm angry with you for leaving us like you did. How could you?" She gave herself permission to cry at the injustice of it, the helplessness of it all, to forgive her father, to forgive herself for not being able to honestly express how she had felt for all those years.

She had to heal her inner child. Be angry at the world and her mother for not giving her a mother. She found that hard to work through because on the flip side she had a better relationship with her grandmothers and aunts than most. She would not have had one without the other. But she had to express that emotional grief all the same.

And then, finally, herself. The dominant pioneering force in her being was a fourteen-year-old girl. At fourteen she had been tested and found what she was capable of. And that fourteen-year-old girl had valiantly stood up to the test. And was the one still standing up to the test. Every setback, every disappointment, every hurdle she had in her life, she said: I can survive this because look what I survived when I was fourteen. How did I survive when I was fourteen? And without even knowing it she was on automatic pilot. She had to reassign the power base in her own being. How utterly terrifying that was. They took weeks working through that. Saying goodbye to that fourteen-year-old girl was like a death. 'Let her be where she needs to be,' Marcus urged. 'That poor child has been overworked for too long. And she's been making decisions in her best interests, not yours.' He was right. She had to let her go. She had to forgive herself for letting her be the almighty crutch in her life. Lindsay felt cast adrift as she tried to find her thirty-four-year old self.

But it was incredible to think a few months ago another birthday had gone whooshing by and it didn't faze her. That was miraculous. Her sense of panic about her own future seemed to have dissipated. A voice inside her soothed her with the words, 'I will be a better mother, when I'm a better person. When I am whole, not fractured or fumbling in darkness.'

32 Dark clouds on the horizon

The swarming dark figures are back.

Because of her mother, and what she had once said, which at the time made as much sense as anything else, Eva always thought the lurking evil force was of the male persuasion. But now she's not so sure and now the forces are multiplying and they're no longer hiding from her. They are there in a group, dressed in black capes and hoods, their faces in shadow, every so often catching a flicker of light as they float past. They move as one, in the same direction, doing the same actions, always keeping their distance but not disappearing either.

She doesn't know what they want from her. They don't talk amongst themselves and they clearly refuse to talk to her. To add injury to insult her reflection in the mirror is no longer cooperating with her either. After one frantic episode when she had calmed down and forced herself to breathe evenly, a thought entered her head. That what she actually was seeing were the spirits of the dead, the benevolent dead, all those in her family who were deceased because of the curse, and they were closing ranks around her to protect her. And this also became her quandary, for if it were true, should she let them in instead of shutting them out?

In her calmed state they subside. Days later when they return she thinks hiding underneath those hoods are the winged Furies with serpentine hair – Alecto, Magaera and Tisiphone. But then their faces morph and twist, recede and re-appear in turbulent. Framed by wild Medusa hair she sees Rebecca, Lindsay and Shane: her mother in her sixties, the age when Eva last saw her; her daughters in their thirties, the faces in the photo she received last month.

She secures her wimple and veil firmly in place. She even sleeps in it, her armour against the world, like a garlic-wreathed cross warding off vampires. White versus black. Good versus evil. Eva versus the world.

33 *We need protection?*

How long could they go without word from Canada? February, March, April and now May. Lindsay and Shane phoned Uncle Jay using both handsets to have another three-way conversation. 'Have you heard anything, Uncle Jay?' Lindsay asked. 'Has she written to you and said, "No, I don't want to have anything to do with them"?'

'No she hasn't but all the same I think that's the message she's sending with her silence.'

'What do you think is going on?' Shane asked. 'Do you think she might have had another episode and admitted herself to another sanatorium somewhere?'

'I doubt it. Who knows?'

'Do you have a phone number for her?' asked Lindsay.

'No and believe me I have searched. None exists.'

'What about a physical address?' she queried.

'No I don't have that either I'm afraid. Only a post office box.'

'Why such secrecy?' Shane wanted to know. 'What's she hiding from?'

'I think the answer to that's obvious.' Lindsay replied. 'Us. Everyone.'

'Clearly, but what's her motivation. Uncle Jay, do you have any insight into that?'

His heavy sigh came down the line.

'Your mother has this warped view that she is cursed. Like her mother was cursed and her mother before her. She believes if you have any connection, any form of contact, then one of you two will also become cursed and suffer a tragic life.'

Part of Lindsay felt like joking and saying, 'Tell her not

to lose sleep over it. That's my life already.' But she knew now was not the time for such dry sarcasm, and besides, that was not her life. Her life had blips of tragedy. But in lots of other ways, her life had been a banquet. While her sister chatted to her uncle, Lindsay thought, if only Gene could have a Marcus in her life, maybe then things could be vastly different.

She heard her uncle say, 'Her silence, her refusal is her way of trying to protect you.'

'Do you think we need protecting?' she asked.

'Did Jesus need protecting?'

34 Counting down the days

In early May Ryan flies to Ketchikan, 250 kilometres north of Prince Rupert, and signs on to a commercial sablefish boat for two months, working in the Clarence Strait and the nearby bays and sounds. Since he turned sixteen he has spent his summers working with Billy, his father, as a long liner in the Alaskan waters, onboard commercial salmon fishing boats, earning big money for his age, which in his first year he put towards the pursuit of sporting happiness: a new sea kayak, a new mountain bike and an Apple Mac. But the next three years he saved for college and for living away from home. Responsible, mature young man that he was, except when he was reckless.

When he first told Eva he wanted to go north for the summer and work on a boat they had the mother of all fights, so monstrous that in her memory it swamps every other fight they ever had. He wanted to go. She of course did not want him to go, for countless reasons, most of which she couldn't tell him and those she could, had little or no impact. In this he would not respect her wishes and she knew if she didn't let him go it would drive a deep divide between them and the prospect of that was almost as bad as the prospect of the unspeakable. What's more how could she deny him spending time with Billy? How to tell Ryan it wasn't Billy, it was the location?

When he is away at sea Eva lives in a perpetual state of panic, nursing a constant bout of nausea. Her appetite, which is poor at best, disappears completely. She lives on cups of peppermint or black tea and the odd piece of toast until the ulcers start to appear in her mouth and she knows she has to force herself to eat otherwise her physical pain will overtake her emotional pain. Last year, he topped and tailed his fishing season with a ten-day stopover on the way up and on the way back to spend time with her. And he flew home for Christmas. For the whole year she saw him for thirty days.

She hates the thought of him flying. She hates the thought of him working on fishing trawlers with those hooks and lines and equipment that can ensnarl a man, indiscriminately wrench off an arm, fling someone unwittingly over the side. One nautical booby-trap after the other. And then there's the booziness and bawdiness that goes with the territory of seafaring. Can he stay impervious to all that?

Though he doesn't say the reason why, this year he has made different plans. After three seasons up north working on salmon boats he has been taken on as a sable fisherman. That prized oily white fish so favoured by the Japanese they will pay an unconscionable premium for it. In two months he hopes to earn what he would normally earn in three. Then he will be back home for five weeks working mostly full-time as a sea-kayaking guide for Pacific Playground, a local adventure tourism operator.

When he's home she knows in what spare time he has he will be busy catching up with friends and his grandfather but she likes to think it is his way of saying to her, 'I know you miss me and I miss you too.'

35 Set free

Lindsay had heard people say from time to time, be careful what you wish for. She never much believed in it, what with all that had happened in her life that she had never wished for, wouldn't wish on her worst enemies even. But it was interesting what the mind could haul in at times.

In the midst of marketing briefs and product launches, in the thick of sales forecast, and distributors meetings, the momentarily lull between reseller presentations and client meetings, Lindsay's heart was becoming increasingly restless. She wished she could disappear to Canada for the northern summer so she could devote all her energy towards finding her long-absent and elusive mother.

And then one Thursday her boss, the ANZ Director of Strategic Partnerships, called her into his office and proceeded to tell her he had good news for her, mostly good news he corrected himself. They had been given budget to grow the channel team, which for her should mean less work, but in the process they were going to decentralise some of her responsibilities, so her national role would no longer be national. Eventually they'd like to make it national but for now they were planning to make her head up a team whereby she would look after Queensland, New South Wales and the ACT and be the first point of contact for two new appointees, one of whom would look after Victoria, Tasmania and the Northern Territory, the other, South Australia and Western Australia.

'So they'll be reporting to me?' Lindsay checked.

'Not exactly. They're dotted to me.'

'Ah, so you get more headcount, while I effectively get none.'

'Well, yes, but look on the bright side, you have less work but the biggest piece of the revenue pie.'

Lindsay could see the logic but she also knew she didn't want to lose the word 'national' from her title. It had nothing to do with ego but everything to do with perception and pay packets and future prospects. She was not going to roll over on that and she sensed she hadn't yet heard all of the mostly good news.

'What other changes will there be?'

'Essentially we have to advertise and interview for the three positions and you'd have to apply for the position you wanted. Though you'll have no problem in securing it.'

Thanks for the vote of confidence, thought Lindsay, dryly. 'And what about the remuneration?'

'You'd be on the same remuneration, but the position is on a lower grade.'

'And where does my salary fit in terms of the salary band for that grade?'

He barely managed to look at her as he muttered, 'At the top.'

Hmm, thought Lindsay with quiet dissatisfaction, no room for further pay increases there. 'I wouldn't be happy about that,' she said.

'I know, but look in no time, we'll have headcount to put a channel manager on in each state and then we'll need a national manager. And before you know it you'll be ahead of the game.'

Lindsay eyed her manager. His body language showed he clearly wanted her to roll over on this. 'What's the redundancy package? You're restructuring my role and effectively making my position redundant. You need to offer me a redundancy option.'

She took the redundancy option. Six week's salary as part of the severance deal, one month for each year she'd worked with the company plus her annual leave entitlements. Nine months salary all up. Who wouldn't take it?

Her friends were equally excited and flabbergasted.

Kristen, who owned her own travel business was quick to say, 'what a bunch of sexist bastards! If you were a guy there's no way they'd be asking you to take a lesser position.'

'That's what I felt.'

'I mean, Lins, it would be different if you weren't a performer and all but you always make your targets.'

'Always. Without fail. Even when times have been tough.'

'What is it about Australian men in business? It's all about feathering their own nest. You wouldn't believe the things some of my clients try and wangle through on their corporate accounts?'

'Like what?' asked Fee.

'Don't ask,' said Kristen with a huff.

'Well what do you do about it?' continued Fee.

'Oh I let them know in no uncertain terms that I know. I say to them,' and she lowered her voice for effect, ' "Let me make sure I'm clear. You want me to extend this booking by another two nights?" And they always pause and you can hear them swallow before saying, "Yes, that's right" and I go, "Okay, no problem," and I add it to my spreadsheet of questionable bookings for that client.'

'You don't!' Ange was aghast.

'The hell I don't,' said Kristen. 'And all my staff do the same.'

'Why do you bother?' asked Ange. 'It's no skin off your nose.'

'I'll tell you why I bother, because it's happened in the past and it will happen again, a large client will call me in and say, "We spent one million dollars on travel with you last year and we're getting pressure to put our business out to tender, is there anything we can do to manage this expense better?" And I say, "Well...you might want to check to see if there have been any abuses of your company travel account?"'

'You didn't!' Ange was still aghast.

'I did.'

'What happened?'

'They signed me up on retainer for five years.'

'Huh.' Ange and Fee looked at each other and then at Kristen.

'How about that for loyalty?' said Lindsay, full of awe at her friend's bravado.

'I may not be a saint in my personal life but I know the value of being scrupulous in business,' Kristen said with a toss of her head.

'Kristen Moore's Introduction to Business 101,' said Fee.

Everyone laughed.

'Yes and 102 is know your client's business intimately, because then you know what's legit and what's not.'

'Oh yes, and you'd be an expert in that,' said Ange nodding her spiky head.

'So, Lins,' said Fee changing the subject, 'Tell us, do you have any plans?'

'Yeah, I do. I'm going back to Canada to try and find our Mum.'

'Are you?' Ange asked in surprise. 'Do you have any new leads? Any leads on that Ross chap either?'

'No, and you can forget him.' Lindsay squinted at her cheeky midget of a friend. 'With respect to my mother I have one lead who hasn't revealed all the findings of his investigation, so I'm going to start with him.'

'Who's that?' asked Fee.

'My uncle. He's being a bit secretive and elusive himself.'

'Doesn't he want to help you?'

'No, that's not it. I don't know what's driving his agenda, but I'm hoping when we're face to face he'll level with me.'

'You sure you're not going on a wild goose chase?' asked Kristen.

'Well, I could be.'

'How will you be if you come back with nothing? No answers, no sighting, no hope.'

'Then I will come back with nothing.'

'Can you live with that?' Kristen queried.

Lindsay was on the verge of saying, "Do I have a choice?" But instead she said, 'I will choose to live with it until I decide I no longer want to live with it. Besides, the hope is in my court.' Dr Brookes was always emphasising the importance of using empowering words rather than powerless words.

'Fair enough. Make sure you have a holiday in there somewhere,' Kristen counselled.

Ange asked her how long she thought she was going to be away. When Lindsay told her about three months, Ange was quick to ask her what she was planning to do with her place while she was away.

'Nothing. Lock it up. Move the plants to Shane's. Why? What's on your mind?'

'How would you feel about letting it out to my in-laws?'

'Alex's parents?'

'Yes.'

'Sure. No problem. Happy to do that.'

'Oh, thank you, thank you.' she gushed. 'You're an angel.'

'Why, such relief?' asked Fee. 'Are they that bad?'

'For two weeks they're not, but for two months, I can't bear the thought. Just when Harry's finally sleeping through the night, I lie awake tossing and turning about how I'm going to cope with the invasion.'

'They can have my car too if you want.'

'Oh, you are heaven sent. Thank you.'

She leant across and kissed Lindsay on the cheek.

'Why are they coming this time of year anyway?' asked Kristen. 'Why leave England in the summer. It's the only time it's decent.'

'Tell me about it,' said Ange, rolling her eyes theatrically. 'The unbearable greyness of it all. They're coming now because they couldn't handle the heat in our summer.' She took a sip of her merlot.

'Haven't they heard of air conditioning?'

'Yes, but trust me this is better, much better. Their

thermostats don't work properly out here. They sweat all the time just getting from the car to the house. It's revolting.' Ange shuddered. 'And I can't bear the alternative of us dragging ourselves over there, dragging Harry halfway around the world. Forget that. Look at the size of him. He's got giant genes.'

'He has,' agreed Lindsay. 'Hard to believe he came out of little you.'

'Another year he'll be even bigger and can have his own plane seat.'

'Another year, and you'll be pregnant again,' cautioned Fee.

'Good. All the better to put it off for a few more years.'

Marcus – as Dr Brookes had invited her to call him – surprisingly, was not as upbeat about Lindsay's plans. 'I'm happy for you Lindsay, that you want to explore this, but are you sure you're up to everything that it might entail?'

'My mental health's a lot healthier than my mother's.'

'Granted. And I know you've come a long way in terms of forgiving your mother and extending compassion to this unknown woman, but are you prepared to do that in the face of her cold hard defiance? Are you at the point when you can forgive your mother for everything – everything – including her not wanting to see Shane or you ever again? You have to go there with an open heart. With Que sera sera. You cannot force your will onto someone.'

'I know. That's not what I want.'

'What do you want?' He leant towards her. 'What are you hoping to achieve?'

'I'm hoping, obviously, to find her and to see her. To meet her under amiable circumstances. Naturally I would hope that she would want to have an ongoing relationship of some description with Shane and I.'

'But what makes you think she wants that? How in all that pounding silence did you decipher she might be keen for that?'

'I think she's confused and frightened, and worried

about unnecessary things. I want to help her deal with that and then I think she will be freer to choose what she wants. Us. I'm hoping some mother daughter bond will at last prevail.'

'You think?'

'Yes. It's like she's in a cage at the moment. She's not free to fly up above and look down from the sky and see how easy it can be, to survey the land and see no danger or threat, to see the beauty on the other side of the mountain.'

'And what if you do all that? What if you have one or two cups of tea with her and she still decides no? What then? What have you gained?'

'A lot more than what I've got now.'

36 Shane's surprise

Three days before she was due to fly to Montreal Sumi, Shane and Kristen joined Lindsay for their annual Yule fest Sunday lunch. Her apartment had sweeping views across Middle Harbour to Middle Head. From both the living and dining area they could see white sailing boats and catamarans and occasionally the Manly Ferry as it cut its way to Circular Quay.

A year after their father disappeared, their grandparents sold his house and put the money into two cash funds to mature when the girls reached twenty-five. They both had a sizeable deposit for their apartments thanks to their grandparent's foresight and generosity. Lindsay's apartment was in one of Sydney's sought-after coastal suburbs. Less than one hundred metres down her road she could join up with the popular Spit Bridge to Manly walkway. In less than two minutes drive she was at the waterfront and could launch her kayak. It was the ideal location for anyone who loved the water and being outdoors.

Today perhaps was not one of those days. Just yesterday there had been snow in The Blue Mountains and Bowral, only two hours south, making the temperature all of a sudden very wintery. Lindsay's faux gas fire was on.

Above it were two old black and white photographs deep-set in wide black modern frames, one of their father, Sonny Marlow, as a young man in his Royal Canadian Airforce uniform, and one of Lindsay and Shane at nine and six in summer dresses with their hands and eyes raised skywards. Born in 1927 two years before the Great Depression, their father grew up on the Canadian prairies. Their grandfather had been a bush pilot and from twelve years of age Sonny learnt to fly and spent what spare time he could hanging around Canadian Airforce bases that were part of the British Commonwealth Air Training Plan. On the day of his eighteenth birthday, the day his parents had agreed he could sign up for the war, was the day the allies declared victory in Europe. Still, he joined and began a career in the military and was soon a pilot of some renown, able to land in difficult snow and ice conditions that other pilots would think twice about. When America committed to saving West Berlin from the Soviets, he was one of 200 Canadian pilots who joined the allied effort in what was the first cold war confrontation. In less than a year they flew over 200,000 flights.

At some point in the operation an American, wanting to help raise the morale of children caught in the cross fire between East and West, started dropping candies from the sky. Planes arrived in Berlin every ninety seconds and to distinguish his cargo from others, he would wiggle the wings of his plane to let the children know he was about to drop mouthfuls of delight. Soon, other pilots got on board, their Dad being one of them, and they became known as the Berlin candy bombers.

A wave of public support led to donations and by the end of the airlift, twenty-five plane crews had dropped twenty-three tons of chocolate, chewing gum, and other candies over various places in Berlin. American and Canadian school children cooperated by attaching the candies to parachutes so the children could spot them easily as they drifted to the ground.

Their father never told Lindsay and Shane about this time in his life until one day, he had his parents drive them to an empty airfield and there for his daughters he dropped parachute candies from the sky. The photograph of Lindsay and Shane was of that day. They had no idea what they were at first and then later no idea of their significance. But after he had landed, Sonny Marlow told them of that time in his life and how it had been one of his happiest and most rewarding experiences ever and he told them that recently he'd realised he was just as happy with his life and the two of them. They were together and whole and content. And it was worth celebrating. She and Shane would always remember that day. Thereafter, every year to mark each and everyone's birthday, they would make up a little bag of candies attached to a handkerchief and go 'Here, catch,' and send a small parachute of sweets flying through the air. Years later Sumi was told the significance of the photograph and the story. That day as he gazed at the two photographs, he said, 'Lindsay, for your birthday this year we should catch a plane from Watson's Bay and fly to Church Point and remember your father.'

'Here, here.' She grinned at the two of them before placing the last of the food on the table that Kristen had spent over an hour dressing in fresh holly, native grevillea, pinecones and cinnamon candles.

They moved to the dining table to enjoy lamb shanks in tamarind with roasted pumpkin in garlic and thyme and a to-die-for Bragado from Chard Farm, New Zealand. Only problem was Shane was barely touching hers.

'What's the matter with you?' asked Lindsay, twenty minutes into the meal. 'Your taste buds gone off?'

'No,' she paused. 'I'm feeling a bit sick.'

'Are you?' Sumi touched her face, clearly concerned.

Shane pursed her lips as she blew out air. It rustled her fringe. She reached for a glass of water.

Alarmed, Lindsay stood up. 'Do you want to lie down?'

'No,' she said. 'I just need to get through this. Please sit down, there's something I have to tell you.'

Suddenly Lindsay felt like the room was too stuffy. She felt clammy herself and reached for her own glass of water. The pained expression on her sister's face was telling her this was going to be bad. The first thing she thought was her mother had died. Uncle Jay had found out and called Shane to break the news to her and save her a trip back to Canada. Wouldn't that be Shakespearian? Her eyes met Kristen's. She took a deep breath. 'You can tell me Shane. It will be all right. Is it about Mum?'

'No,' exhaled Shane. 'Only in the word.' She looked at her sister. 'I'm going to be a mum,' she said with a sad tinge of a smile.

Oh…what tempered relief! Here she was thinking death when the news was all about life. She jumped to her feet and hugged her sister. 'That's fantastic news! I couldn't be happier for you.' And she couldn't.

'You mean it?'

'I absolutely mean it.' And she did. 'I'm going to be an aunty. A new beginning, a new milestone in our lives for us all to look forward to.'

She kissed Sumi. 'Congratulations.' Kristen had come round to hug them both as well.

'Thank you,' Sumi said bowing his head in acknowledgement. 'We were worried it might upset you.'

'I know. Thank you for your concern, but I've moved on.'

'You have.' He smiled.

'When are you due?'

'Middle of December.'

'A Christmas baby,' noted Kristen. 'At least you won't be bloated over summer.'

'We didn't plan it that way. I got pregnant straight away. I thought it would take a few months.'

'Any time will be a good time to welcome a child. Do you know what you're having?'

'No we want to be surprised.'

Later that night as Lindsay was making herself a cup of jasmine tea, she, could not help admit she was excited. Excited for her sister. Excited at the prospect of becoming an aunty. Excited at the prospect of what she might uncover in Canada. Shane's pregnancy felt like a good luck omen. It made her feel like the pieces of the jigsaw were inexplicably and slowly coming together.

37 Happiness can sneak up on you too

The first time Eva had let her one and only husband inside her world was when she was seventeen – well before they were married – when he had asked her to share with him her happiest memory. Many years later he had asked her the question a second time. By then she had actually added some more experiences to her memory bank, even citing the morning visit of two birds on her windowsill.

Once had she asked him why he liked to hone in on these happy memories.

His reply: 'People are too quick to look at their life and remember their pain and misfortune, which only reinforces their pessimistic view of the world.'

Although he was not deliberately talking about her he was completely talking about her.

'Why dwell on the negative?' he asked. 'Why let that live on inside you? Dwell on the positive. Be positive,' he enthused. In Sonny's world, the laws of magnetic forces did not apply to humans. His view: negative people and thoughts attract negative people and thoughts. Ditto positive. Good things happened to positive people was his firm belief. How did that explain his untimely end?

One of the greatest ironies of her life was that her full name, Evangeline, meant good news, from the gospels, 'evangel'. But she knew she wasn't good news, not for him, not for her, not for anyone.

Seeing the positive in any situation was without doubt Gene's biggest challenge in life – on an intellectual level she liked to believe in the concept of equality and balance over the term of one's life, that the positives had to equal the negatives, otherwise one's life would be like an uneven set of scales. How could one go on living life like that? She knew she couldn't.

The two people she had been closest to in life had been eternal optimists, Mary even to her heartbreaking end. And she knew one thing about those friendships – they had fuelled her happiest times. Her father and brother, Jonathan, too had been upbeat people. That, she could not deny. In honour of those two people Gene had made a conscious effort to be positive for Ryan.

For many, many years she had to work at it. When her mind was being assaulted by unwelcome images or thoughts it was virtually impossible. But at other times when things improved, a degree of positivity did prevail; though certainly enthusiasm was not a word one would readily use to describe her. But she liked to think that Ryan had a positive view on the world and had his own memory bank of happy experiences to draw upon. If nothing else in her life, if she accomplished that, it would have been her greatest achievement and the most important thing she ever did. How well she had succeeded she did not know but she did know for a fact that Ryan had some happy memories, for they were also her own.

After he had been living with her for two years on the occasion of his seventh birthday it dawned on him that they had never celebrated Eva's birthday.

'Eva,' he asked, 'when is your birthday?'

She told him the date in August. He asked her how old she would be that August.

'Fifty-one,' she told him.

'Is that old?' he asked.

'No,' she told him, unable to suppress a laugh. 'It's middle aged.'

When her birthday came round he never said a word. She hadn't expected him to remember. But not longer after they arrived home from school, his Grandfather, Ken, turned up with his daughters – Ryan's aunt's, Sarah and Beth, Mary's older sisters – along with their children, his cousins.

Ryan stood at the window watching them pile out of the car, carrying bags and cakes and platters of food. He turned to her and smiled, 'Happy Birthday, Eva.' She smiled at him. He came and hugged her around the waist. She hugged him back, bent down and kissed him on the head. Then she walked to the door and pulled it wide open. 'I guess the secret's out,' she announced.

Another one of her favourite memories came three years later when Ryan received his first permit from the British Columbia Ministry of Water Land and Protection, Fish and Wildlife Branch, giving him the right to hold a captive raptorial bird. It was secured after Ken had signed an affidavit vouching that Ryan, a minor, would conform to all the requirements of the wildlife act. Receiving that first permit had been the proudest day of Ryan's life.

The third, mutual happy moment came when Ryan was accepted into his University degree of choice. He had studied diligently. His marks were in the top percentile. He could have become a vet with his qualifications. She was proud of him because he had applied himself to attaining the highest score he could so he had more options. While he had set his sights on avian studies he hadn't curtailed his studies to just coast in.

These were the big happy memories she stored inside, but on her good days she realised there were many. The simple phone calls she and Ryan shared, the quite cups of coffee she would have with Ken or one of his girls, even when she occasionally came across something rare on one of her bush or beach walks. What she realised about her happy memories was she could never imagine a happy memory. What made a happy memory was something completely unimagined.

Quest

July 1997

38   A homecoming of sorts

Lindsay had a one-way ticket to Canada. She flew with Qantas to Hawaii, then Air Canada to Vancouver. It had been years since she had flown through Vancouver – so long in fact she had forgotten how stunning the international terminal was.

Five seconds after she disembarked she had this overwhelming sense you had arrived somewhere elemental and majestic. The walkways were adorned with First Nations art of the northwest: whales and fishes and birds. As she headed towards Customs she came down an escalator and there to her left was a pounding waterfall, something out of the wilds of Yukon; the water pristine, crashing over a life-like rock wall nearly ten-metres high draped with small native ferns bathed in the faintest freshest mist. Clean fresh moist Canadian air – after the dry and closed-in cabin a welcome like no other. Towering either side of the natural spectacle were two imposing totem poles, their eagle beaks and eager eyes studying all who passed underneath. Lindsay's heart sighed. Oh Canada.

She had a three-hour layover before her connecting flight and then it was an hour late in taking off. She didn't arrive in Montréal–Trudeau till nine pm. Uncle Jay was there to meet her.

In the car on the way home Lindsay asked if he had mixed feelings about her visit.

'I have some concerns about your mission,' he replied, 'but, no, as always, we are delighted to have your company. It is always a pleasure to see you. Having you here with us brings a little bit of Gene and Sonny back into our lives. You don't come alone.'

They were heading towards night, towards Avenue Portland in Mont Royal, along Boulevard Grahame and Chemin Caledonia, past elm and maple and ash trees mesmerising in their softly-lit new season growth, towards truth, for her Uncle brought a little bit of her parents into her own.

Lindsay slept on and off that night. At five she rose early, pulled on her running gear and slipped outside, but rather than run she walked, taking in the summer flowers, the dense foliage, conscious that Australia didn't do seasons the way Canada did. Morton Bay fig trees weren't deciduous. Neither was eucalyptus. Magnolias and crepe myrtles were, but they weren't native.

One September before university started Lindsay had come to Montreal to see the fall colours. She'd always been told fall in Montreal was a particularly beautiful time of year. She had walked up to the parc above the McGill University. From there she had looked out over the city and the St Lawrence River in the distance. But in the foreground had been the colours of crimson and claret dazzling on the maple leaves and liquid amber trees; the pale yellows of the silver beeches; the golden gingko biloba; and the oaks ablaze in fiery autumn hues. They looked even brighter against the grey sky. Her Granny had told her the brighter the fall colours the colder the winter to follow. Back in Winnipeg it was cold regardless.

An hour later, after she had walked off her jetlag Lindsay returned to her uncle's, made a pot of tea like her grandmother had taught her years earlier and took a tray with two cups along to her Granny's room. Knocking lightly she pushed open the door. Her grandmother had the lamp on, reading.

'Ah, Lindsay,' she gasped. 'Hello, my sweet,' she grinned at her. 'I was just about to get up.'

'Stay there a bit longer.' Lindsay put the tray down and gave her Granny a long hug and a kiss, placed some extra pillows behind her to help her sit up and poured them both a cup of tea. She handed one to her grandmother and with hers she sat down on the edge of the bed. 'I'm surprised to find you here and not in Newfoundland,' she said.

'I'm still going!' Her granny was most emphatic. 'I'm just shortening my trip. Decided I'd stay here a bit longer so I could see you my dear. Abby's taking me out there next week.'

'Granny Becca, you're a marvel. And a love.'

'I'm not one hundred yet. While I still have the energy and enthusiasm I go where I can.'

Let that be a lesson for us all Lindsay thought as she smiled at her grandmother in wide-eyed amazement. Over breakfast she shared with them Shane's news. They were thrilled. Granny Becca had ten grandchildren (Abby and Jonathan had had four each, plus Lindsay and Shane made ten) and Shane's baby would make twenty-two great grandchildren. They insisted on calling her immediately to congratulate her and let her know Lindsay had arrived safely. In Montreal they were buzzing with excitement, to Lindsay it felt as if the whole world was going to plan.

That afternoon she brought up the first of the questions she wanted an answer to: 'Uncle Jay, I've asked you before how you found out about our mother but you didn't give me a straight answer. Six months ago you said words to the effect: "At this point in time I can't say." Is that still your reply?'

'No,' he exhaled. 'I will tell you that Gene wrote to me completely out of the blue about a university matter. The timing was quite serendipitous. However, she asked after no one. Her only greeting was, I hope everyone is well.' He paused. 'Her return address is a post office box in some distant location and that's all we've got I'm afraid.'

'Where?' she asked.

Smiling, his lips pressed together, he shook his head at her. 'You know I can't tell you. As soon as I do you're going to hop on the plane, fly to her town and go knocking on every door until you find her. And that will destroy any chance we ever have of hoping for some sort of family reunion with her. She'll pack up overnight and disappear and I will never hear from her again. Never.

'Right now the fact that I'm not giving you that one bit of information you're so desperate for is the only thing that's keeping her trust alive. Her trust is like the most finely spun filament of a spider's web. She'll let it fly and close off her spinneret at the first sign of any breach.'

'I don't want to breach that trust. I don't want to force her retreat,' said Lindsay in utmost gravity.

'I know, but I haven't shared her address with Belle or Mother even – that's how fragile this situation is.' He exhaled deeply. 'If you were to find her how do you see this playing out?'

'I haven't thought it through completely, but I was hoping I could go to where she lives, pop a note in her letter box – I guess post office box now – tell her I'm in town for a week and invite her to come and meet me for a coffee sometime. The choice would be hers, but I'm hoping she'd be curious enough to want to come out of her hole and to acknowledge the earnest effort I'd gone to.'

'If we were talking about a normal person, then that might fly, but you're forgetting something: as painful as it is for me to say this, as painful as it is for you to hear, you have to accept the fact that she knows of your existence, she knows that you want to make contact and she is still not open to that. She is the queen of recidivism.' Her Uncle sighed. 'Why do you think being there right under her nose will make any difference? This is one stubborn and independent woman we're talking about.'

Lindsay had thought about that question all the way across the Pacific. 'Because I feel in my bones that she's stuck, Uncle Jay, stuck in the past. She can't move forward. She can't see the possibilities. I just want her to give it a go. To give me a go. We mightn't work out but I'd like her to try. I'm prepared to try. I just want her to as well.' That was her rousing, heartfelt want. 'Can't you help me a little?'

'I will help you as much as I can without betraying her trust.'

'Thank you.'

'But just so we're clear: you are most likely going on a walk of loneliness and a journey of rejection. Make sure you are prepared for that. I have every faith that if you're meant to find her you will.' He paused, while he ran his hands down his trouser. 'Okay, so forget about me, forget about all your relations in Canada except your father. If you were coming to Canada as a holiday-maker, where would you go, what would you visit?'

'Where do I start, Uncle Jay, the east or the west?'

'Think of your father.'

'He loved the Rockies and everything west of there. The west.'

'Where in the west?'

'I don't know. I can't imagine my mother hiding out in some major tourist attraction, some bustling town that swells under the summer influx of overseas visitors.'

'Think of your father. Where would he have gone?'

'Not to any of those type of places that instantly comes to mind.'

'What then?'

'Smaller, out of the way, beautiful, off the beaten track.'

'Where has he taken you?'

'Has my father ever taken me to the place where my mother now lives?'

'Yes, I know that for a fact.'

'We went with my mother?'

'No, only your father,' he confirmed. 'And if you were coming back to Canada on a holiday, a trip of nostalgia, a meander down memory lane, might you not retrace those special holidays you once had with your father, in honour of him?'

'That time we went to British Columbia was a six week summer holiday. It's not that helpful!'

'It's all the help I can give you I'm sorry. It's something you could have come up with on your own and I have not betrayed any confidence. It is the only path I can walk I'm afraid.'

'Why are you taking her side on this so much? She abandoned you too, remember?'

'In the grand scheme of things she didn't do anything to me. She did what she had to do for herself. To enable her to rebuild her life again which I'm hoping she has been able to achieve even though it's been our loss.'

Underneath her uncle's once firm cheeks the muscles quivered, the faintest sign of his distress.

Lindsay softly asked, 'Why does she mean so much to you?'

'She's my sister!'

'Like Abby is your sister?'

Jonathan paused. 'Yes and no. Abigail never needed me. Gene did.'

'In what way?'

He exhaled at the memory. 'I was fifteen when she was born. I had a childhood, as did Abby. Morton and Gene didn't. Theirs was savagely cut short. Something I'm sure you know plenty about. And if I could have, I would have gladly carried the crosses they had to bear, the crosses you and Shane had to bear even'

Her Uncle leant towards her When she was little your mother was the bravest, most selfless, most impassioned girl you could ever meet. At six years of age I became her rock and my world was never the same after that. She honoured me. She humbled me. To me she is one the most beautiful, fragile, remarkable human beings I've ever had the pleasure of knowing.'

'You must have really loved her,' Lindsay's voice was barely more than a whisper.

'She really loved me too. Once.' His voice caught on the word. He walked away, as tears trickled down his face. And in her uncle's disclosure Lindsay experienced a new form of emptiness and grief, for two estranged siblings, for the love borne through loss and heartache, for the strength they had given each other and for the beauty of the bond they shared, which she had never witnessed and doubted she ever would.

39 Giving notice

Next morning, Lindsay phoned her sister. 'I'm not going to make a habit of this, so don't get your hopes up—'

'Good,' Shane replied.

Lindsay continued without pause, 'I need you to think of all the places we went to on that holiday Dad took us on in 1975 to British Columbia.'

'I was only nine years old!'

'That's right, you weren't a baby. You can remember. Think of all the out of the way places. I'll call you back tomorrow for your list.'

'So, she's in BC then?'

'Yes, that's all I've got to go on. That and the fact that you and I have been there with Dad.'

Uncle Jay went and got her the largest Atlas he had and what maps he could lay his hands on. It was still like trying to find a needle in a wretched haystack. And then she had an idea. 'The postcard wall! What happened to the postcard wall?'

In Uncle Jay's old house, they had a large games room in the basement where they used to play ping-pong and along one wall was a massive corkboard of postcards. It even had postcards dating back to 1925; postcards Granny Becca had sent Uncle Jay from France. Her uncle kept every postcard he'd ever received. Lindsay was hoping he still had them and that somewhere in his collection she would find the postcards they had sent him that summer. She vaguely remembered they had sent him one a week.

They'd driven from Winnipeg to Uncle Morton's place, about thirty kilometres from Regina, stayed there two nights, then from there to Calgary, then Banff, Kamloops, finally, Vancouver. From there they'd caught the ferry across to Vancouver Island, made their way north to Port Hardy, caught the Inside Passage ferry north to Prince Rupert and then out to the Queen Charlotte Islands, back to Prince Rupert, to Prince George, Jasper, Edmonton, Saskatoon, back to Uncle Morton's for two more nights and then home. It was one hell of a road trip. She could rattle off some of the bigger place names but not all the little places in between.

The postcards when she found them were of the totem poles in Stanley Park Vancouver, the butterfly gardens in Victoria, boats at Tofino, whales, which they posted when they got to Prince Rupert, bald eagles in Masset, and horses on the Skyline Trail in Jasper. Clearly nine and twelve-year olds weren't much into scenery. Were any of these places the right place?

One person in four million, one person in a landmass just shy of a million square kilometres – granted a lot of them uninhabitable. She had to narrow the field before she started. Already she was feeling overwhelmed by the task she'd set herself. Was retracing their holiday the right way to crack this? What did that tell her about her mother? What did she know about her mother? She would be turning sixty-four in August, almost at retirement age. Before she had children she had worked for a government agency. Was she in some form of policy development now? Had she remarried? Did she have a different surname?

Lindsay had never entertained that idea before. Why was that? Because she thought her mother incapable of maintaining relationships. But did that stand to reason?

Uncle Jay had told her that her mother had said her life now was complicated. Complicated with another husband and children or stepchildren perhaps?

That idea had merit. How could she face her daughter and say, sorry I didn't raise you, I was too busy raising these. Well it may have merit but it didn't have an opening.

Lindsay gazed out the window at her aunt's garden, watching a white admiral butterfly delicately land on a viburnum flower all the while thinking, what else? What else? She was clutching at invisible straws. Her mother voluntarily checked herself in to Freshwater. What did she make of that? The place was small, village like, with a sense of privacy but community, close to nature, water and trees. That's what she would look for, that was how she would focus her search. Places on a lake or the coast.

Banff, Jasper, she discarded – too touristy, and besides they were in Alberta. It had to be some out of the way place on Vancouver Island or the hundreds of islands around there. Up through the Inland Passage. Queen Charlotte Island perhaps.

'How do you know about this place, Uncle Jay? Did you and I ever have a conversation about it?'

'That, I don't recall. Your father and I talked about it though, after he returned from that holiday.'

Aaagh. It was all so inane. To take her festering mind off little out of the way places, she went and bought herself a Canadian prepaid Sim card for her cell phone – choosing the carrier that was likely to give her the best coverage in distant British Columbia. She wanted to stay in touch with Uncle Jay but more than that she wanted a number that people could call her on once they'd read her notice. She worked up a flyer that she could leave at tourist information centres, local police stations, libraries and bus shelters.

She thought long and hard about its wording, in light of the fact that her mother might be remarried and might never have told her husband that she had two daughters by another husband. Wait a minute! Last summer they had written to all of the thirteen Registrars of Vital Statistics and got thirteen letters back effectively telling them she hadn't married. On this point her uncle was free and happy to dispense with advice. 'Lindsay, do you think the woman who can walk out of a sanatorium without any forwarding address, any contact with her family for what seven years and then twenty, is not the same woman who couldn't falsify her personal details for her personal aim? She's not mean your mother, but she's definitely shrewd.'

He was right. What a nightmare. So she could have remarried. After consulting with her granny, who insisted her mother's hair would be grey by now, the flyer she came up with was this:

Seeking the whereabouts of one Evangeline (Gene) Dalton Marlow.

Age: 64 years
Height: 5 foot 9
Eyes: intensely green blue
Build: slight
Hair: grey

In relation to information regarding a family member.

Thank you for any assistance you can offer.

Lindsay and Shane Aida
Ph 450 379 5102

(And her Uncle's Montreal phone number and address.)

She had used Shane's married name to avoid any connection between a Gene Marlow and a Lindsay and Shane Marlow.

40 He's back

On the 14th of July Eva drives to Prince Rupert to collect Ryan. She meets him at the Digby Island docks. He is no longer a teenager. He turned twenty in April. He is no longer a boy.

In his gait she can still see his gentleness and quiet confidence, but now she sees something else: his self-awareness. He's broader, his forearms muscled, his hair longer, the brown tendrils pulled back in a ponytail. Hard to believe this large man walking towards her, all teeth and bronzed skin and sunglasses exuding such bounty is Ryan.

She smiles at him as she shakes her head at him. It is all she can do. Just the sight of him backlit by the sun forcing its way through the ever-present clouds. What she feels is ineffable. They have a meal in town; catch *The Fifth Element* at the movies, his choice. He drives them home. He tells her about the men he worked with on the boat, the shifts, the food, he tells her little. Who is she, the doyenne of secrets, to pry into his? Eva tries to strike a balance between being interested in his life and being nonchalant.

She changes her routines so she can grab a snatched ten minutes with him here, a quiet cup of coffee there. She drives him into Kitisak even though she doesn't need the car, just because she can have those ten extra minutes with him in the morning and after work. Other days she leaves the car in town for him and walks home, so he can see friends after work. She tries not to be jealous of the time he spends with his pals, of the nights he stays with Ken and his Haisla cousins. He doesn't have a girlfriend or at least not here; she is so grateful for that. If he did, she would almost cease to be.

41   On the road

The night after her grandmother's ninety-eighth birthday Lindsay flew overnight to Vancouver and then in the morning changed planes for Sidney on Vancouver Island. In Sidney-by-the-sea as it was more commonly known she organised a one-way car hire, arranging to leave the car at Port Hardy at the northern tip of the island. Her first flyer went up on the lost and found noticeboard at the airport.

In July 1975, the three of them had come to Sidney, a quiet, picturesque town on the Saanich peninsula, to see the British Columbia Aviation Museum, located at the site of one of the largest aviation bases during WWII. After the surprise attack on Pearl Harbour countless planes had departed from that very airfield to vigilantly survey the Canadian and North American coasts. How could they not come to the museum when flying was their father's passion? Lindsay remembered they'd spent all day at the attraction, breaking for lunch at the coffee shop across the road. In July 1997 she managed with half a day, remembering that holiday, remembering her father.

On the old federal wharf she sat and ate fish and chips, fending off large seagulls, as she gazed across Georgia Strait to the mountains on the mainland and further south to the distant snowcapped summits of the Olympic range in Washington State. The day was superlatively clear. She could see for miles. Then she drove south to Victoria. It had been twenty-two years since she'd been on the holiday with her father and the images she'd retained from that holiday were scant indeed. Was Victoria the most charming city she'd ever encountered? Quite possibly. It seemed to have it all. She felt as if she could live in Victoria. She stayed at The Dalton Hotel. How could she not? The Tourist Office was promoting a special. How could that not be meant to be? She splurged for she knew most nights she'd be staying at backpackers and Youth Hostels and the odd bed and breakfast. Last time she and her father and Shane had camped every night. In Victoria she left notices at the city library, the state legislature office, the police station. That night in her hotel room she went through the phone book. No listings. She didn't think her mother was in Victoria and with a population of 300,000 she would be hard pressed to find her.

The following day she drove to Sooke and onto Port Renfrew and just beyond there to Botanical Beach where they had played in its tidal pools, then back to Victoria. She stayed two nights at the Dalton Hotel.

From Victoria she headed north. First stop Duncan, the town of totem poles, eighty totem poles in fact. She vaguely remembered them because they'd made the ones in Stanley Park seem paltry. At the time she couldn't understand why there weren't more totem poles throughout Canada. It was strange their peculiarity to the west coast of Canada when once upon a time the entire continent was covered by First Nation people. As she discovered, each one was unique, each an emblem of a family or clan, hand carved from magnificent cedar trunks.

After Duncan was Chemainus, famous for its large murals on the town buildings, thirty-three of them depicting the region's native heritage, the Japanese legacy, and early settlers. She went on her own self-guided tour following the footprint markers on the sidewalk. Why couldn't graffiti artists the world over take a leaf out of Chemainus's book? She stayed overnight in Chemainus.

On through Ladysmith and Nanaimo and then she took the Coastal Highway 19A through the towns of Parksville and Qualicum Beach, following the waterfront north. In local coffee shops where there were posters for movies and school plays, community events and upcoming attractions, notices for lost puppies and houses to share she would pin her flyer. She travelled with her own pins. She'd stop at every police station, every tourist office, every library and every local council chamber.

The next day she backtracked to join up with the Alberni Highway, and passed through Cathedral Grove in MacMillan Provincial Park. In 1977 they had stopped there to wander through the well-groomed trails among the giant cedars. Of course, she stopped there again and wandered again. Then onto the Pacific Rim Highway, resting at the timber port of Port Alberni then onto Sproat Lake, home to the Martin Mars water bombers, the largest forest-fire fighting aircraft of their type in the world. Were they there last time? They must have been.

Across the central island mountains she drove, through miles and miles of timber country on a road narrow and windy in places, rough in others – it was called a highway? – some sections surreal, a grey lunar landscape, hillsides completely denuded almost as if they had been reduced to ash before they were replanted. Onto Ucluelet she drove. She ate scones with raspberry jam and clotted cream at the Matterson Tea House, she visited the aquarium and fell in love with the prehistoric-like seahorses – she was on a mission but she was also on holiday she reminded herself – then back in the car and on through the Pacific Rim National Park finally to Tofino. She stayed two nights in Tofino and made the next day a rest day. She read, swam and walked along the beach, popping rockweed under her heels and kicking seersucker kelp and red sea leaves as if she were walking amongst the deciduous leaves of fall.

Back on the road she drove straight to the east coast then north through Courtenay and beyond to Campbell River. The town claimed to be Canada's Salmon Capital. She put them to the test. Grilled with lemon, rosemary and olive oil. It wasn't too bad. She caught a ferry across to Quadra Island. She couldn't remember if they'd done that but the name sounded familiar. Nothing about the island was familiar. With all the stops she was doing it was slow progress.

West to Gold River, through the heart of Strathcona Provincial Park, stopping in at the park office, back to Campbell River. She spotted a few deer and caught the briefest glimpse of an escaping black bear. Then she headed north on the island highway, diverting to Sayward and Woss, into the wilderness, winding through tree-clad mountain passes full of legions of grand firs, the Christmas tree of Christmas trees. The vistas in the late afternoon were breathtaking: an ocean of trees shimmering in the mid-summer light. She had to stop the car and take a long uninterrupted look. The trees were the tallest she'd come across, easily eighty metres high. Bark spotted with resin blisters. Dark green leaves spreading in all directions like a cell under a microscope.

When she came to Port McNeil overlooking Queen Charlotte Strait she put the car on the twenty-minute ferry to Malcolm Island, bound for Sointula. They'd rested there for a few days and gone sea kayaking, she with a guide, Shane with her father. The region was reputedly one of the best spots in all of BC to see orcas. They had not been disappointed. One morning, shortly after six o'clock, their father had roused them from their sleeping bags and as they groggy-eyed stepped outside, they suddenly became alert at the sight of the distinct dorsal fins no further then ten metres from the shore. It had been a magical start to the day.

On Malcolm Island the roads were gravelled. Lindsay saw seals and cormorants, she saw a burnt-orange topped woodpecker, but no one resembling her mother or knowing her mother or even knowing of her mother.

Next stop, Port Hardy. She posted a flyer at the ferry terminal before she boarded a multi-decked BC ferry bound for Prince Rupert.

A great squadron of sooty shearwaters flew past, skimming the ocean's surface with their rapid wing-beats. The excited gasps and delighted hums of other passengers barely registered. Ordinarily the sight of so many birds with their smooth dark bodies and silvery underwings would have captivated Lindsay. But as she glided through the Inside Passage, past rugged coastlines that plunged to the tideline, past humpback whales breaching and log barges dumping, Lindsay was unable to see the spectacular sublime.

Instead, her senses were assaulted with one overwhelming feeling: was that it? Had she overlooked her mother somewhere? Had she missed her in a town she'd been through and not realised? In her sustained campaign, had she perchance scooted by? Did she need to go back and just be in each place for a few days to see what crawled out of the proverbial woodwork, completely ignorant of her presence? Her plan was to go to Prince Rupert, do a small side trip inland then back to Prince Rupert, out to the Queen Charlotte Isles and then what? As the ferry cut its path through the bluest of blues, she decided she would retrace her steps and spend more time playing the waiting game in each location.

For fifteen hours on that ferry, all of them in the long hours of summer daylight, Lindsay alternatively sat and walked while the world pulled away from her and the boat's wake caused ripples to reach unknown sounds and remote bays. She whispered, 'Come to me, come to me.' But what came to her were her uncle's words, "Walk of loneliness. Journey of rejection." And she thought maybe this is it, my "Voyage of acceptance."

The day wore on, thoughts of her sister flitted across her mind. Lindsay wondered if she was just tired or lonely or despondent or all three. On her last day on Vancouver Island she had come across a small tree with a trunk so red it reminded her of the Australian outback and pink cockatoos. At a gas station when she had refilled she described the tree to the female attendant, inquiring as to its name. She looked at her as if Lindsay were on drugs. Was she homesick for the sunburnt country?

Not long before they berthed, the epiphany of holidays past came to her. It wasn't so much the places one sees, or the things one does but the people one meets along the way that make the journey so worthwhile. At the rate she was going, she wasn't meeting anyone. She was barely enjoying the sights let alone relaxing, letting her hair down, laughing and getting to know people. At some point she needed to pull up and put down for a few days, to make this trip count for something at least.

42 A mistake

Prince Rupert, deepest natural harbour in all of Canada, guaranteed year-round ice-free harbour. It was a port town but as port towns went, this one was a cut above the rest. How is it when you're young you don't see the beauty of a place, Lindsay wondered, for there wasn't a single thing about Prince Rupert that had lodged in her memory from two decades earlier.

She vividly recalled seeing the Port Kembla coal terminal on her first trip south of Sydney, just past Wollongong – smoke stacks to the sky binding with the cloying smells of the blast furnaces from the Port Kembla Steelworks – heavy industry right on the coast. It felt like the beginning of the end. She was dating David at the time. They were on their way to Jervis Bay, in fact to Point Perpendicular, the northern cliffs at the entrance of the bay, to spend the weekend rock-climbing. It was such a contrast: two places a world apart, right on each other's doorstep.

South of Prince Rupert there was the odd pulp mill sending a ballooning white cloud skywards that seemed to purposefully mingle with the other ballooning white clouds that clung to the west coast in summer. But mostly it was picturesque, the town built half on the flat and half on the winding foothills of mountains covered with native spruce trees, no doubt in winter draped with soft alabaster snow. Snow, settling on pinecones, anoraks, letterboxes and antlers – images of a northern winter.

But this frontier town, like all frontier towns had an inherent excitement about it. It was a meeting point, a hub. Giant cruise ships docked on their way north to Alaskan waters, on route to legendary Juneau and Anchorage, to galloping glaciers that calved into the abundant sea. The resident population of Prince Rupert was less than fifteen thousand but over the summer months the town more than doubled. It became a melting pot for every nationality in the world.

There was a colour and vitality to the place that other destinations lacked, the buildings brightly painted to offset any impending grey. Lindsay stayed at The Black Rooster Guesthouse, nothing black about it. Floatplanes circled the sky. Deer wandered the street. She felt like she was on the edge of the world but the world wasn't just in front of her, it was behind her and above her. She had come to a place where eagles, bears, and whales purportedly outnumbered people. How thrilling to be in a place where she was in the minority.

She called Shane and updated her. She asked after the bump. Shane said, 'Hard to believe I'm halfway along.' Lindsay said the same.

At the café where she dined she struck up a conversation with a South African couple from Johannesburg – Jo'berg, as they called it – on their honeymoon. They told her: 'now we know what people say about Alaska is true. You have to save it, put it off, for once you've been there the world is spoilt for you.' This from people who had game parks in their back yard. Mental note, said Lindsay, don't go to Alaska for another thirty years.

After two days of wandering around Prince Rupert, enjoying cappuccinos and smoked salmon bagels, putting up her notices, chatting to other travellers, a night in a pub with a live band and talented locals who took to the stage at random, Lindsay caught the Skeena train through to Salvern. There she disembarked and waited for the local postman after being told at the tourist Information Centre in Prince Rupert that he operated a casual bus service between Salvern and Kitisak every day bar Sunday. Otherwise, she could catch a bus that left on Tuesdays, Thursdays and Saturdays.

She'd forgotten completely about Kitisak until Shane

mentioned it. Back in 1975, they'd actually been on their way to Kitimat to see a reportedly giant Sitka spruce when their father in his excitement saw a sign for Kitisak and by mistake took that turn-off. An hour later they ended up on an inlet on the Queen Charlotte Sound that fed into the Pacific Ocean, surrounded by many Sitka spruces but not the giant one they were searching for.

Yet, there was something about the quaintness of the township that appealed to all of them: its small marina, its wooden buildings, its coastal walkways – a heritage town in the making. They ended up staying for two nights and spent the day sea kayaking around evergreen headlands and shallow bays.

Two hours and several chapters later in the book she was reading, *Fall on Your Knees,* by Canadian writer, Ann-Marie MacDonald, the postman turned up and was happy to give her a lift for fifteen dollars. She sat in the front seat with him yet glanced more than once over her shoulder at his mailbag, casually thrown across the floor of his van. She had half a mind to climb over and search through its contents to see what she might uncover, but instead, she asked if he knew of an Evangeline Marlow or Evangeline Dalton, perhaps a lady called Gene?

He answered her with a single shake of his head. He dropped her in front of the Kitisak Spires Guesthouse recommending she try there for a room, but pointed down the road to The Sheltered Inn and told her that the campground also had cabins that were respectable. As she threw her pack on her back, she thought, well, he wasn't totally unhelpful.

That afternoon she visited the local information office come heritage centre. Lindsay had found from previous trials and errors, it was best to amble through and appreciate the displays and comment on them before cornering a customer service assistant with her irregular enquiry. Some days she had to feign interest in a piece of sculpture, a painting, a shell and driftwood mobile, but today she was drawn to the realism of the bird mannequins on displays: an evening grosbeak with yellow and black and white plumage, the white belted blue-grey kingfisher, but mostly the regal peregrine falcon, its charcoal hood tapering to a fawn collar and wings that featured fine black bars and spots.

'Where do you get your birds from?' Lindsay inquired.

'They're all local. There's a woman who's a fine taxidermist when she puts her mind to it.'

'It must be quite a skill,' Lindsay commented.

'Yes. Takes a lot of patience and I guess it helps if you love birds.'

'I love birds,' laughed Lindsay, 'I don't know about being patient.'

Martha was the amiable and helpful lady at the information desk who couldn't help with any information on an Evangeline or Gene Marlow or Dalton. 'When do you think she may have moved here?' she asked.

'Oh, I don't know that she's here, specifically,' said Lindsay. 'We got a vague and cryptic message that she was living in some small coastal community in British Columbia.'"

'That could be anywhere!'

'Tell me about it,' Lindsay said, with a hopeful smile.

'Oh, well.' She glanced down at the flyer and Lindsay's handwritten note – at Kitisak Spires till 4th August. 'I'll ask around and be in touch if we find anything.'

The heritage centre was across the road from what seemed to be the most popular attraction in town, the Kitisak Shack, though this two-storey bar and eating establishment with a large jetty jutting over the water, looked far from a shack. Next door to it was Pacific Playground, a sea kayaking and adventure operation.

She looked around at the Sitka spruce trees lining the bay, the picnic tables dotted here and there, the little sandy swimming beach, the escarpments piercing the pine and cedar and fir-flanked mountains in the distance and thought, yes, this is even more picturesque than I remember and with the knowledge that this was the cheapest accommodation she'd found to date, she decided here might be a place to chill out for a few days. She walked to the Shack with her pins and flyers, looking for a noticeboard to tack her despairing plea.

43 A friend of the family's

Lindsay never relished walking into a strange bar by herself, knowing no one, expecting no one, the potential awkwardness of being too old, too young, too female or too foreign. Fortunately, for her, today was not one of those days. There was a good mix of people in and outside flowing onto the deck. She blended well.

She smiled at the bartender. 'Hi. I'd like a…' Her eyes searched the lineup. 'Beer. What do you have on tap? Something light.' One always stood out less with a drink in one's hand.

'Do you want to try Kokanee? It's made here in BC. A lot of women go for it.'

'That sounds fine,' she said. 'Can I have a middie please?'

'Jake, she means a pint.' The guy to her right turned and said, 'Been away for a bit.' He was a New Zealander. She knew by the way his 'bit' sounded like 'but'.

'Yes,' she smiled. 'Left twelve years ago. What about you?'

'Been here four years. Need to head back one of these days else I'll end up with a life sentence.'

'I'd say, as sentences go, here's pretty good.'

He smiled in acknowledgement.

'What do you do?'

'I guide, sea kayaking mostly. Go to Whistler or Kelowna to work on the slopes in the winter.'

'You must be fit.'

'It helps.' He raised an eyebrow. 'You here with friends?'

Lindsay shook her head.

'Come out the back, we're shooting the breeze with

some folk we had out on the water today. I'm Andy by the way.'

'Lindsay.' She smiled into his suntanned face. His blue eyes were ringed in pale skin above bronze cheeks feathered with the faint redness of broken capillaries, the telltale sign of man who spent his days outdoors, his shades permanently in place.

Carrying a jug of beer in each hand he led her outside. He placed the jugs on the table. 'Everyone, this here is Lindsay, all the way from–' He looked at her.

'Sydney, Australia' she supplied. 'Originally Winnipeg.'

'Hi, I'm Phil,' said the Canadian at the end of the table.

'Penny,' said a Scottish woman with, 'Brian.'

'Michael. How do you do?' No guessing where he came from.

'Jane.'

'Toby.' Two more English travellers.

'Kiki' and 'Katie', two young Canadian girls in their early twenties, either side of the other guide, 'Ryan,' wearing the same logo shirt as Andy, and 'Jemma' who handled the bookings for Pacific Playground.

She sat between Andy and Jemma, opposite Ryan and the KK girls who seemed engrossed in a conversation about Jeff Buckley, Kurt Cobain and other dead rock stars. She doubted they would mention Elvis. They were discussing the likelihood of drowning in the Mississippi river. Katie had been and seen. 'It's massive,' she said, 'brown and roiling, like an enormous river in perpetual flood. All it would take would be a submerged log.'

Lindsay hadn't seen the Mississippi. She'd seen fast-flowing rivers in Nepal. The Sun Kosi for one. But it wasn't brown. At least the section she'd rafted on wasn't. It was glacially fed, white and pale blue. And cold.

Andy dragged her back from the Indian sub-continent to ask her what she did in Sydney. She told him. Then Jemma asked, 'where're you staying? How long are you in town for?' Which was followed by Andy's, 'are you into sea kayaking?'

'Why yes,' she replied. 'I have my own prijon.' A ten-minute conversation with Andy ensued about paddling in Australia until Jemma managed to ask in the briefest of breaks 'what brings you to the West Coast? Do you have family here?'

So fed up with her fruitless search, Lindsay almost said, 'yes, my mother.' But she remembered the vow she had made to her uncle. 'A friend of the family's actually.'

'Who's that?'

She stuck to her story. 'A woman who knows my mother.'

'And where does she live?'

Now came the part that made Lindsay sound a bit crazy. 'I don't know. I'm trying to find her.' Her voice was even and calm.

At that point the young guide who for the past fifteen minutes had been looking into his half-drunk beer glass, indifferent to his female companions' best attempts to engage with him, suddenly raised his head and peered at her with what felt like uncanny recognition.

'Who is this woman? What's her name?'

'Well,' said Lindsay, a slight grimace on her face, 'we think she goes by the name Evangeline or Gene and by the surname Dalton or Marlow.' Lindsay pulled a notice from her bag and handed it over. 'Do you know this woman by chance?'

Ryan read her flyer. When he finished, he dropped it on the table and ran his hand down his thigh, as if the paper had been sticky or dirty. He eyed her intently. Lindsay eyed him intently. He had a well-defined oval face. A solid forehead, the brow and dark eyebrows shadowing the eyes, his nose was long but not too long, his lips generous and full. His teeth were large with the slightest of gaps between the top front four. Dark stubble covered his smile lines and his chin. His eyes were the lightest, gentlest brown. Right then they were remarkably earnest.

'Why are you trying to track her down?'

'I'm hoping she can help me find someone.'

'The family member?'

'Yes, someone we last saw about twenty years ago.'

'Whereabouts?'

'At a hospital.'

'And when was the last time you saw this Evangeline woman?'

'Me?' Lindsay looked into Ryan's questioning face. 'About thirty years ago.'

'So who was the 'we' who last saw her twenty years ago?'

Lindsay swallowed. 'My Uncle.'

'And were this Evangeline woman and the family member you're trying to locate together then?'

'That's what we believe.' Lindsay hated this charade for making her lie in such a way to this innocent and interested young man. She abhorred lying – and thieving she reminded herself, two traits she wouldn't condone in anyone let alone herself and here she was misleading and deceiving the one person who had shown more genuine interest in her quest than anyone she had encountered to date.

'Do you know her?' Lindsay asked, her eagerness clearly apparent.

'No,' he said, 'but there's a few people I can ask for you. Can I keep this?'

'Please.'

Ryan's hair was pulled back from his face, his glasses hung around his neck, the strap made of neoprene but Lindsay was only conscious of his eyes searching her eyes. They shared an intimacy normally reserved for best friends or lovers. Oddly it didn't make her feel uncomfortable. It made her feel completely the opposite. There was something about this guy. He was almost buzzing.

Ryan wanted to know how long she had been looking for the mysterious Evangeline and where her detective-work had taken her. As they talked the others slowly drifted away. Kiki and Katie moved with Andy to another table.

When Lindsay told him she had been on the road for three solid weeks trying to locate this woman his eyes glowed. They looked dreamy and spellbound. Lindsay couldn't tell if he was interested in the specific nature of her search or the romance of her search or just interested in her? It had been a long time since she had such highly-focused attention from such a striking young man. In fact she'd go as far to say that she had never had such attention.

She put him in his early twenties. Most of the twenty-year-old guys she'd ever known were of two persuasions. One, fickle: if they weren't interested in bedding you or if you weren't interested in bedding them, they moved on faster than a roadrunner. Two: they were interested in bedding you all right but knew you weren't interested in bedding them so they set out to become your new best friend in an attempt to bed you in a moment of drunken it-just-happened-ness. She quickly saw through both ploys which was why twenty-year old guys – in fact in her experience those men, cough cough, boys in the eighteen to twenty-six-year-old range – had never much featured on her dating radar. Most were so transparent. It was refreshing to meet someone who seemed to break the mould. Maybe his generation was different.

Ryan's voice interrupted her musing. 'I heard you mention earlier you were into sea kayaking. I'd love to take you with us tomorrow but we're completely booked out.'

'Are you?'

'Got a West Coast Connections tour group coming in for two days. We're actually doing an overnight trip.'

'That's too bad.'

'Maybe after that?'

'Maybe,' she said. 'I was going to head back to Prince Rupert and go out to the Queen Charlotte Islands after here. Maybe I should duck off and do that and come back when you're free.'

'Maybe I could come with you. Be your tour guide.' His eyes twinkled at her. 'I've got two days off after these two days, maybe I can wrangle a few more. Have you been there before?'

'Yes, years ago, when I was thirteen. When was the last time you were there?'

'Three summers ago. Before I started Uni in Vancouver. I love the place. Not an easy place to get around though. You need a mountain bike or a car.'

'I have neither,' said Lindsay.

'Luckily, I have access to both.' He smiled at her, such an easy smile.

'Do you want another beer?' she asked.

'No, thanks – two's enough. I need to move onto water else I'll be too dehydrated tomorrow. I could go a meal though. Would you like to share a fisherman's basket?'

'Sounds great.'

Over fish and chips, crumbed scallops and prawns they talked a little about his life in Vancouver and avian studies.

She asked, 'Any bird courses in your bird course?'

'Couldn't resist, could you?' He grinned at her with all his teeth. 'No one can.' In Canada a bird course was a university subject one could cruise through, a gift from the academics powers that be, an easy A.

'Are you into falconry?'

'Yes,' he replied. 'But I don't have birds any more. I can't look after them when they're up here and I'm down there.'

'No place to keep them in Vancouver?'

'Falconry isn't about keeping birds for pets, and I don't keep birds for the sake of it. The pinnacle of falconry is hunting with your bird. If you're not hunting with a bird, you're not a falconer.'

Lindsay smiled inside. Here was a purist.

'And you've got to have a bird that fits the locale and has an appetite for the local quarry.'

'Why's that? I didn't realise birds were so choosy.'

'Most people think that,' he smiled. 'What you want is for your bird to hunt regularly and to fly it at the highest weight possible. That way you can be confident your bird will focus on the quarry and not you and the feed bag.' He raised his eyebrows in emphasis.

Lindsay laughed. 'Has that ever happened to you?'

He showed her a scar on the back of his right hand.

'What type of birds did you have?'

He swallowed a mouthful of water. 'I had a bald eagle and a northern goshawk. Started with Aragorn, the goshawk, then got the baldie three years later.'

'What was his, her name?'

'Her. Skye.'

Lindsay's heart sighed. 'After *The Stonor Eagles?*' Their eyes were drawn to each other as if they had travelled together to those distant landmarks in Scotland and Scandinavia with all that shared history between them.

'Yep, my favourite book of all time,' Ryan said.

'It's up there. Tell me, are you only a true falconer if you fly an eagle?'

'Not at all. There are many competent falconers out there who don't fly large longwings. It's all in the mastery between man and bird, or woman and bird. Eagles are very hard for women to manage because of their weight. Four, five, six kilograms is very hard for most women to hold steady with just one arm. A goshawk is better. They're just over a kilogram and still large enough, around sixty centimeters from head to tail.' He took another mouthful of water, wiping his mouth with the back of his hand. 'I could see you with a goshawk. It would be the ideal bird for you.'

And in that moment Lindsay could too. Her heart sighed for the second time in a few minutes.

After that he moved the conversation back to her life in Sydney. How she came to settle there, what she liked about the place, what she did on her weekends. Around nine o'clock Ryan glanced at his watch. 'I've got to make tracks.' He was almost apologetic. 'Would you like me to walk you back to your guest house?'

'I don't know,' Lindsay laughed. 'Does danger lurk here after dark?'

'It's safe.'

'Yes and it's only a few hundred yards down the road, and it's still light. I think I'll manage. Thanks anyway.'

Outside, as they were about to say goodbye and go their separate directions, Ryan turned to her. 'Promise me you won't leave. Promise me you'll meet me here in two nights time.' His eyes seemed almost to plead.

'Sure.' In the dwindling daylight she offered him an encouraging smile. 'I promise.' It *was* something to look forward to and also a relief to be able to give her word to him; as if in some way it offset the fraudulent words she'd hidden behind earlier. 'What time?'

'Shall we say six? I'll have to have one round with clients, but I should be able to make myself scarce after that.'

44   *Under her very nose*

In the kitchen Eva was making an omelette for breakfast for herself and Ryan when in the midst of whisking the eggs she happened to glance at the miscellaneous bits and pieces lying on the bench and that is when she saw the flyer. How did this come to be in her home! What were those girls up to now? Or was it the furies? She glanced around seeing if she could see any cloaked figures.

She picked it up, roughly folded it in half, and folded it in half again and was midway though putting it in the rubbish when Ryan asked, 'What are you doing?' She'd been so inside her head she hadn't heard him come down the stairs. She dropped the paper in the bin regardless.

'What does it look like? I'm cleaning up.'

Ryan rescued the note that was resting on broken eggshells. 'I wanted to talk to you about this.'

'Me? Why, for heaven's sake?'

'This woman sounds a lot like you.'

'Don't be ridiculous.'

He started reading the physical description. When he finished he gave her a look.

'So? A lot of women would fit that bill. You age, you go grey, you lose weight.'

'Intensely blue eyes, Eva?'

'Where did you get this note from?'

'From the Shack. Straight from the hands of the woman Lindsay whose name is on the bottom of that flyer.'

Jonathan! How dare he! Eva's hands clenched tightly around the metal egg whisker.

'What was this Lindsay doing there?'

'She's been all over British Columbia, all over

Vancouver Island. She's retracing a holiday she did with her father once and at the same time trying to locate this woman.'

'Did she seek you out?'

'Yes,' he eyeballed her.

He was looking for a reaction. She wasn't going to give him one.

'No ' he confessed. 'I'm just stirring you. But don't you think it's a coincidence, the description and your first name being Evangeline and all.'

'And that's where the coincidence ends. Grab me some butter please. What were their names again?'

'Lindsay and Shane Aida,' he read.

'I have never heard of a Lindsay and Shane Aida.' Eva replied. 'As God is my witness.' She made the sign of the cross on her body.

'Lindsay has been looking for this woman Evangeline for over a year. To her this woman holds the key to someone they lost in the past, someone they haven't seen for twenty years – think about that, Eva? Imagine trying to find a loved one you haven't seen for twenty years?'

Eva didn't have to imagine. 'What in that note makes you think she's trying to find a loved one? She could have other motives. This note could just be a ruse. You need to be on guard, Ryan. More conscious of how the world operates.'

'You think the world is devious and cruel?'

'Yes, at times. Why do you think I live how I do? Live where I do. Raised you like I have. There are reasons why I stay away from the world.'

'Which are?'

She didn't answer him. In her mind, she said: I hope you never find out. She wasn't thinking of her reasons. She was hoping he never had just cause to walk away from life like she had.

As soon as he left, she took the offending paper outside and burnt it.

45   Four days of togetherness

Like Prince Rupert, something about Kitisak made Lindsay feel more alive, more sentient. It rained but that did nothing to dampen her spirits. After the morning storm, she walked around the townlet then followed a trail along the northern shore, into a dripping forest full of towering silver firs, shining willows and alders shaking their serrated leaves. Large droplets dislodging from drenched branches would splash on her face and head. Each time they did she felt herself baptised by the pure waters of pristine pine.

Green and silver foliage shimmered in the diaphanous light. The opposite shoreline would appear and then disappear as the mist slowly lifted from the ocean and crept back up to the peaks. Birds that had sought dry shelter once more braved the world. Two humming birds with shocking pink hoods and throats entranced her. Another, a thrush she concluded, for her searching eyes could not locate it, bewitched her with its melody of short whistles followed by an ascending series flute-like notes. *Po po tu tu tu tureel tureel tiree tree tree.*

Two nights later when Lindsay walked to The Shack, so relaxed and at peace did she feel it was as if she had emerged from a long luxuriating bath.

Ryan was already outside, waiting.

'Hi.' She smiled. 'Got an early pass?'

'Yes and I got my leave application approved as well.' His eyes shone.

'Well done!'

'Are you hungry?'

'Not particularly.'

'How do you feel about heading away tonight? There's a

ferry sailing that leaves at ten pm from Prince Rupert. Gets into Skidegate at six am. The next one's not till eleven a.m. on Wednesday.'

Thirty-six hours time. 'No wonder you're an eager beaver. Are there bunks? I'm not going to sleep on a chair all night.'

'I believe there are private cabins. Nothing flash. They sleep two.'

'Fine, I'll pay.'

'Can you be ready in thirty minutes?'

'I can be ready in twenty.'

'I'll pick you up outside Spires.'

'We'll get back into Prince Rupert on Friday is that the plan?'

'Yes, the boat gets in at six p.m. But you're coming back here right? I haven't had a chance to show you Kitisak yet.'

'I'd thought I'd seen it already,' she joked.

'You haven't seen it till you've seen it from the water.'

She smiled. 'I guess I haven't seen it then.'

She was outside waiting when he pulled up in a stationwagon with two mountain bikes on a rack at the back.

'What are we taking on the ferry?' she asked. 'Just the bikes?'

'Only if we can't get the car on. I haven't booked so here's hoping there's some free vehicle spots.'

On the way to Prince Rupert, Lindsay told Ryan how she first came to Kitisak all those years ago.

'When was that?' he asked.

'When you were a toddler. Maybe before you were born even.'

'What year?'

'1975.'

'I was born in 1977,' he said, taking his eyes off the road to look at her. After a few moments he asked, 'Who's Shane?'

'My sister.'

'Older or younger?'

188

'Older than you, younger than me.'

'How old is that?'

Lindsay hesitated. Why did she not want to tell Ryan her age? This was a first for her. Get over it Lindsay she told herself. 'Thirty-four,' she almost whispered the words.

He whistled in jest.

'Old, hey?'

'No,' he said, 'Amazing.'

Lindsay didn't quite know what to make of that. 'Tell me,' she said, 'Do you make a habit of sneaking away with older women?'

'Who said I was sneaking away?'

'Okay, forget that, what about the older women part?'

'Haven't you noticed by now Lindsay most girls my age don't interest me all that much? It's like they haven't lived enough. Wouldn't you prefer to spend time with someone who opened up your world rather than someone who maintained the status quo?'

'Undoubtedly.'

'Tell me about Shane.'

Half an hour later she was still talking about her sister. 'Enough of me. Do you have any siblings?'

'No. But I have cousins who are like brothers and sisters to me.'

'Tell me about your cousins. Tell me about your friends.'

He told her about Jesse, Mickey and Terry. 'Have you ever seen the movie *Stand by Me?*'

'Yes, River Phoenix, Richard Dreyfus. I love that movie.'

'Well that was us.'

'Did you see a dead body?'

'No we didn't need to. We used to scare each other shitless as it was telling stories when we were out camping in the wilds.'

'Any close encounters with any leeches?'

'Had one between my toes once. But no, fortunately I haven't been scarred for life.

What about you? Many leeches in Australia.'

'I'm sure there are but I can tell you the place for leeches.'

'Queen Charlotte Islands!'

'No!' She laughed but looked at him to check if he was serious.

'If you're lucky. But I interrupted you, sorry. Go on.'

'The greatest concentration of jugars as they are called in their native country, is Nepal. I went there on a trekking expedition once for a month towards the end of the monsoon. There was a place we went through, miles from villages, on the way to the Barun Glacier and Makalu, the fifth highest mountain in the world. We made our way up these hills, past great groves of rhododendrons, towards high passes that would lead to even higher passes, and the little buggers were everywhere. And they weren't little. All the porters had them on their legs and could hardly do a thing about them. They used to carry their loads on their heads with straps, only using their hands to steady things if their loads became unbalanced. They could barely manage to bend over and flick them off. They'd call out to a fellow porter, "jugar, jugar," so their friends would come along and try and swipe them off with a switch or swipe them with a foot if they could manage. Even we would try and flick them off if we saw their grimacing faces.'

'Weren't they used to them?'

'Would you ever get used to something crawling over your body, sucking your blood?'

'I guess not.'

'We had one day where they were incessant. Every time rain or sweat trickled down a part of your body you instantly thought it was a jugar. We couldn't escape them. They were three inches long, a pale green colour, so well camouflaged, one end firmly attached to a leaf and the other leaning outwards over the path hoping to snare a victim. They were on the ground as well. They were everywhere.' Lindsay shivered at the thought. 'I peed standing up that day.'

'Scarred for life?'

'Could have been.' Lindsay laughed. 'Luckily someone told us to take Dettol. We would wipe that around the tops of our boots and all over our legs as a deterrent.' She drifted off, then said, 'I don't think I've ever seen anyone work so hard as those porters, the conditions,' she blew the air out of her mouth as if she had just spent the day portering loads. 'They get paid two US dollars a day. It's inhuman, supporting a family on that.'

'Did you tip them?'

'Of course. And left them some clothes.'

'Despite all that, did you enjoy your time there?'

Lindsay paused, reflecting. 'Yeah, I did. It's a place you have to visit at least once in your life. The mountains in Canada are breathtaking but over there they are something else. And photographs don't do them justice. You simply can't photograph a mountain in a single shot, no matter how you try. Here you look at a mountain. There you look up and look up and look up. It's like looking at the Grand Canyon or Ayer's Rock in the centre of Australia. Nothing captures the scale. Or the majesty. Only your mind and your memory.'

'Eight kilometers doesn't sound that far in distance on the ground does it, but vertically. Yes, that would be quite something.'

'Nearly nine kilometers.'

'I stand corrected.'

They made the ferry, cost them $200 to take the car over and back. Lindsay insisted on paying. Fortuitously they secured the last cabin, an inboard one.

'You won't get to see any water, I'm afraid,' Ryan said.

'If I wake early enough I'll stroll out to a deck. Besides, we'll see the view on the way back, won't we?'

'Definitely.'

'Don't worry about it then.'

The cabin was tiny but it had its own tiny bathroom cubicle and the bunk beds were not on top of each other, but either side, otherwise it would have been extraordinarily claustrophobic. At the end of the room was a small table between the two bunks and above that a framed photograph of Gwaii Haanas National Park Reserve. Further above were air vents.

Did Lindsay feel uncomfortable sharing such a small space with a man she had only known for a total of eight hours? Not in the slightest. He could not have been more courteous or respectful or companionable. Falling asleep, she felt as if she were finally, nearly five weeks after the fact, on holiday.

When she woke the next morning, she turned her head torch on not wanting to disturb him, but he was already up, his sleeping sheet and blanket rumpled on the bed. She flicked on the light switch and grabbed a quick shower. When she came out he was back. Two cups and two papers bags were on the small table.

'I got us some cream cheese bagels. I didn't know if you drank tea or coffee. I hope it's coffee.'

'Coffee will be great. Thank you.'

'Do you want to take it up top. It's a beautiful morning. Still as. We'll be there in thirty minutes.'

He stepped outside the cabin while she finished dressing. She joined him two minutes later carrying the bagels. She locked the cabin behind them and followed Ryan as he led them through to the main deck at the front of the vessel towards the bow. There they stood surveying the sea.

Lindsay couldn't help asking. 'Are you the king of the world?'

'Some days.' He grinned at her. 'Maybe the prince.'

Off to starboard was the low-lying, densely forested landscape of Graham Island. Like Canada, the mountains of the Queen Charlotte Islands were on the west coast; the tops of a submerged range that plummeted into the ocean. A few kilometers offshore it gave way to the continental shelf that dropped off even more dramatically to unknown depths. This side had the shallow sea but to Lindsay there was nothing shallow about it.

'Xaadala Gwayee,' said Ryan. 'The original name for the

Queen Charlottes. Islands on the boundary between two worlds: the sea and the sky.'

The name could not be more apt. From her vantage point the island was like a long thin magnetic band that pulled the sky and the sea together. Today that sky was a warming blue, the sea a calm green blue, the island the result of their rapturous union: the silhouetted spires of cedar and pine and hemlock their climactic sonograph. Was it a land old and untouched or was it new?

Before long there was an announcement asking them to return to their vehicle. Once they'd docked they drove over the boat's metal ramp, shuddering onto the island. But rather than vibrations what they felt was a sense of wonder. Perched casually on two of the pier's wooden poles, almost like centurions vetting new arrivals, were two bald eagles.

'Where else in the world would you see such a sight?' Lindsay whispered in awe.

'Nowhere,' grinned Ryan.

Leaving the car behind they took their bikes onto the twenty-minute ferry crossing to Moresby Island and road to Sandspit for some exercise and fresh air. Lindsay's family hadn't gone to Sandspit last time. Moresby had less than twenty-five kilometres of roads that were not well used, making the whole island feel like one giant national park.

They returned and visited the Skidegate carving longhouse where two whiskered old men were carving a killer whale from argillite, which they were told was a rare slate available only to the Haida people. The eyes were being inlaid with pearly abalone shell. Afterwards, they drove to Charlotte City, city being somewhat of a misnomer. They pottered around, went to another carving studio and a convenience store. Lindsay chatted to people, warmed them up and finally asked her questions, leaving her flyers with many who were more than happy to help if only they could.

Around four, Ryan asked, 'Are we done for a while?'

She nodded. 'Let's take a break.'

'Good. There's some place I want to show you.'

They got back in the car and he took the road towards Masset, and after a few kilometres turned down the road to the dump.

'You're taking me to the local dump?' Lindsay asked. 'You're all class, Ryan.' She laughed.

'Believe me, this is a dump like no other.'

He stopped the car about one hundred metres from the fence. 'Come,' he said, 'we'll go by foot.' He opened the back door and pulled out a ground sheet.

They walked along the bitumen road then veered through the gates on their right. Seconds later Lindsay stopped, put her hands on her heart, and just silently shook her head in amazement. With tears springing to her eyes, she looked at Ryan. He was smiling such a beautiful, sad smile. He shrugged his shoulders. 'You said you loved eagles.'

She slowly nodded as she gazed in wonder. 'Thank you,' she whispered.

In front of them perched on mounting piles of garbage were easily thirty bald eagles and to her right lording on the branches of a lone Cyprus tree were easily another twenty more.

'How fitting, a cemetery tree in the middle of man's dumping ground.'

'The end of the road in more ways than one,' Ryan murmured.

But here as ancient eagles circled the sky and their shadows flitted over them Lindsay felt it was a place where life began. Distant relatives of Cuillin's offspring, Askaval and Mourne and Hekla. Who could forget Hekla?

Ryan led her round to a small rise on the left and lay out the groundsheet. They talked little and when they did in whispers. After any major movement or change, their eyes would pull away from the eagles and towards each other, a morse of understanding. For two hours, till the mosquitos started to bite, they sat, mostly in silence, and watched the most amazing display of wildlife Lindsay had ever seen and doubted would ever be bested.

On dusk they left and found a spot to camp for the night, set up their tent and went back to Charlotte for a meal of crab chowder. The last time Lindsay had come to the Queen Charlotte Islands she had camped and here she was camping again. She couldn't remember the last time she had camped. Her father would be pleased.

The next morning on the high tide they swam in the calm ocean, until Ryan started hurling sea felt at her, those soft green mossy buds that reminded her of cotton wool left in a swamp to ferment. She liked it floating in her hands but not splat on her back and definitely not on her face.

And so the games had begun, the dance men and women do, touching each other first with objects, then using those objects as an excuse to touch with fingers, the tactile mating prelude: the holding of hands to climb rocks, the hands around the waist to swing someone down from a branch, the wiping of a crumb near someone's lip.

While Lindsay packed up their tent and belongings Ryan made ham and egg waffles for breakfast. The male territorial habit the same the world over: men loved to cook outdoors and Lindsay loved for them to do so. Was that part of the stratagem – a message that says, I can provide for us.

They headed north towards Tlell, driving slowly. There was no rush; they could be in Masset at the top of the island within two hours if they didn't stop. As it was, the cedars and pines and copper bushes swirled by, flashes of red, the fruit of a rowan tree, reminding her of her last meal with her sister.

She asked him when he knew working with birds was to be his calling in life.

'From a very young age,' he replied. 'I must have been about six at the time and we came across this injured bird and nursed it back to health. And so began the mystery. From then I always wanted to be up close to them, to be able to hold them and stroke them. And birds of prey soon became my favourites. They're just so imperial.'

'They are, aren't they?'

'True masters.' He sighed. 'How they catch thermals and soar and spot a mouse in the grass from four kilometres up in the sky.' He glanced at her. 'Half way up Everest hey? It just blows my mind. How they can live to be sixty-years old. What other land creature lives that long? How could anyone not love them? Not want to learn about them, protect them?' He paused. 'What about you?'

She looked out the window at more old growth forests that flickered in varying shades of green. 'My father was born to the skies. He learnt to fly when he was twelve and flying was his life. Little wonder we were airborne at a young age. When other families went driving in their car on the weekend we would go flying in one of his Cessnas. That sense of freedom, that perspective, what comes close? And I think therein began a fascination with birds and like you the larger ones.'

A little later Lindsay added, 'When I was eight he gave me a copy of Jonathan Livingston Seagull. It was all the rage. The seagull that flew for the love of flying rather than merely to catch food. What a life!'

'What happened to your father?'

'What makes you think something happened to my father?'

'Your voice. It's so sad when you talk about him.'

Lindsay lightly shook her head. 'The story of my life,' she mumbled. Later she quietly said, 'he died, in an accident more than twenty years ago. My life was never the same after that.' She bit her lip before continuing. 'It kind of unravelled.'

'Who was there for you then?'

'My grandparents, aunts and uncles.'

'What about your mother?'

Lindsay didn't answer. She stared out the window shaking her head. After a few kilometres, she turned back to him. 'How did you get on with my flyer? Did you uncover anything?'

'No,' he shook his head. 'I wish I could tell you I had. I know someone who kind of matched the description of the lady in your write-up. It was worth a shot. I left it with her. Maybe it will jog something. Don't get your hopes up.'

'Trust me, I won't. Thank you for trying all the same.'

On the outskirts of Tlell, Lindsay came out of herself and asked, 'you said you didn't have any siblings. What about your parents?'

'My parents? Now, that's complicated.'

'How's that?'

'Well, I was adopted by a couple called Mary and Billy. Then, when I was five, my mum died of cancer and my dad went off the rails for a few years. On her deathbed my mum asked her best friend, Eva, to look after me. So she more or less raised me along with my Grandfather, Ken – Mary's dad. My father got sober and went back to being a commercial fisherman. He's away for seven months of the year, roughly mid-April to mid-November. When he comes back I spend time with him, bunk down at his place. So you could say I was raised by four people.'

Lindsay was unsure how to respond, but after some moments she said, 'they didn't do too badly. Raising you and all.'

'No,' said Ryan. 'I think they did their best. We're kind of a bunch of misfits that go together.'

'If you're a misfit then we're all misfits.'

Ryan caught her eye. 'We're not so different, you and I?'

Lindsay held his gaze as her chest rose and fell. 'No,' she whispered.

After Tlell they drove north to Port Clements where, on the west bank of the Yakoun River, a logging protestor just earlier that year had cut down a sacred giant Sitka spruce, reportedly a thousand years old.

'Like that helped the cause,' said Lindsay when she heard the story. 'How sad that it didn't crash on top of him.'

'The stump's still there...' He looked at her questioningly.

'Please no, Ryan.'

They drove onto Masset the biggest commercial centre

on the island, but still only a village of less than a thousand, then onto the Haida village of Old Masset, on the eastern shore of Masset Inlet, where they saw the largest log barge in the world in operation – so the sign said – 129 metres long, 26 metes wide capable of transporting the contents of 400 logging trucks the equivalent of 12,000 telephone poles. It was like a floating runway.

'It's a good job large tracts of the island are protected,' noted Lindsay.

'I think they manage it quite well here. They've a reasonable balance. People get up in arms about the logging, but the Haida have it in check and they're pragmatic. They need to make a living to survive. And most of the logging happens on the west coast, which gets the highest rainfall, so the trees grow fairly quickly. And they plant again as soon as they cut the trees down to minimise erosion.'

'And maximise their returns.'

'True, but the cycle works. The rotting stumps eventually break down and provide valuable compost. A hillside that's completely denuded will be covered in young growth within three to four years. And we all need timber in our homes, for furniture.'

'True,' said Lindsay. She didn't want to be arguing with him.

Afterwards they headed to North Beach and spent the afternoon beachcombing along the vast expanse of the northern shore. It was a fusion of faded driftwood, scallop shells, the odd sperm whale tooth and orca skeleton, sand dollars with their distinctive petal patterns and Ryan's most prized find, three Japanese glass fishing floats. They lugged them back to the car.

'This person you are looking for, Lindsay,' Ryan said, 'would you recognise them if you saw them?'

'Unlikely, Ryan. That's why I need this woman to come forward and help me.'

'What made you decide to start this search after all this time?'

'That's a question and a half.' Lindsay pulled her hair back into a rough ponytail while she thought about her answer. 'I woke up one day and saw things for what they were. Maybe I felt this person might be open to meeting me and getting to know me after all these years. We lost all the formative years but maybe there is something to salvage for the future.' She glanced away. 'What about you? Have you ever tried to track down your biological parents?'

'I've been thinking about it,' he said. 'I don't have much to go on. Apparently I came from Vancouver – I'm not sure if I was born there or not but now that I study there I wonder where my biological parents are. What became of them? I think my mother couldn't take care of me,' he paused, 'or her family didn't want her to keep me.' He looked at her then, his eyes thoughtful. 'This summer I asked my Dad if he would mind if I looked into things. He was cool with it. I would like to know where I came from, to know my history. I don't think it will change anything. I know who I am all right. I don't have this sense of being lost or of missing out. Unlike you, I think it's hard to miss what you've never had. You had a father. I had Billy. I missed Mum – Mary – a lot after she died but all the others have been constants in my life. If something were to happen to them, well, I would miss them for sure.'

Lindsay gave him an understanding smile.

'One day I would like to fill in the blanks. Who knows it may open up a whole new world to me. I'd certainly be open to it. I wouldn't hold a grudge or blame anyone for what's in the past.'

They returned to scour the pools at the base of a headland jutting out into the sea at the end of a long stretch of sand. Lindsay was torn between watching the tide of Ryan's movements and all the exquisite sea life he was pointing out to her. Beautiful specimens that were enthralling in their environment but not quite the same when removed from their saltwater home. Still beautiful though, but somehow diminished. Feather boa algae, charcoal-coloured sea stag horns, the delicate northern sea fan, a sanguine symbol of snow, and her favourite, the iridescent coral-like blue, yellow and green branching seaweed. She wished she had her dive gear with her and they could come back at high tide. Beyond the low-tide mark there was sure to be a mesmerising abundance of marine life.

Around six they went fishing for salmon in one of the rivers feeding into Masset Inlet. In the Charlottes there were five different species apparently as well as trout and char. Lindsay tried to fish but after awhile abandoned all efforts. Mostly she watched Ryan fly fish. He had the knack with his wrist and the way he lassoed the line to make it sail in the breeze like a web that was cast off. It took her back to holidays she'd had with her Uncle Morton, resting by summer streams and watching him become lost in the pure pleasure of fishing. He had been a master at it, sensitive and patient, landing fish that, judging by their size, had escaped many other keen fishermen for years.

Ryan would enjoy fishing with her uncle, Lindsay decided. Uncle Morton could teach him a thing or two. After an hour when they hadn't had a single bite, she corrected herself…definitely teach him a thing or two.

'Do you think we should have asked someone back in Masset where the good fishing holes were?' Ryan gave her a look as if she were a lost cause. 'What?'

'You don't know much about fishing do you?'

'I will concede you know more.'

'The golden rule of fishing is you never tell anyone where you find your best catches.'

'You just have to be a sleuth around the locals?'

'Exactly.'

A little while later she asked, 'what are we going to do if we don't catch any fish?'

'Don't worry, I have a treat in mind as a back-up.'

'What's that?'

'Jugar soup.'

'Ha de ha ha. Well, for entrée I'm going to make up some crackers and cheese. Want some?'

'I'll come with you. We'll try somewhere else.'

Half an hour later at another hole near a thicket of salmonberries festooned with cerise summer flowers, Ryan was rewarded with a Coho salmon, followed shortly by another. He removed the hook, grinned in boyish delight and gleefully announced, 'we've got dinner.'

'Obviously we should have looked for the salmonberries at the very beginning,' Lindsay mumbled in jest.

They built a campfire and roasted fish fillets over the coals.

While they pulled the flesh apart with their fingers Lindsay asked Ryan what he hoped to do when he finished uni. 'I know you want to work with birds obviously, but do you have any ideas?'

'I want to build a bird of prey heritage park just outside of Prince Rupert, dare I say it, right on the tourist route.' Lindsay was impressed – not just with his certainty but his vision. 'It would be a place where we would rehabilitate injured birds and eventually release them to the wild,' Ryan continued. 'I'd make it open to the public and let them get up close to giant raptors and kestrels, falcons and eagles, all manner of birds. I think when someone has a close encounter with a bird they can't help but become a convert. They'll no longer hunt them. I'd make it an education park so people are aware of how fertilisers and chemicals damage their eggs. That's my pipe dream,' he mused.

'I love it!'

'Haven't got a hope in hell of bankrolling it.'

'It will come together. You can be the birdman. You need your own television show like Steve Irwin, have you heard of him?'

'Is he that croc guy?'

'Yeah. Come to Australia and talk to him. I imagine he'd be more than happy to help another eco-warrior. I'll help you. In fact I'd love to. Start with applying for government grants but then get large corporations to sponsor a bird. Chrysler for example, they could sponsor the eagle. You'll have to write a mountain of letters but it will pay off. Most large organisations have a slush fund that they give to charities. Two thousand here, five thousand dollars there – doesn't come out of their marketing budgets but out of their philanthropic pots.

'And you could have a gift shop with books and videos, postcards–'

'Already thought of that.'

Lindsay continued without pause. 'Good. Binoculars, an apparel line, clothing patches, car stickers. I'm so excited for you! You would be good in front of the camera. What's your surname?'

'Adair.'

'Ryan Adair,' Lindsay said then repeated the name in her head. 'That's great!' she exclaimed. 'Ryan Adair, Birdman Extraordinaire. I like it,' said Lindsay grinning at Ryan. 'It rhymes. We'll have to get a website up and running as well. Oh, and you could have school groups come and visit. And you could have university students like yourself come and do part of their prac there. What do you reckon?'

'Sounds great. I need a location first.'

'Maybe when we go back to the mainland we can have a look.'

'Are you loaded?'

Lindsay laughed, shaking her head. 'No. Maybe I could be an investor though. Are you looking for a business partner?'

'Maybe.'

'How much land will you need?'

'Thirty hectares. For starters.'

'Looks like you already thought it through,' she said.

'Got the plans already drawn up.'

'Have you? Can I see?'

'When we get back to Kitisak I'll show you.'

'Oh, I love it already. Can you teach me falconry?'

'One day when I've got my own birds again.'

'You're incredible.' She studied his face, the slow burning embers painting it a sienna shade, a loose tendril lifting in the faintest of breezes. More than her eyes were drawn to that face. Not wanting to come across as fawning she gave him her reasons. 'I love how you think big, I really do. It's an attribute my father always loved. He always used to say: small people talk about other people. Average people talk about material things. Great people talk about ideas. And look at the idea you've come up with.'

'I don't just want to talk about it. I want to make it happen.'

'You will. You will.'

'What did you get up to at uni? Drawing crazy plans on serviettes? Or were you in a club of some description – bird watching, canoeing – or just into lots of wild parties?"

'You know I did my best to avoid wild parties when I was at uni. Not because I didn't want to go but because I felt so bad not being able to take my sister. So mostly I had my wild partying days with her when she was going through university and we lived in Toronto. We used to go to these passport parties. Ever heard of them?'

'No.'

'Held just a few days before Christmas but sold out weeks before. It would cost you $100 bucks and that paid for all your drinks and food and, for two lucky people, one guy and one girl, a holiday to the Bahamas. So there would be fifty guys and fifty girls at these events and the idea was you took your passport with you and a light bag – because you only needed light summer clothes where you were going– and at midnight, one a.m., they would draw the names out of the hat. You had to be there or you forfeited your prize. Then, a few hours later, the lucky pair would be on a plane jetting off to some warmth and sunshine.'

'Nice job if you can get it. One hundred dollars though is a lot for struggling university students.'

'So too is the lure of the tropics in the middle of a Torontonian winter.'

'How cold does it get in Sydney in winter?'

'By Canadian standards it doesn't get cold at all. Lows of around seven or eight Celsius, highs around sixteen, eighteen degrees.'

Ryan whistled.

'I know. I'm a wimp now when it comes to the cold.'

'So winter's not your favourite season?'

'I love October when the jacarandas come into flower. They're large trees with thousands of tiny rice like leaves and soft lilac flowers that line the footpaths in mauve. And I love summer nights, the balminess of them, sweet summer breezes that come off the ocean. They're so sensuous.'

'In what way?'

'The way they caress your body, the way they make you feel. So light, so free and flowing.' She looked at him across the warm glowing coals. 'Breezes to make love by.' What am I saying? She quickly averted her eyes, cleared her throat and asked, 'What's your favourite time of the year?'

'I don't know if I have a favourite. I like it all. I like the variety. How did you end up working in computing?'

'I stumbled into it. After uni I went travelling for a few months but before I left I applied for an internship with IBM in Toronto. What do you know it came through and it kind of rolled on from there.'

'Do you like what you do?'

'Yes and no. For many years it was fine. It was fun. It was fast-paced. It's a young industry full of a lot of young people. Outside of banking it's one of the highest paid industries around. But after awhile it's just a series of new products after new products, of higher and higher sales targets. You're on this elevator. When you're in the middle of it you can live with it. But when you get some distance like I have now, it's hard to go back to it. I love long holidays. I always save my holidays up so I can take a long holiday every second year but it's a drag to get back into the swing of things.

'When I came back from Nepal I had culture shock. All I could think of was, what would a Sherpa think of the Sydney Harbour Bridge, of the Opera House?' Magnificent feats of engineering but a world away from their mountains and their lifestyle. In a big city you create a lifestyle based on a certain income level and you become compelled to maintain that lifestyle, particularly if you're single. You kind of have to put yourself out there.'

'So there's no man in your life right now?'

'No. Thanks to my brother-in-law, I've been single for the past eighteen months.'

Ryan laughed. 'What does your brother-in-law have to do with your being single?'

'He challenged me to be single for a while. Said it would be good for me.'

'Has it been?'

'Yes. It's created some room in my life for other things.'

'Such as?'

'Me. Understanding my past, my actions, their consequences. That's partly why I'm here today, on this crazy mission.'

'So what's next for you?'

'Ryan, your questions don't get any easier!' After several self-conscious moments she said, 'would that I knew what I really wanted to do. My father used to always say if you do what you're passionate about that is what you'll be best at.'

'Makes good sense to me. So what's your passion? What are you good at?'

She let out a deep sigh. 'I don't know if it's my passion, but I'd like to be a mother, I'd like to have family around me and watch them grow up, and somehow protect them, give them a better life than the one I knew. I think there were things in my life that have prevented me from doing that till now. Stuff that happened in my teens that I needed to deal with. But I'm ready now. I just need the right person to come along.'

'You never know, Lindsay. When you least expect a miracle, it can happen.'

In the chill just before dawn Lindsay awakens in a world of Persian blue. Wrapped in silk, her sleeping bag unzipped beneath her, she stretches her hand above trying to touch the damp dew from inside the tent. Next to her Ryan is lying on top of his bedding wearing only his boxers. His eyebrows move to the rhythms of a dream.

She raises herself until she is fully seated. Her eyes are lured to his unguarded form. They settle on the dark crease of his elbow then the bronze of his wrist. She glances at his left arm and wonders what colour the skin under his watch is, that and other skin that is never uncovered. Her eyes travel up to the dark cavity of his underarm and dilate at the sight of his well-formed, mostly hairless chest. Her nipples twinge with an ache to press themselves up against his. She holds her breath but she can't hold back the tingling and quickening that happens in other parts of her body, denied too long from such physical pleasures.

If they had been intimate the night before she wouldn't restrain herself now. Much to her disappointment they hadn't. It had seemed such a waste: the night, the stars, this earthly utopia, the two of them so obviously drawn to each other. With her back to him it had taken her a long while to fall asleep. She lay there virtuous as a sister, curious to know how he would moan making love to a woman. Now she is awake and cannot linger.

She sneaks outside, walks a little distance away, crouches behind a Western Yew and pees with satisfaction. She walks through the tree line, enjoying the carpet of pine needles underfoot. At a juniper tree she pauses to bring a branch to her nose and inhale deeply. The last stars are in the sky, the world slowly starting to take shape.

On the beach she gazes at the ocean, noticing that the tide has just turned. In this bay, the water barely licks the shore, so calm and peaceful and windless is the breaking day. She peels off her tank top, her hipsters and walks forward to greet its kiss. It is wet and bracing but it is welcome. She swims till she is breathless, the blood firing her veins, fighting the numbing cold.

With her back to the ocean, she watches the sun's elevation cast gilded rays on the western hemlocks and yellow cedars, wishing that the touch of light will persuade their drooping branches to strain upwards, to reach for the light, to say yes. He comes to her then, along the path of her discarded clothes, the timid rays drawn to him, consecration in motion.

She turns and breaststrokes into the deep. She hears him dive under and turns to see where he'll surface. When he does he has maintained a distance but the smile on his face is a song of elation. He slowly twirls around in the water, savouring a full three-sixty view, impervious to the cold. When he looks at her, he says, 'does it get any more beautiful than this?'

She smiles back. Her eyes soften. Her heart whispers, 'come to me, come to me.' But he doesn't venture any closer.

Soon after, he asks if she wants to get out first, an opening for her to dress discreetly. She rises from the ocean, her goose bumps subduing as the seawater rolls down her skin in delicious beads. She scoops up her clothes but doesn't put them on, walking across the beach towards their campsite. She resists the urge to glance over her shoulder to see if he resists the urge to glance over his.

They drove back to Charlotte City via Juskatia and the inland route, along the logging highway, a private road but the boom gates were up meaning that that day it was open for public access. From time to time they'd stop and go for a hike following one of the side paths. The rainforests they encountered were undisturbed. The forest floors covered with hundreds of species of salal bushes, huckleberry, ferns and mosses. Lindsay had never felt anything spongier underfoot. At one point she said to Ryan, 'wait up. I've just got to try this.' She lay down on the ground and he lay down beside her. They stared up at trees draped in witches hair and horsehair and other forms of lichen, patches of blue light in a sky mostly full of varying shades of green webbing.

'This is heavenly,' she whispered.

'Yeah, we should have camped here. We wouldn't have needed the Thermarests.'

'I feel like I'm in a Tolkien landscape or as if we're Hansel and Gretel.'

'Careful. We don't have any pebbles to mark our way back,' he warned.

They stayed side by side while Ryan asked her question after question and she complied with vivid answers as if she were a modern day Scheherazade and her life depended on the quality of her stories. She never embellished. She spoke plainly but freely and when she would tire, she would say, 'enough of me. I want to hear about you. Your turn.'

She had no idea how long they spent talking beside reindeer lichen and miniature toy soldier lichens with their red helmets, liverworts that looked like tiny aliens with green heads and multiple eyes, apple green moss balls that were surely related, fire moss with its long red needles smothering decaying wood, the occasional waft of fecundity on a sleepy wind. Lindsay wanted to get lost in that forest.

They faced each other and Ryan brushed her hair back from her face. He told her she had beautiful eyes. So clear, so striking. They reminded him of someone else but said she was the complete opposite of that person. They stared into each other's eyes for what seemed like an eternity. They didn't kiss. At times Lindsay wondered if she was still breathing, but she told herself, slowly, slowly, how many more times in your life will you fall in love. Savour this.

He rolled onto his back and pulled her into the crook of his arm and they stared up at the indecipherable sky, their indecipherable future.

She doesn't know what is happening to her? Is it him? Or this place? There are times she feels she is part of a lost world, elusive and spiritual, primeval, almost as if she is coming back to her very roots. Here in the Galapagos of the north where nature and wildlife abounded – on the earth, in the sea and across the sky – her senses were being caressed, her very being stimulated, her base instincts tumbling. In the short time she had been on the island she had become so at one with its unique environment. She wanted to protect it, worship it. Had Ryan become at one with the place as well? Was that what flowed between them, a mysterious life force?

An eight-hour ferry ride was all that separated this Shangri-La from the outside world. Here she felt ageless amongst the aged. Hopefully the distance to the mainland would act as a deterrent for decades to come and those who came would honour what they came to. Certainly for her it was ethereal and inspired, an experience that had surpassed many others, certainly a match for the Barun Glacier and Makalu.

That night they ate hamburgers at the Misty Isles Café in Charlotte City sitting on the verandah overlooking Bearskin Bay, the sky painted in pinks and purples and lilac and every hue in between. In the morning they would catch the ferry back to Prince Rupert but had decided to camp north of Skidegate, rise early, go beachcombing and swimming once more. After they had ordered their second round of lemon, lime and bitters, Lindsay took Ryan's hand in hers, looked into his eyes and said, 'I won't forget this trip. In the midst of this madness that is my life right now, you pulled me aside and showed me something real and beautiful and magnificent. You reminded me what there is to be grateful for: the purest and simplest pleasures of life. And while some things refuse to yield, others offer light and life. The Charlottes. The eagles. You. Thank you. Thank you for sharing your passion with me. I don't know why I've been so blessed to have your company. I can't tell you how much I appreciate it. Come to Australia one day and I will return your kindness.'

'Is that a promise?'

'Yes.' She squeezed his hand. 'A promise I look forward to keeping.'

Ryan squeezed back. 'Why return to Sydney? Stay in Canada! Couldn't you do what you do in Vancouver?'

'Possibly. But Sydney is my home now. And my sister lives there. And soon my niece or nephew.' She gave Ryan a mixed smile. 'Would you rather I live in Vancouver than

Sydney?' She didn't know whether to be hopeful when she asked that question. They definitely had unfinished business. She so wanted to be in his life but wondered how quickly he would tire of having her in his. How soon she would fade in comparison to his other female companions, the intoxicating allure of winsome teenagers.

But he simply said, 'yes.' He smiled at her. His eyes twinkled. His teeth gleamed. She wanted him to put away his smile or kiss her. She didn't know what to do. She squeezed his hand once more then they released their grasps at the same time.

46   The eagle has landed

The next day was still and grey, casting a mellowness that seemed to suspend the soul, as if the spirits, were saying, we know you're leaving, today, we will be suitably melancholic.

In the early morning dawn they saw two more eagles both with a fish in their talons returning to a nest high in a hemlock. Lindsay and Ryan swam in the calm, cold ocean, floating as if they were in the Red Sea. She kept her underwear on and they pulled each other through the water and walked hand and hand along the beach. They rinsed off under fresh water, the last of their camping supplies. Afterwards when they boarded the ferry Ryan led Lindsay to the stern on the second deck where they had it all to themselves. They sat, mostly in silence, and watched the island become smaller and smaller as they drew away from it until there was nothing left but the boat's wake through the oily grey surface and the faint discolouration where the water met the opaque sky above. It was oddly warm and comforting. Easier on the eye than an intense blue.

'I guess that was the Queen Charlotte Islands,' said Lindsay, her voice wistful.

'Not quite.' Ryan reached into his short pocket. 'Hold out your hand.'

Lindsay was expecting a shell, something that he had found on the foreshore that morning. But resting on her palm was a small, carved wooden box.

'Open it,' he urged.

She prised the lid off. Inside was a silver eagle's head carved in relief in the Haida design, one of their mythical messengers that also appeared on the Canadian twenty-dollar bill.

She rubbed her thumb across it. 'It's beautiful.'

'I wanted you to remember me and our time here.' He said, his voice low.

She looked at him and was bewildered by the emotions flowing through her and what was surfacing and retreating on his face: hope, joy, and sadness – such an unsettling mix of feelings. Part of her wanted to kiss him and not just kiss him, really kiss him. But there was something about this young man. He was of uncommon strength, self-sufficient, anchored in his own being. It floored her that he was only twenty years old yet so in control of himself and the situation. He was so interested in her, so attentive, so thoughtful, so tender, so innocent and earnest, such a gentleman. He seemed to be able to bring her to an edge but kept her there. As if there was a boundary that she couldn't cross. It was like the ocean that day, coalescing and deceptive in dull amorphous light.

She had never felt less in control in a relationship and she wasn't sure why. Was it because of his mastery of the situation? Was it because she was in his environment and he enthralled her? Enthralled her in a way that she couldn't fault. Was it because she felt something stronger pulling her towards him? What sane woman wouldn't be swept off her feet by his combination of youth and maturity, his abundance of masculinity and good looks?

Was he waiting for her to make a move or was he waiting to make his move? Modern girl that she was Lindsay still preferred the man to be the first to reveal his intentions. But if nothing happened soon, she would have to level with him and tell him, she did not know how to read him. Or did she have the completely wrong end of the stick and best err on the side of caution less she embarrass herself and compromise their fledgling friendship. After all, she was thirty-four, thirty-five in November yelled a second voice inside her, which she mentally slapped away. Granted she was in good shape for thirty-four, even better than Jackie Onassis at forty-three on her Greek isle, and that was saying something. But he was only twenty for crying out loud. What was he thinking? She had to suppress a sigh of frustration. Whoever knew abstinence from dating would make her so rusty.

'Here,' he said taking it from her and placing the leather strap over her head. He pulled the loops of the leather around her neck till the bird sat just below her clavicle and then he secured them in place. 'It's not coming off in a hurry.'

She smiled in reply as she wrapped her hand around it. 'I should have been the one to buy you a gift for all you've done for me.'

'Another time.' He was looking at her like there would be a million other times. She had to look away.

Absent-mindedly she said, 'I wonder if there will be any messages waiting for me when I get back.' Her cell phone had had no coverage for the past four days. 'I should ring my uncle and Shane – see how she's getting on.'

'Lindsay,' said Ryan, 'it doesn't matter if you don't find this woman you're searching for.'

His caramel eyes melted into her blue green ones, together their irises the colour of the iridescent seaweed she had marveled at just two days earlier. What an illustrious union they would make. 'You're right,' she said at last. 'To be honest, I've barely thought of her since we've been away. Only when I've talked to people has she been front of mind. Right now you are a lot more real to me than she is.'

'That's because I am more real than she is.'

'I know. You're flesh and bones,' said Lindsay putting her arm around him and squeezing his left shoulder while resting her head on the other.

'I'm the one you're looking for.'

Lindsay looked at him, wondering if he really was that intuitive. Her personal anthem – U2's *I still haven't found what I'm looking for* – flashed through her mind. Was he really the one then? Was this what he was trying to tell her? Was this where her search had led her?

'You are?'

'Yes!' he said, his voice full of conviction. 'I'm yours.'

He paused. 'Your child. The one you had to give up all those years ago.'

She leant toward him, all eyes and ears, certain she had not heard him properly,

'It's okay,' he smiled encouragingly. 'I know your secret. I know why you're trying to track down that woman. To find the baby that your uncle handed over to her. To find me.'

Lindsay slumped back in her chair, her eyes closed.

...And were this Evangeline woman and the family member you're trying to locate together then?

That's what we believe...

...Maybe I felt this person might be open to meeting me and getting to know me after all these years. We lost all the formative years but maybe there is something to salvage for the future...

...I wouldn't hold a grudge or blame anyone for what's in the past...

She put her hands over her face. 'Oh, Ryan,' she exhaled. 'I don't know what to say.'

'It's okay. Hard to believe what you've been looking for all this time has been right under your very nose. I'm sorry I didn't say anything sooner.'

She pulled her hands away from her face and took his hands in hers. 'Listen to me now.' Her eyes latched onto his and held. 'It grieves me to tell you this, Ryan, because I know how much you want to find your mother, believe me I do. But I'm not your mother!' He was shaking his head at her as if she was wrong or in denial.

'I'm not.' She was emphatic. 'In all my life I've only ever been pregnant once – and that was two years ago when I had an ectopic pregnancy, which nature took care of.' Lindsay shook her own head. Oh Ryan, poor Ryan. She squeezed his hands. 'If I had a son though, I would want him to be like you. I would be immensely proud and beside-myself happy. I would be in awe. You are the perfect son.

But I'm sorry. You're not my son.'

'But we are so alike! We're so comfortable together. We love nature. Wildlife. Birds! It's as if there are magnetic forces pulling us together. Don't you feel that?'

'Yes,' she exhaled, 'but how much is that you wanting me to be someone I'm not. Is what pulls us together real or imagined?'

'If you're not looking for your child then who are you looking for?'

'Like you, my mother. Ironic, hey? See how alike we are!' Lindsay looked away to the water trailing in a vee behind the boat. 'I could never quite grasp why you were bending over backwards to help me and be with me and now I know. More fool me.'

'Lindsay, come on...'

'I'm sorry, Ryan. Excuse me. I need to be by myself for a while.' She picked up her daypack, opened the door and walked inside.

It wasn't even twelve o'clock, but she needed a drink. She headed for the nearest bar. She ordered a gin and tonic. 'With lots of lemon and ice' she added. Had she ever been more humiliated or delusional? As if, as if, she kept repeating to herself. What normal twenty-year old guy would be interested in a normal thirty-four year old woman? She had her answer. She so needed to get a grip on reality. She seriously had been contemplating starting something with this guy but holding her back was all the progress she had made with Dr Brookes. Don't choose to become involved in a relationship that isn't healthy for you. And here they were, separated by the vast Pacific Ocean, geographically unavailable, financially at opposite ends of the spectrum, their different ages driving incompatible emotional needs. But if she were honest, the only thing holding her back was his lack of initiation.

She sat there spiking her lemon with her straw, doing her all to hold herself together. What she was feeling was more profound than simple disappointment at the unlikelihood of a reckless misadventure, more disturbing

215

than the bile of rejection and the sting of deception.

The last four days she'd spent with Ryan gave her a glimpse of the teenage life she wished she had had. Where there was no emotional pain and uncertainty, no overwhelming sense of being her sister's keeper, no awkward shyness and lack of confidence. Her hours were filled with a sense of freedom and lightness. Being with Ryan had made her feel eighteen again, but a new eighteen when life was full of the most uncomplicated possibilities and a new eighteen where she was not just a player but a spectator to the beauty and power of young love, first love. For a few fleeting days he had been like this mythical Greek God, endowed with physical gifts rarely bestowed, innocent and pure of heart, wholly devoted to her. And she had found herself falling for this young man in a way she had never quite fallen for another.

Was this life's taunting swansong, her own personal elegy? She left the bar, blindly scrambling for the restrooms. Inside the tears flowed as she surrendered to one of her saddest realisations ever: that her youth was irretrievably over. She mourned deeply for the young teenage girl who once was, but never was, and certainly never again would float on the springtide of love. She leant over the washbasins and cried into the sink. She folded her arms around her body, feebly trying to comfort herself.

After a while she blew her nose and splashed water on her face. She stared at her image in the mirror and with no one else in any of the cubicles, she said out loud, 'you're pathetic. You're vain.' And then more quietly, 'at least you don't lie to yourself, Lindsay.'

Half an hour later Ryan found her walking the decks.
'Can we talk?'
She nodded but kept walking.
'Lindsay, I'm sorry I didn't level with you but I wanted to get to know the real you, not someone who had to hide behind something else or be in fear of recriminations. And despite what's transpired, I want you to know I've enjoyed

your company for who you are, not just who you might have been.'

'That's something.' She glanced his way but not at his face. 'Did I get to know the real Ryan or someone else?'

'I believe you got all of me.'

Lindsay sucked in her cheeks.

'Do you want to grab some lunch? I'm starving.'

Slowly she acquiesced.

Over lunch she placed the little wooden box on the table. 'This is beautiful, but I can no longer accept it. It's meant for another.'

'No,' he said, shaking his head. 'I bought it for you.'

'You bought it for a woman who you thought was your mother.'

'I bought it for a someone who shares my passion for eagles, in memory of those two hours we shared watching those great birds guarding the scraps of humanity. I bought it in honour of the communion of souls – theirs and ours. It's meant for you.'

By leaving the box on the table she would be saying their whole time together had been a sham. When it hadn't. There had been many real moments, beautiful and unforgettable. She closed her eyes. She couldn't deny him that. If she could just get over herself and her hurt she could admit that. And then she realised with flashing insight, that he was hurt too. Beneath his calm exterior he'd been hurt for a long time and was still hurting. Did she want to perpetuate his pain?

She opened her eyes and opened the box, and let Ryan place the pendant around her neck for the second time that day.

Reckoning

August 1997

47 Avoidance

Ryan had been excited before his four-day break but now he just seemed sad. He'd told Eva before he left that he'd been going and going and going and just needed some time out for a few days to do his own thing.

She understood completely. 'Of course you can take the wagon,' she'd said to him.

Now she asked him, 'what happened over there?'

'The usual.'

'Did you have a good time?'

'Mostly. The eagles were plentiful.'

When he left she was glad he had disappeared. She had as well – inside one of her mind traps. Ever since that damn flyer turned up she'd been unsettled. She'd gone into hiding, walking in the woods during the day, submerged in silvery brown swales of white spruce and silver firs and scatterings of snowberries, avoiding the ocean path, the beach, the road, avoiding her own house even. At night she went to bed when the sun went down, pulled the curtains and played music on Ryan's CD Walkman listening with the earplugs. If someone by chance came knocking she wouldn't hear them. She wouldn't hear the dog barking either. She could truthfully say, 'I never heard anyone, I never saw anyone.' Who was she preparing those justifications for?

When the music wouldn't distract her she started thinking about leaving. If she had to leave, where would she go? What other part of Canada could she see herself living in? She liked the rawness of British Columbia. She liked the sense of being overwhelmed by nature. She would find it hard to give that up. The older she got the more Eva realised she wasn't a devotee of wide-open spaces, unlike her brother Morton, who found solace in such places. She liked to shelter in the lee of mountains, near their buffering proximity, restful and reassuring. She didn't mind that the light fell fast in their shadows. She needed mountains to form ranks behind her and trees to surround her like a four-pointer blanket she could draw close to keep warm, close out the elements and ward off whatever else might attack if she was left exposed.

And what about Ryan? This was his home. Could she sell their home, such as it was, out from underneath him? Could she abandon him like she had once abandoned others? But she wouldn't be abandoning, she would be leaving him to others – his grandfather, his father, his aunts and cousins. My God that sounded familiar. Was she still that woman? One thing she knew, she was a woman who, until a few days ago, liked her limpid life just the way it was, thank you very much.

48 Human nature

Lindsay spent her first day back on the mainland reliving everything that had happened on the Charlottes. After hours of soul-searching she realised, had she been Ryan, she would have played things out just as he had. What she wouldn't give to spend four days with her mother, relaxing with her, chatting with her, building memories and for her mother to be her complete unencumbered self and revel in the time they were having together. Once she had come to that conclusion she instantly and completely forgave Ryan.

She called her Uncle Jay. She called Shane and spared no details. She even managed to laugh with her about the state of events.

'In an obtuse way,' said Shane, 'maybe it's a sign that things are looking up for you. I don't know…connecting with someone who's also looking for their mother.'

'Hmm,' said Lindsay, 'I wonder if deep down inside I want to be with a Canadian man.'

'Who wants to live in Sydney,' said Shane, categorically stating her vested interests. 'I miss you already. When are you coming home?'

'I don't know. Before I went to the Charlottes I was thinking of retracing my steps completely, but now I feel like bailing altogether and going to Hawaii or somewhere and then home.'

'Sounds like a plan. Honestly, I think if you are meant to find her, you will. And who knows, maybe in six months time, something will come to light and you can go back next summer, if that's how things transpire.'

Lindsay was inclined to agree.

Around five o'clock on her second day back, she was

just about to have a shower and head down to The Shack to see if Ryan was about when there was a knock on her door.

It was him. He looked cautious.

'Hi,' she said giving him what she thought was her stock standard smile.

'I was wondering if you'd like to go for a twilight paddle.' Their recovering, unsure eyes met and held, a defining moment.

'Yeah. I'd like that very much.'

They went in a twin sea kayak, Lindsay in the front and Ryan in the back. They headed out of Kitisak Bay down the Queen Charlotte Sound, following the coniferous coastline, as they worked their way down the inlet. There were a few islands here and there that they paddled past. The largest one, a conglomerate of boulders and foreboding ribbon kelp, had a small rookery of Steller sea lions. They could smell them before they saw them. And then they heard their raucous cries.

'I don't think we want to get too close,' said Lindsay over her shoulder.

'No,' Ryan agreed. 'With all their new pups they won't welcome our presence beyond a certain point.' They glided by close enough to see the young ones launching themselves into the sea and hauling themselves out again as if it was the best game ever invented.

'When they're a bit older you can go swimming with them. They're quite friendly.'

'Are they?'

'Would you like to do that?'

'Sure. I've been swimming with dolphins before. It was wonderful.'

'Where was that?'

'In Jervis Bay, a few hours south of Sydney, near a beach called Huskisson. We'd gone down there for the week-end to go diving and on the Saturday about five o'clock in the afternoon, we were just hanging out in the boat after our dive, enjoying drifting on the water, talking about what we'd seen down below. Then someone decided to play some music so they put on Joshua Kadison, *Beautiful in my eyes*, and then out of nowhere these Hector Dolphins appeared wanting to sing and dance with the music.'

'Incredible.'

'It was. Everyone just quietly peeled over the sides. There was this one woman, who hadn't gone diving because she was six months pregnant, you'll never guess what happened to her.'

'What?'

'The dolphins were attracted to her like a homing beacon. Around her and only around her, they would swim slow enough and close enough for her to stroke them. It was as if they could sense the other heart beat inside her and recognised that they needed to be extra gentle around her.'

'Wow.'

'Wow doesn't even come close. When I'm pregnant I'm going swimming with dolphins.'

After circumnavigating the islands, they headed south, hugging the coastline. In places there were sea cliffs with stands of silver firs but in other places there were tracts of beaches with sea grasses and other native groundcover.

'Can you walk to these beaches from Kitisak?' asked Lindsay.

'Sure can. The path starts just after 7-eleven.'

They approached another headland and as Lindsay glanced up she saw someone walking along the coastal track. She slowed her paddling, as she studied the figure trying to work out what the person was wearing. A cape? A wimple? Was she a nurse? A nun? Such an incongruous image.

Behind her Ryan called out, 'paddle, Lindsay. Hard!' They were approaching the end of the point where the ocean heaved as it rode the cliff and then tumbled as it fell away, its backwash crashing into the swell coming forward, sending up revolts of water and spray. If they weren't careful they would get caught up in the opposing seas and be smashed against the rock face. Paddling wide and fast was the only way to stay in control. They paddled with determination and once they were past the headland and danger Lindsay turned to look over her shoulder, as did Ryan. The figure was now standing about fifty metres away at the very end of the promontory.

It was a woman. She waved.

Ryan waved in return.

Who's that?' asked Lindsay.

'A local.'

After two more kilometers they beached the kayaks and lifted themselves out to stretch their legs.

A large bleached trunk lay to their right, striated from its passage at sea. Lindsay walked over for a closer inspection. Timber like that made for interesting beachcombing but she could see with its enormous size how it would be a constant menace to pilots of small craft. 'I guess you're never short of wood for fires around here.'

Ryan agreed. 'This wood burns blue like the sea it came from…as if the spirits of the original tree are still alive and come out to dance. If you hang around long enough we'll camp out one night and I'll show you.'

They hadn't mentioned her leaving or staying. Lindsay did not know how to reply.

She turned and started walking backwards, facing Ryan. 'Has this beach got a name?'

'I call it Osprey Beach. This beach is where my interest in birds first started. The first injured bird I ever found and nursed back to health was an Osprey that we rescued on this beach when I was six years old.'

'Have you brought me out here under false pretenses again?' Lindsay asked, but she laughed as she asked.

'That wasn't my primary reason for taking you paddling tonight but now that you mention it, are you still interested in helping me with my bird of prey heritage park? There's absolutely no obligation. You're not my mother and all.' His eyes narrowed. Was he prepping himself for her refusal?

The wind played with wisps of her hair, rogue escapees from her ponytail, feathering her cheeks and lips. With her fingers she tried to put them back in place. 'There was absolutely no obligation before when I offered. Remember I was a complete stranger, someone you had known for only a few days and happy to help you back then. Why should my response be any different now?'

'Is it?'

Lindsay exhaled. This was a surprising test of commitment. She had not been expecting it. 'Tell me why do you want my help?'

'Because you've got good ideas. You've got experience in business.' He paused. 'Because you love big birds, maybe nearly as much as I do.'

'Is that all?'

This time he exhaled. 'It would give us a reason to work together and get to know each other more.'

Lindsay half-wondered where it was all leading to, but...enough, she said to herself. Just accept this for what it is, take it on face value.

She looked up at him. 'Let's do it.' She broke into a wide smile. 'Even though I have no architecture experience, I would love to see your plans.'

They walked along further as dried knots of sea grass scampered ahead of them. When they reached the end of the beach they turned back towards their kayaks. The iris sky was darkening, perhaps, if they were lucky, an orca sunset.

Midway between the beach and the headland they had given a wide berth to earlier, Lindsay came across a small floating object. Had she been nearer the tropics she would have guessed sea roses. From a distance they looked like badminton shuttlecocks, but when the first one came alongside and she scooped it up with her paddle and dropped it on her spray skirt, she realised with a sense of foreboding it was something else entirely: a checked handkerchief, two of its corners tied together and tied around something small and hard. Lindsay didn't need to untie them to know what they were. Parachute candies. Candy bombs.

She sighed deeply. 'Unbelievable,' she softly said, mostly to herself.

'What is it?' asked Ryan.

'Something man-made,' said Lindsay. 'Not garbage.'

She paddled on towards the next one and the next: they were easy to spot; trailing in a twilight current that was coming straight towards them. All up they collected ten. Lindsay shoved each one down her front between her life-vest and her T-shirt.

'These weren't here before, were they?' She turned seeking Ryan's confirmation.

'No,' he said.

'They must have come from that lady wearing the wimple. Do you know her?' Lindsay tried to keep the urgency out of her voice.

'Not very well,' said Ryan solemnly.

'What's the date today?' she asked.

'The sixteenth.'

Lindsay groaned.

'What?' demanded Ryan.

After a few seconds she said. 'I need to call my sister.'

When they got back into Kitisak, Ryan asked her if he could have a look at what she had collected. She handed one over. 'Go ahead and unwrap it.'

'What do you think's inside?'

'Candy.' Inside was candy. Butterscotch in fancy wrappings, maple fudge in clear plastic, minties in waxed white and green paper.

'How did you know?'

'I just knew.'

'How?'

Lindsay took a deep breath before exhaling. 'During the Berlin blockade in 1948 not long after the end of the war, as part of the food parcel drops, American, French, British and Canadian pilots used to also drop bags like these from the sky for the children below. If you have a tradition of flying in your family chances are at some point you'll come across the story.' Lindsay pressed her lips together. A few moments later she asked, 'Do you want to keep some?' She had offloaded their haul from her vest onto the picnic table in front of them.

Ryan picked one up, weighing it in his hand, his expression pensive. 'No,' he said, dropping it to the table. 'I don't want to keep a single one of them.'

Lindsay was perplexed. 'I'm sure they'll be fine to eat.'

'You keep them.' He unzipped his own life vest. 'About my sketches, shall we look at them another night?'

'Sure, tomorrow night's good.'

'Sorry, got a prior engagement. Catching up with my cousins. I can do Tuesday night.'

'Okay.'

Lindsay didn't need to ring Shane to think through the improbability of what she'd just encountered. But she called her anyway. After she said, 'Hi, it's me again.'

Shane said, 'you've made a decision. You're coming home.'

'Quite the opposite actually. Do you know what today is?'

'Do you mean do I know what yesterday was?'

'Right, sorry, I'm a day behind. But it's the sixteenth over here.'

'Are you feeling sad and maudlin?'

'No, but get this. I've just come back from a paddle with Ryan.'

'Oh yeah?'

'Yeah. It was fine. Anyway, as we rounded this headland there was this woman staring out to sea wearing jeans and a nun's wimple. That's all I could see really.'

'Different,' offered Shane. 'But how is she relevant?'

'When we came back she was gone, but floating in the ocean below where she had been were these parachute candies.'

'No way!'

'Don't you think that's a connection?'

'It's the closest connection you've had so far. I'd say it

definitely has to do with the Berlin candy bombers, but that might be the extent of the connection.'

'But today's date.'

'Okay, say it is her and it is the anniversary of Dad's service. Why is she remembering Dad's death? She hadn't seen or been in touch with him since 1969.'

'That we know of.'

'That anyone who's anyone knows of.'

'Yes, but she came to his funeral remember. She knows that date. She or a friend had read the paper or kept tabs on him. Maybe both.'

Shane paused. 'It doesn't quite compute for me I'm afraid. And besides for us it was a symbol for happiness. Is she happy that Dad died?'

'Who knows, but I want some answers.'

'You go get us some answers, Lins.'

49 Confrontation

The next morning over breakfast at the Spires, Lindsay asked the landlady if there was a convent just outside Kitisak. She knew there wasn't one in Kitisak. She'd re-walked all the streets before breakfast.

'No,' said Jill. 'Why do you ask?'

'Well because I thought I saw a nun atop of one of the sea cliffs I paddled past last night.'

'That would be Sister Eva,' said Lorna, a woman in her mid-twenties, Jill's helper. 'She teaches at the local High School from time to time.'

'Kitisak has a high school?' Lindsay asked.

'No, nearest one's at Salvern.'

'Does Sister Eva have a surname?'

'Adair, isn't it Jill?'

'No, that's Ryan's name. I believe it's St Clair or St Anne. St Something.'

'She's part of Ryan Adair's family?' asked Lindsay, trying not to inflect her voice too much.

'Yes.' The two of them looked at her, their eyes questioning. Lindsay could say no more. She let out a sigh and looked away to the window and beyond.

After breakfast she went back to the local tourist information centre, where she had first left her flyer, and asked if there was a local phone directory. She didn't want to do it back at The Spires and draw more attention to matters. There was no St Anne E or G. Nor a St Clair for that matter. There was an Adair B and an Adair R. There were no listings for any Marlows or Daltons. Why would there be? She wrote down the phone number. The address gave nothing away. Pulp Bay Road, Kitisak. She went and

231

admired the bird models once more. They made her feel connected to Ryan, confusing her feelings for him all over again. Sighing she said to the woman behind the counter, a different one this time, 'who's the woman who makes these mounts for you?'

'Eva St Anne,' the woman replied, matter-of-factly.

'Eva St Anne?' Lindsay replied, her voice a mix of disbelief and dread.

'Yes,' she said, 'do you know her?'

'Um,' Lindsay paused. 'Know of her. Ryan's Eva, right?'

'That's the one.'

Unbelieveable. 'How much does she charge for a private commission?'

'She doesn't do them anymore,' the lady replied.

'That's too bad,' said Lindsay quietly.

Outside she exhaled. Of course, she thought, it now made sense. He flies eagles; she stuffs them. What was she going to say to Ryan when she saw him next? What she wanted to say was: 'Ryan, when I asked you if you knew her, you said not very well. But she's your foster mother! Why would you say that?'

Two nights later she met him outside The Shack at six p.m.

'Hey,' he said, 'I thought we'd grab some supplies and head home and cook some dinner.'

Holy Crap! At the moment of reckoning, Lindsay didn't think she could face it. Tentatively she asked, 'There won't be dinner waiting for you at home?'

'No. Eva's gone to Prince Rupert with Ken. Won't be back till late tonight.'

They went to the fish wholesalers to see what was fresh in. After scanning the offerings, Lindsay offered to cook fettuccine marinara. They bought what they needed. Lindsay bought a bottle of Frascati. On their drive to Ryan's home she tried to make note of the turns Ryan took. When they finally arrived outside his house, she thought: who would know this was here?

'It's very quiet,' she noted. 'Tucked out of the way.'

The first thing Lindsay saw when she walked inside was a great grey owl on a branch. She instantly felt as if she'd been caught out. The yellow eyes were penetrating, even though they were glass. She glanced around and then she noted the golden eagle, perched on a rock.

'These birds, where did you get them from?' She had walked over to the golden eagle.

'Well, the eagle came from Sawtooth Ridge. It had been shot. The owl I found on the side of the road – about six miles south towards Pulp Bay.'

'Did you … I don't know what you call it when you convert them into stuffed displays? Taxidermy isn't exactly a verb.'

'These are Eva's creations.'

Yes, Lindsay whispered to herself. 'She's very good,' she said aloud.

'She is.'

'They're her birds in the information centre?' Lindsay asked, stating what she already knew.

'They are.'

Lindsay glanced around the room. The walls inside Eva and Ryan's home were lined with fake wood paneling. It was a small, open-plan lounge and dining room, with a potbelly fire in the middle against the back living room wall, to the left was the kitchen. Heavy dark-olive drapes lined the windows in the lounge and dining. Lindsay imagined when they were pulled in winter the room would be dark and subdued. On one wall was a wall hanging of the Ten Indian Commandments, on another the Ten Commandments from the Bible.

They deposited the groceries on the bench. Ryan put on some music. The Verve. Out came chopping boards and knives. Lindsay started on the onion and garlic. Ryan poured the wine then poured a little into the marinara mix. They couldn't get any fresh basil, so they had bought a small tub of pesto and added some of that to saucepan, but once at home, he walked outside and came back in with a few sprigs in his hand.

'I thought we had some, but I wasn't sure.' When it was cooked, Ryan served the meal in two large wooden bowls and put a small loaf of bread they had reheated into another. They walked out the back, through a glassed-in sun porch to a small outdoor table setting that overlooked two raised garden beds and a small orchard of citrus and fruit trees. The food was good, the company as well.

'You know,' said Lindsay, 'this is very pleasant.'

'Which part?'

'All of it,' she said. 'I can't get over how at ease I feel with you.'

'I know.' He tore off a piece of bread, then tore off a smaller piece and put it in his mouth, chewing a few times before swallowing. 'It's amazing how quickly you recovered from last week.'

'Me!' She gave him a shove. 'What about you?'

Gently he shoved her back. 'It kind of feels as if a weight has been lifted.' Her eyes met his. 'I think I always held out hope that my mother would come and find me one day. On reflection I don't think that's likely. I think what we had together was better than it would ever be in reality and I'm okay with that. Plus, every cloud has a silver lining.'

'Which is?'

'I don't have to worry about developing an Oedipus complex.'

Lindsay laughed.

'Don't you think it's made it easier. Our friendship can just be whatever it's going to be.'

'It can.' She took a sip of her wine, put down her glass. 'So that part about your penchant for older women, was that true?'

'Mostly. I don't discount girls my age completely. They would just have to be quite exceptional.

'Subjective term exceptional.'

'Highly,' said Ryan, his face friendly but unreadable.

'Ambiguous,' replied Lindsay. She didn't know what to do with his smile and that look in his eye. She averted her gaze.

After dinner, Lindsay cleared up while Ryan went and got his plans and laid them out on the table outside. His dream park property would back onto a hill forming a natural amphitheatre overlooking a cleared area that he would use for shows and presentations. With funds he'd build seating for a stadium possibly made out of river stones. Each cage would be a minimum of twenty metres long by ten wide by ten high and be built around juvenile trees and a natural habitat. He'd also like to create an island for injured, flightless birds to nest on, so they wouldn't need to be in a cage. There was a cafeteria, toilets, a cinema for guests to watch David Attenborough type movies, a medical/veterinary wing, a maintenance and supplies building, a food depot for the birds, a gift shop, a donations box – very important noted Lindsay – as well as an office, his house and staff accommodation.

'What do you think?' he asked after he had talked through every element with her.

'You think big, don't you? You sure you're not doing a minor in landscape design?' Ryan had not just drawn aerial representations but many sketchings of what each building would look like, as well as the amphitheatre from different angles and some close up detail shots he had in mind for some of the features. 'It's going to be costly,' Lindsay said. 'This perimeter fence alone will set you back thousands.'

'I know. I'd love not to have to build it on all sides. I thought if I could find a property that was at the base of a cliff then I could maybe get away with building two sides in a V with a long rock wall being the third part of the enclosure.

'Or maybe you just plant trees for your borders. Plant them closer than you would normally so they create an impenetrable hedge. They'd grow quickly with the amount of rain you get here on the west coast.'

They talked on and on, discussing how the park could be built in stages according to funding. To Lindsay, Ryan's project was the most exciting endeavour she'd come across in years. Sailing across the Pacific, buying her Sydney apartment paled in comparison. His dream had promise and potential, a bold adventure that would give his life focus and possibly his children's as well. How could she help him make it happen? How could she be a part of it?

'Do you have any friends that are designers?' she asked. 'You know graphic artists?'

'No.' He shook his head.

'Would you be open to me getting a friend to come up with some possible logo designs and theming elements? I'll wear whatever costs arise from that. Why don't I Xerox some of your drawings and she can use that as a basis, but she might also come up with something completely off the wall as well.'

'That would be great…but you don't think we're putting the cart before the horse so to speak.'

'No, we're going to be sending letters out to people, asking them for their money and telling them we'll give them appropriate recognition of their funding and their logo. You need to show them that you're professional and you understand branding.'

'I don't.'

'But I do.' Lindsay glanced at her watch. It was nine pm. They could talk for hours more but Lindsay decided she did not want to risk meeting Eva St Anne that night. She didn't want to spoil what had been a wonderful evening. And although Eva could be a complete red herring, Lindsay didn't want to take that chance. There would be other nights. Twilight was resigning to darkness. Lindsay glanced to the east where the moon was shining brightly.

'Ryan,' she said. 'Have you ever been paddling at night?'

'Would you like to go paddling tonight by the light of the full moon?'

'Yes,' she whispered. 'I'd like that very much.'

He drove her back into Kitisak. They stopped in briefly to see Andy and borrow his twin kayak and skirts and then Lindsay ducked into her room and changed into her tracks and a jacket.

They put in a little way beyond the town, further down

the inlet. Tonight they were going to go to the mouth of the inlet and a short way north up the coast.

'Is there anything particular you're hoping to see?'

'Phosphorescence,' she said.

'I'll see what I can manage. Best time of year for that is spring, particularly if you come across any red algae.'

'Doesn't matter if we don't,' she said, 'I just love the feeling of gliding through moonbeams.' A little while later she added, 'And seeing the silhouettes of pines against the skyline.' To her left was a splash. 'And flying fish.' She twisted half-round to Ryan. 'Maybe you should have some of them in your park,' she mused. The night was still and mild. Lindsay unzipped her wind-jacket as she warmed up with the paddling down Queen Charlotte Sound. She suggested a change of plan. 'How about we head to the seal colony? See if they're sleeping or playing in the moonlight.'

About eighty metres from the rocky island Ryan suddenly lifted his paddle out of the water, 'Lindsay,' his voice quiet but urgent. 'Stop paddling. Listen, what do you hear?'

She lifted her paddle completely out of the water and rested it on the kayak. What she heard was air being expelled.

'Where?' she whispered.

'To your right. About forty metres ahead.'

She peered through the dark, knowing what she was looking for but unable to see it. 'Does it know we're here?'

'I doubt it. Can you see its head?'

Lindsay trained her eyes and that is when she noticed the narrow telltale white markings in the wet blackness, then a luminescent flash of the underside of its fin. 'Yes, it's bobbing up and down. Why do you think it's doing that? Do you think it's feeding?'

'Could be but I would have thought the plankton would have been better further out in the Inland Passage.'

'Don't they normally just come up for air and then dive back down for another ten minutes or so?'

'That is one of their behavioural patterns but as I'm not

237

an expert on whales, your guess is as good as mine.'

'Maybe it's like us and just chilling out in the moonlight.'

'Or maybe it's a she and she's about to give birth to her calf. She's expelling a lot of air, which means she must also be taking in a lot of air.'

Lindsay gasped again. 'Wouldn't that be something?'

'Do you want to jump in and go swimming with her?'

'Are you crazy?'

'Yeah, but not that crazy.'

'I'm pleased to hear that.'

'Do you want to go any closer?'

'I'd love to, but I don't think we should. How would you like someone staring at you while you were trying to give birth?'

'It's an image I can't quite get my head around.'

Lindsay laughed. 'I can't get my head around how they mate in the first place.'

'Oh, they have all the necessary equipment.'

'You know this for a fact?' She quickly turned her head to look at Ryan. 'Have you actually seen them mating?'

'No. I wish. Apparently only the grey whale mates close to the surface. And they mate in winter down near Mexico.'

'How do you know that?

'Last summer I got chatting to some whale scientists in Juneau between shifts.'

'And what did they tell you?'

'That whales have penises that are permanently erect and rolled up like a fern frond inside their body. They just plop them out when they need them.'

'No way! So they just free willy and it's all on.'

'Not quite. They don't mate until a pod of dolphins turn up.'

'You're kidding.'

'I'm serious.' In the moonlight his face seemed as if it were full of devilment. '

What do they do, sing to get them into the mood?'

'Would you believe, they scrape lice away from their genitals?'

238

'Charming.' She turned to the front. It was too uncomfortable the other way. 'The whales can't scrape the lice away from their own genitals?'

'No. Nor each other's. Besides, it might spoil the romance, don't you think? In any case, they don't have the right mouths for it. The dolphins use their lower jaws to rake—'

'Ryan! I'm not that gullible.' But Lindsay couldn't quell her laughter.

'It's a real delicacy, to the dolphins apparently.'

'Remind me not to try it. Next thing you'll be telling me they follow up their de-licing service with a massage.'

'More or less. Apparently, when they're cleaning, they make loud low-frequency noises that make their heads shake like vibrators.'

Lindsay leant over and laughed so hard she almost cramped. When she could find her breath she managed to say, 'Are you finished?'

'I could be.'

'Good.'

But then he quickly said, 'Lindsay, would you rather have been born a whale?' And followed it with, 'What do you really think those dolphins were doing with your pregnant friend?'

She picked up her paddle and gently swung it over her head to hit Ryan on his. 'Stop it, stop it.'

'Not till you tell me you believe me.'

'I believe you,' she gushed, hoping to recapture her breath.

'You're just saying that to shut me up.'

'Yes, and it's working.'

'I'll start again. Apparently if you are near mating greys in a kayak, every time they do it, it feels like someone is touching your boat with a powerful vibrator. Can you imagine what that must feel like?'

'Wait,' said Lindsay, 'you have to give me a moment. I can't breathe.' She rested her paddle across her skirt as she wiped her wet eyes with her hands. Taking a deep breath, she said, 'I'll tell you a story, a true story,' she said for emphasis, 'about a formidable woman, an Australian called Kay Cottee who in 1988, the year of Australia's bicentenary, was the first female sailor to sail single-handedly around the world. She sailed in her eleven-metre sloop called First Lady and did her circumnavigation in just over six months, an incredible feat.

After she had rounded Cape Horn and was coming up the east coast of South America, she was overcome with exhaustion, having to be on constant guard for icebergs, so she would set her alarm to wake up every hour, which she would do, check all her equipment, check the horizon for any looming catastrophes and go back to sleep. One night, she slept through her alarm and was woken four, maybe five hours later by loud and urgent squawking noises. She rushed up above and there in the water just next to her boat was a semi circle of dolphins, loudly singing, sending their sonar chorus back through the icy depths to deter a sperm whale oblivious to the presence of her boat and on a path that would smash it in two. She survived because of those dolphins. So if you're telling me the truth, I believe you because they are amazing creatures.'

'That's, an amazing story.'

'Yes, and you know what?' She half turned as she lowered her voice. 'She did that voyage with a hole in her heart. What an amazing woman.'

'How old was she?'

'Mid thirties.' Lindsay paused. My age, she thought. She lifted her eyes to the whale in the near distance still heaving with inhalations, thinking, I hope it doesn't have a hole in its heart. 'Have you ever been up close to a whale like this before?' she asked.

'Yes.'

'Of course you have. Look where you live.'

'Actually the last time was last year in Alaska just a few weeks before I spoke to those scientists. I was working on that fishing trawler I told you about and we had to take refuge from some bad weather in Stephen's Passage. After it cleared we discovered we were in an area where the tide had a giant pull around these headlands and islands.' He paused. 'It would be a mean place to kayak, only for the very brave or stupid. Anyway, the ocean there is full of deep valleys and rising peaks that forces the water through at incredible velocity, stirring up nutrients, plankton, krill and the like.

'If you could take a column view it would blow your mind: silver herring near the bottom layer, thousands of salmon chasing their tails, and then porpoises, killer whales and humpbacks, while above the water, the seagulls teem and eagles hover waiting for the feeding frenzy to begin.'

'Does it happen at a certain time of day?'

'When I was young I used to think feeding times were at dawn and dusk but when you learn how much these creatures consume – nearly a third of their body weight a day – then you realise they eat whenever the opportunity presents itself.'

'Can you imagine eating a third of your body weight?'

'They're big animals and they eat to keep warm. They're mammals remember. But no.'

'So how does it work?'

'Well the whales dive deep down to the herring layer and start circling and as they do they release air from their blowholes. The air bubbles form a net around the herring to prevent them from escaping. What is the normal reaction to any animal that is threatened?'

'They try to escape.'

'Exactly. So the herring swim away from the bubble to the centre, congregating into one massive crowd with no avenue for escape. The whales tighten their circle. Then they rush to the surface, their mouths gaped wide as they swim up through the column It's like a mountain range suddenly erupting from the deep, an explosive black mass. Silver herring everywhere, in their mouths, in the sky, streaming down their sides like waterfalls, a sea of quicksilver, thousands of flashing scales swirling in all that tumult.'

'That, sounds amazing. How close did you get?'

'At one stage about twenty metres away.'

Lindsay gasped in wonder. 'And how long did they feed for?'

'Over three hours in that sitting.'

'Three hours!' She turned to look at Ryan. 'Shall we call it a night? Nothing can quite top this.'

'Don't you want to hear my stories of eagles mating?'

'Promise me you'll tell me those another night.'

'I promise.'

Ryan dropped Lindsay outside her guesthouse around midnight. As he said goodbye he reached for her hand and squeezed it. 'Thank you.' he said.

She squeezed back. 'No. Thank you.'

50   Take two

The next morning Lindsay woke up and wondered what she was going to do. Last night at Ryan's place there had been photographs of him on the walls, with his leather gloved-hand holding a sleek bald eagle, him as a young boy with Ken and his Haisla cousins and one of him with a group of other male friends, but none of the mysterious Eva.

Why was Lindsay hanging around Kitisak? For Ryan? Or for the weird wimple lady? As the day wore on she decided it was for both and worse, why did the two have to be connected. If a "meeting", accidental or otherwise, with Eva, did not go well, how was that going to affect her budding friendship with Ryan? A few more hours she decided she was procrastinating and possibly worrying unnecessarily. Eva could be completely innocent of a hidden past and she, Lindsay, could be unnecessarily complicating matters.

Lindsay knew one thing for sure, however. Beautiful as the location was, she was becoming increasingly bored during the day with no companion to do anything with. Jill, her landlady, told her she had to go to Salvern to run some errands. Would Lindsay like to come along for the ride?

'Can you do any photocopying in Salvern?' she asked.

'Yes,' replied Jill. 'Where do you think you've landed? On the moon?'

They drove along straight hemmed in roads, through preserves of forests, light blinking through the narrowest of rows.

Lindsay contemplated the soundness of her going out to Ryan's place during the day and seeing Eva without Ryan being present. How would that go over she wondered? Thirty minutes later she decided that would be just the same as Uncle Jay giving her their mother's address and her going knocking on the door unannounced. She actually had an in with Ryan. One way or another she had to use it. That night when she came home there was a note from him.

Lindsay, we are taking some clients to the Quaal Indian Reserve tomorrow and will be going paddling in one of their dugout canoes. Would you like to join us? Be at the Playground office by 8 if you do. I hope you do. Ryan

They travelled in the company's mini bus. At Quaal they were given a guided tour of how they still carved canoes in the traditional manner using an adze, an axe, a planer and a drawknife. The Quaal people had carved canoes for centuries from ten-feet-long small canoes for clam digging through to large, rarer, freight canoes that were fifty-feet-long. More common was the one they would be paddling in that day – a thirty-foot vessel typically used for travel, warfare and whale-hunting. Lindsay and Ryan's eyes collided almost in panicked desperation when their guide said that.

The canoe was made from a cedar log that had been six feet in diameter. Fortunately, there were rollers on the ramp to push it into the water. To Lindsay it felt as if it still weighed a tonne. To paddle they sat on little padded seats and even with ten people paddling it took some work. The water was only about six inches from the gunnel and they were hardly carrying anything, noted Lindsay. She wondered how the craft would ever manage to tow a humpback whale behind it.

When they returned to Kitisak, Lindsay mentioned to Ryan that she had photocopied his logo designs and asked if he wanted to take the originals home.

'Yeah, I may as well. I've got the car today.'

'It's not your car?' Lindsay asked.

'No, it's Eva's. If she needs it I ride my bike in. It only takes about twenty minutes.'

'What are you doing tonight?' Lindsay asked.

'Not a lot. Catching up with Eva. I head back to Vancouver in a few weeks and won't be back till next summer. I need to make some time for her.'

'She doesn't come to Vancouver to visit you?'

'No. Eva rarely goes anywhere. Hop in the car and I'll drive you to the Spires and you can run in and get the designs.'

When she returned, she asked him, 'when you go back to Vancouver, I was thinking we could maybe travel back together. Take the ferry down the Inland Passage and I'll hire a car to get us down Vancouver Island. Have a think about it.'

He told her he would.

An hour later, from the phone booth outside the Shack, Lindsay called Ryan at home. She tapped her fingers nervously against the window wondering who was going to pick up. He answered the phone.

'Hi, it's Lindsay.'

'Hi,' he said. 'What's up?'

'I was ringing to see if you've thought about it?'

'Thought about what?'

'Thought about going to back to Vancouver with me.'

'Hmm' he said, 'it has crossed my mind.'

'Really,' said Lindsay, unable to mask the surprise in her voice. 'That's great. But seriously the reason I'm calling right now is I've lost my sunglasses. I've spent the last hour turning everything upside down. I didn't leave them in your car by chance?'

'Hang on. I'll check.'

He came back after about a minute. 'Yes, they were on the front seat.'

'Thank you. That's a relief.'

'Well I guess that's one less pair we'll be selling in the shop.'

'Too bad. I hate to be a pain but Lorna from here's

taking me hiking in the morning up Nesbitt's Ridge and we're leaving early.'

'Do you want me to drop them back in tonight?'

'No, I don't want you to go to any trouble. Jill said I could borrow one of her bikes. I think I can remember my way. I'll ride out and pick them up, if that's okay.'

'Okay,' he said. 'If I don't see you in an hour I'll come looking for you.'

Lindsay grabbed her head torch in case she needed it. She found his road after thirty-five minutes. Twenty minutes to town, my foot. Was she riding cautiously? Yes but not that cautiously. More slowly than normal? Double yes. Did she think this was a good idea? She wasn't sure but she was on this path now and the way she justified it to herself was, she wasn't going to rock up and go, 'Hi, I was wondering if Gene Marlow lives here by chance.' She had a legitimate reason – albeit rigged – for calling in. And she knew already that even if it were her mother, she wouldn't come out with it in front of Ryan. But she was determined to let this Eva woman know that she knew...

The dog barked as she approached. Ryan came out to meet her and for a second Lindsay thought, maybe he's going to give me my glasses and expect that I'll turn tail and leave. But he didn't have the glasses in his hand. He just held the dog as he said, 'now Axel, you met Lindsay the other night. Go and have a sniff.'

'Didn't make any wrong turns?' he asked.

'No.' she smiled. 'Just took my time.'

'Do you want a cold drink?'

'I'd love one. Thanks.'

'Go round the back and sit at the table and I'll join you in a sec.'

Lindsay walked round the back, her heart pounding. Her breath tight in her throat but there was no one there. She could hear Ryan talking to someone inside. It was now or never.

The back door was wide open. She knocked nonetheless. 'Ryan,' she called out, and when he didn't reply she called out, 'may I use your bathroom please?'

'Sure,' he called back. 'Come through.'

She walked through the sun-porch into the kitchen. The light was on and standing at the sink doing the dishes with her back to her was a thin woman wearing jeans, a green cotton shirt with the sleeves rolled up to just under her elbows, and, as she had feared, a nun's wimple.

'I'm glad I'm not interrupting your dinner,' said Lindsay.

'No, we were eating when you called.' He glanced at her. He looked uncomfortable. Understandably she thought. She'd just sprung him for the liar he was, as he clearly knew the wimple lady better than "not very well". The woman in question still had not turned around to look at her. Did she know already? 'Eva, this is Lindsay, who's on holidays from Australia.'

Lindsay was not looking at Ryan but at Eva. She saw her back stiffen and watched her raise her head from the sink and look straight out the window. At that moment she wished her sister were by her side so she could clutch her hand for strength. 'Lindsay,' said Ryan, 'this is Eva.'

With that introduction Eva was given no choice but to turn around and acknowledge her. The room was dimly lit but even so Lindsay could swear the woman was pale. But it was her mother, no doubt about it. The eyes, the nose, the lips, the forehead were all the same. Her eyebrows had lightened, her cheeks had sagged and her face was lined, but it was her, undeniably.

Lindsay stepped forward and held out her hand. 'Very pleased to meet you.'

Eva stared at her. Yep, thought Lindsay, trying to not crumble under her withering gaze, still the same power there. After what seemed like an ice age Eva looked down at her hand, wiped it on her jeans and held out her hand. 'Hello,' she muttered.

Lindsay wanted to say, 'hello, Gene.' Mother wasn't actually forthcoming but she wanted to out her just the same. She wanted to say, 'Gene the wimple lady, where have you been all my life?' Her handshake was a non-event.

There was no clasping or squeezing. There was no welcome. Was there a rebuke?

She looked over Lindsay's shoulder. 'The toilet's just behind you.' Did she even look at Lindsay's face for more than a second? No. Lindsay didn't think so. If that wasn't a dismissal, what was? Lindsay turned and walked away, determining her shoulders not to shake. She could feel her face reddening, she could feel a lump stretched to breaking point across her throat but she willed herself not to cry. She told herself. Remember you asked for this Lindsay. You have done this. You have thrust yourself into this woman's home.

Lindsay barely peed but stayed in there for a good two minutes just the same, staring blindly at the calendar. She came out and splashed water on her face and then wiped it with some toilet paper and flushed it all down the toilet.

When she walked back into the kitchen there was no one there. She made her way outside. There was only Ryan sitting down with a pitcher of ice tea and two glasses on the table in front of him.

'Where's Eva?' Lindsay asked.

'She's up in her room.'

Lindsay looked at Ryan wanting him to divulge more.

'She normally makes herself scarce when I have friends pop by.'

'Really?'

'Nine times out of ten. There are only a few exceptions. She would need to know you for about ten years before she would hang out with you.'

She never knew me for ten years. Lindsay let out a sigh then took a sip of her drink, wanting to ask Ryan what she had wanted to ask him days ago. She asked him.

'Ryan, the other day when I asked you–'

He cut her off. 'I know, Lindsay. I'm sorry.'

'Why?'

'Because I couldn't answer the questions that would surely come next: what was she doing? And why? I have no idea. I told you my truth. Eva may be the woman who raised me but she's an enigma to me in many ways. And besides, she values her privacy. She always has. It sacrosanct. That's Eva and I respect that. I don't inflict people on her. I made an assumption about her and you, just like I made an assumption about you and me. I was wrong on both accounts.'

'How do you know you were wrong about her and me?'

'After that first night I met you I showed her your flyer and I asked her if she knew a Lindsay and Shane Aida and she categorically said no.'

'Did you show her the flyer to see if she would be forthcoming about your real mother?'

'Yes. I told her she looked like the woman you were looking for based on your description. Do you think she lied to me?'

Yes! Lindsay wanted to say. She wanted to tell Ryan everything. Because he had told her everything and right at the moment she felt like she needed someone to help her and by telling Ryan he might become that someone. She wanted to tell him that her surname was Marlow, that that woman upstairs who called herself Eva St Anne was actually Evangeline – Gene – Marlow – her mother. What held her back? What held her back was she desperately wanted this precarious situation to slide in her favour. Not against her. How could she do that? She needed to be like her Uncle Jay and give that hostile, threatened woman upstairs a reason to trust her. So that in a day or two she might be forthcoming and seek her out and talk to her, with Ryan being none the wiser to any interaction.

Lindsay closed her eyes then opened them to look at Ryan. 'She's telling you her truth. Aida is not our surname, it's Shane's married name. We didn't want our name to be so obviously connected to the name of the woman we are looking for, for a whole host of reasons.'

'Is Eva the woman you're looking for?'

Lindsay looked at Ryan and looked away. She took a breath and turned back, her eyes meeting his as she parted her mouth.

'How did you come to be in Kitisak?' The voice was disconcerting, surprisingly loud and authoritative.

Lindsay was startled but tried not to show it. She turned around to see Eva leaning up against the doorjamb, her arms crossed in front, her body language yelling at her. 'It's such an out of the way place and all.'

'Not as much as it used to be, Eva,' said Ryan, 'else Pacific Playground wouldn't have a business. Would you like to join us?'

'I'll take a glass of ice tea if you can spare one.'

Ryan rose and walked past Eva into the kitchen.

Lindsay looked at her. There weren't butterflies fluttering in her stomach, there was a flock of injured ospreys madly flapping. Even so, Lindsay willed her voice to be calm. 'I came here once years ago with my father and my sister, Shane. It was a very special time in our lives. I thought I'd like to come here again.'

'Do you have more than one sister?' she asked.

Ryan was back outside.

'No,' said Lindsay, shaking her head. 'Why do you ask that?'

'Because the way you specified her name. Most people only do that when they have a number of sisters or brothers to be clear which one they're talking about.'

'No,' said Lindsay. 'I only have the one. Shane's thirty-one years old, lives not far from me in Sydney, works as an osteopath. She's married.' If you read our letter you would know all that, but not this bit. 'She's pregnant. Going to have her first baby in December.'

'Is that so?'

Lindsay was looking for a spark, a sign of interest, a thawing of her icy facade, an awakening of the torpor around her clamped heart. But there was nothing.

Ryan said, 'Eva would you like to sit down?'

'No thank you. I'd rather stand. Do you have any relatives still living here in Canada?'

Lindsay stared at her. Was this a test? 'Yes. Lots of family on my mother's side.'

'And when was the last time you saw any of them?'

'I saw my grandmother who just turned ninety-eight a few weeks ago. I was with her on the day. She is amazing.' Lindsay emphasised amazing. She didn't care. She was proud of her Granny Becca and at that moment pitied her for having such an unmoving, unloving daughter.

Ryan said, 'I didn't know your grandmother was still alive. That would be so special.'

Eva looked at Ryan. Lindsay looked at Eva looking at Ryan and the way he had said, 'I didn't know…' as if there was a lot about her that he did know. Lindsay continued. 'I saw my Uncle Jay at the same time. My Granny lives with him. Mostly,' she added. 'I haven't managed on this visit to catch up with my Aunty Abby or my Uncle Morton.'

She had to know those names. Lindsay waited for a reaction, or another question. Wouldn't a person normally follow up such a statement like the one she'd just made with: 'and where do they live? Or when do you hope to do that? Or, how old is your Uncle Jay?' But then Lindsay paused as she remembered: when had her mother ever been normal?

But finally, Eva asked, 'And what does your Uncle Jay do when he's not looking after your grandmother?'

Was she having a dig at Uncle Jay? Lindsay wasn't sure but she was going to have a dig at her. 'The most recent memory I have of my Uncle Jay is he telling me a story that dates back to 1939 of this young girl who stole his heart and begged him not to leave her.'

'What happened to her?' asked Ryan.

Lindsay looked at Eva. 'She left him in the end.'

No one said anything for quite a while until Ryan glanced at his watch. 'Lindsay, I don't think you should ride the bike back. It'll be dark before you get there.'

'It's okay. I brought my head torch,' She patted her bum bag.

Ryan smiled at her. 'No,' he shook his head. 'We'll throw your bike into the back of the stationwagon and I'll drive you.'

'Thanks for the offer, but it's okay.'

'No,' said Eva. 'It's what we'll do. Big trucks go down that road often at night. I'll come with you, Ryan. I want to pick up a few things from the 7-eleven.'

Lindsay sat in the back seat, Eva, Gene, whatever she called herself, in the front. Ryan asked Lindsay what time they were starting their hike.

'Six,' she replied. 'Lorna's bringing brunch.'

'Lorna Patterson?' queried Eva.

Lindsay said she didn't know her surname.

Ryan said, 'Yes, Eva.'

Eva said, 'She's got a set of legs on her that girl.'

They barely exchanged another word. When they pulled up, Ryan got out, pulled the bike out of the back, and using her head torch fitted the front wheel back on. 'Now, have you got your sunglasses?' Lindsay tapped her bum bag. 'I'll see you sometime,' he said.

'Yes,' she said. 'Bye.' Lindsay walked back down the passenger side of the vehicle, pushing the bike. Eva's window was one third of the way down. 'Bye, Eva,' she said. 'I'm in town for another week or two. Maybe we'll run into each other sometime.'

Eva stared at her. Lindsay doubted she was going to say goodbye even. She put her head down to walk away and in that moment Eva said, 'I walk fast. But I don't run.'

51 Holding her tongue

They called in at 7-eleven. Eva bought things she didn't need.

On the way home she asked Ryan, when was his next day off.

'I don't know. I need to check. Why?'

'I just thought it would be good to do something together before you disappear.'

'Yes,' he said, 'that would be good. Any thoughts?'

'I'll think about it,' she said.

She talked about their future and his departure to stop her from talking about other things more distressing.

She wanted to tell Ryan that he was never, ever, to bring that woman into her house again. But that would be a first for Eva – a statement more extreme than any other – it would instantly make him suspicious, provoke questions.

She wanted to say, what are you doing hanging around with her? She's much too old for you. That was almost as bad as her first train of thought. No, she had to do what she always did with his other friends. She had to retreat and disappear, be happy to give him his space and safeguard her own. Lindsay had pointed her invisible finger but she had also held her tongue. She would do likewise.

After that phone call during dinner Eva hadn't asked, '2ho was that?' She never asked. When he was younger if it concerned her he would tell her as in, can I go to Jesse's place for the weekend? Occasionally he would tell her who was on the phone and what they wanted. Tonight he said, 'one of our clients left her sunglasses in the car.'

That wasn't a first.

'How does she know where you live?' she had asked.

'We swung by here the other day when you were in Prince Rupert.'

At the time it was immaterial.

Should she just let it go completely? Let it be water off a duck's back. Let tomorrow be a new day and put today behind. Be relieved that is was behind her now, once and for all. And that it would never come again...would it?

Eva was so wired she couldn't sleep. In the middle of the night she walked to the main highway and back two times. At four-thirty she came inside and did what she hadn't done for more than two decades. She took not one but two Valium. The very taking of it worried her. Took her back to a time and a place she did not want to go back to, but once it subdued her, she could surrender to oblivion for eight to ten hours and hopefully, when she woke, what was frantically running through her system would be slower in wakening.

52   All this way

Lindsay was relieved she had arranged to go walking with Lorna the next morning. She had struggled to sleep the night before replaying conversations and expressions over and over in her head. She wondered what had happened after they had dropped her off. Maybe Ryan would tell her. Certainly Gene or Eva – whatever she called herself – never would.

It was such a hollow end to her search. To think all her determination and planning and action had led to this anticlimax. A part of Lindsay, the four-year-old child, had been holding out for her mother to take one look at her and take her in her arms. Lindsay laughed bitterly, such a foolish whim. Not even a furtive glance was on offer.

Could her mother have been more apathetic to her last night? Eva feigned interest in her life merely to prevent Lindsay and Ryan from talking about her, shifting the focus back on to Lindsay in a managed way.

Not that she was one to give up but Lindsay felt proceeding was pointless. At the same time she felt she had to stay in Kitisak for another week at least, like she had flagged, but would it be like serving a sentence, doing time, regardless of whether she was innocent or guilty.

At least there was Ryan. After last night's reception, Lindsay wished, if only there was Ryan. Over the preceding days she had come to the conclusion that had she lived in Vancouver she would gladly dive into a relationship with Ryan, go with what she was feeling. So positive had been each and every one of her experiences with him she had decided that he was truly exceptional. Vastly more mature than your average twenty year-old male. The fact that his life had vision and drive was a testament to that. It had been years since she had felt so inspired being around someone. The last person was David, the mountaineer, but his pursuits had been a solo mission. Ryan's were ones she could share and support. She had no ties to Sydney other than her sister Shane, Sumi and the baby – which were big ties – and the weather. Still, Lindsay warmed to the idea of a new life in Vancouver with Ryan and helping make his avian dream a reality.

She wondered how he really felt about her now that the mother son relationship had been resolved. Did he still see her as a mother figure or was he open to other possibilities?

Lindsay felt she could sit on Dr Brooke's couch and say: the only thing that makes him unavailable is geography…and perhaps she could change that. That was all before the complication that was Eva, the wimple lady, her mother, who clearly did not want Lindsay in her or Ryan's life.

53 Numbness

When Eva woke she felt groggy, her tongue heavy. She made her way downstairs to the bathroom and showered, washing her hair. Still wet, she pulled it back in a hairband as she sat on a stool at the island bench, drinking peppermint tea, staring through the open backdoor. It was early afternoon.

Could she will this problem away? In the past she would walk away from something this emotionally overbearing. She had to for her own survival. At times she completely vanished. This is what she wanted to do now except she wanted to flip the order of things. She wanted to make Lindsay completely vanish. It wasn't Lindsay per se. It was the situation. She had managed to create a life for herself and Ryan up here on the edge of the northern wilderness and she was happy enough with that. Mostly she was sane enough with that. Mostly. That was what counted.

What preoccupied her was how she felt about Lindsay, which honestly, was not much at all. It had been more than thirty-years since they had seen each other face to face, and if she were honest they had never looked at each other as two cognisant people. She had given birth to Lindsay, but she had hardly mothered her. Other people had mothered her. There was a time once when she was stronger and in good shape, possibly the best she had ever been, and she had strong maternal feelings. She wanted to mother Lindsay and Shane. She walked in that direction but then the earth shook and the ground gave way beneath her and she had to drag herself out of the dismal abyss and retreat. It was not safe to cross. It never would be. She knew her place.

With Mary's family she found refuge in that place.

Except for Ryan, she was alone and she had to manage. With Ryan she had actually made something of her life.

Eva could sense images swarming her, crowding her mind, grinding on the base of her skull, pressing up against her temples. Today was not going to be a good day. Before long she would need to go back to her room and take another Valium. What she'd like to do was swim in a cool mountain pool, glide across the shaded surface, submerge then slowly come up for air. What she needed to do was to ward off the attacks and marshall her reserves so that she could go see Lindsay and tell her to leave. Tell her they had no future together. Perhaps she owed her that conversation and with that Lindsay would leave. And hopefully Eva would survive the onslaught that would come later.

In the darkness Ryan came to her bringing freshly sliced nectarines and iced tea.

'Eva,' he whispered, or did he whisper? 'I've brought you some fruit.'

'What time is it?' she somehow managed to wrap her tongue around the words. The hallway light cast a slice of lemon into her darkened room.

'It's nine o'clock.'

'Did you just get home?'

'No. I came home at six. I'm here in case you need me.'

He knows. But what does he know. 'Thank you,' her voice rough. 'Hopefully I'll be right by the morning.' He rose and kissed her on the forehead. It had been a long time since he had done that. She ate the fruit and drank her tea. Got up and pulled back the drape to see what kind of night it was. At least the moon was at the window. She left the drape half-opened and walked over to close the door.

The next morning when she woke, she could hear him moving around downstairs. She waited till he left and then she said, 'I'll be right once this is behind me,' and then she got up. She showered again, secured her wimple, ate another nectarine and a wedge of avocado spritzed with lemon on toast. Ryan had ridden his bike and left her the car. But she wasn't going to need her car.

54   A beachside encounter

Late yesterday afternoon, Ryan had come across Lindsay sitting at one of the picnic tables by the waterfront halfway between The Spires and The Shack, writing overdue postcards to Shane and her friends back in Sydney.

'Hi,' he had said. 'How was your walk?'

'The climb,' Lindsay smiled for emphasis, 'was good. But I think my quads will know it tomorrow. Did you know Lorna is a fern lover? She pointed out fifteen different ferns to me, can you believe that?'

'That sounds a lot.'

'Yes. I think her spying for ferns was a way of her passing the time till I caught up. How was your day?'

'Cruisy,' he said. 'Tomorrow, I've got an overnighter up the inlet to Kitimat village.'

'Oh, okay.' Lindsay smiled.

'I'd invite you but we're full up again, I'm sorry.'

'Don't be sorry. I should get myself organised and book myself on one of your trips. I just don't want to be in your face all the time.'

'I wouldn't mind.'

Lindsay leant forward so her face was only about two inches from Ryan's. She felt like pressing her nose up against his and rubbing it together like how Inuit people supposedly kissed. She longed to give into the amorous pull inside her.

But then he kissed her. Once, twice, three times and as he pulled away he smiled and his hand stroked her face. She smiled and when she did she felt herself dissolving. This, she thought, this is my blessing.

When he spoke, he spoke quietly.

'I can't stop thinking about you. I don't know what to do with what's between us.'

She wanted to say, don't think. Do. But that was how she had lived her life till now and look where that had gotten her. She replied just as quietly. 'We'll just take it slowly. One day it might become clear to us what we do.'

'I can't have dinner with you I'm afraid. I've got to head home. But I want to make a date for two nights time.'

'Yes please,' said Lindsay grinning into Ryan's smiling face and slowly letting her eyes trail down his lips, chin and to the soft brown flesh at the base of his neck, that most sensuous of hollows. She wanted to roll her face there under his chin. She could smell the ocean and Ryan's scent and was tingling with anticipation, a sense that she was finally coming out of her own self-imposed Arctic. She took a deep breath before she exhaled, 'How was Eva this morning?'

'I didn't see her.'

Lindsay looked at him waiting for more.

'Which means she was in a bad place.'

Ah.

'I've got to go.' He stood but then he bent down and gently kissed her once more on the lips. 'You're so beautiful,' he whispered.

With her lips close to his Lindsay smiled. 'Does that line always work for you?'

'I've never used it before.'

The next morning Lindsay's calf muscles were saying: so you think you can do this once in a blue moon and get away with it, think again. She needed to go for another walk to warm them up and stretch them out, though this time on the flat. She decided she'd take the coast path behind 7-eleven and head towards the headland where she had first spotted the wimple lady. That's how Lindsay had to think of her from now on.

After about forty-five minutes of weaving in and out of clusters of conifers she came to the headland and looked north across to the small islands she and Ryan had paddled out to. She slugged her water and continued walking. Perhaps she would walk to the beach Ryan had taken her to that evening, where he had rescued his first bird.

A few headlands later the path dropped down to the beach. On her right were a number of tidal pools. She wandered over and started ambling from one dry rock to the next. In one, she found a purple sea star, in another an orange one, then in the next, one that was smaller and magenta, another almost silver. She stood up and quickly hopped from rock to rock and in every shallow liquid indentation were more and more sea stars, brightly coloured, some iridescent, slowly edging themselves along. Bat stars that looked like fat maple leaves, but came in a range of colours, the common blood stars which were some of her favourites because of their more rigid asymmetrical shape, the ochre stars and the brittle star which really did look like it could break at any point.

Lindsay was enchanted. She had never seen such a concentration of sea stars. Could they have a saltwater rock pool in the bird of prey heritage park for people to marvel at the wonderful marine life, maybe an aquarium? Children would love that, especially if large birds intimidated them; it would give them something else to enjoy.

She bent down and picked up a burgundy specimen, plucking it quickly, less it suck itself onto the rocks with its powerful muscles and little tubed-feet. She turned it over to look at the suction points underneath, the slits inside each leg, and the tiny mouth in the centre where the creature consumed food. She turned it back to look at its top side, the colour less intense out of the water. As she did she glanced up. Twenty metres from her, on the edge of the beach, was the wimple lady, looking at her. Lindsay placed the sea star back in the water. She stood up, wiped her hands on her cargo pants and walked towards Eva.

'I wasn't looking for you,' she said by way of greeting.

'I know,' Eva said. 'I was looking for you. Those sea stars are something else aren't they? The British Columbia coast has the greatest variety of sea stars in the world.'

'I've just been thinking how I'd love to have a big aquarium full of them.'

'Do you see many sea stars in Australia?'

'Rarely on the beach like this. I scuba dive sometimes in Jervis Bay – that's a place about three hours south of Sydney and you see them there. Lots more nudebranches. Who knew sea slugs could be so beautiful?'

'Come, walk with me,' she said. 'I take it you like walking along the beach.'

'I have for years,' said Lindsay, 'I used to love walking along the beach listening to music on my Walkman.'

'What would you listen to?'

'Simple Minds, *Biko*, U2, *The Unforgettable Fire, A sort of Homecoming.* '

'I don't believe I've ever heard that one. I've heard of U2. How does it go?

'I'm not a very good singer.'

'Sing for me anyway.'

Lindsay sang a few bars and then said, 'it sounds better with a band behind and with Bono singing it.'

'You did fine.' Eva said.

'At the beginning of the song there are birds squawking. They sound like seagulls. That's why I used to love playing it while walking along the beach.'

They walked on until Lindsay said, 'I hope you can forgive me for coming here and trying to find you.'

Eva didn't look at her, merely kept walking. 'I had my doubts about Jonathan's discretion.'

'Uncle Jay told me zip. The only thing he told me was I had been to this place once with my father. Do you know how many places I have been to with my father?'

Their eyes met and peeled away.

'Did you come here once with Dad?'

'No,' she said, her voice just above a whisper.

'I didn't think so,' said Lindsay, 'as our trip here was his first. Bizarre that you ended up here. '

'How long have you called Jonathan, Uncle Jay?'

'Since I couldn't get my tongue around Jonathan. Since I was about three-years old.'

'I must have missed that.'

'How long have you been wearing a nun's wimple?'

'Many years now.'

'Were you a nun once?'

'I've spent some time in convents over the years. It's who I am these days. Helps my frame of mind.'

Lindsay waited for what Eva had to say. Clearly she had come searching for her because she had made a decision of some sort. But then all of a sudden Lindsay didn't want to give her that opportunity because once she said her piece, everything might well be over. 'Where did you learn to do taxidermy?' she asked

'In Alberta,' Eva replied. 'But with everything it's practise.'

'You seem to have a gift for it.'

Eva tilted her head ever so slightly in acknowledgement.

'Do you think you could do taxidermy on sea stars?'

'I don't know,' said Eva. 'I've never given it any thought.'

'Maybe it's something we could try together.'

Eva made no commitment. After a few minutes she said, 'Lindsay, this is very difficult for me. I don't think you know how difficult.'

Lindsay hesitated. 'You're doing very well.'

Eva stopped walking and half-turned towards her. 'When your holiday is over I want you to go back to Australia and forget about me, forget about Ryan. Get on with your life. Help Shane get on with hers.'

'I can't forget you, especially now. And why should I?'

'I can't handle you in my life. I can't handle Shane. I'm sorry. My life is constructed in such a way for my own survival and my own sanity. You have no idea how your very presence here threatens it. If you have any feelings of compassion towards me you will walk away and accept what I say as gospel.

'I know it seems selfish but I don't see it like that.

Intellectually I know I am your mother and you are my daughter. I loved you when you were born and part of me will always love you. But I don't think it would be wise to establish a bond. I think it's better if we forget about that connection.'

'Fine, forget about being my mother. Be my friend.'

'What do we have in common as friends?' asked Eva.

'I'd say like Ryan we share a love of birds. Your creations are beautiful. I can admire you as an artist.'

'Ryan is the only common thread.'

'Couldn't he be enough?'

Her mother looked at her but didn't speak.

'What about our history? Your mother is my grandmother.'

'You don't need me to have a relationship with your grandmother.'

'No, but wouldn't it be wonderful for the three of us to sit down and have a cup of tea together while she's still alive.'

'I'm not a person who sits round and plays happy families.'

'Your mother's life is drawing to a close. You can't have a relationship with her when she's dead.'

'I did have a relationship with my mother Lindsay. I had thirty-six years of a relationship.'

'That's more than I had with mine.'

They walked on some more neither wanting to concede to the other. Lindsay tried a different tack.

'Why do you begrudge your mother?'

'I don't begrudge her any more.'

'She doesn't know what she's done for you to ostracise her and your whole family the way you have.'

'It hasn't been them. It's mostly been me. I couldn't give what other people gave and I couldn't have what other people had. I live this way because I can manage my world like this. The women in our family are cursed, Lindsay. First Grandma Crowe, then my mother, then me. They all end up losing their loved ones.'

'You didn't lose us,' said Lindsay 'You walked away.'

'I sacrificed my life to give you your life. If I hadn't it may have been very short-lived. Years ago I mourned you as if you had died. If I hadn't done that I no doubt would have mourned you at a time when it would have completely severed my heart. You or Shane or both would have gone down on that ill-fated flight with your father. I know it to this day.

'So in living my life, I have tried to break this pattern by removing myself from you, and by removing you from my life. It has worked because you and Shane are still alive. But now you have come here against my wishes and placed your life and Shane's in jeopardy and I won't have that on my shoulders. You are ignorant of the pain and suffering that will surely come your way.'

'Well now you have enlightened me and done what you can to warn us. Is not the choice ours to make given we are forewarned and forearmed?'

'Lindsay, have you ever lost a sibling, a lover, a child?' Her eyes were demanding. 'People who were your world and whose lives were snatched from you way before their time?'

'I lost a father.'

'I know,' she said dryly. 'That is one of the greatest losses.'

They walked on in silence.

'With or without this so-called jinx Shane and I could go on to have lives that are marred and scarred or have lives that are blessed and bountiful. Ultimately, it is out of our hands. It is out of your hands.'

'Believe me, it's in someone's hands.'

'I refuse to live my life in fear of what might happen! I would rather love and lose. I have suffered in the past and chances are I will suffer in the future. The living take care of the living that's what I know. And I would rather have the memories to sustain me and enrich my days, no matter how great my loss. The fourteen years I had with my father are incomparable. When I'm Granny Becca's age, if I ever live to be that age, those memories will be gold.'

'That's absolutely fine and you will have memories whether I am part of those memories or not.'

Lindsay stopped walking. 'Did you ever love us?'

Her mother who was three paces ahead of her stopped and turned. 'Of course I loved you once. And I set you free – some say that is the greatest love of all.' She looked at Lindsay then, before looking away.

'Well I came back, like the saying goes. That means I am yours.'

Her mother shook her head. 'It's now your turn to test your love then. To set me free.'

They reached the end of the long stretch of beach; ahead the path wove through the woods.

'I suggest we leave each other here.'

Lindsay didn't know what to say. Such a short-lived interlude then this dismissal. 'I'm glad you've had Ryan in your life. I want you to know I don't resent that at all. I'm glad you haven't been alone all these years. I think he has helped you come alive again…all I can remember of you was you being in a trance-like state for most of the time.'

'You should end your association with him. It's not in your or his best interests.'

'What's in Ryan's best interests would be finding out about his real mother and father. I can empathise with him. I know what the search for family is like. Are you capable of helping him in that?'

Eva stopped walking, but looked as if she were desperate to continue. 'What are you talking about?'

'He mentioned that he's interested in knowing where he came from. That his father Billy is okay with him trying to find out the details.'

Eva glared at her. When she spoke her voice was clipped. 'You know the world is not so black and white and picture perfect like you imagine. Sometimes it is not in our best interests to know everything. I don't know of many searches that end in happy endings.'

'Well maybe that's a matter of perspective. I found out

you're alive and well and not alone – that's something. That you've had Ryan and his family in your life. I seem to recall Granny saying that you had wanted a son.'

Eva stared at Lindsay, to her it seemed the way she held her mouth was as if she were debating whether to disclose something or not. But Lindsay had never been able to read her mother and she wasn't going to start trying now. After a few moments Eva said, 'it was true when I was pregnant with both of you I wanted a son. But now I know the best thing I could have done with my life was not to have children. I should have joined the convent as an eighteen year old like I had seriously contemplated and taken a vow of celibacy. Everyone's life would have been spared. That, I didn't do.'

Eva spoke a truth. She wasn't cut out for motherhood. Had Lindsay and Shane been born to a different mother, everyone probably would have been happier, including her father. What Eva said next though Lindsay would never have predicted.

'But what is done is done and despite what you think, Lindsay, the second best thing I could have done was to have you girls.'

'Why?'

Her mother shook her head, not interested in explaining herself. She took one step forward her head aslant as she looked sideways at Lindsay, her expression saying, 'are we done here?'

Lindsay took off her hat and held it between her hands, squeezing it for support. 'Is this goodbye then?'

'Yes. This is goodbye.' Eva stepped towards Lindsay and placed her hands on her shoulders and kissed her on the forehead. She stepped back. 'Have a good life, Lindsay. Say hello to Shane for me. Tell her I hope motherhood agrees with her.'

And then she turned around and walked off. Lindsay stood and watched her till she could no longer see her. Eva never turned back.

55 *Rejection never gets easier*

In less than an hour the weather changed dramatically. As Lindsay walked, the wind picked up, almost as if it were blowing her out of there. Grits of sand attacked her scalp and neck. Sandpipers hopped nervously about, while gulls sought shelter behind the shifting dunes. Overhead dark clouds raced across the sky ahead of the front coming her way. Branches and tips of trees bowed and flexed between strong gusts, their leaves as one trying to form a shield to deflect the worst of it. The external battering parallelled what Lindsay was enduring inside. After all this time, her heart was still the young and tender heart of a child who wanted her mother to give her the love she had never given her. What made her think that thirty years down the line her mother would suddenly have a change of heart? At least Eva hadn't excoriated her for tracking her down, but that was little comfort.

Set me free, set me free was the refrain in her head as she slowly walked back to town. This whole endeavour had come back on her and she knew it was of her making. For the first time since that day in Dr Brookes' office when Lindsay had walked through her old front door in Winnipeg, did she long for her father. She wanted to walk into his chest, have his arms fold around her and make her feel all right.

When she got back to Kitisak she knew she had to leave, staying would just prolong her sense of unworthiness. Worse, Ryan was away on that overnight trip. Perhaps that was best. To say goodbye she would have to wait another day or two. She couldn't.

She didn't want things to be over. And that upset her

doubly: that her mother could refuse her and at the same time force her to walk away from something so heartfelt and promising. From that first night when he said, *'I could see you with a goshawk. It would be the ideal bird for you,'* he gave voice to his vision for her and it had melted her heart. Only one other man had ever done that.

She wrote him a short note:

Dear Ryan

I'm sorry I've had to leave all of a sudden. I hope we meet again one day. Herewith my contact details in Australia. Come visit and I will show you our eagles, although they are not as plentiful as here. Love and dreams, Lindsay.

P.S. Could you please pass the enclosed onto Eva.

The package was sealed and contained a sealed envelope within. On her note Lindsay wrote:

I don't know what I should call you. Eva feels so foreign.

But regardless, thank you for seeking me out today. I had hoped our meeting would fare differently and I would have the opportunity to pass on the enclosed from Granny Becca, but that was not to be.

Afterwards I felt very alone and I ached for my father. It saddens me immensely that you don't want to give us a second chance. If not for me or Shane, will you do this for Sonny Marlow? For the man you threw parachute candies into the sea to mark the 21st anniversary of his death. Lindsay.

56 Her father's wings

Lindsay stayed in Prince Rupert that night and flew to Vancouver the next afternoon. She wanted to get far away as quickly as possible. After Vancouver she didn't know her next move. To stay put, go back to Montreal, to Hawaii or back to Sydney?

At the airport she scanned the hundreds of brochures for hotel listings and settled on the Renaissance Harbourside. It had a "stay for three nights pay for two special". She hoped she would know what she was doing by then. She dumped her bags, had a shower, put on a dress and walked into Gastown where she found herself a bar and ordered herself a glass of wine that she knew would not disappoint. She took it outside and watched the sun set over Grouse Mountain. She should call Uncle Jay. Her phone had been turned off since she boarded the plane in Prince Rupert. She turned it on. There was a message from Ryan.

"Lindsay. Where are you? I miss you already. Don't leave. Stay in Vancouver and I'll come to you."

Bittersweet solace. Tears sprung to her eyes – the very first of her tears – and she turned her face away from other patrons to surreptitiously wipe them away. She would call Uncle Jay in the morning and her sister. She didn't have it in her to call anyone that night. She had nearly finished her wine when two men approached. She stood as they came near. 'We thought you might like some company,' said one.

'I was just leaving,' she said giving them the briefest smile. Theirs was not the company she would enjoy, at least not that night. A drinking and pinking session with Kristen and the girls was what she was after. She had had enough of her mother dictating the terms of her life. To hell with that. Why was Lindsay always so deferential? All her life her mother has had this power over her, by withholding herself, and she was still doing it now, denying Lindsay her birthright.

She grabbed a meal and another glass of wine at another establishment down the road and then found herself a cinema. She wasn't ready to go back to her hotel room and lie awake and dissect her life. Blandly she chose GI Jane, a woman up against her own military. Strange how just a few words at the right time can have such an impact.

I never saw a wild thing   sorry for itself. A small bird will drop frozen dead from a bough   without ever having felt sorry for itself.

Lindsay didn't remember much else about the movie other than Command Master Chief's words of encouragement.

The next morning she peeled back the curtains in her room and gazed out at the harbour below. Her hotel was not far from the Convention Centre overlooking Coal Harbour and as she discovered its floatplane marina. How poetic.

After a shower and breakfast she strolled down to the marina to watch the Otters and the Beavers and the Cessnas move up the jetty ready for their next lot of passengers and departures. This was the aorta of her father's life. Two days before she had wanted her father and now she almost had him. It was like he was saying, 'Come fly with me Lindsay, let's talk.' She booked a ticket on the alpine lakes tour, over the hanging glaciers and knife-edge ridges of Mount Mamquam. They landed on a small, elevated lake where she braved the chilled waters and swam before having a picnic lunch at a table under the shade of an airplane wing.

She loved these times. She missed them. It was as if her father were saying to her, 'If this is what you want Lindsay, go for it. You only have one life – go out and live it. Honour me this way.'

They returned to Vancouver. With her eagle-eye view Lindsay looked down at alpine meadows and craggy cliffs and thought, I am so ready for the next stage, whatever the next stage is, and she knew she couldn't be like the little people down there waiting for it to miraculously fall out of the sky, she had to find the spot and choose to go land there herself. And then at one point she blinked and when she opened her eyes, she saw a magnificent bald eagle soaring less than one hundred metres below the aircraft. She blinked again. Did she conjure up that heraldic image? But, no there was the bird in full flight, its wing outstretched, the tips of its feathers, its sarcels, slanting upwards. Lindsay took in a deep breath and let it out slowly. Such a poignant reminder, or was it a sign from her father, like the eagle volant from his RCAF days, wanting her to embrace his spirit more.

57 A mother's prayer

My dear Evangeline

You were named after a beautiful French woman your father met during The Great War. At the time, his feet were in a bad way, blistered and bloodied and fungal. She, a young widow of eighteen, took pity on this hobbling stranger and invited him into the home of her in-laws. There, she removed his socks and bandages, went to a well and pumped water into a bucket, poured it into a basin and gently cleansed his feet. She sat opposite him as she held his foot in her lap and tenderly patted it dry before rubbing it with a salve.

This story he carried inside him for fifteen years until I was pregnant with you in the height of a Torontonian summer. He arrived home to my frazzled state, after I had been on my feet all day looking after Abigail and Morton. He took one look at me, led me out the back to the table under the cherry tree in our garden, poured me a cold glass of lemonade, filled a small tub with cool water, dropped lavender oil into it and gave me Walt Whitman's The Leaves of Grass to read. Forty minutes later he came back after he'd fed Abby and Morton and assigned Jonathan to reading duties.

Then he proceeded to bend down and trickle water all over my hot, aching legs. In his retelling, the beauty and simplicity of this girl's act of kindness moved me to tears: her servitude so unexpected, so biblical. And we decided there and then to name you Evangeline if you were a girl in honour of this woman who had shown such pity on a stranger.

I don't need to tell you how long ago that was. We were overjoyed to welcome you into our lives and for many years that life was blissful. You weren't blessed with the joys of motherhood in the same way as I, but I want to tell you the joys of being a grandparent are just as sweet. It is like what they say about love being wasted on the young. You don't see the beauty of it yourself when you are in the thick of it. You see it from middle age when it has slipped through your fingers. You see it in the life of others – your own children even.

One day very soon you will be a grandmother. It's the greatest joy. Truly one of life's pleasures. You get to enjoy the young without all the responsibility. I would wish for you to enjoy this blessing. Embrace it and may it be the path that brings you back to your own children.

This is what my heart desires for you.

Love always, love still

Mom

58   Trying not to pry

Ryan asked Eva, 'did you go in to Kitisak and see Lindsay?'

'No,' she said. He glared at her. She glared at him. 'I ran into her on the beach.'

'What did you say?'

'I told her to go back to Australia and forget everything about here.'

'You have no right to tell her what to do when it comes to me! I am the one who will do the telling. What is she to you? What's the connection? Because there is a connection between you and the woman she's searching for, I know it.'

'What did she tell you?'

'She told me that her mother and this woman, Gene Marlow, were very close and that her mother had disappeared a long time ago and she believed if she found this woman, Gene Marlow, she would find her mother.'

'Well I once was that woman, Gene Marlow, but I haven't been that woman for decades and I can't help her in her quest for her mother. It's in the past, Ryan, and that's where it needs to stay, buried in the past.'

He was silent and stayed silent for the rest of the evening as they watched an episode of Silent Witness. How fitting. But as she got up to leave, Eva said, 'Ryan, earlier you asked me what Lindsay was to me and I told you. I ask you, what is she to you?'

He looked at her, unanswering. 'Someone important,' he said in the end.

'More important than all the girls in Vancouver?'

'Yes.'

'In British Columbia?'

He didn't reply.

Eva took a deep breath. 'You're not seriously considering having a relationship with her, are you? I mean you live in Canada. She lives in Australia. Long distance relationships are fraught with heartaches and headaches.'

'You're an expert on relationships, are you?'

'Just hear me out. She's an older woman, mixed up and hardened by life's experiences. By her age most women have settled down and had a family. I don't want to see you get hurt that's all.'

'Don't worry about me. I'm a grown up.'

'Grown ups hurt most of all.'

He glanced at her.

She gave it one more shot. 'I know this is none of my business—'

'You're right it's not.'

'Tell me you haven't started anything with her?'

He ignored her.

She walked away wishing he could see that she only wanted the best for him.

When she was halfway up the stairs he softly said, 'the answer you are looking for is no.'

59 Saving Ryan

Why did her mother choose her, Eva, to share her ill-considered conclusions on life? That she, Rebecca, and her mother before her, Morna, had loved their men too much, and that God was a jealous God and took them away from them. In that conversation Gene had thought her mother was speaking of her sons, but later she realised she was also speaking of the husbands, and after her experience she drew the conclusion that any male whom you loved was unfair game, it had nothing to do with blood connection, Sonny, and Andrew before him, being prime examples.

When he was eight, Ryan asked her if he could call her Mom.

'You already had a Mom. Mary, remember?'

'I know but she's gone.'

'I know. I'm sorry. I will always be sorry for that.' In those early dark days when Mary was diagnosed with cancer Eva had worried that by moving north she had brought this curse upon her.

What was she going to tell Ryan now? For his survival she needed to construct their life in a certain way. She needed to care for and love him yet keep him at a distance, keep him safe.

'You know my name Eva means life. It's the Latin form of Eve. You know about Eve in the Bible, how she was the first woman God created. She became the mother of many children; they say the mother of all civilization. Until the flood when Noah's wife whose name we don't even know took over that mantle. She really should be the mother of all but I digress. Anyway, I am a bit like Eve, an ancient mother of sorts.'

And like her, she thinks, I am a rebellious sinner.

'I know for all intents and purposes I am the closest thing you have to a mother. I am like my namesake, Eva. Life enabler. So when you call me Eva, that's kind of what you are calling me anyway.'

'Eva,' he said.

'Eva. Yes,' she had said, 'that is what I like to be called, even by you, especially by you. I like it when you say my name. Say it,' she said with a smile.

'It,' he said with a grin.

'It's not my name. I'm not an it. Are you an it?'

'No.'

'That's right. You're a boy. A cheeky, inquisitive, speedy Gonzales, ticklish, if you're not careful, wet your pants, boy.' She was tickling him. He could barely breathe, he was laughing and squirming so much.

'Did you ever know an Adam?' he managed to ask.

'No. I never knew an Adam,' she said, giving in to laughter herself.

Situation aborted.

When he was ten, on the occasion of his birthday, he asked 'Eva, how do you know it's my birthday?'

'Because I know the day you were born.'

'Were you there?'

'I was living in Vancouver and I know you were born at the Grey Nuns Community Hospital also in Vancouver. It was from there that I took you to bring you up here to be with Mary and Billy.'

'Do you think my real mother loved me?'

'Of course,' she had replied, automatically. 'She would have held you for a little while. She would have said hello to you while she was saying goodbye in the only way she knew how: by pouring out her love for you and praying that you were going to go to a good home. She would have cried tears over you. Giving up a child is the hardest thing a woman can ever do.'

'Then how can they do it?'

'Because they want what is best for their children and they hope and pray that by giving up their child, he or she will have a life that is better, filled with more comforts and opportunities and support than they can ever possibly give.'

'Was my mother a young girl like Mary said?'

She exhaled. 'When you were born she would have been younger that's for sure.'

'How long did it take us to get from Vancouver to here?'

'Four days. We stopped overnight at Clinton, Prince George and Smithers. Stayed in motels along the way. You had to be fed and changed every few hours.'

'Were Mary and Billy excited to meet me?'

'Everyone was so excited they cried.'

'Even Grandad?'

'No,' Eva laughed, shaking her head at the memory.

'I didn't think he would,' laughed Ryan in return.

'But your mother and father and I cried.'

When he was sixteen he needed to procure his birth certificate to apply for his driver's license. She had his vaccination card and medical records and all his bird permits from the Ministry of Water Land and Protection but they had to go to Billy's place and rifle through his paperwork until they found it, his amended Birth Certificate, approved by the Prince Rupert judge, stating Billy and Mary as his legal parents.

Date of birth: 12 April 1977.

Place of birth: Vancouver.

Gender: Male.

It stated nothing he did not know. He'd glanced at it casually then lifted his eyes to hers. 'Everything about my life is one big mystery.'

'No,' she said, 'not at all. A mystery would be if you could not remember your own life. Mary may have died at an early age and Bill may not have been around much but the rest of us – your grandfather, me, your aunts – remember a great deal of your life, so if you ever forget you can ask us. Some children are less fortunate than you – they are passed around from one foster home to the next with no one to be the keeper of their memories, no one to really love them for the joy they bring to their lives.

'You have been stuck with me for eleven years. I know they haven't always been the most brilliant of years, but we have lived life, enjoyed life, granted we have endured it at times, but we have each other. That is more than some people can say. And I for one am grateful everyday for that. To have been given this opportunity to have you in my life.' Uncharacteristically she was on the verge of tears. 'I count myself richly blessed.'

'Sshh.' Uncharacteristically he pulled her into his arms and pressed his cheek into her head. He was taller than her by then. 'I am blessed too. I am just curious about the unknown. That is all.'

What did Joni Mitchell say about tears and fears and feeling proud?

She would like to be able to tell him she loves him. But that would be tempting fate or something more sinister. She knows he knows. But one day she'd like to be able to say the word, for him to hear them. When...on her deathbed?

60 Disturbances in the night

Ryan had come home and asked her had there been any phone calls or messages.

'You think she'd ring here? If she calls you it will be at your work and she'll leave a message. But she won't be calling.'

He said, 'I'm thinking of heading off next week. Chill out on Vancouver Island on my way down. I've only had those four days over at QC, hardly a break.'

He doesn't mention their barely mentioned little get away or a pre-birthday dinner that they normally have before he goes away. Neither does she. Right now she needs him to go. She was quite good the first day after she told Lindsay to leave, but since Ryan had come back, agitated himself, she'd been on edge. She went to bed early and took a sleeping pill every night so she wasn't wired all night long. During the days she resumed her habit of walking. Some days she'd take the car and drive away so she could walk in less familiar spots, returning around five in the afternoon with dinner in tow or at least in mind.

That night she'd thrown together BLT toasted sandwiches and chips. As she placed it on the table in front of them he said, 'there's another reason I want to head back to Vancouver early.' He paused waiting for her to look at him. 'I've decided I want to find out whatever details I can on my birth parents.'

In this one thing Eva was grateful for the conversation she had had with Lindsay on the beach that day. 'Is that so?' she replied, forcing herself to smile, even if half-hearted. 'How do you plan to go about that?'

'Well there's this guy at college who's also adopted and

he's already started the process. Apparently last year the Adoption Act was amended to provide more information to adopted children and their birth parents. If you are over the age of nineteen you can apply to the Vital Statistics Agency for an adoption record to be made available.'

He handed her over some official paperwork.

She read the details:

An individual, who was born and adopted in British Columbia, will receive a copy of their original birth registration in their birth name (including the names of any birth parents on record) and a copy of their adoption order provided a disclosure veto has not been filed.

'How does Billy feel about this? Have you asked him?'

'Yeah. He was on board. But he wanted me to talk to you about it first.'

'Did he?'

'Yes.' He paused. 'He said the original birth certificate they received didn't reveal a great deal and he didn't know whether the Vital Statistics details would add much to that. He told me where to find it.' He lay it down in front of her.

DOB:	12 April 1977
Time:	16:44 hours
Gender:	Male
Name:	Golden Boy
Place of Birth:	Grey Nurse Hospital, Oak Street
City:	Vancouver
Province:	British Columbia
Agency:	Salvation Army Community Services
Mother's Name:	
Age:	
DOB:	
Father's Name:	
Age:	
DOB:	
Consulting Physician:	Doctor Arthur Boyne

She read the paper, nodded slowly, her eyes downcast.

'Billy never said anything exactly but I sensed he

thought you knew more about my adoption than you ever told him and Mary.'

Eva cut her BLT sandwich into quarters avoiding Ryan's eyes. She didn't like to spill secrets. In fact the one thing in life, maybe the only thing in life she was truly good at, was keeping secrets.

'Do you?' asked Ryan 'Is there anything you can tell me that you may not have told Billy and Mary?' He waited for her to look at him. 'Eva?'

For the first time ever he had asked her outright. How would it look if she denied him now? She couldn't stop him digging. She knew the official records would hardly elucidate matters for him. But she knew how voracious Ryan could be when searching for knowledge. He'd ask anyone and everyone he could. He'd track down the doctor who delivered him. He'd go to the hospital and want to find out who were the nurses on duty. And ultimately how angry would he be when he found out she had not been completely truthful with him. She sighed deeply. Maybe at his age he would understand. Maybe Billy would understand too. Certainly after last week it was time he knew.

'You're right,' she said, maintaining eye contact. 'There is something I did keep from Billy and Mary.' She paused while she chose her words, 'and that is…the truth of your parentage. And the reason I did that was because if they knew the truth I don't think they would have ever accepted you. They would have been torn in two and that would have doubly broken their hearts all over again.'

'I'm not following you,' said Ryan.

Gene sighed. She tried to keep her face passive and her eyes glued to Ryan's. 'As you know I knew Mary when we both lived in Vancouver in the early seventies. I was a schoolteacher and at the time she was one of the cleaners at Burnaby High. She was married to your father and he worked as a taxi driver. Your parents and I became very close friends and I knew all about Mary's heartache over not being able to have a baby. She miscarried nine times. Nine times! Not only is that a sad and tragic loss for a woman it is also an incredibly painful one physically. Then, when she and your father decided they would adopt, they were told that being over thirty-five she was too old. The rules were quite archaic back then. Consequently your parents then had another battle on their hands. With the help of their local minister they fought that ruling and gained special dispensation.

'When she was thirty-six and living back here in Kitisak your mother received the wonderful news that she and your father would be given a child. They flew down to Vancouver and went to the adoption agency only to be told that the birth mother had decided within the first twenty-four hours to not give up her child. Your mother and father were devastated. They went back to Kitisak and went on the waiting list again. But in the midst of all those heartaches and setbacks your mother had fallen pregnant again. The comfort of knowing she was going to be a mother at last through adoption had taken the pressure off her own body. She relaxed and what do you know without noticing she had missed three monthlies. They were overjoyed. At the same time they decided that they would keep their name on the list for adoption, because your mother had once lost a child before, when she was quite a way along and she wasn't convinced she wouldn't lose another. So Mary didn't tell the adoption agency she was pregnant out of fear that they might remove her name off the list and by some stroke of foul luck she would also lose this baby and end up with no child.

'In January 1977 I called your mother from Vancouver and she told me the exciting news that her own baby was to be born in mid April and her adoptive baby was due to be born around the same time – what an exciting dilemma. I can't tell you how thrilled I was to hear this news from her. By this stage she had come clean with the adoption agency and told them the miracle that had happened and that she would be able to breast-feed their adopted baby as well. The agency was on board. But then as your mother's pregnancy progressed she started to spot and her doctor ordered absolute bed rest. She and your father rang the adoption agency and me to ask if it would be possible for me to bring their adopted baby up to them in Kitisak. I told her I would be honoured to do that and that she might want to line up her sisters to help once we arrived.

'Then just a few days before she was about to give birth tragedy struck. The baby's heartbeat became fainter and fainter. Unbeknownst to them their little girl had chorded herself inside Mary's womb.'

Eva saw a curtain of sadness fall across Ryan's face. It gave her the strength to continue.

'Your father rang me. He was so upset. He said, "Eva, I don't need to tell you we could do with that Vancouver baby yesterday." I rang the agency handling the adoption to tell them of Mary's heartache and to check that everything was in order for the adoption. There was silence down the phone line, then the lady said, "I have bad news too I'm afraid. This latest girl has reunited with the father of her child and they want to make a go of things. She no longer wants to surrender her baby."

'I couldn't ring up Mary and Billy and tell them that. There were secrets I had kept from Mary throughout my life but that one would be forever at the top of the list. I had been handed this grave, unpalatable problem, what was I to do?'

Ryan's eyes were equal parts empathy and curiosity.

'Paradoxically I did know of a solution. There was this woman who happened to be pregnant and close to full term herself. She was single and discovering she was pregnant had come as a great shock. She had had mixed feelings about her pregnancy because she didn't see herself as mother material. She had had a difficult time coming to terms with why she was pregnant – what purpose that was to serve in her life? Yet at the same time she had never thought of giving up her child, because she knew it was a precious gift.

'But in her early years this woman had had a formative experience with some aboriginal people. And she tried to live by the motto: *If you give an Indian something, give him the best you have, because he will always give you his best.*

'And so after some fast soul-searching she made the decision to give up her son to this worthy woman, for Mary. She came to see that that was the reason why she was pregnant. And that son was you.'

Ryan stared at her, slowly nodding his head in understanding. He opened his mouth to speak. She opened her mouth to say, 'Yes, I did deceive them,' but the dog barking suddenly masked their words. Her face posed the question. His expression said he wasn't expecting anyone. Then they heard the car pull up. Ryan stood and walked towards the window.

'Who is it?' Eva asked.

'I don't know the car,' he replied. 'But I know the driver,' his voice suddenly joyful.

Eva's fork clanged on her plate.

Ryan was already out the door.

'Hi,' he said. 'Leave something behind again?'

Eva could hear the happiness in his voice. It made her stomach clench.

'As a matter of fact I did.'

'Do you want to come in?'

Eva scraped her chair back as she stood up. This, she wasn't having. She walked to the door as she heard Lindsay say, 'no, I don't want to come in. This is Eva's home and I respect that.'

She halted. Ryan walked down the stairs. Eva walked to the doorway. She watched him walk towards Lindsay and embrace her and then they kissed. They KISSED. Not in the way platonic friends kissed.

'That's enough!' she called out. 'What are you doing here, Lindsay?'

'Isn't that obvious?' She was smiling up at Ryan and hugging him.

'You're doing this to get at me.'

'Eva!' Ryan gave her a look.

'I'm not doing this to get at you, Eva. I'm doing this for

me. The world has to be defined and constructed your way in order for it to work for you. And because of that we all have to bow down to your commands and wishes or else you'll go off the deep-end. How is that going to affect me? It might affect Ryan as he is still in your clutches but I'm not. I have been banished from your life for all eternity, therefore I don't have your condemnation to fear nor absolutely anything to lose.'

In no time Eva was three feet away from Lindsay.

'You ignore my wishes yet you want to play in my world. Did I travel half way across the world to disturb your life? How would you feel if I landed on your doorstep with all types of demands?' In Lindsay's face she saw her own brilliant blue green eyes staring back at her.

'How disturbed is your world going to be if I don't stay? I am merely here for one reason only, and it's a free world. You can't deny me this.'

Lindsay reached for Ryan's hand and held it in both of hers as her venerating eyes gazed into his. 'In all my life there has been only one man who has been truly exceptional, and that was my father. Now there is you. And I don't want to live without you. If you're willing to give our relationship a shot, so am I. There's only one condition: Either you have to move to Sydney or I have move to Vancouver because I'm not going to have a long-distance relationship. And as you've got one year still to do of your study and all these amazing plans for a bird park, I think it's best I move to Vancouver and start things moving along for what we both want.'

Eva pushed Lindsay away. 'You can't do that.'

'Eva!' said Ryan, reaching to restrain her. 'What are you doing?'

'What about your sister? Shouldn't you be with her in Sydney with the baby coming? She will need you.'

'I know the timing's terrible but she has her husband and she will understand. More than anything she would want me to be happy.'

'You've come here to rub my nose in this haven't you?'

'Eva, calm down.' That was Ryan.

'Eva, I haven't.'

'Yes you have. Why else would you not leave a message for Ryan to meet you in Vancouver? You wanted to wave this under my very nose.'

'I've come here to give Ryan what I can of myself. I didn't want him to have to wait anxiously and wonder. And why shouldn't you know where things are at? I don't want to live my life in secrecy and deception.'

That was a jab aimed squarely at her. Inside her mind a sinister voice snickered, "oh, I could tell you about secrecy and deception." Eva did a three sixty on the spot, her hand pressed to her forehead.

'I know I'm older than Ryan but is there any other reason why we shouldn't be together? Don't you want your child to be happy, no matter how that child is tied to you?'

Ryan pulled Lindsay to his side. 'Lindsay makes me happy like eagles make me happy, Eva. You just need to get to know her.'

Eva stared at them, panic-stricken not sure how she was going to begin her protest. Lindsay misread her state of mind.

'This day was always going to come. The day Ryan walked out of your life – I'm not saying for good – but there was always going to come a day when Ryan would put another woman ahead of you. You need to see this for what it is. I am a woman who would be happy to come and spend time here in Kitisak and for you to continue to be a close part of his life. The dice doesn't always roll that way.'

Eva turned her back to them. In the evening breeze the tail of her wimple tapped irritatingly at her shoulders as her hands covered her face and her eyelids covered her eyes but they couldn't block the images of the life she had lived twenty, thirty years ago. Did she have it in her to say what was in her? Five minutes ago she had but now Lindsay's unwelcome arrival had sent her scrambling into withdrawal. The truth would upset both of them, deeply. They may never talk to her again. Which on one hand might be the best thing. Ironically, might she be the one to find that cost too high?

Her chest was tight. Her heart felt as if it were burning, and her head too. Was she having a heart attack, an angina attack perhaps? She tried to relax her body. She tried to imagine herself walking Axel outside on a winter's day.

Two questions were before her: Would she maintain her silence that night? Or would she crack the wax and break the seal? For this was the night that would make all the difference. After tonight there could never be any turning back.

After several moments she took a deep breath, lowered her hands and walked inside.

61 *Let go – it ain't worth it if it hurts you*

A few days earlier Eva had told Lindsay she needed to let go. But what this was about was her, Eva, letting go, letting go of Ryan. She needed to do that. She'd done it before and she could do it again. Those years they had together were, after all, a bonus. She would find herself a new convent. Who knows, this time she might stay. Or perhaps she might end up doing what she'd never quite managed to do before.

Even though Gene had worn her wimple for years she had had a love hate relationship with the Almighty.

Is this how Mary the mother of Jesus felt?

Even though she knew all along she would lose her son to a higher order.

What am I losing him to?

I have lived my life worried something would happen to him. Is my benevolent yet potentially doomed daughter the chimera I feared? How Greek!

She went upstairs to her room and returned with a torch. They were sitting on the front steps, Ryan with his arm around Lindsay talking about her time in Vancouver.

'I'm going for a walk,' she said.

Ryan stood and stepped towards her. 'Eva.' He held out a hand in supplication.

'No, Ryan, I need some fresh air. Go and stay at your grandfather's tonight. I think he might be able to help with what we talked about earlier. Take Lindsay with you too, introduce her to Ken. Do that for me, please. Don't go crashing anywhere else. Promise me that.'

'Okay,' he said.

She gave him a half smile and a nod. She stepped forward and kissed him lightly on the cheek. She gave

Lindsay the briefest glance and turned away.

She walked to the ocean, along sandy shores littered with seaweed, under a night sky that was milky with clouds, thinking about how many nights the satellites and stars had kept her company. She used to try and draw them towards her, those suns of other solar systems, permanent and reliable in a world that in all other ways was the opposite of that.

She took in great gulps of the sticky ocean air. It was clean and briny, the waves, tumbling across the shore, timeless. These things survived. So could she, she told herself and she managed quite well until her mind meandered and she imagined Ryan and Lindsay making love on a blanket on a beach beside a driftwood fire, Lindsay's hands in Ryan's unruly hair, the blue flames reaching for the sky, arcing and twisting to match their fervour.

He had been on the verge of asking her, who the woman was.

She had been on the verge of telling him.

In her mirror at night she used to try to assuage her guilt over her at arm's length treatment of him. Her deception. She would remember the Last Supper, of Jesus's words to Peter: "You will deny me thrice before the cock crows.' And he did. And Peter wept bitterly when he realised. And so did she. There was nothing Peter could do to halt what was written in the Scriptures, the fate in store for Jesus. Why did Eva think she had half a chance?

Because the boy was a gift that came to her in her absolute darkest days? When she was lost and reeling. Conceived when she was almost forty-three, when having a child was the last thing on her mind. Conceived out of compassion and grace and something far more deeply interfused that was not meant to be. If not given by God, then who else and for what purpose? To prolong her personal suffering. To mock her. Where was the reason in that? This one, God would protect. This one, she would protect.

This was her creed: to never acknowledge to another soul, not even the boy, that he was her son, her own flesh and blood. She loved him. She adored him. She adored him for the child he was and the man he was turning into, so like her own brothers in many ways. But for his own protection and survival, for hers as well, she had constructed this artifice that kept him at a distance. He would love her as a mother but have no idea that she was. She would care for him like a nephew, withhold herself, withhold love where she could. She practiced detachment, so she could believe he was not her son, merely someone she was raising. Nowhere did there exist any record that they were related. By following this modus vivendi she hoped he would be saved.

Occasionally this scripture would haunt her: *Do not deceive yourselves: no one makes a fool of God.'* At times like that she wanted to scratch out those eyes that stared back at her in the mirror, taunting her – her very own.

She had wanted to instantly decry their union. Who wouldn't? But she knew, the more she opposed it the more they would rebel and dig in their heels. She doubted they would ever believe her if she told them the truth, so blinded by their own passions, so Byronic. And what proof did she have. She had made absolutely sure she had none. They would most likely regard her as she had once regarded her mother: artful.

And when Lindsay had turned up at the precise moment she was going to tell Ryan, was that God's will? Like Mary's dying – was that God's will too? So that Ryan would come back to her.

At times in her life – when she lived in the sanctuary of the convent or those months at Freshwater by the lake – and times since – she had taken comfort in the Bible, in verses and scriptures. Now what she remembered was the story of Lot and his two daughters. How Lot had been willing to turn his two virgin daughters over to the wanton lust of a horde of men to be gang raped – therein was part of her hate relationship with God – in this we should trust?

And then how God had allowed what came after: Lot's two daughters getting their father drunk, sleeping with him so that they could each conceive a child, both sons.

Who was she to cry foul?

The idea of the two of them together abhorred her yet she wondered was it God's will for her to hold her peace and let it run its course for surely it would run its course. Lindsay would want from Ryan what a young man in his early twenties would not be ready to give. Ryan would want from Lindsay what she would not be able to give him: variety; casual, carefree love; youth. The two would drift apart. They would fall away and get on with their lives and in years to come they would struggle to remember the other person's name, certainly their surname. And she would never ask a single question about any of it.

Hejira

August 1997 – May 2001

62 Fleeing

The next twenty-four hours were filled with such trauma, such pain and guilt and shame Eva decided she could never find peace in her house again. She packed a few things and recorded a new phone message for Ryan when – if ever – he phoned from Vancouver.

'Ryan,' it said 'I've taken myself on a holiday. I'll send you a postcard to your Vancouver address.' She left no other message to any other caller. Who else would phone? Would he still live in the same place again this year or would he shack up with Lindsay? She shuddered.

She knew he would be in disbelief when he picked up that message, but then she knew he would reflect and if he could he would tell her, 'good for you.'

If she could, she would reply, 'yes, I'm going on a little trip. Time to see some more of Canada while I still can.' Under her breath she'd say, 'a reconnaissance mission. Who knows, maybe a last goodbye to my mother and siblings?'

'When will you be back?' would be his next question.

'I'm not sure,' would be her reply.

This way she wouldn't need to reply. The refuge of the road.

After one month she sent him a postcard from Grimshaw, Alberta. She sent one to Ken as well, realising, possibly way too late that in the epoch that was the fourth stage of her life, the stages ending with her bouts in an institution, that next to Mary, his daughter, he had become the closest anyone had ever come to being her friend for a long time. The only relationships that had ever taken root in her soul were the ones that had been smelted in a furnace of shared trauma and loss. There had been few and with the exception of Mary, they had all been male. Jonathan. Morton. Andrew. Sonny. Ryan. And Ken.

Ken had not only been Ryan's stalwart at Mary's funeral. He had been hers. She worried how the funeral would affect Ryan but afterwards she was silently relieved that the first funeral he was to witness was a Haisla one. Even though they grieved they were accepting. Life was returning to the Great Spirit.

She thought Ryan had traversed that crossing remarkably well for one so young but not long after, they had come across that that injured osprey on the beach and he became more and more sullen over the ensuing days till finally she was able to prise from him what was causing him such unrest. What would happen if she were to die? Who would look after him then?

She wanted to say to him: I can guarantee you I'm not going to die any time soon. There were few things she was certain of. Ironically, that was one of them. So she had gone to Ken and Ken had finally persuaded him that there would always be people there for him. Twenty years Eva's senior, he was still a man she could always count on.

In October she drove as far north as Peace River then turned south and then east again. She liked being on her own. She still wore her wimple everyday. Once a week, sometimes twice, she'd find somewhere to have a shower, or wash. She set down at Slave Lake for several weeks, another postcard, then Athabasca, another postcard then bypassing Edmonton, east into Meadow Lake Provincial Park, Saskatchewan. For a pittance she rented out a log cabin for the winter.

The postcards became fewer and fewer, further and further apart until there was none. She suspected by then Lindsay would have told him all about her. How she had checked out of her daughters' lives many years ago and how Ryan was fortunate to have had her in his for the twenty years he did. There was an odd Catch 22 comfort in that.

She wondered if he missed her. If he worried about her

or had he moved on, already caught up in his new life? Mostly, she didn't want him to miss her. After the way she had raised him, she had no right. Some days she missed Ryan, but as he had already been living away from home for three years, she didn't miss him as much as she had feared. Strangely she missed him most when she burnt her toast. He always liked his bread well toasted.

She thought of Lindsay more than she wanted to, more than she had for years, but in truth not much at all. One day she thought of Shane and wondered if she had had the baby? Did she have a boy or a girl? Was it healthy? What did she call it?

She read The Bible from Revelations to Genesis. She read Hardy, Hemingway, Hawkins, and Hoeg. She crossed her words. She walked Axel diurnally, avoiding the day's full brightness when the desolate landscape, the burning white would sear her eyes. She viewed the world with a permanent scowl and a permanent squint. When there were blizzards, she paced a path inside the cabin. Physical exertion the key to sleep, her body too tired to power her mind. She listened to the night sky, to snow sliding off leaves and thudding on the ground, trying to steady her breathing, her mind, and find her equilibrium. She lived in the world of a colder dark, so she didn't have to live in hers, an artifice, but one she knew would ensure her survival.

In the spring she tossed a coin to decide whether to head north or south but who was she kidding? Emerging from isolation was always disorientating, but all roads went south. Still, she stayed as far north as possible, Prince Albert, White Fox, down to Dauphin in Winnipeg and then she said, 'What am I doing? I'm not going to Winnipeg.' So she turned and headed west back into Alberta towards Yorkton, Melville, towards Regina. Late one day, she found herself outside of Lumsden, outside her brother Morton's place. Was it still her brother's place? There were still dogs barking to wake Lucifer. She knocked on the front door. He came to stand on the other side of the screen, wearing a flannel lumberjack shirt, his grey hair rumpled as if he he'd been sleeping on the lounge, his face creased and red from where it had been resting.

'Hello, Morton.'

'Is that you, Gene?' his voice raspy as if he hadn't spoken to anyone in days. Neither had she.

'Yes.' She replied. 'I was just passing, thought I'd call in for a cup of tea or something.'

He rubbed his head. 'It'll be something.' He held the door open for her.

'Still got your dogs,' she noted.

'Yeah, still got 'em.'

He led her inside, out the back to the kitchen and opened the fridge. He stared inside. After about five seconds he reached for a bottle of soda. Then he opened a cupboard door and pulled down a bottle of Canadian Club.

'This okay?' He looked at her.

She rarely touched alcohol, certainly nothing that hard. 'It will be fine.'

'Do you remember Flint and Sooty?' One thing about her brother, he knew never to ask questions. Certainly none that was invasive.

'How could I forget?' He handed her a cold glass, iced and three-quarters full.

'I spent the past winter drawing up the family tree for all the dogs I've ever had.'

'Did you?' she asked, her eyes alight. 'Can I see?'

'Yeah. I even wrote some notes on several of the trips I had with each pack. Thought I'd best do it while I can still remember.'

'Are there things you're forgetting?' she asked.

'Things have started to fade,' he said. Their eyes met. 'Strangely I can still remember Granpa Dalton though.'

'They were dears the two of them,' said Eva.

'No, I'm talking about Granpa Dalton. My namesake. He died when he was ninety-eight and I was five. Do you still remember him?'

Eva shook her head. 'No. I only remember Granddad and Nana Dalton. She was a ball of energy.'

'And didn't he have the patience of a saint?'

'He was patient with you,' noted Eva.

'Had to be,' Morton replied. He swallowed a mouthful and brushed his bottom lip with the back of his hand. His stubble was completely white, a few days old. 'I wonder if I had had children would I have turned out like him.'

Eva didn't answer straight away. 'Depends if you would enjoy lavishing all your time on your grandchildren. They had the knack of including you in so many things. It was as if they lived their lives solely for their grandchildren's pleasure.'

After some moments Morton said, 'I think they mostly did.'

Eva was close to saying, 'unlike someone else.' She didn't but it was as if she did for Morton eyeballed her and said, 'she did okay.'

'Yeah,' Eva sighed in admission. 'She did okay.'

'She did,' said Morton. 'You missed seeing her at her best.'

Eva couldn't reply. Instead she swallowed a mouthful herself. After a while she said, 'Would you have liked to have been a grandfather?'

They were sitting around his kitchen table. Morton's eyes were downcast as his hands palmed the beveled glass. 'Paul's grandchildren call me their great uncle. That counts for something.' He raised his eyes not to meet hers but to stare out the back door. 'Some days when you have one of them perched on your knee looking at you with their big button eyes, all innocence and interest, I have moments when I feel I let a good thing pass me by. Do you know what I mean?'

Then he steered his eyes back towards hers. She forced herself to hold his gaze, to see his lifeline. She bit down on her lip. She wanted to say, 'no. No, I don't know what you mean. No, I don't want to hear this anymore.'

The next morning she said she had to be pushing on.

'You just got here. What's the rush?'

'Alright,' she said, 'what are we going to do? I'm not

sitting around the house all day.' She couldn't do that. She'd walk ten miles in one direction and ten miles back along unchanging fields of wheat rather than stay seated all day at the table and the lounge and then one or other of the porches.

'I hear there's a movie playing in Regina. Paul tells me I gotta go see.'

'What's that?'

'The Horse Whisperer. It's got Robert Redford in it.' As if that were enough for him. 'We could drive over and have lunch and see the matinee.'

She looked at him.

'Have you seen any movies lately?' She shook her head. 'Well, what do you say?'

She smiled in submission. 'Okay dog whisperer, let's check it out.'

Morton drove. 'Do you remember the first time you came here?'

'I remember.' Three days of train travel, how could she forget?

'Do you remember your last?'

Eva stared out the window at the monotonous fields that stretched onto forever. She didn't want to remember. But she did. The winter she told him about Andrew...after she'd told Sonny. Would this be her last? One thing was for certain: she could never live here.

Outside, when the film was over and they'd left Montana behind, Eva said, 'I didn't know Paul and you were into romances.'

'Neither did I,' Morton mumbled.

And Eva laughed. For the first time in a long time she laughed. Still, they both agreed it was a fine movie.

And afterwards on the drive back home, the song from the movie played on in her head, a strange comfort. Morton was definitely her soft place to fall.

The next morning he suggested taking her fishing at the lake.

302

Eva looked at him. She could do fishing and she could do a lake but she couldn't do a lake with her brother. That was too much.

'Any goldeye left in that waterhole by the river we used to go to?'

'Could be. Haven't fished there for a while.'

He never said to her, 'Lindsay's back in Canada. She's living in Vancouver.' He never asked if she had seen her daughter or daughters lately. She didn't know what he knew. With Morton those things really didn't concern him and that was why she could bring herself to visit him.

But the next morning at breakfast she felt Joni Mitchell's word's taunting her: 'the prairies are so empty – you have to fill it and the only thing you can fill it with is your mind.' That was her problem. She had to get out of there.

This time he didn't try and talk her out of it. He said, 'are you heading east?'

'I might be.'

'Jonathan and Mom would welcome a visit.'

'We'll see,' she said, giving him a hint of a smile. She came closer to kiss him on the cheek. He patted her on the back. 'Thank you.'

'Any time.'

She opened the car door. 'Genie,' he called out. She raised her head to look at him.

'Don't leave it twenty years till I see you again.'

She nodded, the lump in her throat, preventing her from replying. She looked into the distance and back at him. His eyes were watery. Could he see that hers were too?

She held up her hand than curled down the middle and ring finger.

He did the same.

She went back to Freshwater on the Lake. She wondered if it would still be there but it was. She sat by the water's edge and ate a sandwich. In a few months she would be turning sixty-five, qualify for the old age security, though being a low-income senior she had received a benefit since she was sixty. Still, she was not far from the age that her mother had been when she used to visit Eva in her vegetated state. How did she cope with a daughter like her? How did her mother view her own life back then? With Wyatt by her side, no doubt with more promise than how Eva now viewed hers.

On the outskirts of Montreal she parked her car at a rail station, tied Axel to a tree and left him a bowl of water then caught a train into the centre. She was glad that she had. It had been more than thirty years since she'd been to Montreal and it was too chaotic for her. Like she had all those years ago, she found solace in the Notre Dame Cathedral. She prayed for guidance. At the same time she prayed for forgiveness. Outside her feet led her in the direction of the train station. She thought she was going back to her car, but at the very last, she took the train to the suburb where Jonathan lived. She got out of the station and studied the plan des rues. She found his street easy enough. She ambled slowly in that direction, and when she found his street and the numbers she crossed over to be on the opposite side to his house. She stood next to a small-leafed linden tree blooming with creamy yellow flowers that smelled of honey. It was a stately residence. What she imagined were once leadlight panes had been replaced with modern double or triple glazed windows. She could see no one inside. She stood and waited for more than two hours for someone to come out and collect the mail. At some other place they may have come out and watered the garden. Maybe there was a garden out the back Certainly there was no garden at the front, only a hedge to be trimmed. She told herself if someone came outside then that was a sign and she would approach. But no one did. She couldn't find it inside herself to cross the street and walk up to that front door and knock. With Jonathan and her mother she would feel the need to explain and she could not explain. Somehow with Morton things were different. Perhaps another day she told herself.

She returned to her car and drove north to Quebec and

the further her car got from Montreal the better she felt: her chest less tight, her breathing more at ease. Across the Saint Lawrence and through every Saint-named town imaginable, a big arc round to Grand Falls and down to Moncton and then across Confederation Bridge to Prince Edward Island, which, like Nova Scotia still ahead of her, was a place she had never been before.

When she was five they were meant to spend their summer holidays at Cavendish on Prince Edward Island, but something had happened to change that and they went to Newfoundland instead. If only they had never gone to Newfoundland that summer. She wouldn't be going to Newfoundland this summer either. The farthest east she ventured was Cape Breton Highlands National Park. In places it was rugged, but mostly it felt tamed. Trees and nature didn't seem to dominate here. She missed the west coast. She turned tail, back through Nova Scotia. She spent that winter in a convent near a place called Sainte-Anne – thirty-minutes outside Quebec City – it seemed to call to her. A frugal existence inside an unheated two-foot-thick stonewalled building made every meager austere winter Eva had ever experienced seem extravagant. It was almost as if she were serving some penance.

When she walked outside during the day it was the coldest winter she could ever recall, the cold somehow managing to permeate her thick-soled sorrels, her clothes not suited to this eastern chill. Spiny frazils hung from larch branches dwarfing the hoar frost of months earlier. In the paleness a skylark flew in an arc. *Alouette, gentille alouette, Alouette, je te plumerai*. When she was a little girl her nana had taught her that song with all the zest of a true French Canadian.

Axel gave up on her there. She took him to hospital so he could be burned in their incinerator. She hoped something of him would end up back on the west coast. When spring came she left and headed towards Montreal but took the 158 at Berthierville and drove all the way to Ottawa. She had enjoyed living in Ottawa in her twenties.

She liked Parliament Hill and the Native American Indian statues in Major's Hill Park.

After Ottawa she drove north on highway 11, far north of Lake Superior, through to Thunder Bay and back into Manitoba, south of Winnipeg, West to Weyburn in Saskatchewan, to Moose Jaw, close to Morton, but so far. This time he might ask her why she didn't call in and see their soon-to-be and she tried to calculate what age her mother would be in a few months if she were still alive and then she had to pull off to the side of the road as it came to her.

One hundred! Surely not! She couldn't call in and see Morton now and so she drove and drove until she crossed the border into Alberta and at Medicine Hat she stopped and bought her mother a card and sent it to Jonathan's address. So what if it was April and a few months early. She didn't know if her mother was still alive and she didn't pose the question in her card. She merely said:

Mom, Congratulations on reaching one hundred. I hope there have been many good years in there. Happy Birthday. Love Gene.

She drove on, trying to assuage her guilt over not calling in and seeing her. Why? Because she felt it would be too painful. For her mom or for her? She could not say. She believed she had put her past behind her. But why couldn't she start anew? What kind of person stayed away from their one-hundred-year old mother?

Those thoughts refused to leave her be. She got to the point where she needed to know if her mother was still alive or not, yet she couldn't bring herself to call. What she did instead was force herself to go back to Kitisak. When the town slept she cleared her post office box, such that there was to clear. There was an envelope from her brother, the post date quite recent, one from Lindsay, months old.

She went home to what once used to be her sanctuary. She still felt far removed from it. The phone rang. It startled her. Ryan must have kept paying the bills. It was him. Did he have some security monitor hooked up to the house? He asked this, he asked that. He said this. He said that. He wanted this. He wanted that. She didn't know what to say. Lindsay came on the phone to talk to her as well. All she could manage was an, 'I'll think about it,' as she looked at Jonathan's unopened envelope on the table.

A little while later she hit the road again, her hejira continuing, back and forth across the country. This time she wounded up in Nelson on the western arm of Kootenay Lake. She found she quite liked it there and with the harbingering signs of the changing season, she located a bedsit and a job as a cleaner and holed up another winter. The millennium came and went.

The following spring she woke tense from a dream about Shane. In her dream Shane was with two children. Was something happening to Shane like something happened to her? Who would be there to look after Shane's child? Sonny and his parents and her family had been there to look after hers but there is so little she knows about Shane and her situation. After this gnawing away at her for several weeks she writes to Shane care of the clinic in Newtown. She doesn't know if she has the address right. Certainly she doesn't know the postcode. But maybe it will get there and maybe they will pass it on. In the left hand corner she writes personal. Are you all right, she asks? Are you coping with motherhood? She doesn't know what she will do if she gets an answer back to say she is not.

But several weeks later, towards the end of summer she does get a reply and some photos. All is well. She writes of a baby boy, Raiden, made in Canada, she says, born on 11th April 2000, now three months old, how his sister Tamiko thinks he looks like a monkey. She encloses photos of the two of them. She writes of her life and of the exciting developments with Ryan and Lindsay's bird park. How it's coming together, of the people who have joined them this summer for various working bees: Ari, Sian, Sam and Taylor. Had she met them?

On a whim Eva wrote to Morton suggesting they meet

in Medicine Hat for Christmas. He brought two dogs with him, unable to be separated from them completely. It was as if Eva's life rolled back fifty years. The dogs slept in his car, while Eva and Morton shared a motel room.

In May 2001, nearly four years after she started her travels, she returned for good to her home outside of Kitisak. She nearly didn't return at all in the end. Nelson had grown on her; she liked being on the water nestled amongst ridges, white in winter, green at others times, the dim light of morning, the shadows of pines, the world viewed through a quadrant of light. Except the place was too big and while they had black spruce and rocky mountain maple and wolf willow she missed the groan of familiar trees that would send her to sleep when she was well.

Her home was tended but not lived in. Winter killed grass was starting to recover. Inside the ammonia of mildew and mould stung her nostrils. After four damp and drizzling Decembers sans a wood fire, what did she expect? The hydro was still connected but the fridge was off. Her room was untouched. In Ryan's, the twin mattress and bed had gone – she later found it in the shed – to be replaced by a queen. It was his room in every other way. Outside there were wild tomatoes and cucumbers that needed picking and weeding. The herb garden she expected to be worse off, but surprisingly the rosemary, thyme and sage had survived.

She called over to see Ken on the reservation. They shared a pot of coffee. He told her Ryan and Lindsay were doing well. Yes, she nodded as if she knew that already. 'He's in his element. He's never been happier. They're making good progress with their bird park.'

When Ken talked about the bird of prey heritage park, Eva could see it clearly, as if she had been there before, walked over the land, staring at Lindsay and Ryan and Ken's faces as they all were nodding their heads, saying this is the one. And her, confounded at how they could afford it. And their telling her, don't worry we can. She shook her head as if to clear the fog.

Ken said he went up to see them occasionally, wished he was younger so he could help more. Still, Ari and Sian were there now helping as well. Had she met them? Said they must go up there together soon.

She told him she'd lost some things with all her moving around. 'Did he have their phone number?'

He asked her when was the last time she spoken to them.

'Oh, a little while ago,' she mumbled.

'Well maybe you don't know?'

'Don't know what?'

'Maybe I shouldn't be the one to tell you.'

She stared at Ken until he told her. 'Lindsay's pregnant. Due in September.'

Eva slowly blinked. Behind her lids she tried not to think the word but it came to mind even so. I've come back for this. But, and she blinked again, it wouldn't be the first and it won't be the last. And it won't be the only secret she would take with her to the grave. She blinked a third time, but then, what do I know anymore?

The piece of paper lay on the kitchen bench for days. She told herself she should ring and let them know she was back home for a while. Save an uncomfortable scene like the last time they were all together.

But then one day, weeks later, curiosity got the better of her or was it something else, like the pull she felt all those years ago, or perhaps her brother saying, *'Some days when you have one of them perched on your knee looking at you with their big button eyes, all innocence and interest.'*

She called. They invited her up for a visit. They sounded happy to hear from her. She might just go.

Reframing

August 1997 – September 2001

63 The road less travelled

There are days when Eva remembers events very differently, almost as if she is living in a parallel universe. She tries to follow the train of thought and when she has the whole sequence clear she thinks, next time I see Ryan or Lindsay I'm going to ask them if that is what actually happened but there she always hesitates, waits a minute, thinks: that will give her away, they will think she is losing it – undeniably some days she is – they will think she won't be able to take care of herself. They will want to put her away.

Did Eva return that night from the beach determined to get in her car and drive over to Ken's to find Ryan? Did she meet Lindsay's car driving up their gravel road as she was driving out. Did they return to her house and once inside were words torn from her at great personal cost? Dragging buried roots with them like a North Pacific landslide leaving more scarred faces and untold detritus in its wake. Some places, some people never recover from such forces of nature.

'Ryan,' she says, *'you should know Lindsay is my daughter, my eldest daughter. Her sister Shane is my youngest daughter.'*

'Figures.'

She could have told him the car needed new tyres.

'Did you really abandon them when they were little children?'

'I left them to others who could take better care of them. I was sick! I was committed to an institution!'

'She was not well. She is much better now.'

'Who are you to judge my state of wellness?'

A flash of her as a judge, doing her circuits, presiding over strangers, innocent and not so innocent, forming her own wrangled rulings.

She catches glimpses, like shadows flittering by, of her marching back and forth, pivoting on her feet, as if she is inside an invisible prison cell. Then a tribunal in front of Ryan and Lindsay, backed into a corner, forced to contravene her one imperative. How does she manage to say it? But say it she does.

'Yes.'

The question Ryan asked was:

'Are you my mother?'

'I was going to tell you earlier, but we were interrupted.' She swallows. That was the truth. She wants to stare pointedly at Lindsay but restrains herself. *'Did Ken tell you?'*

'All Grandad said was the day you first arrived with me, when I was little more than a week old, I started to cry and the next minute your shirt became wet and you hastily made excuses that you needed to get something out of the car, and only he saw the damp patches.'

Gene would never forget that day. Five minutes later Ken had come up to her while she was leaning against the car trying to get a hold of herself. He never asked a question, he just said, *'tomorrow or the next day, I'd like to help you find a place to live so you can be close by. You are family now.'*

But she is brought back to the present with Ryan's incredulous question. *'How could you have kept this from me for all these years? Did you ever tell anyone?'*

'You think I'd tell anyone anything?'

Ryan shakes his head at her.

'Do you think you would have been ready to hear this before? Are you ready to hear this now even?'

'What? That you lied to me for years! You know I can't even see you as my mother. You're some cold, calculating sick woman.'

'Is that what you really think of me? I know that's what Lindsay thinks of me.'

'Not all the time,' says Lindsay. Or does Eva want her to say that?

'I gave you up to my best friend! To a woman who desperately wanted to be a mother, to have her own baby. To a woman I loved and cared for and admired greatly. If she knew the truth she never would have let me give her my baby. I gave you up to a safer, better place because the last time I had been

a mother I had been a woeful mother. I gave you up knowing I would still see you, still be able to watch you grow up, knowing that hopefully on those occasions you would get the best parts of me. I gave you up when my heart didn't want to but my head did. I still loved you. Your not being with me never negated the fact, it never made me love you any less.'

'You have a funny way of showing your love, Eva.'

'I know.' She barely manages to mumble.

A recorded message on her answer phone that she hasn't got round to deleting: "Eva, Lindsay took me to Montreal to meet her grandmother and Uncle Jay. They couldn't have been more welcoming. They thought I reminded them of Matthew Dalton, Lindsay's great uncle."

She hears voices, others and her own.

'Where was Ryan's father when you were giving birth to his son?'

She becomes even more restless, riffles in all directions, to the kitchen bench for support then back, then around to the kitchen sink, pours herself a glass of water, gulps down a few mouthfuls. From the distance of six metres, she looks at Ryan but then she has to look away. A crank turns in her heart.

'Ryan was conceived out of...pure...hard-won...short-lived...love.' Every word a stone around her neck.

But then the room suddenly hushed.

Into silence that is heavy and stilted, Lindsay says, 'I'm sorry that relationship didn't last for you.'

Eva shrugs. 'I think it was a matter of I couldn't have both. You, Ryan, were a consolation for not getting the man.'

'So you would rather have had the man than me – is that why you gave me up. Is that why you always kept me at a distance?'

'No!' she yells turning to look at him. 'That is not the reason why I've always kept you at a distance. I've kept you at a distance to keep you safe.'

Ryan's eyebrows ripple in incomprehension.

Lindsay eyes glare. 'Your life would be in danger if she were to love you too much.'

'Oh go ahead and mock me!'

What she had wanted to say was: 'finding out I was pregnant with you saved my life.' Did she say that in the end?

Was that her story or a story someone had told her, or something she had read, somewhere, sometime, someplace? Perhaps a movie she had seen on the television or in the cinema?

Ryan is shaking his head, his eyes wild. 'If what you are saying is true, did this man know he was going to be my father?'

'No.' Her voice is almost inaudible.

'So why didn't you tell him?'

Eva closes her eyes and bites down on her lips. When she opens her eyes again she says, 'I wasn't able to tell him.' Her eyes dart from Ryan to Lindsay. She reaches for her glass, but her hand is unsteady and she knocks it over. She goes to grab the glass lying on its side but leaves it, staring instead into the water drooling in all directions. Herself reflected.

'He would have loved to have been your father,' she murmurs.

'So why didn't you tell him? What happened?'

She looks away to the stairwell. She wants to race upstairs. Was that a memory? A dream? A nightmare? Their demanding faces pinning her down. That massive lobed scar.

She cannot stop the waver in her voice. 'His life was cut short.'

'How?' asks Ryan and Lindsay in unison, coming at her and at her and at her. Lindsay on her feet on the opposite side of the kitchen bench, ready to pounce.

Eva starts to sob, to drown, gulping for breath to save her from this ordeal, to save her from her own life. 'He died. In a plane crash.' She manages between gasps for air.

Ryan is on his feet. Does he say, 'Oh, Eva, I'm sorry'? All she can see is the blood draining from Lindsay's face, a fury herself in the making, as she cries, 'no! No. Don't tell me. Not Dad!'

'Don't tell you!' Eva cries back. 'What am I meant to tell you? Of course it was your father. I killed him. As certain as if I struck down his plane with lightning.'

'What are you talking about?' Ryan is totally bewildered.

'You didn't kill him,' counters Lindsay. 'You didn't make him fly the plane that day.' She is yelling.

And Eva is yelling. 'He left me there at Lake Temagami at the cabin where we had spent the week-end and he flew out to bring you girls back so we could be together again as a family during your school holidays, because that was what I wanted!'

'He wanted it just as much! He called from Sault Sainte Marie and I spoke to him. He said he had the most amazing news. The best news in the known universe.

' "What?" I asked him.'

' "I can't tell you," he said. "I have to show you." And then he told us he wouldn't get in till late so we were to stay on with our grandparents and he'd come by early in the morning and we would be going on an adventure.'

Eva turns her back on them, presses her hands against her ears, her eyes shut, wanting to make this stop, go away. Her shoulders shake with the avalanche of her emotion.

'Mom. Come here.' Who is Mom? Where is Mom? She opens her eyes and Lindsay is standing in front of her, arms outstretched, and Eva is trembling, trembling like an aspen but as she falls she topples like an ancient Sitka spruce, the last of an old growth forest, not wanting to yield to the passage of time. As they cry anew over the death of the man they loved so deeply, it is the first time anyone has hugged Eva as she cries over the death of her husband, twenty-one years before.

Ryan comes near but stands just away. Minutes later when Lindsay and Eva break apart, Lindsay through her tears, says, 'I wish you weren't my brother.' She goes to him, presses her damp face against his chest, while Ryan hugs her tight and kisses her head.

'This way, he'll always be a part of your life,' Eva cries.

Was that reality? Or some deep-seated wish hurled at her from the depths of her subconscious?

64 Son of the disappeared

The next day Lindsay flew to Montreal with Ryan. She wanted him to meet his ninety-eight year old grandmother before it was too late. The fact that she was still alive and in good health was not something Lindsay wanted them to take for granted. Their timing was such that they converged on Montreal together, Rebecca having just returned from Newfoundland. They were unable to convince Eva to accompany them. She was in a state. 'Tell them I said "Hi",' was all she could manage in farewell.

Lindsay had called her uncle and said she was coming and bringing a friend – not her mother – she emphasised, so he wouldn't get his hopes up.

On their layover in Vancouver airport she called her five-month pregnant sister and broke the news of finding her mother and the unbelievable discovery that Ryan was their brother, their full brother. 'Do you want to say, Hi?' Lindsay asked.

'This is all so random, Lins.'

'I know. Just go with it.'

They spoke for five minutes. He handed the phone back to Lindsay. 'I'll call you from Montreal. Fill Markus in for me.' She hung up and turned to Ryan. He was grinning his hopeful, it-will-be-alright smile at her. She walked up and rested her forehead against his chest. He wrapped his arms around her. She hugged him back.

On the flight across, Ryan asked, 'do you think Eva will ever make this trip?'

'Maybe after we've broken the ice for her, she can.'

'She can't face them and explain me.'

'And everything else.'

They arrived in the evening and Granny Becca was already asleep or as is the way with the elderly, lying in bed chasing sleep. Jonathan and Annabelle listened to Lindsay's remarkable story. When she finished, Aunty Belle said, 'that's incredible.' She turned to Jonathan. 'To think Gene had a tubal ligation years before.'

Jonathan's eyes met his wife's. 'Yes, well, some doctors in the seventies knotted the tubes rather than cutting them. I heard reports that some did come undone.'

'I wasn't ever meant to be?' queried Ryan.

'I'd say, quite the contrary. You were. Que sera.' He smiled warmly at this nephew. 'You're into ornithology, aren't you?'

The next morning Lindsay introduced her Granny Becca to Ryan and then proceeded to tell her how she had tracked down her mother and what she had discovered. All the time she spoke, Granny Becca's eyes were far off as if she was with Lindsay walking by her side reliving her quest. It ended with the revelation of her mother and father's short-lived union and the surprising issue of that union. Beyond what Eva had told them they had not been able to extract any details of when or where her parents had hooked up. But it warmed her heart, knowing her father had found love again, with his wife, her mother, no less. Lindsay wished she had known her back then – she must have been someone amazing to enthrall her father.

When Lindsay finished, her Granny said, 'come here and let me have a close look at you, young man.'

Ryan kneeled in front of his grandmother. Rebecca's eyes slowly scanned his face. Her hands touched his forehead, ran down the sides of his face and rested on his shoulders. 'Are you really Gene's boy?'

'Yes,' Ryan said. 'Except now she calls herself Eva.'

'Well, give your Granny a hug. Lord knows it's way over due.'

She broke into the brightest smile, her face full of pure delight, her eyes sparkling in all their exquisite intensity.

'He doesn't have your eyes, Granny.'

'No,' said Jonathan. 'He has his father's hair though, the same but darker like Don's, your father's father.' But now that they were together everyone could see a striking resemblance between Ryan and Jonathan.

'How can that be?' asked Lindsay.

'The face shape is more Samuel's, more Leonard's,' said Granny Becca, 'but the olive colouring is Lottie's, his wife, my mother-in law's, your great grandmother.'

'She died in fifty-four,' said Jonathan. 'She was something.'

'Obviously, I didn't get to meet her either,' said Lindsay to Ryan in consolation.

Ryan asked if there were any photographs of his mother and father he could see.

'Of course!' they all replied. Out came the photographs of Sonny and Gene Marlow, their young daughters, then ones of Lindsay and Shane with just their Dad, and even ones of Don and Elin, Ryan's paternal grandparents, taken thirty-nine years ago, in 1958, at Parry Sound.

Over the next few days Ryan and Lindsay were immersed in stories of Sonny's life, for it was Jonathan who knew Sonny the longest and first introduced him to Gene and they in turn were immersed in stories of Ryan's life with his mother, their daughter, sister, mother, living on the edge of the northwestern wilderness where eagles soared.

65 Déjà vu

Ryan's anger at Eva, his mother, was short-lived. He had tried to call her – several times – from Montreal to check how she was doing but she wasn't home or she didn't pick up. He tried again when he returned to Vancouver but to no avail. There was only an infuriating recorded message. He phoned his grandfather. Ken called back, said there was no sign of her or the car or the dog.

He looked at Lindsay with concern.

She said, 'welcome to 1969 all over again.' After a pause she added, 'sorry. Try not to worry about her, Ryan. She will be all right. She always seems to manage.'

In September 1997 Lindsay returned briefly to Sydney, caught up with her sister, friends and Marcus, put her belongings in storage, rented out her unit then returned to Ryan in Vancouver where they found an apartment to share. She told him what captured her heart and imagination most was making his avian dream a reality. He told her it could be her dream too, their dream together and that it was. They agreed they would stay in Vancouver for two years – three at the most, work hard, save money, make contacts then head north.

That Christmas she flew with Ryan back to Sydney to introduce him to Shane and Sumi and meet baby Tamiko. They would have invited Eva but they didn't know where she was, even though Ryan still had had his mail redirected from his old place in Vancouver.

They hear from Eva infrequently, via an occasional postcard, but they don't know how to contact her. Apparently she used to pick up the phone and call Ryan. Now he calls Kitisak regularly on the odd chance she is at home. If they could speak to her they'd tell her to go and buy a cell phone, dammit.

Lindsay sends her mother a letter to her post office in Kitisak. She doesn't know if she will ever receive it or ever get a reply but she has nothing to lose:

Eva, one day when you are ready I would like to know about the time you spent with my father, the man you got to know again back in 1976, your last days together that summer. I know you might see that as an invasion of your privacy. Please don't. I don't want to take away from you what you shared together. I just would like to know some more about my father and what he told you of our life back then.

66   Pinned down

On Eva's noticeboard above the island bench where she has pinned a Gary Larson calendar, her shopping list, any bills to be paid, old school listings and the handful of numbers she infrequently calls there is a business card:

Lindsay Marlow
Manager, Corporate Sales
Business Objects
910 Mainland Street, Vancouver BC V6B 1A9

How long has Lindsay lived in Vancouver? Next to it is a letter with a pin through its centre. She doesn't now how she can ever begin to reply to that.

She has days when she is angry with Lindsay for coming back into her life and starting her on this slide. That day on the beach she had tried to tell her that her life was finely balanced. She tried to warn of that and other things. Then and later.

'You will rue the day, Lindsay.' Eva has moved closer to them but still in the kitchen standing behind the bench.

'When it comes,' says Lindsay, 'I will remember you and thank you for having taught me to make the most of each and every day, for having told me that life is too short and bad things happen to good people for no apparent reason.'

'There are reasons. They are just unfathomable and unchangeable.'

This anger she doesn't quite know how to channel. Is it her anger she is holding inside her or someone else's? Ryan's? Ahh...the memory comes back. Lindsay was not there – she'd gone to Kitisak to buy some groceries, to give them some time together. It was Ryan who was storming around their kitchen.

'You're angry with me. I'm sorry you're angry with me.'

'I am angry with you. How could you have lied to me all these years, denied me all these years? What type of evil witch are you to do that to your own son?'

Eva doesn't answer him.

'What did I ever do to you?'

He is in pain. This is exactly what she had dreaded. She wants to disappear, she wants the furies to swoop down once and for all and take her away with them. She forces herself to meet his glare. 'You did nothing but good.'

'You denied me my own mother! You denied me my own father! My own sisters!'

'Did you feel unloved growing up, Ryan?'

'I always felt my real mother would have loved me more; she would have hugged me more. Jesse would run out of kindergarten and his mother would greet him crouched at his level with her arms wide open. You would stand there and smile your closed lipped smile and if I was lucky or you were in a good mood, you would hold out your hand to me.'

'You didn't get the best, but you got the best I could give you.' Then she looks away. His wounded intensity is too much. 'I did such a disastrous job mothering Lindsay and Shane. I was catatonic. When I was pregnant with you I worried whether I would ever be in a fit enough state to be your mother. Somehow I willed myself to be well for you. But I knew if I fell too hard in love with you, my child, my fears and anxieties would get the better of me and I would have to give you up. I wouldn't be able to care for you, like I wasn't able to care for Lindsay and Shane. It's impossible for you to comprehend what I once was like, the edge I teeter above some days. That complication with that baby your parents were meant to adopt seemed to be ordained by God, shining a light on the path you, me and Mary had to take.'

He stares at her, not responding.

'You kept me alive all these years.'

'Is it all about you, Eva? What did you do for me?'

'Everything I could.'

He whips the tea towel down on the bench in front of them. 'Horseshit!,' he yells. 'From the moment I was born I could *have had older sisters in my life. We could have been a family.'*

'You had cousins to play with that were more your age. That were boys and into what you were into.'

'That doesn't change the fact.'

'Look, you think I never thought about that. I thought about that for years but in the end I decided this was best for you, for them and for me. You've had a good life here surrounded by the ocean and mountains and wildlife. Not too many bald eagles in Winnipeg. Not too many men like Ken who pardon the pun, would take you under their wing.'

'Except my father by all reports.'

'Who died before I even knew you were a living thing inside me. My choices were not so black and white. The world I live in is shaded in every gradation of grey. The girls would have left home a few years after you were born.'

'Who says? And even if they did, they would have come back from time to time. Don't you have any remorse over the way you have treated them?'

'When I was forty-one I wanted to be a mother to them again. And that is when I got in touch with their father.'

'Sonny Marlow, Eva, say his name.'

'Sonny,' she swallows. 'I got in touch with him and slowly over time he came to trust me again. I never expected we would end up in a relationship after all that time but we did. But then when he disappeared, I regretted that I had been so selfish, so selfish wanting to be with my children because I was the angel of death that re-entered his life. So for months I regretted my actions, my lack of will power, which I mistook for courage. But then I discovered I was carrying you, as if it was his parting gift, knowing how I ached to be a mother and I came to accept what it was and I tried not to regret it any longer.'

'I still could have known the truth about my family. That I had one and where they lived.'

67   Her prophecy

After a week of looking at that crisp white envelope she eventually opened it. A fancy invitation from her brother to celebrate the centenary birthday of Rebecca Dalton Kingston on Sunday 11th July 1999, a luncheon affair at the Fairmont Le Château Frontenac in Quebec City. La de da! How could she not go? How could she go? Perhaps, if Morton were to take her...

When Eva was Gene and at Freshwater all those years ago, she was encouraged to keep a journal to write down how she was feeling, what she was thinking. On her first visit she never committed anything to paper. Her second and third visits were different, but she always made sure she hid her journal in her pillowslip under her bed so no one could ever read it, even if she fell asleep. She'd write to try and make sense of things. She'd write to remember things so she could come back to them later. It has been many years since Eva has written anything in her journal until one day she opens her last unfinished notebook and finds a number of unfamiliar entries, all recent.

I tried to warn Lindsay this would happen, but she wouldn't listen to me. She wouldn't take no for an answer.

And days later, one short entry:

Mont St Anne. What do they know of the little mountain village of St Anne? Were they following me?

Downstairs she says to the owl. Did you see anything?

St Anne, the patron saint of Quebec and women in labour – for many years her surname, an appropriate offering of gratitude at the time she had thought.

68   The celebration of a century

Rebecca's one-hundredth birthday celebration, held at Quebec's grandest hotel, perched at the top of Cap Diamant, on a mild, cloudless summer day, commenced with French champagne and hors d'oeuvres served on the terrace. The guest of honour was positioned on a chair under a large calico umbrella emblazoned with a Dom Perignon logo welcoming guests as they arrived. Jonathan was by her side. As Lindsay kissed her, she had to stop herself from apologising for her mother's absence.

Forty-five minutes later they moved inside to a ballroom where there were display boards, covered with photographs of Granny Becca, the first one taken on the day of her marriage in 1919 – eighty years earlier – one by herself and one with her handsome golden-haired groom, Samuel. Another taken in 1949 with her silver-haired groom, Wyatt, then mixed family shots and shots of her with her eleven grandchildren and twenty-two great grandchildren. Every single member of Rebecca's family was in attendance except for her daughter Evangeline.

Even the second cousins were there, the children of Jean-Paul and René Sibonne, who had been very close to their Granny during all the years she lived in Montreal, Uncle Paul, Wyatt's nephew, and his wife Aunty Nadine, and just a handful of friends, none of them their Granny's age. From the Crowe side there was a table of relatives from Newfoundland, most in their seventies. How could they tell a one-hundred-year old, they were too old to travel? Another table representing the Daltons from Toronto, more specifically the descendants of Analeise Dalton, the sister of Granny's first husband, Samuel.

The children of Evangeline Dalton were seated with their Uncle Morton and Paul and Nadine. The entrée was cleared. Their mother hadn't shown, clearly wasn't going to be showing. Lindsay sat, drowning in a niagara of disbelief. Uncle Jay came over, placed his hand on her shoulders and said, loud enough for the whole table to hear, 'I want you to forget about who's not here and think about who is. This day will never come again. Don't spoil it for yourselves.'

Between the main course and dessert, Jonathan spoke on the life and loves of Rebecca Dalton Kingston. There was no greater tribute of love and admiration. It could have almost been her eulogy. And with a heart-warming sigh, Lindsay thought, well so be it, eulogies are wasted on the dead. What is said should be said to the living while they are still alive to hear it. Their Aunt Abby followed Jonathan reading telegrams finishing with a letter from the Queen. Shane and Lindsay looked at each other, mouths agape.

Finally, the guest of honour royally enchanted them. Her voice reminded Lindsay of the skin of an old peach, withered but still intact, holding inside the mouthwatering sweetness of one of life's delicacies.

'I wanted to thank you all for coming along to help me celebrate my birthday, particularly those of you who travelled such a long way to be here. Those of you from Newfoundland, from British Columbia and all the way from Australia: Shane, Sumi and my youngest great-grandchild, Tamiko.'

'The first time I came to this fine establishment was on the second anniversary of my wedding. I suspect my experiences tonight might not quite live up to that occasion. Never mind. I grew up in a home where we had a mistrust of mirrors and the room we had that night had mirrors on the ceiling – you can imagine my horror. I was a superstitious young woman but I'm pleased to say I'm superstitious no longer. The magic of that night aside, the fact that I came here at all was certainly beyond the wildest imaginings of a young girl who grew up in a remote Newfoundland outport at the beginning of this century.

'The day after tomorrow I fly out there to the home I was born in so I can be there on Wednesday the actual day of my birthday. I will have my first ride in a helicopter. We will land at the front door as we are agreed that I probably can't manage those steps from the cove any more. I have promised Jonathan this will be the last time I make this journey. In return he has promised to put me on life support in the event I should die before my actual birthday. There's no way I'm not making one hundred.'

The room erupted in cheers and whistles.

'When I was a young girl I had a goal to escape the bounds of the island I grew up on. No disrespect to any Newfies here today. My next major goal after that was to have children. That didn't come as easy as you might expect. But then for many years, I couldn't say I had any goals at all. My first exhibition – that was a goal and a deadline. But then I drifted along for many years till I arrived at the incomprehensible age of ninety-six and something clicked for me and I said I want to live to one hundred. And I made sure I did.'

She had to pause and let more raucous whistling and cheers take their course.

'The reason I'm telling you this is to emphasise something you may well know but don't practice and that is, it truly is amazing what you can achieve when you set your mind to it. When I was a young girl of fourteen, the most influential man of my life said to me, "Never give up hope, Rebecca, sometimes it's all we've got." That man was Samuel. Given what he'd just been through those words couldn't have been more apt.

However, mostly, we have a lot more than just hope. First and foremost we have family. Even today there are things I still hope for and I have faith that these will come to pass.

'And what else have I learned of life from the sage old age of one hundred. That it's still mysterious, mostly it is joyful and abundant, sadness fades, attitude is everything, as is forgiveness.

'I know Jonathan has touched on this but I just want to take some time to remember some dear people whom many of you have never met but in the spirit of remembering absent friends and all. My parents, Silas and Morna Crowe; my sisters, Esther and Rachel and their husbands David and Andrew; Ronnie and Margaret Evans; Samuel, my wonderful first husband; his parents Lottie and Leonard; Addie and Jerome; Granpa Morton Dalton; Uncle Michel Sibonne and Aunt Marguerite; Matthew and Lenore; Analeise and Randall; my dear Wyatt, my surprising second husband, and his family; my three lost boys, Samson, Henri and Joel; and last but certainly not least: Jonathan and Annabelle, Abigail and Will, Morton, Gene and Sonny, and all of you who descend from them. You are my life. Thank you.'

69   Random images

Eva has at long last got the pungent smell of damp out of her house after burning citrus oil and having the doors open for four weeks – one for each year she was away. She has decided she is going to get a new dog: an Italian greyhound. It won't shed hair and she can have it inside with her for company. They are good with young children too apparently. She saw one in the Art Gallery of Alberta, which she visited with Morton last winter. It was in a painting of Catherine the Great. She had called her dog, Zemire. Eva liked that. She thought she would call her dog the same. After Christmas, they'd driven up from Calgary to see an exhibition of the Idtarod. They'd gone through it two times they enjoyed it that much and decided to stay in Edmonton to see in 2001 in the Festival City.

She wrote to Morton telling him of her plans. He wrote back saying, *'you call that animal a dog?'*

She looks at a photograph of her with Shane and an Asian man and child. She turns it over and reads Vancouver July 1999, Tamiko 18 months old. Then one of Lindsay, Shane and Ryan in Quebec also July 1999. Their outfits look vaguely familiar. She squints as she looks at it and thinks Lindsay's turquoise dress suited her eyes perfectly, her ash brown hair layered almost to her elbows. She squints again and in her mind can see them walking up cobbled stones while she waves at them from a petit balcony with a cigarette in her hand.

Then a photograph of her wearing a white shirt, a dark-blue skirt and a new wimple. She can't remember where that outfit came from. Did Lindsay buy it for her?

Another day she comes across a letter from Jonathan, a short covering note:

Gene, I thought you'd like a copy of Mum's speech.

It's familiar; that line about attitude and forgiveness – was it aimed at her? But she can't picture her mother at all giving her deliberated monologue. She should, shouldn't she?

But she hasn't the vaguest recollection of what her mother was even wearing, let alone the ballroom where she gave such an address. Was she standing outside? She shakes the envelope and out falls a photo of her regal looking mother in a dress of elven green lace and taffeta with a mauve ribbon and jasmine corsage. She has never seen it before.

But she does have an image in her mind of her two brothers ensconced in armchairs at the far end of a long hotel lobby, each with a scotch and a cigar in their hands, under the soft light of an antique chandelier.

Her saying 'Look at the two of you.'

And their saying 'Look at you.'

And then an image of her walking down a short, dimly-lit hallway, past an open door, into a room where there is a bed, and her sleeping in a chair next to that bed, while another form slept silently in it.

A conversation with Ryan…

'Have you ever been to Newfoundland?'

'Yes, of course I've been to Newfoundland.'

'Have you been to Rebecca's house on Second Chance Island?'

'No,' she says. *'Never.'*

'Would you like to go?'

'No,' she says. *'Never.'*

70 The dashing of high hopes

When Lindsay had planned the trip east for her Grandma's one-hundredth birthday party, she also booked tickets for Ryan and herself to fly to Newfoundland to be there on the actual day. After living his entire life on the west coast Ryan jumped at Lindsay's suggestion to take a week to explore the other edge of the country. It might be the one and only chance he got to go there with the last surviving original inhabitant of the property. After hearing Rebecca's birthday announcement he had been right.

The morning after her grandmother's birthday party, Lindsay woke with a numbness that came from years of unconscious neglect by her mother – her cross in life. A sensibility, that was both indignant and embarrassed, mixed with incomprehension as to how Eva could be so callous towards her mother, and siblings, let alone her children. Lindsay gave her sister a single despairing look. 'I know. I know,' Shane replied. Ryan came over and wrapped her in his arms. A week earlier things had looked so promising.

Back in May when they received their invitations they had phoned Eva and, as luck would have it, she had been home. The first conversation they had had with her in over twenty months. Ryan said, 'you've got to go, Eva. No one's taking no this time. And Lindsay wants to talk to you.'

Lindsay took the phone from her brother. 'Eva,' she said, 'I've been talking to Shane and we've been thinking if you're up to it, will you come to Vancouver first to meet Shane and Sumi and Tamiko? They want to stay here for a few days to break up their journey and Shane would like to meet you without everyone being around.'

'I'll think about it,' she promised.

'And I thought we could go shopping together when you're here. Buy something to wear to Granny's do.'

'I'll think about that too,' she had said.

She drove to Vancouver and stayed in their study. Lindsay asked her if she would like to be alone when she met Shane for the first time.

'Please, no,' she'd said, 'I'm done with explaining.'

Lindsay had wanted to say, 'actually, no you haven't,' but she held her tongue. Instead she said, 'your presence here is enough,' and tried her best to smile reassuringly.

That was how it unfolded. They met like they caught up regularly with one another. It had gone as well as could be expected.

In Quebec Lindsay had reserved two, two-bedroom apartments at the Chateau de Lery Inn, a nineteenth century European style inn in Old Quebec just a few minutes walk from the Chateau Frontenac. She could have got good rates at the legendary Chateau but Eva has specifically requested that they not stay there. It was no problem – they were happy with their accommodations: old style sandstone walls inside but with high ceilings and modern fixtures and furnishing, the living rooms of each apartment light and airy, opening on to two petit balconies.

For Eva's outfit, Lindsay and Eva chose a white polished-cotton finely pleated button down shirt with three-quarter sleeves and a full yet flowing midnight blue silk skirt with black and silver sandals. She even let the girls talk her in to having her toenails painted. The morning of the lunch she was uneasy. Understandably. They noticed she was the last to get dressed.

'Are you ready, Eva?' Ryan called out. 'We want to take some photos before we head off.'

Their mother had walked into the living room wearing a new white wimple, nervously brushing down her skirt. She looked elegant and smart thought Lindsay with pride.

'That really suits you,' said Ryan, his voice genuine. He was wearing a fawn coloured-jacket, a white shirt himself, open-collared above charcoal-coloured trousers. His hair was clean and pulled back, an odd ringlet escaping here and there. He handed Eva a glass of champagne.

'It's not midday yet,' she said.

Lindsay told her to drink it. 'It will settle your nerves.' A little while later she said, 'Would you like to borrow some of my make-up?'

'I haven't worn make-up for years.'

'Suit yourself. I have a pearl lipstick that would be your colour. I'll leave it on the vanity in our bathroom.'

When Shane and Sumi and Tamiko joined them Shane handed over a small thin package for Eva. 'This is from Australia.'

Eva had smiled, taken aback. 'You didn't have to do that.'

'I wanted to.'

Inside was a band of irregular pieces of dark wood joined by silver clasps. Eva looked closer and saw it was a watch. She let Shane place it around her wrist. It was a little loose but Shane told her that was the idea. She readily posed with her children as they snapped away but when they went to leave, she said, 'you go on ahead, I'll be there shortly.'

She walked to her room and came out holding a cigarette and lighter and waved it at them.

They all stared at each other but said nothing. After a few moments, Lindsay said, 'you'll have to smoke it on the balcony, Eva. There are smoke alarms in here.'

She had nodded and waved them off.

'You have your key?' Ryan asked.

She nodded as her hand closed round the balcony door, the cigarette pressed between her lips.

'There's still some champagne left in the bottle,' said Lindsay.

'Ha,' she managed, her back to them.

Outside as they walk up the cobbled stones they glanced back at her. She waved, inhaling sharply as she did.

She never showed. That night Lindsay, Shane and Ryan stayed out till nearly one a.m., dancing in a nightclub, partly to party, partly to let off steam – none of them was ready to face Eva and not say something vitriolic that they would later regret.

When Lindsay and Ryan stepped inside their apartment they took off their shoes and crept along the hall past their mother's room. The door was open, but their mother wasn't in her bed. Lindsay turned on the light. Her suitcase was still there, but her outfit wasn't.

On the kitchen bench the next morning was a note:

'Thank you, Lindsay, for treating me to this trip. Don't worry about me. I'll see you some time. x Eva'

She had avoided their vehemence. By that stage Lindsay had to admit it was a relief she had disappeared.

When she had planned this trip east, they had asked Eva whether she would like to join them in Newfoundland but she had declined. 'You two go,' she had said. 'Don't mind me. I might spend a day or two with Morton and then head home after that.' Lindsay had organised her an open ticket. Now, she doubted that Eva had even headed off somewhere with Morton.

71 Heartache's companion — joy

As part of the Quebec celebrations her uncle had organised two buses to take everyone to Mont St-Anne for lunch – thirty minutes from Quebec city, a ski field in winter but in summer a mecca for mountain-bike riders and paragliders who launched from a site close to its eight-hundred-metre peak. At the top of the mountain was a restaurant accessible by walking trails or a gondola. To rid herself of her pent-up anger Lindsay hiked with Ryan while the others caught the gondola.

At the top they walked along the sundeck. In winter it would be full of skiers resting between runs enjoying café latte's or glasses of cabernet franc or chablis. Today it was nearly as popular, with commanding views of the Saint Lawrence River and Quebec City to the south and the Laurentian Mountains to the north. The right end of the platform overlooked a cleared grass area where paragliders were laying out their brightly-coloured canopies and in quick succession running down the short slip, their wings aloft. After watching two pilots take off, both flying tandems, Ryan said, 'that's it! Let's do it!'

Shane wasn't keen. Sumi was tempted. Lindsay was tempted but afraid. 'Come on, Lindsay, my treat.'

'You don't have to pay, Ryan.' She looked at him not wanting to give voice to her fears, that sense of having no control whatsoever.

'But I want to. Please let me.'

How did she suddenly go from that short conversation to signing a waiver form and having Sumi eight metres in front of her and Ryan eight metres behind her, all three of them wearing harnesses and helmets and strapped to a stranger? Her pilot tried to set her at ease. 'Where are you from?' he asked.

'Vancouver,' she mumbled.

'No kidding,' he said, 'I'm heading there in ten days time for my sister's wedding.'

'How long will you be there for?' she asked.

'I figure a week.'

'Will you do any paragliding when you're there?' asked Lindsay, her voice somewhat distracted, her eyes glued to Sumi's takeoff.'

'Would you like me to take you paragliding over Grouse Mountain?' he teased.

'Ask me again, when I get to the bottom.' Sumi and his pilot were rising slowly, drifting upwards and to the left. 'Sorry, what did you say your name was again?' The past few days her concentration had definitely strayed.

'You don't remember?' he joked.

'Sorry,' she mumbled. Lindsay's back was against his front making it near impossible to turn and see his face.

'I'm Ari,' he said.

'Ari, short for Ariel?" she asked.

'Mais oui.'

This time it was she who said, 'no kidding.' She tried to turn and smile at him. He was wearing green tinged shades that were highly reflective. In the Bible Arial was an angel and that day she was flying with Ariel's Wings.

'Is this your operation?'

'Mais oui. I'm the man,' he teased, smiling broadly. 'Do you like flying?' he asked.

'I used to love flying,' she said, thinking of the times with her father.

'Used to! What's this used to business?'

Once airborne she surrendered, wishing she could remove her helmet and let the wind rush through her hair. They didn't fly straight down; they drifted along the mountain range then rode a thermal as they corkscrewed upwards. She'd seen eagles do that, their primaries angled to maximise their lift, and now here she was riding invisible skyways, floating over conifers, different shades of green flashing by on a slow shutter speed, a grand sweeping motion, part of a symphony; after the downheartedness of her mother's disappointment this unexpected, surreal lightness of being. Uplifting. She never wanted it to end.

When they touched down and gathered together, Sumi, ever a man of understatement, his eyes glowing, said, 'very peaceful.'

Ryan, his face alive, his body electric, said, 'I'm hooked.'

Lindsay smiled at him. She shook her head at such a lost cause, before giving way to laughter.

'I'm going to become a paraglider. No two ways about it. This is me.'

'It is you.' She smiled and the smile stayed on her face as she gazed at this miracle of a man, now twenty-two years of age, who had the unique ability to shoulder his pain and hers and not be weighed down by it.

Some moments later she walked over to thank her pilot. He was busy packing up his paraglider. 'My brother is a convert,' Lindsay said, smiling and buzzing still with the exhilaration.

'Is he?' Ari pulled the pack on his back and stood up, his smile reflecting her own. She could see herself in his glasses; one thing she couldn't see though were his eyes. 'What about you?'

'I could become a convert,' she felt a nervous flutter in her stomach, '…though I don't know if I'd ever be game enough to fly solo like that, with nothing between me and the ground. Maybe a light aircraft.'

'Much more expensive,' he said. 'Lots more controls.'

'True, but I think I'd pick it up pretty quickly.'

'Confident,' he noted. 'Have you been in the cockpit of a light aircraft before?'

'Yes.' And suddenly Lindsay was filled with another rush of happiness.

Something in her expression must have pierced those reflector shades. 'Many times I take it,' he said.

Lindsay nodded.

'Alright then, which one was the most thrilling?'

'You know,' she drawled, or did she tease? 'They both were, for different reasons.' Then softly she said, in all seriousness, 'thank you, sincerely. That was the best adventure I've had in a long time. And it could not have come at a better time.'

His brow lifted in acknowledgement. 'How's that then?'

'Long story,' Lindsay replied. 'Immaterial really.'

Ari tightened his harness straps. 'Maybe we should catch up in Vancouver?'

'Maybe. Depends.'

'On what?'

'You bringing your tandem harness along.'

He laughed at that.

'And,' she said, feeling exceedingly adventurous, 'you taking off your glasses so I can see the colour of your eyes.'

He laughed even more at that as he walked away from her, all the time walking backwards, facing her. When he was about seven metres away he stopped. You tease, she thought. Now he shows me his eyes. But he made no move to lift his shades.

'I guess that's a no then, Ari,' she called after him, feeling a tad humiliated.

Then he smiled, the broadest smile. 'They pale in comparison to yours.'

How was she to reply to that?

'Lindsay, I have your number on our waiver form. Now you'll have two things to look forward to.' And with that he turned his back and walked towards the chairlift.

What was she to make of that?

72 Seldom we come

The next morning Lindsay and Ryan farewelled Shane, Sumi and Tamiko as they headed south to stay with friends in Toronto and have a few days by themselves at Canada's most famous waterfall. Meanwhile she and Ryan flew with Jonathan, Belle and Rebecca to Gander. As the others boarded their helicopter she and Ryan took the much slower shuttle bus then ferry to Seldom Come By and Second Chance Island. They were the ones to walk up the steep stony path this year. The only difference between now and three years ago was this time Lindsay's luggage had gone on ahead.

At the top of the steps they stopped to catch their breath. They turned and looked back at the cove, an oily grey framed on either side by steep cliffs of grey and taupe-coloured rock. The sun was behind them sliding over the island and into the ocean beyond. The little wooden stage, weathered and barnacled, was neatly poised at the head of the bay on the left hand side; in the distance, the motorboat that had dropped them off was barely visible.

Someone had mowed a path from the top of the steps above the cove up to and around the old saltbox house and barn. Though the house did not look too old and shabby with its grey painted weatherboards and white trim. To the right was a large stand of pine trees near the end of a rocky promontory.

'We'll walk out there sometime,' said Lindsay, nodding in its direction. 'You can see bay after bay to the north, rocky headlands that guard the sea. The view is quite magnificent. Some days you see icebergs.'

'Let's hope,' he said.

The back door was open. They walked in. The short hallway had a door on the left to what was a small extension to the original house, where the downstairs bathroom was located, with a second bathroom above on the first floor. At the end of the hall was a door to the pantry, and to the right a doorway to the kitchen, which was one step down.

'Good crossing?' Aunty Belle asked in greeting.

'Not too bad,' said Lindsay.

'How was the helicopter ride?' asked Ryan. 'Granny Becca, did you look down at all or were you too scared?'

'Of course I looked down. First time I ever saw this part of the country from the air. I wasn't going to not look down.'

'Did you spot any icebergs?' asked Lindsay.

Uncle Jay shook his head.

'Still time for that,' mumbled Rebecca. 'Besides, I've seen icebergs from the air when I turned...fifty. I can't believe it was that long ago!' Her Grandmother sounded put out. Lindsay laughed.

'It was mother, but don't worry, neither can I. By the way,' said Jonathan looking at Ryan and Lindsay, 'your bags are upstairs in the room on the right.'

'Thank you,' said Ryan. 'I could have done that for you. Saved you that effort.'

'The effort is good for me,' said Jonathan.

'It's small but cosy,' Annabelle said.

'No smaller than the house I grew up in.' Ryan looked around at the kitchen. 'In fact, I'd say bigger.'

'It's back to nature,' said Rebecca, clearly delighted as she sat slowly swinging in a rocking chair. 'Jonathan, do you remember the first time we went to the cabin at Lake Temagami?'

'You mean when I rushed up to you and said, "I don't think you are going to like it here, Mom. They have an outside toilet and it doesn't flush and it's a bit smelly." '

'That's the time. And I said something like, "goodness me, how will we ever cope? Is there running water inside?" '

'And I said, "yes, only cold though. Dad said we have to

boil up hot water in a pot if we want to have a warm bath. There are no showers or anything like that, no electricity either." '

Lindsay gasped. 'Shock horror, no electricity.' Everyone laughed.

'Not unlike here,' noted Belle. The power had only been connected just over a decade ago.

'Do you remember what you said next, Mother?'

'Something along the lines of well, if you have to boil up your own hot water then I would expect not.'

'And,' said Jonathan winking at Lindsay and Ryan, 'I kept at her trying to get her to fold. I said, "it's got those kerosene lamps and candles like you have to use in a blackout." '

'Oh, I'm sure we will survive,' said Granny Becca, thrilled with being caught up in the re-enactment.

'And there's no mirror, not a single mirror in the whole place,' said Jonathan. '"What!" said Dad. "No mirror? Rebecca, you know how I love mirrors. I demand a refund! Let's go and get our money back." '

Jonathan and his mother chuckled at the memory. He leant across and clasped her hands as he looked into her clear eyes. 'So what do you think, Mom? Do you want to bother unpacking?'

Lindsay's heart sighed. She watched her Granny pull her son's hands to her lips and kiss them.

When they came out of their reverie, Ryan asked, 'are there any mirrors here?'

'No,' said Granny Becca.

'Seriously?' asked Ryan.

'Haven't you heard that joke, Ryan?' asked Jonathan.

'Which one?'

'The one where a man is signing a hotel registrar and the publican says to him, "do you have a good memory for faces?" And the guest replies, "yes. I pride myself on the fact." And the publican replies, "good, you'll need it in the morning. There's no mirror in your bathroom."'

They all broke into laughter.

Over a supper of cold meats and cheese and light pickles, Ryan asked Rebecca what her first memory of the place was.

'The red fox,' she said without hesitation. 'I was three, maybe four, looking out that window,' she pointed to the window over her left shoulder, 'on a winter's morning and I saw it sitting there looking back at me with its pointy face and ears and long bushy tail and I called out doggie. My mother came to have a look and she said, "it's a fox." Then she bent down and whispered to me, "don't tell your father." And then more loudly, "I hope he stays away from my hens."'

'Would your father have killed the fox if he saw it?' asked Ryan.

'Oh yes, my father was quick to kill and he hated dogs. Got bitten by a dog when he was a little boy and his leg got so badly infected he nearly died. They didn't have antibiotics in those days, not like they have now. For years he was convinced dogs had venomous fangs like snakes. Thought they were onside with the Devil.'

'Did you ever meet him?' Ryan asked Jonathan.

'No. People didn't travel as much back in those days.' Jonathan and his mother exchanged glances. 'I knew Granma Crowe though for over forty-years.'

'She lived till she was nearly one hundred too, didn't she?' asked Lindsay.

'Ninety-eight,' said Granny Becca.

'Did you meet her?' Ryan asked Lindsay.

'No, I spoke to her on the phone a few times. She would send us cards for our birthday and Christmas.'

'Do you remember how old you were when you saw your first iceberg?' asked Ryan.

'It must have been the next summer or the one after. I didn't know what they were at first. My sister Rachel had to explain them to me, told me they were pure frozen water from the North Pole and if you got up close, you could scrape some off and put it in a cup and when it melted it would be the sweetest water you ever tasted.'

'Was it?' he asked.

'You know, I never tasted it.' She hesitated, her mouth open as if she was going to say more, but then she closed it without another word.

Lindsay jumped to her feet. 'That reminds me. Guess what I bought at Gander airport while we were waiting for our bags to come through?'

'What?' asked Belle.

'Wait till I fetch it.' She ran up the stairs and returned in less than a minute. 'This is what the label reads: Iceberg Vodka, a vodka manufactured by the Newfoundland and Labrador Liquor Corporation, produced using water from icebergs harvested off the coast of Newfoundland. Who wants to try some?' Lindsay, an imp incarnate, grinned invitingly at everyone.

'Let's all have a small nip,' said Jonathan.

'Do we have any ice?' Lindsay asked.

'We do as a matter of fact,' said Belle. 'Bought some in Gander at the supermarket. Wanted it for the icebox for all the meats and cheeses.'

Ryan went to the freezer while Jonathan and Lindsay grabbed glasses.

'Just a tiny one for me, please, Lindsay,' said Belle, 'I'm not a big drinker.'

'What about you, Granny, want to try some?'

'Yes, why not? After Sunday I think I should try more.' She paused her eyes along way off. Then she said, 'you know, Jonathan, I don't think I told you, I woke up the night after my party and I thought I saw an angel sitting in a chair by my bed. I went back to sleep but sometime later I woke again and the angel was asleep, her head resting on my bed and just for a moment or two I thought the angel was Gene.'

'Was it?'

'Yes, either that, or she visited me in my dreams.'

Lindsay looks at her Uncle but he is inscrutable. Her Aunt's eyes are locked on her mother-in-law. Lindsay can't tell if she is inscrutable or not. Ryan spoons in the ice. She picks up the bottle and pours normal nips for her uncle, Ryan and herself, and two smaller ones for her aunty and grandmother, then lets out the sigh she is holding inside.

Lindsay knows her relationship with her mother drifts back into the shadows more often than not. Only in recent months has it been anything at all. After her long overdue, and difficult disclosure her mother had typically, disappeared. At least this time she did return. That was something.

In those intervening months Lindsay had a few long-distant sessions with Marcus, worried that perhaps she had done the wrong thing after all. Perhaps she should have left well enough alone – her mother. She felt a heavy sense of guilt that she had destroyed her mother's life and what few relationships she had. She didn't believe that wholeheartedly but she felt that her mother's behaviour was once again her censure and Lindsay's punishment – Ryan, unfortunately happened to have been caught in the cross fire.

She and Marcus had talked at length. 'Lindsay,' he had said to her, 'to an extent you are right. That is something you do have to take responsibility for but you also have to balance that with other considerations. Try and detach yourself from what is not happening between you and your mother. She is only one person in this dynamic. Think about this in relation to the others involved, you, Shane, Ryan, your relatives and dare I say it, your father. Would they have wanted for you three siblings to be reunited? Absolutely. Does that hold sway in this discussion? Absolutely. Will your mother come round one day? The odds are she's already been to the point of no return and she's on her way back. By her reclusion she is hurting herself the most. She learnt that before. I'm sure she'll learn it again. If you had never embarked on this exercise you wouldn't have Ryan in your life.'

'But I didn't know he was going to be the reward when I set out on this path and caused this calamity.'

'And if he hadn't existed there would not be this calamity. You can't have one without the other. Come to terms with it. And know while you're feeling judged and damned, she is mostly likely feeling that ten-fold. Remember our sessions on forgiveness?'

'Yes.'

'You're going to have to forgive her for everything she's done. Now that you know everything that she's done and all that she's still doing.'

'I forgive her more than most people think, more than she thinks. Although she wasn't there for us and she gave up Ryan, I think what she did for her best friend was incredibly magnanimous, incredibly selfless. It took immense fortitude.'

'Have you told her that?'

'I haven't had the chance.'

'Well I hope one day you get that chance. We all seek approval and love no matter what messages we give to the contrary. I hope your mother has the courage to walk towards you, to seek and grant forgiveness. I wish she had the courage or the insight to get some professional help, maybe that would help her come to terms with everything.'

'Ha,' said Lindsay down the line. 'If only.'

Lindsay felt her mother's personality was becoming more and more divergent by the day.

In early June she and Ryan had flown back to Prince Rupert – the first time they had seen Eva in twenty-two months. With Ken and Eva they had traipsed over blocks of land within a 100-kilometre radius trying to find the perfect acreage for their bird of prey endeavour. When they found it, she and Ryan hugged each other with glee and her mother had looked at her as if to say, 'take your hands off him, you slut'. Then five minutes later Eva had confided in her, 'your father would have loved to have been involved in this too.'

Later that day Lindsay had asked her, 'did it take you some time to get over everything? Did you go back to Freshwater or some place else?' Lindsay desperately wanted to know if she had tipped her mother over the edge; if Eva had seen a psychiatrist or someone. Eva had looked at

Lindsay, dazed and confused as if she had no recollection of that night and that morning they had spent in her house trying their best not to break each other, trying their best to restrain their anger, suppress their pain, sort through the wreckage of their own shared histories.

'Don't know what you mean,' she'd said to Lindsay. It was as if she'd had a lobotomy the way she couldn't remember or refused to remember. Maybe her words were a euphemism for: 'I'm never talking about this ever again. You're never talking about this ever again.'

When Lindsay returned to Vancouver she once more had phoned Marcus out of concern.

What he'd said was: 'not having your mother as a patient it's difficult for me to diagnose what's going on. But from what you're telling me it sounds like she has experienced a fugue episode. A pathological amnesiac condition during which one is apparently conscious of one's actions but has no recollection of them after returning to a normal state. The condition, usually results from severe mental stress and may persist for several months.'

Not for the first time did Lindsay wish she could bring Doctor Brookes to Canada to be her mother's personal psychiatrist.

Still, just in the past two months, she was starting to realise that although her relationship with her mother was not all that it could be it was more than it was. No one came as close to Eva as Ryan. And it was this that Lindsay took away from it – the gift of a brother – a full-blooded brother who was the very best of the Daltons and the Marlows. And that was the biggest bonus of all. She was grateful they had that time together at the start to cement a friendship and a bond bound by truth and intimacy and shared longing – a meeting of hearts and minds. Now, whenever she had the opportunity to observe Ryan without him noticing her she was filled with wonder that this man was her brother, her father's son. Oddly no one came as close to Ryan as Lindsay, that inexplicable dynamic of sibling relationships. Belated. Beloved.

They had welcomed him with the arms of giants. When Granny Becca heard all about their dream to create a bird of prey heritage park she gave Ryan a painting of hers to auction off to raise funds. He thanked her but said he couldn't part with it. 'Fine,' she said, and proceeded to hand over another one. 'Keep whichever you like best and sell the other. Jonathan will take care of matters.' Then a dawning. 'Would you like me to paint you an eagle love?' she said. 'Though I don't know if I'd be any good at that.'

Shane and Lindsay had drawn down one hundred thousand dollars each from their mortgages and given that money to Ryan. It had been part of their inheritance from their father and their father's parents; he had a right to some of it. Jonathan and Abby and Morton also got into the spirit handing over fifty thousand between them, so they could create this inspired endeavour on the north west coast of Canada where falcons and ospreys and eagles filled the skies.

Now they were on a coastline where eagles were rare, but majestic mountains of ice sometimes graced the seas.

'Raise your glasses,' says Lindsay. 'To Rebecca Dalton Kingston and her love of icebergs.'

They all take a sip, except Ryan who downs his in a single swallow, not quite slamming his empty glass on the table, the ice cubes skate around inside.

Lindsay looks at him trying to suppress a laugh.

What?' he says, 'I thought we were having shots!'

'You remind me of my husband, Samuel' says an amused Rebecca, her eyes relucent.

Jonathan tosses his down and pushes his glass towards Lindsay. 'Come on, keep up, girl.'

She pours the burning liquid down her throat, catches the ice in her teeth and slams her glass down on the table, its echo ricocheting throughout the ancestral home...or is that a knock on the door?

73 A journey to life's end

A page torn out of a notebook, folded and refolded with unfamiliar place names: Clarke's Head, Wings Point, Rodgers Cove, Stoneville, Port Albert, Man of War Cove, Farewell, Seldom, Deception, Serious Cove.

Calling all angels...

Another one with names of people hastily scribbled over it.

'You want to know the truth about your family. Hand me a piece of paper and a pen,' she says.

She starts back in the late 1800s with Silas and Morna Crowe at the top of the page and then she lists all the names and partners with a straight line linking Morna, Rebecca and her, Eva. And then she shoves it across the bench at him.

Some minutes later she says, 'hand it back,' and then she starts putting crosses through nearly half of the names and then she hands it back to him.

'All of these, dead before their time, as babies, in their youth or their prime. This one,' she points, 'adopted. This one,' she points, 'scarred for life.' She swallows. 'Not unlike me.' She glares at him, till what she isn't saying sinks in.

'You think that is my fate.'

She looks at him, while she bites her lip and her eyes water. 'Do not give voice to it, Ryan. That is why I have lived my life the way I have. Put up a wall between you and me, between the girls and me, trying to stop whatever it is moving down the line.'

'But they're all male.'

'Don't say it. Don't even think it.'

Their eyes lock on each other, not a silent battle of wills,

350

but a bridge of understanding. He, more than any other person she had ever known, understood her, more than Jonathan and Morton even. He would never call her crazy.

Ryan glances down at the paper in front of them.

'And what about your mother and your siblings?' He raises his eyes again to her. 'How does all this affect them now? They are all past their prime.'

'The road back to my family is a torturous one,' she says, almost inaudibly.

'They are bad people?'

'No,' she whispers. 'They are good people. It is I who is the bad one.'

'I want to meet them.'

'Of course you do.'

'Will you take me to meet them?'

'You ask of me more than I am capable of giving.'

'Are you ashamed of me?'

'No. I am ashamed of myself.'

He glances again at the paper he is holding in his hand.

'Your mother, she could die any day.'

There is a lump in Eva's throat preventing her from speaking.

'When was the last time you saw her?'

He is waiting for her to answer.

'Nineteen sixty-nine,' she manages to say, her voice hoarse. Twenty-eight years ago.'

'You should see her before she dies.'

She can't avoid his eyes.

'Have you spoken to her in all that time?'

'I called her after Sonny disappeared. She sent a letter through Lindsay.'

'What did she say?'

She can no longer look at him. 'Love always, Love still.'

'Eva,' he sighs.

An irretrievable loss.

An immeasurable sadness.

Zemire nudges her. She knows.

When Eva stares in the mirror at night, sometimes she swears she can once more see her mother staring back at her, sitting in a rocking chair in some strange house…and with a tremor in her voice, Eva says, 'are you waiting for someone?'

And her mother slowly pulls herself out of her rocking chair and walks towards her. 'Yes,' she says, her hands outstretched, her eyes aglow. 'You.'

74 *Come full circle*

On Tuesday 13th July 1999, on the eve of her one-hundredth birthday, Rebecca turns in for the night in the very bedroom, the very bed, she slept in as a child. Same bed, different mattress. She saw to that in the fifties and once more in the nineties.

At the age of one hundred it has been a night of surprises and firsts. Members of her family are sprinkled around the house. Jonathan and Annabelle share the double bed in what used to be her parent's room. In the room next door in two singles are Lindsay and Gene – Eva as she calls herself now. The baby her mother helped deliver at their home in Toronto when Rebecca was thirty-four years of age. The one and only time her mother ever left Newfoundland. Samuel had crouched behind her and she had tensed her body into his as she struggled through each wave, till she cried, 'Samuel, come round in front and catch our baby.' His hands were the first to hold her. 'Our children have another sister to play with,' he said.

Tonight Evangeline had stood in the middle of the kitchen doorway wearing jeans, a light, travelling zip-jacket, and a scarf around her head, holding a duffel bag at her front. On her face the expression of the hopeful five-year old girl Rebecca had once known. 'God bless you, Samuel,' she whispers. 'You, who always told me to keep my hopes alive. Tonight my hopes have been rewarded. I can think of no greater sign for what is to come.'

Gene now has a granddaughter of her own and been blessed in other ways – Ryan, her son, on the day bed downstairs. It pleases Rebecca immensely that he is lying there. She wonders whom he might be thinking of before he is taken over by sleep, where his mind lingers. His very presence reminds her of another young man, of a similar age, of a similar build, light not dark like this one, lying on the same day bed: both an unforeseen brightness, an unforeseen joy, the most bounteous gift.

Tonight her thoughts drift to him and before she knows it her dreams and her memories become one. She is in that plane, the one she was in back in the 1950s only this time it is a floatplane and she is the pilot. She's flying up over Iceberg Alley and she knows this time the berg she's looking for will be there, the one with the nautilus shell at its end. And this time she will coax the plane down, glide through the water and bring it up inside to moor on the icy shore. Because inside is Samuel, waiting for her, in a massive ice cave floating along with the sea.

THE END

Epilogue

Queenstown, New Zealand, December 2006

New circles, new skies

The girl stood erect with her left eye pressed to the viewfinder, her right eye closed, peering into the telescope as if she were a seasoned bird watcher – something her uncle would be very proud of. But today the telescope was directed towards Frankton, Queenstown Airport more precisely, where she had been watching and naming the Qantas and Air New Zealand aircraft, the Beeches and Airbuses coming into land – something her grandfather no doubt would have been proud of.

Deftly she tilted the angle and adjusted the focal length while Lindsay and Shane stood nearby, silently watching. Her hair, the colour of spun honey – just like her father's – was pulled into a long plait down the middle of her back. Suddenly she gasped. 'They're coming! I see Daddy's car, it's driving along Frankton Road.'

She turned her brilliant blue green eyes towards her mother. 'Can I go up to the road and wait for them?

'Sure thing,' said Lindsay. 'Go round up the welcoming party.'

'Nina,' called Shane. 'Tell Tamiko I said it's time to put down her book.'

'Oui,' she replied, as she shot down the stairs.

Shane turned to Lindsay, frowning an apology. 'Sorry, she's witch-mad at the moment.'

'*Harry Potter?*'

'No, *Wintersmith*. She has promised she will play with her cousins as soon as she's finished.'

'That's fine. They've got three weeks together.'

'So, Eva came, how 'bout that?'

'Yes,' inhaled Lindsay. 'Miracles will never cease.' She

gave way to a faint smile.

'What did Ari's text say?'

'Party of five on its way. Told you she'd come.'

Shane chuckled. 'Why was he so sure?'

'Don't you know, Shane?' Lindsay smiled. 'Very few women can resist him.'

'Did he say that?'

Lindsay smiled again, this time rolling her eyes.

'Cocky.' Shane chuckled once more. 'True, though.' She straightened the magazines on the coffee table. 'Do you think we should prepare them?'

'Why? We've kept it a surprise all this time.'

'We've kept it a surprise all this time because we didn't want to disappoint them,' Shane reminded her. Which was true. This was only the third time in thirty years that Eva had been in a plane. Given her fear of flying they really had expected her to renege.

'No, let's not let the cat out of the bag, but, you're right, I should talk to Nina.'

'Mum, I'm thirsty.' Lindsay glanced up as two boys walked towards her; the first, her five-year old son, Marlow, Nina's twin; the second, Raiden, his dark-haired seven-year old cousin.

'And sweaty, too,' said Lindsay touching his head. Go wash your hands and face. Ryan and everyone will be here soon.'

'Mum, I said I'm thirsty. Can I have a drink.'

'Marlow Luc Valin, the water coming from the tap is perfectly drinkable. It's from a mountain spring. Drink up when you go and wash. Off you go.'

'You too, Raiden,' urged Shane. 'You can have some juice at lunch.'

'Is it lunch time already?' The question came from a slim, nine year-old, Eurasian girl, pulling her sleek black hair back in an elastic band. Tamiko. She trailed Nina into the living room. 'I'm starving!'

'How could you be starving? You've done nothing all morning.'

'Mum, we've been fighting off winter!'

'And a good job you've done, Miko,' quipped Lindsay. 'Look at the day,' she gestured towards the windows.

The land of the long white cloud had banished the clouds on this auspicious day and held the ever-present breeze at bay. The double-glazed windows of their house were expansive, as were the decks. To the left, behind the airport you could see the tussocked slopes of The Remarkables with a few small and persistent patches of determined snow. To the right was Lake Wakitipu, framed in light green poplars, and if you walked to the far right end of the deck and turned to your right you could see Ben Lomond and the Skyline Gondola where Ari worked his tandem paragliding business from November through to March every year.

'Nina, Beccalina, come here for a sec,' said Lindsay, popping down on a lounge and patting the seat next to her.'

'What?' the girl asked, almost in frustration. Lindsay raised her eyebrows. Sighing, Nina Rebecca, the golden child named in honour of her great grandmother, came to stand in front of her mother, but she did not sit down. Rather, she bounced on her toes, impatient to be outside, greeting their guests with fanfare.

'Now,' said Lindsay, placing her palm on her cheek to calm her. 'I know this is a big day for you. Ryan will be here any minute and I know you've been counting down the sleeps till he arrives. But I want you to remember to say hello to everyone, okay? And give everyone a welcome hug too. Don't forget Sian and Macey.' Macey was her fourteen year-old half sister. 'It's her first time here and it could feel a little bit strange for her being so far away from home.'

'Strange?' queried, Nina. 'We're not strangers,' she muttered.

'You're right, we're not. It's just they might be exhausted and out of sorts. Remember how tired you were when we got here? And Macey has flown all the way from Montreal.'

Ari's daughter had flown unaccompanied to Vancouver,

where Ryan and his long-term girlfriend, Sian, joined her to fly to Auckland. Meantime, Morton and Eva had broken their trip by flying to Tahiti; a place they hoped would be less touristy than Hawaii. But also where Morton could spend a few days fishing for rainbow runners and giant trevally. Sumi had big plans to take him fly-fishing up the Makarora. Lindsay and Shane had big plans to take Eva on a walk to Mt Aspiring Hut, which until now had been a big if.

Her mother though, to be truthful, had become much better at committing to something and sticking to it, unlike their strained trip to Quebec for Granny Becca's 100th birthday. Most of those commitments however revolved around meeting Lindsay, Ari and the kids at Ryan's place, at Gwaihir Raptor Park – whenever they visited, which, if Lindsay could swing it, was twice a year.

Gwaihir – named after the great eagles from Lord of the Rings, and because Ryan liked the symmetry of Haida Gwaii, the Charlottes, where he and Lindsay had delighted in the congregation of bald eagles – was a family enterprise that had brought everyone together and, fortuitously, had been a stirring success.

At its entrance was a spectacular wrought iron gate of an eagle's head, made with dedication and zeal one wintry January when Uncle Jay and Uncle Morton had visited and partnered with Ryan's adoptive father, Billy, and grandfather, Ken, to weld Ryan's vision to life. Not to be outdone, in the last year, Ari and Ryan had put together a short film called, On the Wings of an Eagle – a ten-minute voyeuristic video they'd filmed by attaching a miniature camera to one of their friendly baldies, interspersed with paragliding shots of the guys flying, almost in symmetry with some giant raptors. It had quite the wow factor.

Lindsay had taken on marketing the business, building its website, attracting sponsors and travel TV shows – not just in Canada but in Australia as well – using any and all contacts they had. She'd not long linked in to the Cruise liners visiting the Pacific Northwest, offering day trips to their park, lining up tour coaches for holiday makers. On top of that they had regular school trips. Everyone loved the birds, everyone walked away in awe and excitement about getting within a few feet of the birds of prey that Ryan and Sian or their helpers held on their wrists. Lindsay continued to manage the marketing from wherever she was based.

Much like Canada's wild geese, not long after Lindsay and Ari got together she had surrendered her corporate job to live a life of migration across the northern and southern hemispheres, wherever Arial's Wings flew, detouring via Sydney and Vancouver and Prince Rupert whenever they could manage it. Every spring and fall she would spend a month on the West Coast with her brother and her mother, whom, the kids called Neva after stumbling so long over Nana Eva. Secretly, Lindsay thought Nina called her this as it sounded like her name and was her way of claiming a degree of ownership.

The twins had arrived in September 2001, three weeks shy of full term, six weeks after her dearly beloved grandmother had departed. Lindsay counted her blessings that the timing was such that she was in Canada and only had to drive a few hours to Montreal for her funeral. Surprisingly her mother, Eva, had been at Granny Becca's side when she died, having driven 15 hours to Edmonton so she could fly in a large aircraft direct to Montreal, even though she could have caught an airplane from Prince Rupert, two hours drive away. All of Granny Becca's remaining children had been at her side: two stalwart brothers, two recovering sisters.

When she found out she was expecting twins, Lindsay took her doctors advice and had a Caesarean. She asked Eva if she could be there when she came out of hospital and be there she was – to her credit. Eva's only condition being that she bring along her puppy, Zemire.

And that really was a turning point for Lindsay and her mother. Lindsay no longer gave Eva an out. Whenever she was in BC, she simply said, '*I need you.*' And Eva came. '*I need you to help teach the children French. I need them to be comfortable around dogs. I need you to look after them while I have this meeting with potential sponsors, do you mind? Can Ken help you?'* God bless Ken! *'I need you to teach them the names of Canadian trees – I've forgotten so much. Can you take them to the beach and show them all the sea stars?'*

And on it went. The zombiism that Lindsay had witnessed as a child had long vanished. Her mother seemed to be imbued with a new sense of lightness. Around her grandchildren there was a sparkle in her eye and some days Lindsay felt the presence of her grandmother in Eva. Nina and Marlow were certainly getting the best of her and it was in those moments that Lindsay most missed her father and what could have been.

Two years ago Lindsay had decided to write a memoir of the famous Canadian seascape artist, Rebecca Dalton Kingston. She was still working on it. *'Eva, I need you to help with the research of Granny Becca's first gallery opening.'* Eva had baulked at that. A week later, she called and said, 'Jonathan remembers the opening much better than I. He'll write to you.' Which he did, but a few weeks later, Lindsay was surprised to receive from her a mother a long letter describing how her Granny Becca had returned from a holiday in Newfoundland in the summer of 1949 like a woman possessed. She had been painting for close to a decade, but always landscapes, suddenly she burned like dry ice with her iceberg creations that were almost too real. Eva recalled how her mother set up her studio at the front of their home in Avenue de Lorimier, clearing out Jonathan's old room which had large windows facing the street letting natural light pour in. But, Eva wrote, the light was nothing compared to the light that came to life on mom's canvases.

Though Eva had little interest in talking about icebergs, the project bonded them in a way that was completely unexpected – over the topic of light. Eva talked about the midnight sun in the Arctic Circle, about the pewter reflections and purple tinged heather, she talked about the white light cresting the peaks of the rocky mountains in the early morning dawn, turning into vignettes of pale blue and amber, and the gilded, hallowed rays deep inside a conifer forest. Once, she also talked about the way the sunlight always glinted on his hair. Whose hair? Lindsay had queried. 'I was thinking of Sonny's,' her mother had volunteered, 'but,' she paused, 'also on Dad's hair. Always, anytime.' Eva drifted through her own mental snapshots before exhaling a wistful admission. 'Sonny drew the light and shone the light.'

Lindsay could picture that completely. The way her mother talked made Lindsay think Eva really did have her mother's artistic eye. And for a woman who, for many years it seemed, had lived a life of oblivion, she certainly had a knack for recalling some of nature's finest elements.

When Lindsay decided to invite her mother on a sojourn to New Zealand's South Island, she didn't say to her Eva: *'I need you to come.'* Instead, she said: *'we want you to come. We want you to celebrate Christmas with all your children and your grandchildren. Bring Uncle Morton as well.'* And then they had slowly waged a war of email enticements, suggesting all the things they could do and see on the way, and when they got there.

'I'm not going tandem paragliding with you, Ariel,' Eva had replied. 'You can count on that.'

'One day,' he joked, 'One day, Eva.'

What Lindsay had done though, was to book both her mother and Morton onto a twilight trip with the Queenstown Centre for Creative Photography. She thought they'd like that, creating their own photographs under the guidance of some of New Zealand's best landscape photographers.

'Lins, come on, the kids are yelling at us to hurry up.'

Lindsay stirred and followed Shane out the front door and across their driveway, spying their LandCruiser a few hundred metres away, followed by Sumi in her run-about. He'd told Nina he had to go to the supermarket. In reality he'd followed Ari to the airport to pick up two of their guests. Lindsay could see Uncle Morton in the front with

Ari. Nina was jumping up and down waving her arms in the air like she was a pilot signaller on a busy runway, making sure they turned into the right driveway. Ari was playing with the horn, egging her on. Nina saw her father at the wheel and then her eyes jumped to the passenger seat. Morton was waving at her, waving at them all. Nina twirled round to her, somehow knowing exactly where to look.

'Uncle Morton!'

'Yes,' Lindsay nodded.

'What's he doing here?'

'He's come for Christmas too. He and Neva.'

'Neva too!' squealed Nina. 'And Ken and Billy?'

'No. They're looking after the eagles.'

Ari pulled the car to a stop and Marlow ran up and placed his hand onto the passenger window. Macey's larger hand met his from the inside. His green eyes, his pearly smile, were shining bright. Shane's kids were on the other side, tapping at Neva's window. These are the images Lindsay saw. What she heard was the excited babble of children. And then she saw her brother, leap out of Sumi's car, blurring towards her, snatching Nina up in one arm as he wrapped his other arm round her.

'Kia ora,' she said. 'So great to have you here.'

'So great to be here,' said Ryan as they hugged each other. 'It's beautiful.'

'I told you it was.'

Ryan released her to hug Shane and his other nieces and nephews.

Shane and Lindsay walked towards their mother who had stepped out of the car.

'Hi, Lindsay. Hello, Shane,' she smiled.

'Hello, Eva,' said Shane.

'Hello, Mom,' said Lindsay. 'Thanks for coming all this way.' She went and gave her a warm hug. Her mother was seventy-three after all. It was a big thing to travel half way around the world at her age.'

'Thanks for having me,' she said. 'I like the name of your street.' Their house was on Birch Lane.

'Yeah, we organised that specially for you,' quipped Lindsay.

They settled Eva and Morton in with Shane and Sumi, just two houses along. After everyone had showered they re-joined them with Christmas presents in tow to place under the tree, much to the kids amazement – the excitement of visitors having temporarily banished all thought of Santa Claus. Shane and Lindsay started bringing out bread rolls and bowls of salad, along with jugs of cranberry juice and iced tea. Ari took Macey out to the southern end of the deck. His feet were bare, his tan marks showing his Teva strap lines. He was wearing grey cargo shorts, and a navy polo shirt, with his trademark Maui Jim shades perched on his sun-streaked head. Macey had changed into a white sundress. Their arms were casually thrown around each other. Ari raised his left arm and pointed in the distance. Lindsay heard him say, 'the bungee jumping is that way.'

'The Nevis one?'

'No, the original Kawarau Bridge Bungee. Forget the Nevis – you can do that next time or you can do The Ledge off the top of the Gondola.'

Lindsay chuckled. Watching her fearless husband be measured in his free rein with his children was refreshing and comforting.

He turned around. 'I amuse you?'

'You do,' she replied. But you also re-assure me.' Their eyes held then he gave her the faintest nod in understanding.

He went to grab some beers for those who wanted them. Welcoming everyone with a toast, he clicked bottles with his brother-in-laws and uncle. And with his arm around Macey and in a voice loud enough for everyone to hear, he said in his trademark Québécois accent: 'ladies and gentleman, if you will allow me one little indulgence – I just have to say, it's going to be the best Christmas ever. For I have all the women I love in the one place.'

And just like that her husband, master of evasion, told all the women present that he adored them – even her mother.

'Look out, Ryan,' joked Shane.

'Charmer' murmured Lindsay.

As if he had heard, Ari turned towards her. She couldn't suppress her smile nor the adoration she felt for him. He sauntered up to her, pulling his sunglasses down over his face, their own private joke, but even so she caught his teasing wink, his teasing smile as he lowered his head and kissed her, like he always kissed her, full of life, full of love.

Acknowledgements

Fortunately less research went into **Come Full Circle** than its predecessors because in part it followed a journey I took with my partner to British Columbia and other parts of the world. Still, research was involved to name the magnificent trees and sea life of the Pacific Northwest. Any mistakes are entirely my own.

It feels both strange and sad to be drawing to a close this chapter of my life and leaving these characters who have been such a part of it for the past decade.

Thanks most of all to the stranger who became my Gene and the genesis of *The Iceberg Trilogy*, and who oddly, tangentially, gave me the freedom to create Rebecca and Samuel in their own image.

I am also deeply grateful to my partner, Mark, and my sister, Anita, for reading **Come Full Circle** throughout its various iterations, and for all the help they provide with my books and my life in making this possible.

To the wonderful women who helped me finesse **Come Full Circle** – Ruth Schaffer, Carolyn Wood, Jane Brisbane, Leah Sparks, Svetlana Stankovic, Jenny Gillis, Mel Kettle, Katherine Hooton and Sheree Davey – thank you for being part of this journey.

To my family and friends who have been tireless in their support of The Iceberg Trilogy, with a special nod to my mother who champions my books and who also had a surprise baby later in life.

Finally, thanks also to the readers and bloggers who have embraced The Iceberg Trilogy, especially The Eclectic Reader, The Book Bosses and Honey Lemon Tea. I appreciate your support very much.

Resources

You can find more information about Sherryl and her books on her website: www.sherrylcaulfield.com.

This includes:

- Discussion Topics for book clubs on Come Full Circle.

- Frequently Asked Questions on Come Full Circle

- Music links for the soundtrack of Come Full Circle

On her website you can also sign up for her newsletter to be kept up to date with major book releases.

If you want to get in touch with Sherryl you can do so by:

Sending her an email to: info@sherrylcaulfield.com

Or by visiting her Facebook page: SherrylCaulfieldAuthor where she often runs giveaways, posts images from her books, provides project updates and chats to her readers.